MEGA-DOGS OF NEW KANSAS

For Tracy, always —D.J.

To my folks, for letting me draw at the dinner table —J.K.

Text copyright © 2020 by Dan Jolley
Illustrations copyright © 2020 by Jacques Khouri

Graphic Universe™ is a trademark of Lerner Publishing Group, Inc.

Graphic Universe™
An imprint of Lerner Publishing Group, Inc.
241 First Avenue North
Minneapolis, MN 55401 USA

For reading levels and more information, look up this title at
www.lernerbooks.com.

Designed by Lindsey Owens.
Main body text is set in CCDaveGibbonsLower. Typeface provided by Comicraft.

Library of Congress Cataloging-in-Publication Data

Names: Jolley, Dan, writer. | Khouri, Jacques, illustrator.
Title: Mega-dogs of New Kansas / written by Dan Jolley ; illustrated by Jacques Khouri.
Description: Minneapolis : Graphic Universe, [2020] | Audience: Ages 7–11 | Audience: Grades 4–6 | Summary: "When an official threatens the mega-dog program, Sienna Barlow sneaks away with her dog, Gus, and begins an adventure across New Kansas." –Provided by publisher.
Identifiers: LCCN 2019039452 (print) | LCCN 2019039453 (ebook) | ISBN 9781541517332 (library binding) | ISBN 9781541599475 (ebook)
Subjects: LCSH: Graphic novels. | CYAC: Graphic novels. | Science fiction. | Adventure and adventurers–Fiction.
Classification: LCC PZ7.7.J65 Me 2020 (print) | LCC PZ7.7.J65 (ebook) | DDC 741.5/973–dc23

LC record available at
    https://lccn.loc.gov/2019039452
LC ebook record available at
    https://lccn.loc.gov/2019039453

Manufactured in the United States of America
1-44296-34557-3/5/2020

MEGA-DOGS OF NEW KANSAS

DAN JOLLEY

JACQUES KHOURI

Graphic Universe™ • Minneapolis

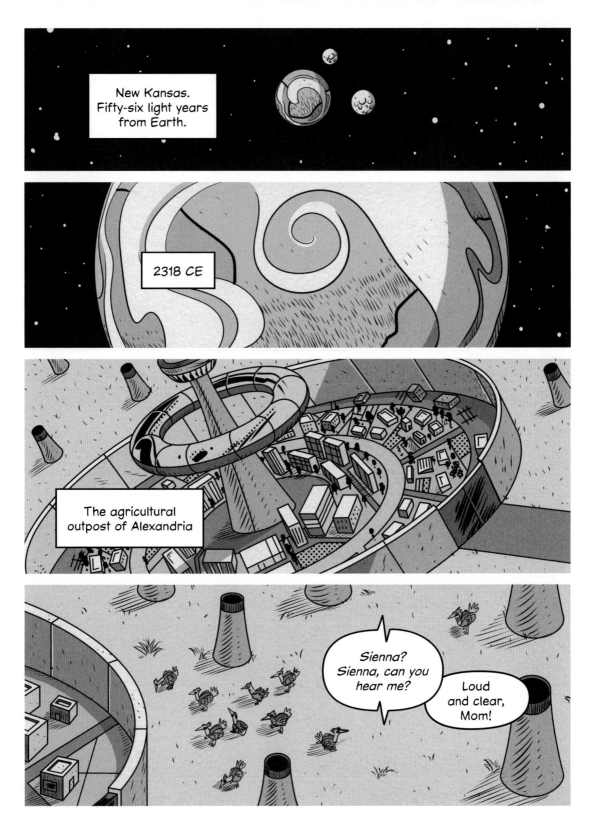

New Kansas.
Fifty-six light years
from Earth.

2318 CE

The agricultural
outpost of Alexandria

Sienna?
Sienna, can you
hear me?

Loud
and clear,
Mom!

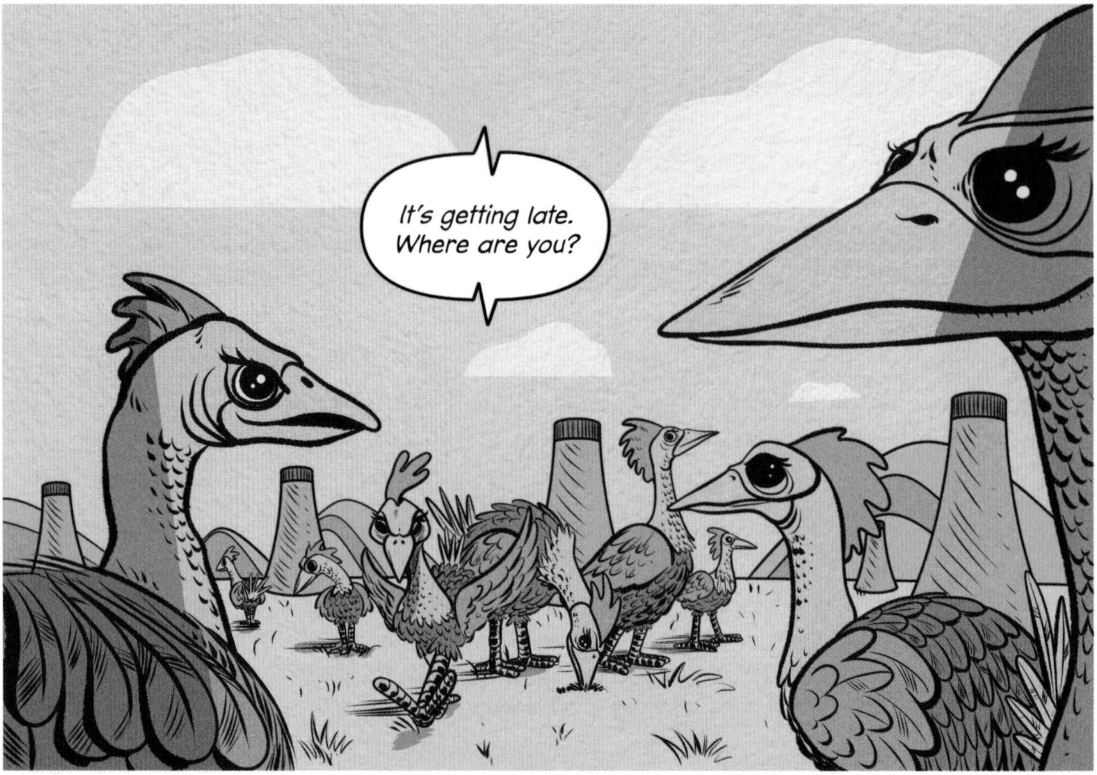
It's getting late.
Where are you?

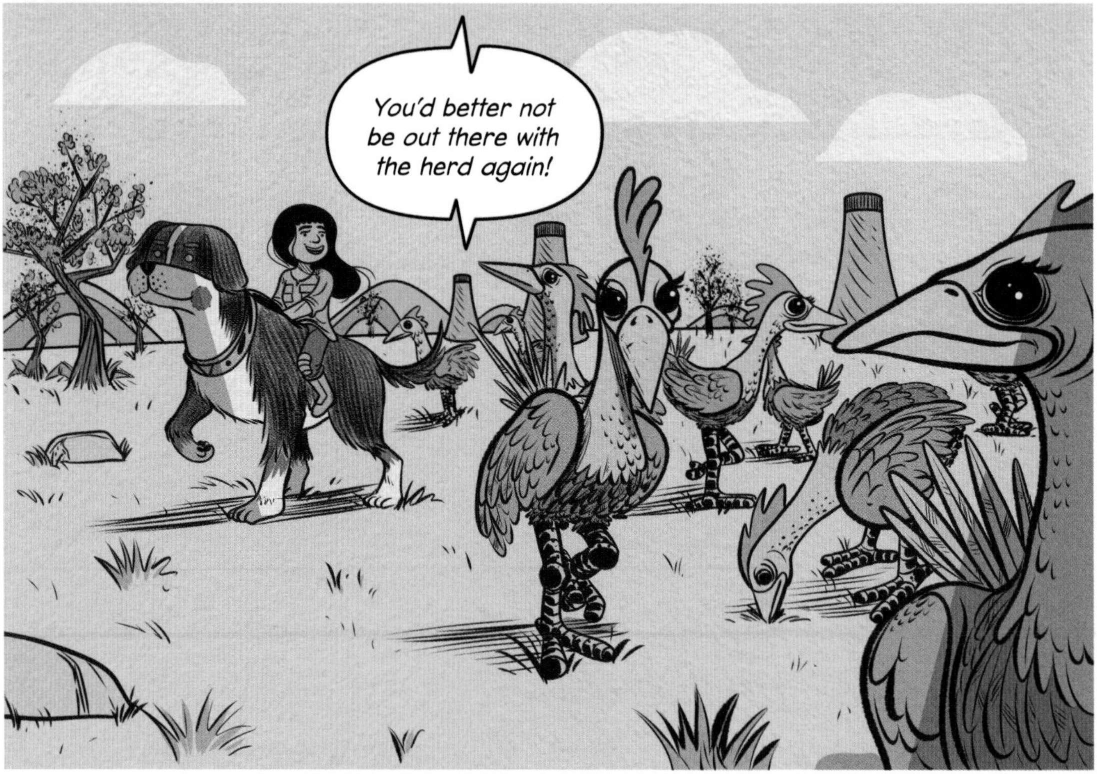
You'd better not
be out there with
the herd again!

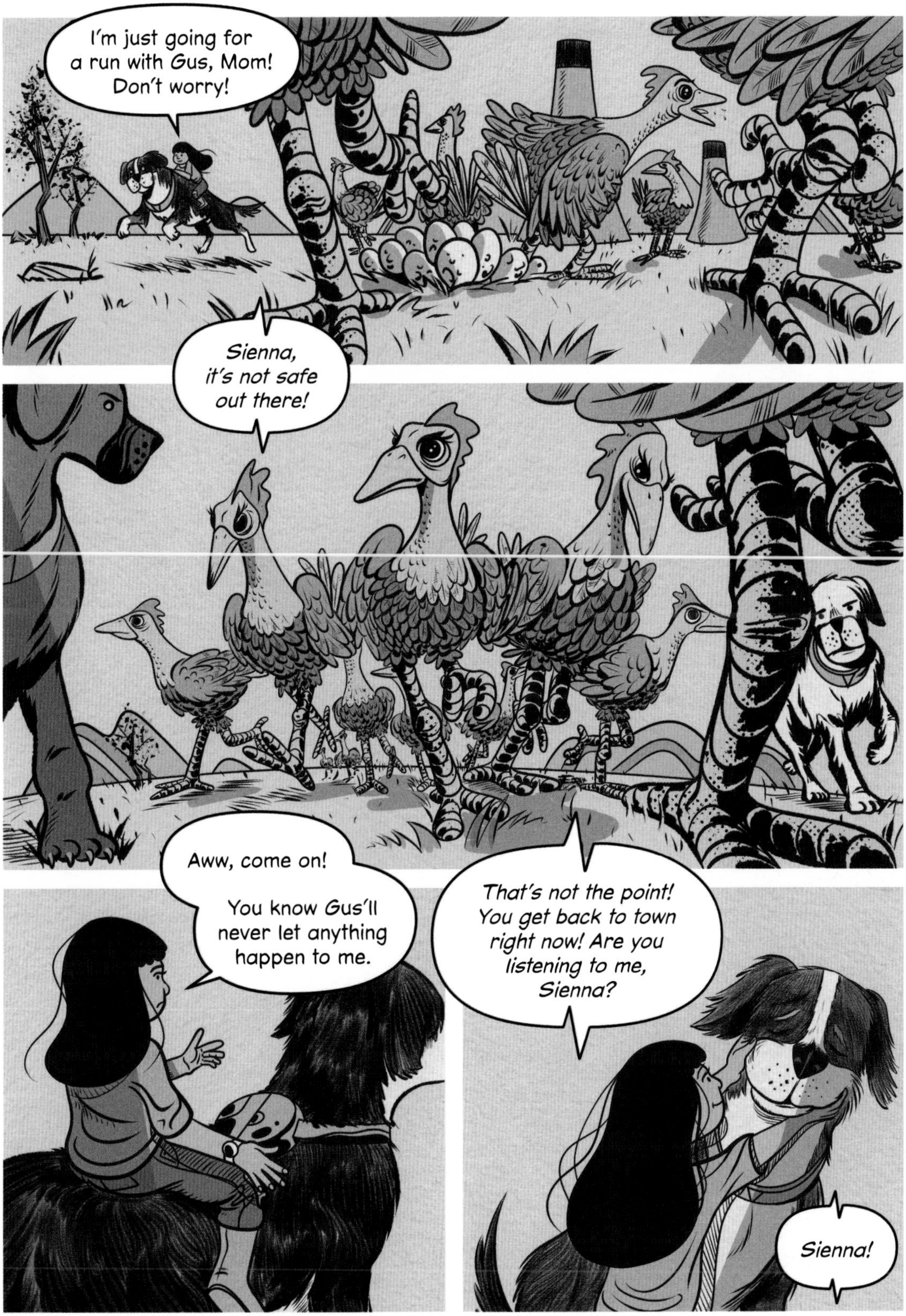
I'm just going for a run with Gus, Mom! Don't worry!
Sienna, it's not safe out there!
Aww, come on!
You know Gus'll never let anything happen to me.
That's not the point! You get back to town right now! Are you listening to me, Sienna?
Sienna!

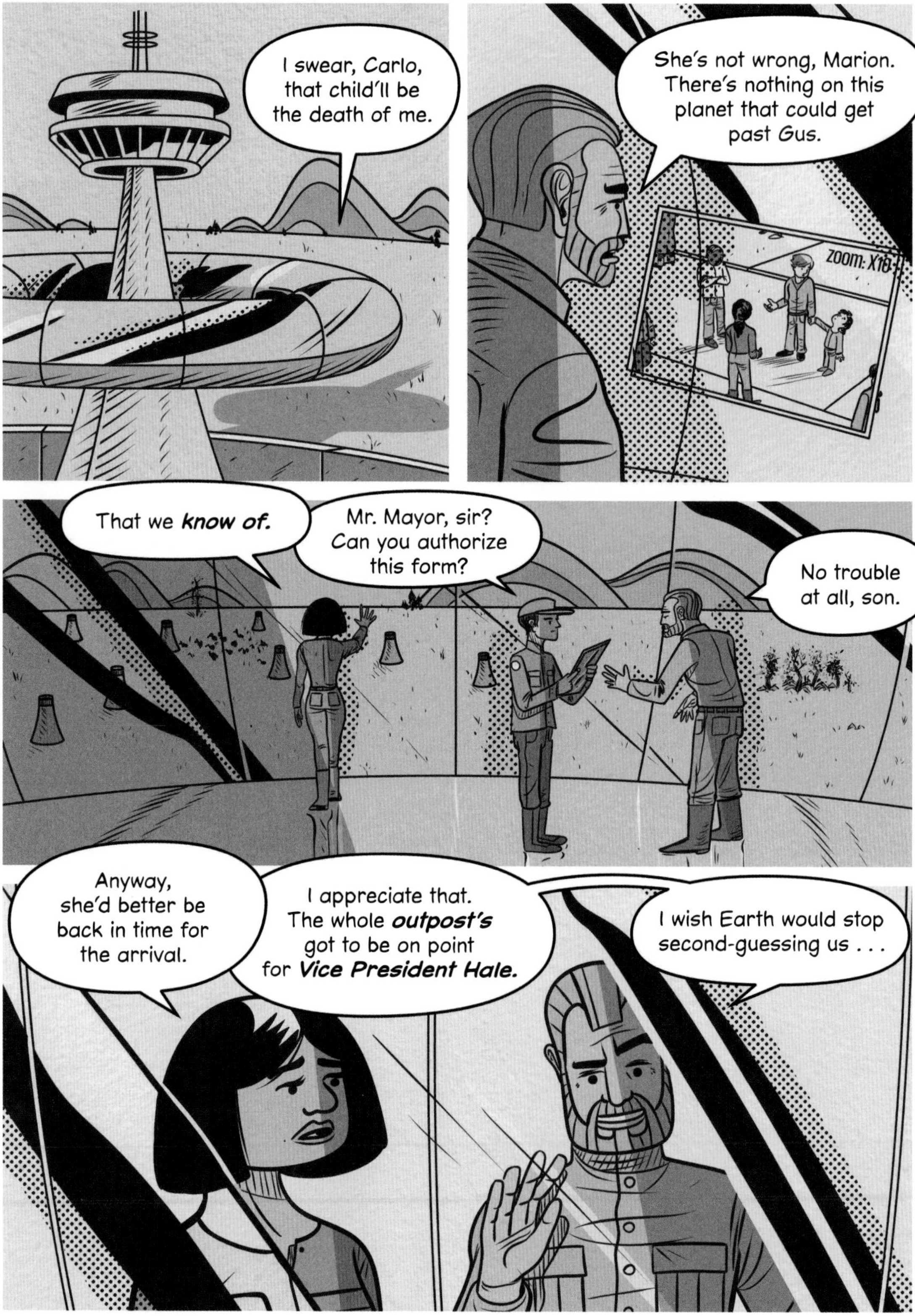
I swear, Carlo, that child'll be the death of me.
She's not wrong, Marion. There's nothing on this planet that could get past Gus.
ZOOM: X10
That we **know of.**
Mr. Mayor, sir? Can you authorize this form?
No trouble at all, son.
Anyway, she'd better be back in time for the arrival.
I appreciate that. The whole **outpost's** got to be on point for **Vice President Hale.**
I wish Earth would stop second-guessing us . . .

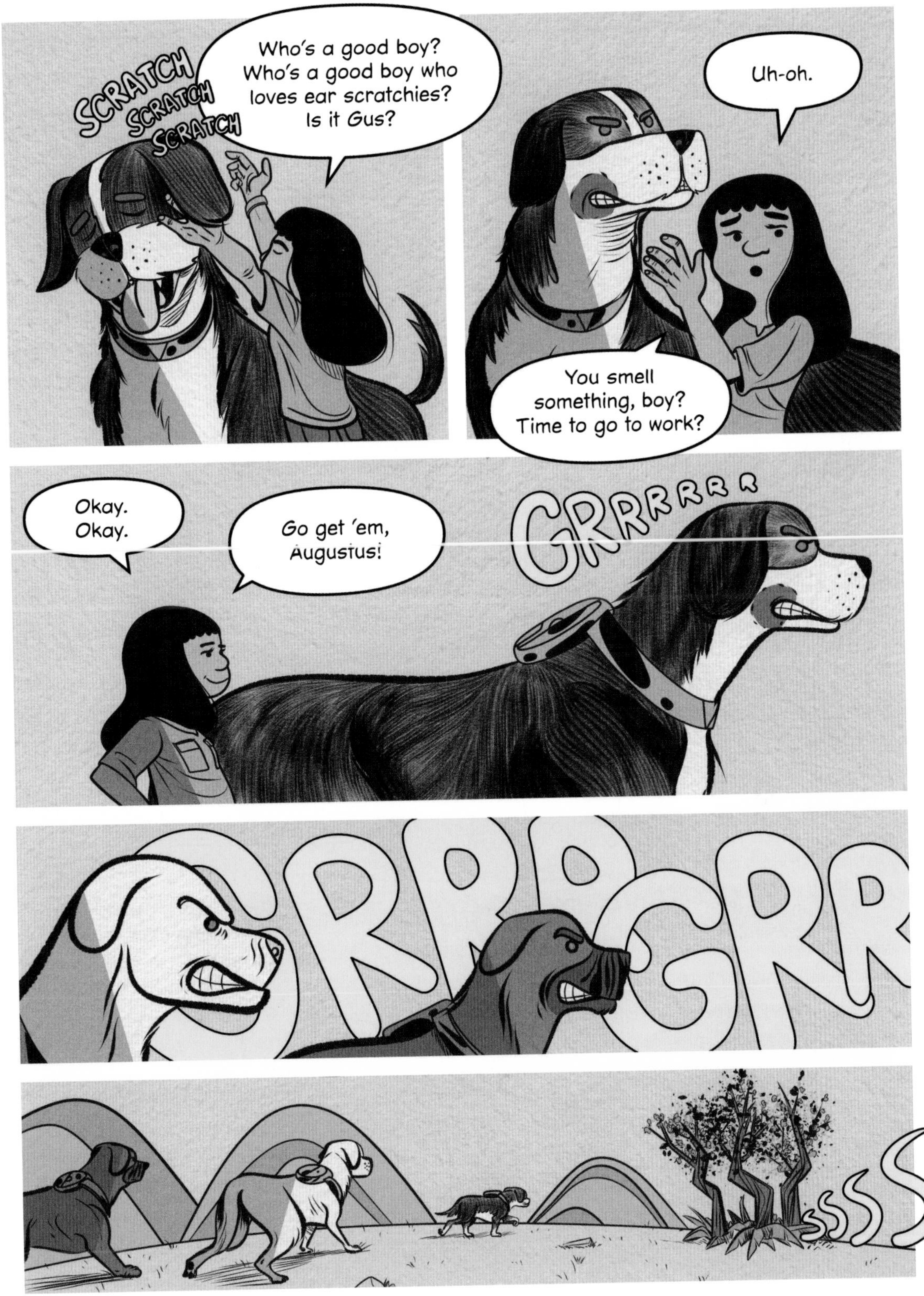
SCRATCH SCRATCH SCRATCH
Who's a good boy? Who's a good boy who loves ear scratchies? Is it Gus?
Uh-oh.
You smell something, boy? Time to go to work?
Okay. Okay.
Go get 'em, Augustus!
GRRRRRR
GRR GRR
SSSS

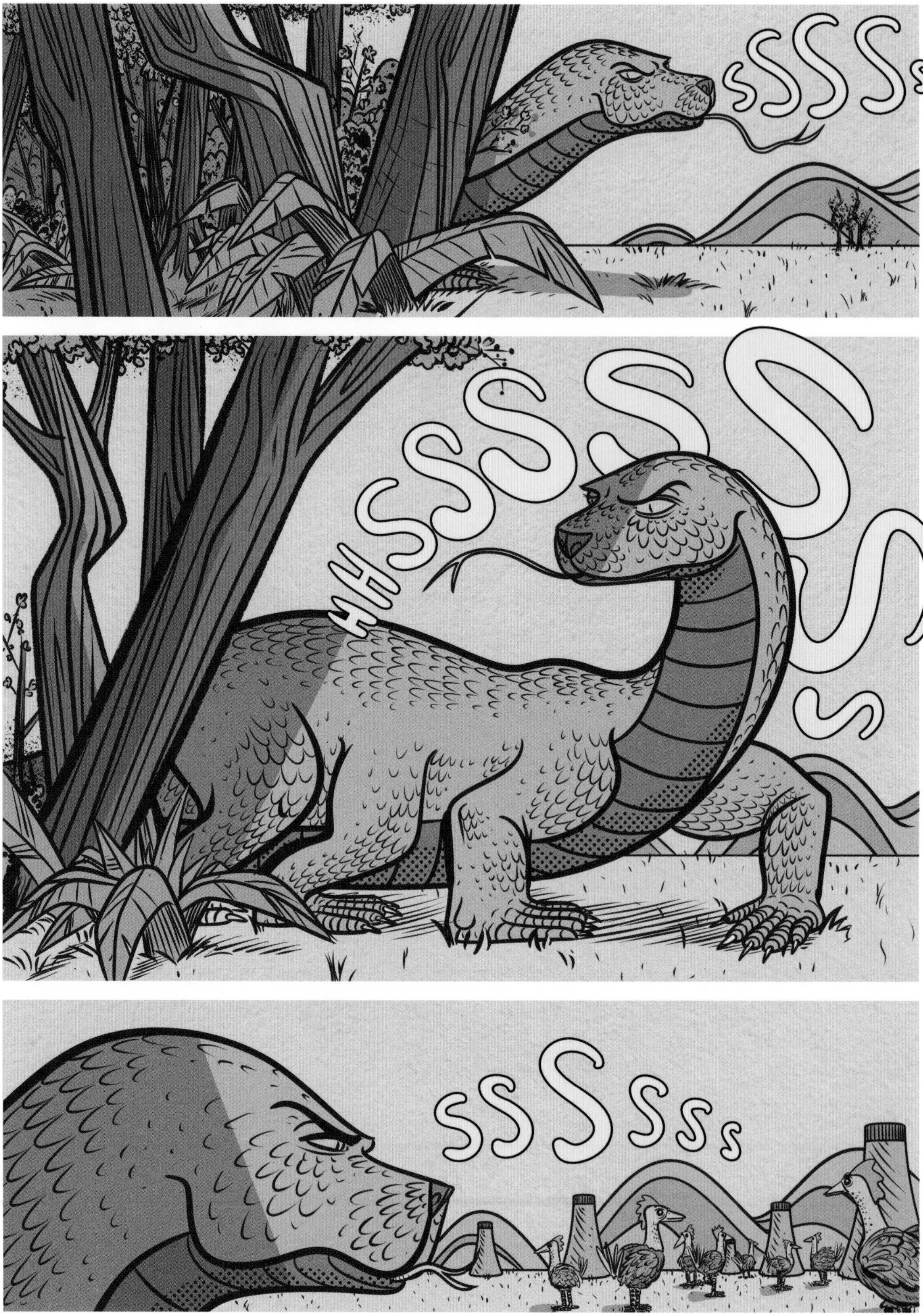
sSSSs
HHSSSSSs
sSSSs

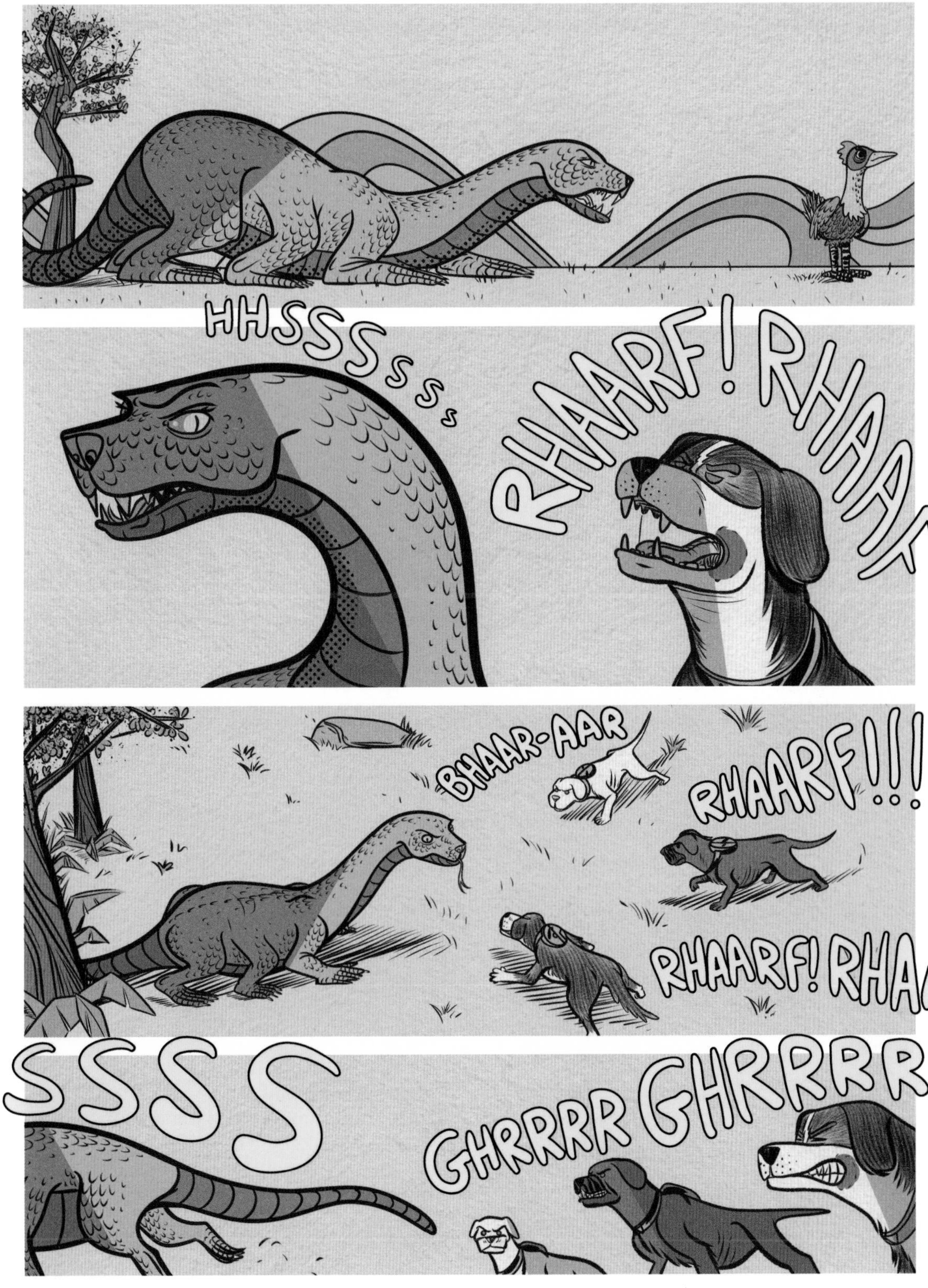
HHSSSsss
RHAARF! RHAAF
BHAAR-AAR
RHAARF!!!
RHAARF! RHAa
SSSS
GHRRRR GHRRRR

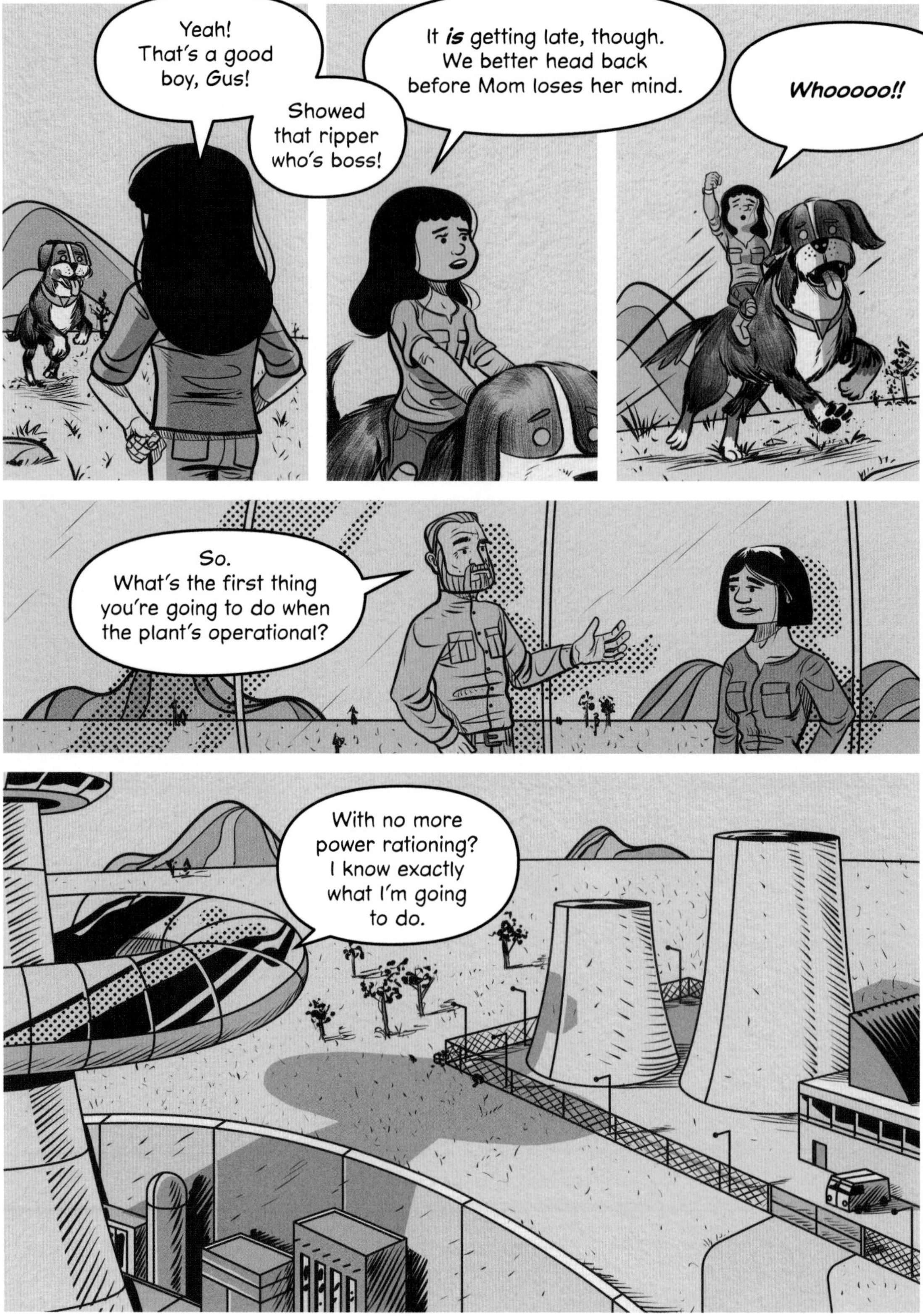
Yeah! That's a good boy, Gus!
Showed that ripper who's boss!
It *is* getting late, though. We better head back before Mom loses her mind.
Whoooooo!!
So. What's the first thing you're going to do when the plant's operational?
With no more power rationing? I know exactly what I'm going to do.

I'm going to take the longest, hottest shower in Alexandria's history.

Good choice.

C'mon, boy, let's see how your better half is doing!

NURSERY

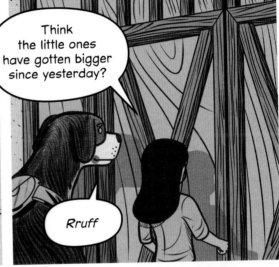

Think the little ones have gotten bigger since yesterday?

Rruff

There they are!

There's my fluff-bundles! Mimi, you outdid yourself with these guys!

Hey there, Cuthbert!

Look how *tall* you're getting! You want some belly rubs? Huh? Huh?

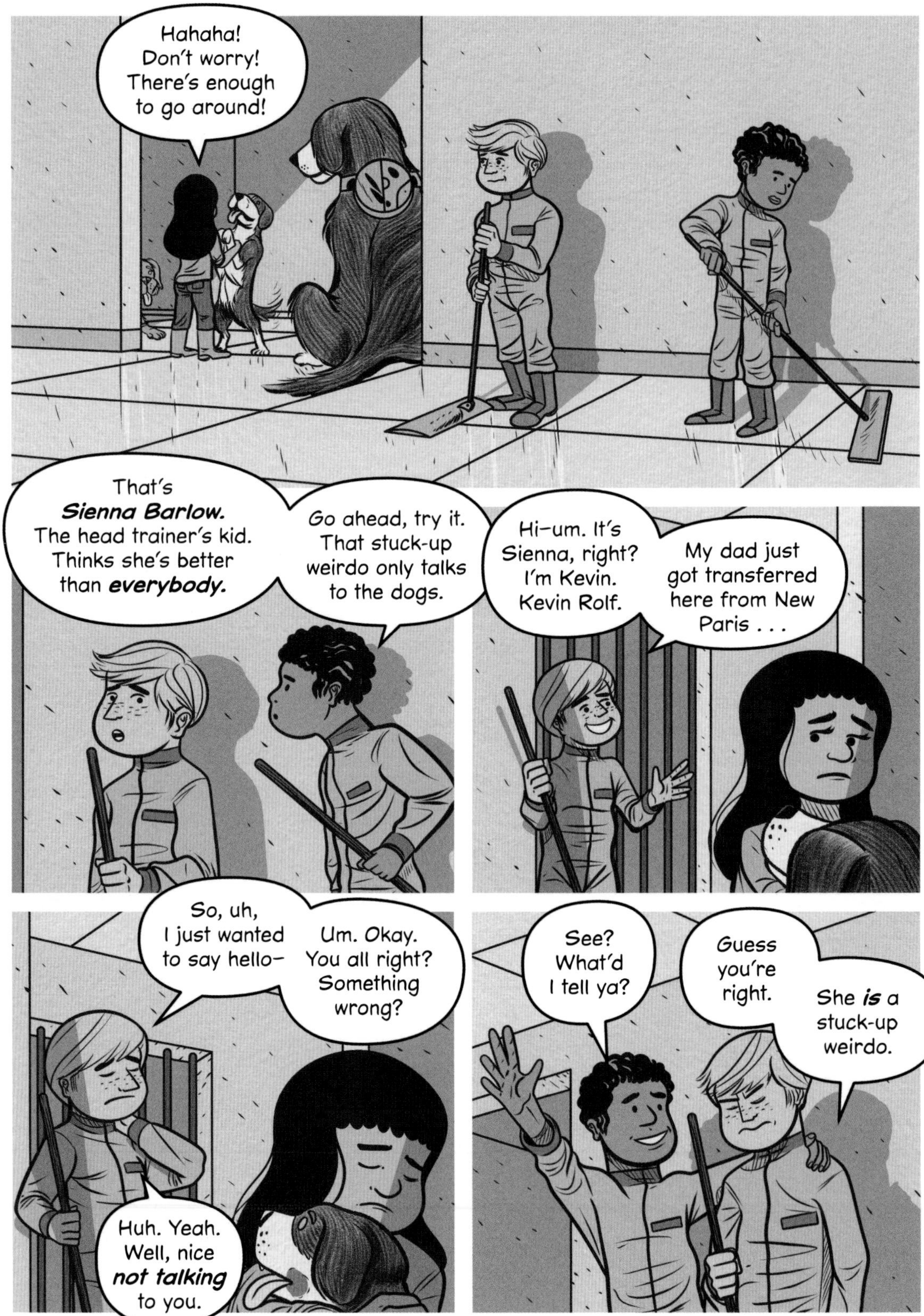

Hahaha! Don't worry! There's enough to go around!
That's **Sienna Barlow.** The head trainer's kid. Thinks she's better than **everybody.**
Go ahead, try it. That stuck-up weirdo only talks to the dogs.
Hi—um. It's Sienna, right? I'm Kevin. Kevin Rolf.
My dad just got transferred here from New Paris . . .
So, uh, I just wanted to say hello—
Um. Okay. You all right? Something wrong?
Huh. Yeah. Well, nice **not talking** to you.
See? What'd I tell ya?
Guess you're right.
She ***is*** a stuck-up weirdo.

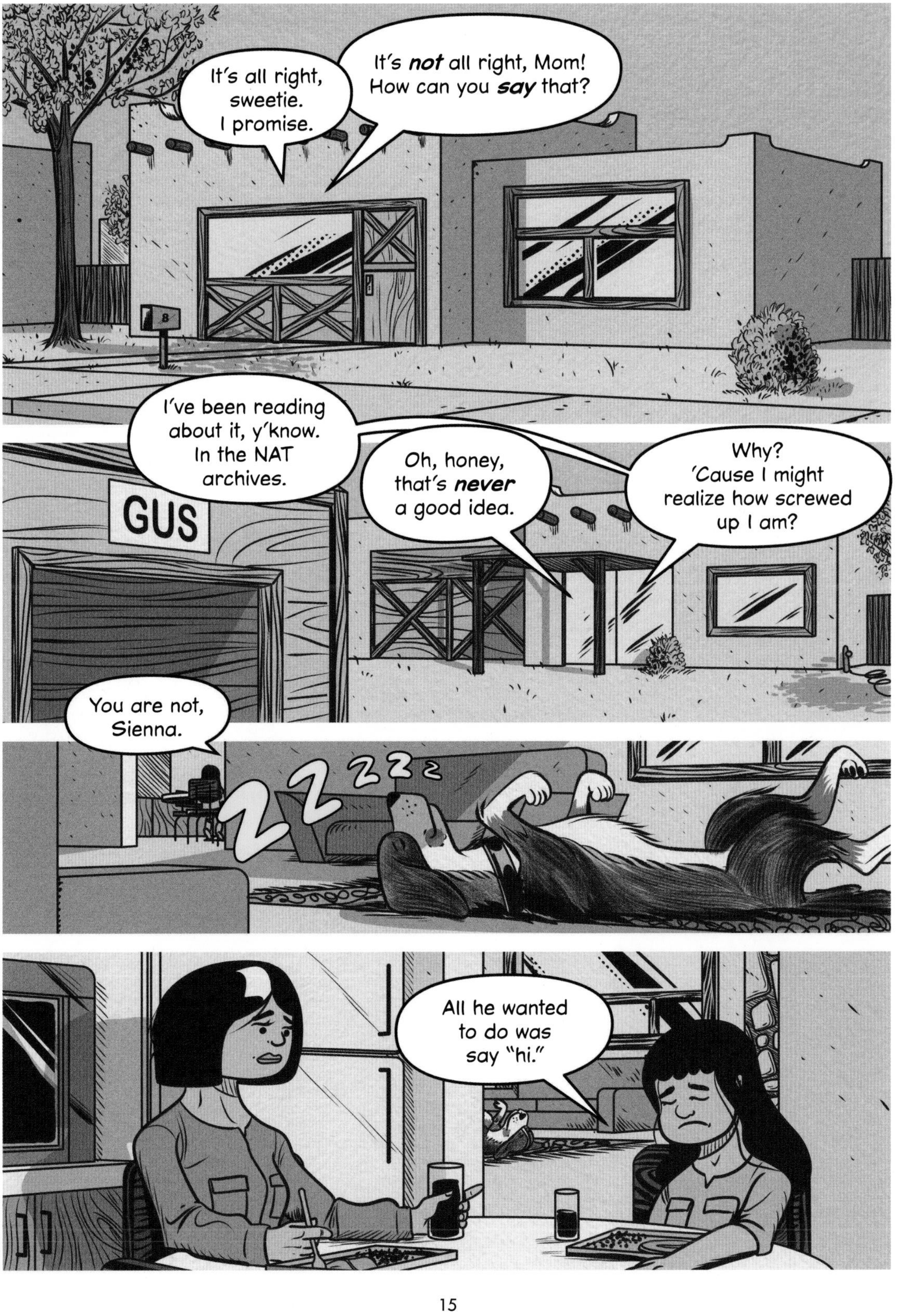
It's all right, sweetie. I promise.
It's **not** all right, Mom! How can you **say** that?
I've been reading about it, y'know. In the NAT archives.
GUS
Oh, honey, that's **never** a good idea.
Why? 'Cause I might realize how screwed up I am?
You are not, Sienna.
ZZZZZZ
All he wanted to do was say "hi."

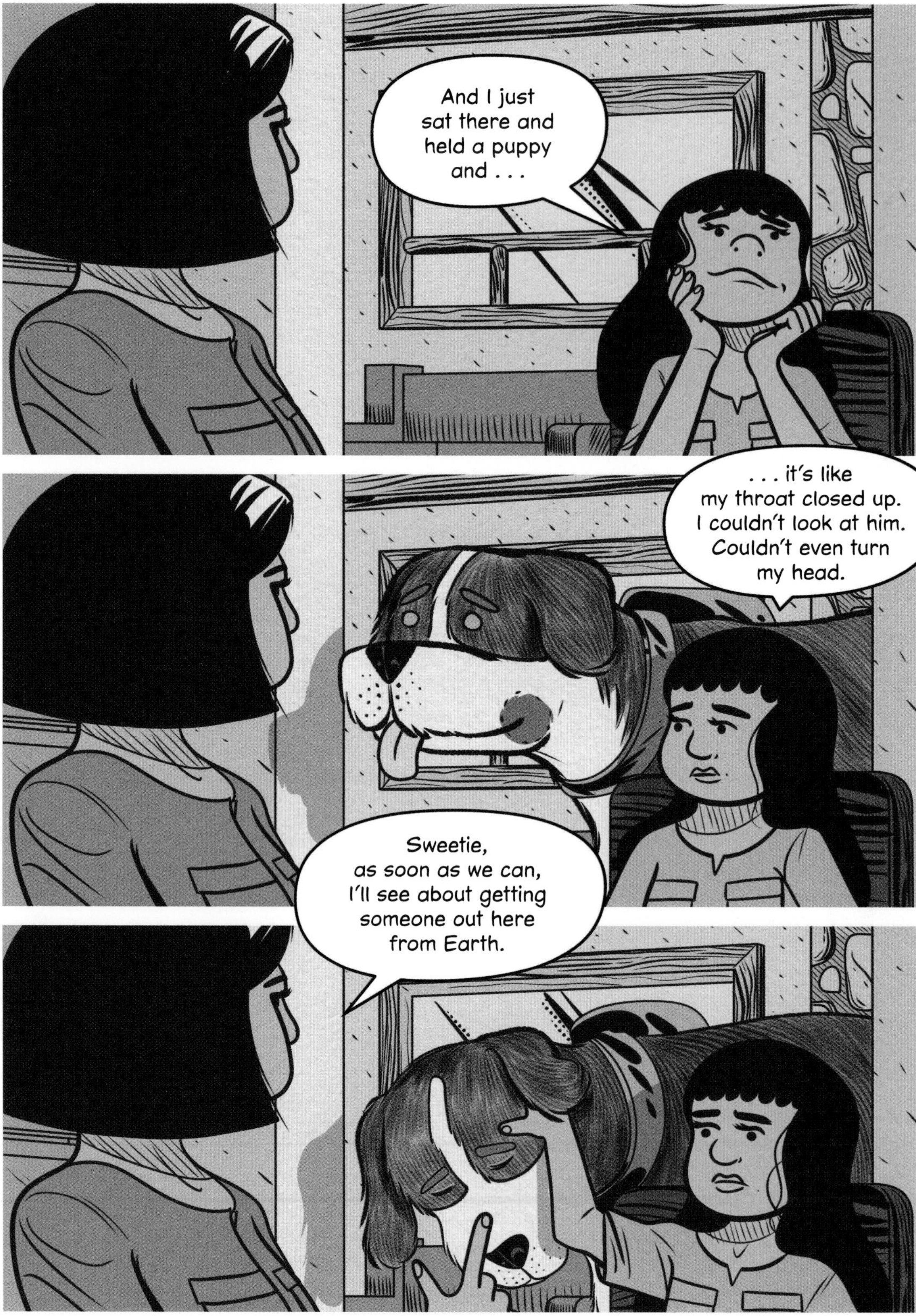
And I just sat there and held a puppy and . . .
. . . it's like my throat closed up. I couldn't look at him. Couldn't even turn my head.
Sweetie, as soon as we can, I'll see about getting someone out here from Earth.

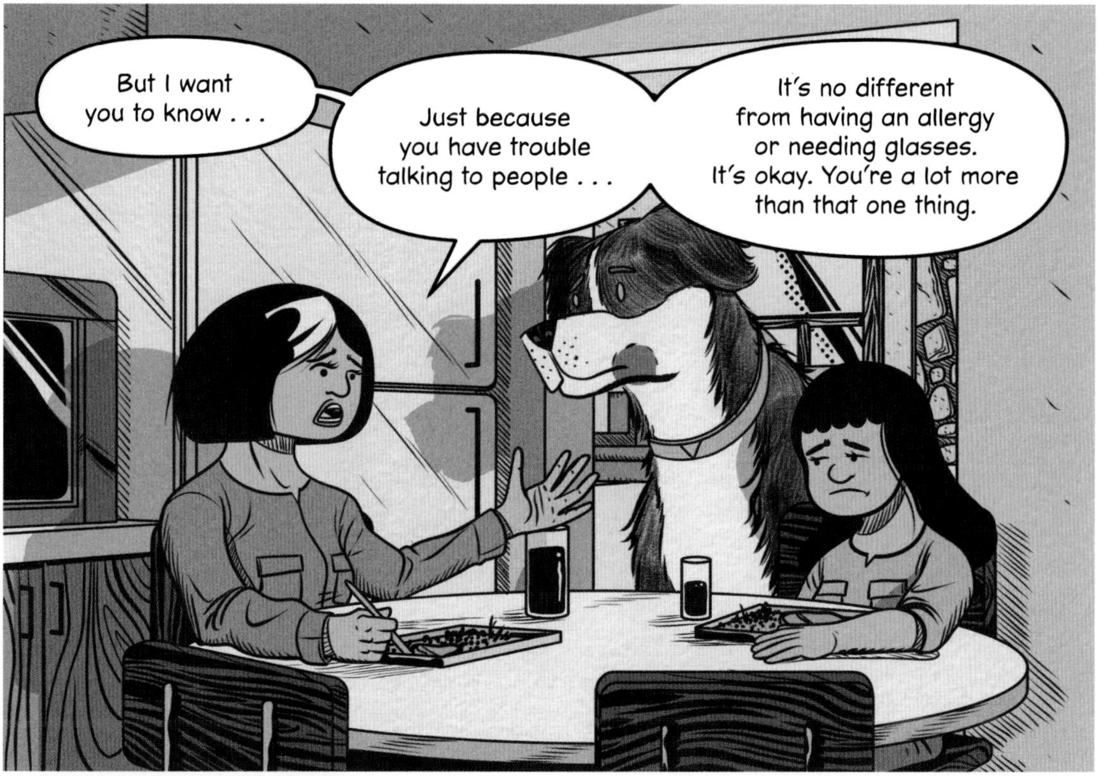
But I want you to know . . .
Just because you have trouble talking to people . . .
It's no different from having an allergy or needing glasses. It's okay. You're a lot more than that one thing.

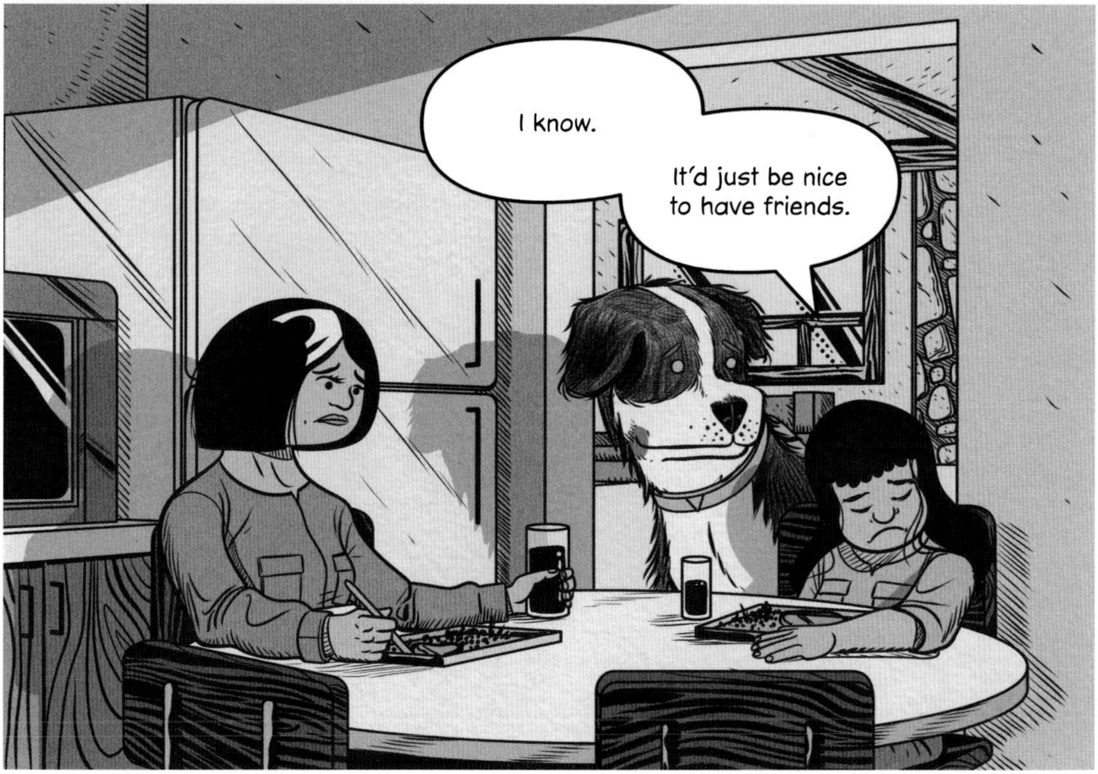
I know.
It'd just be nice to have friends.

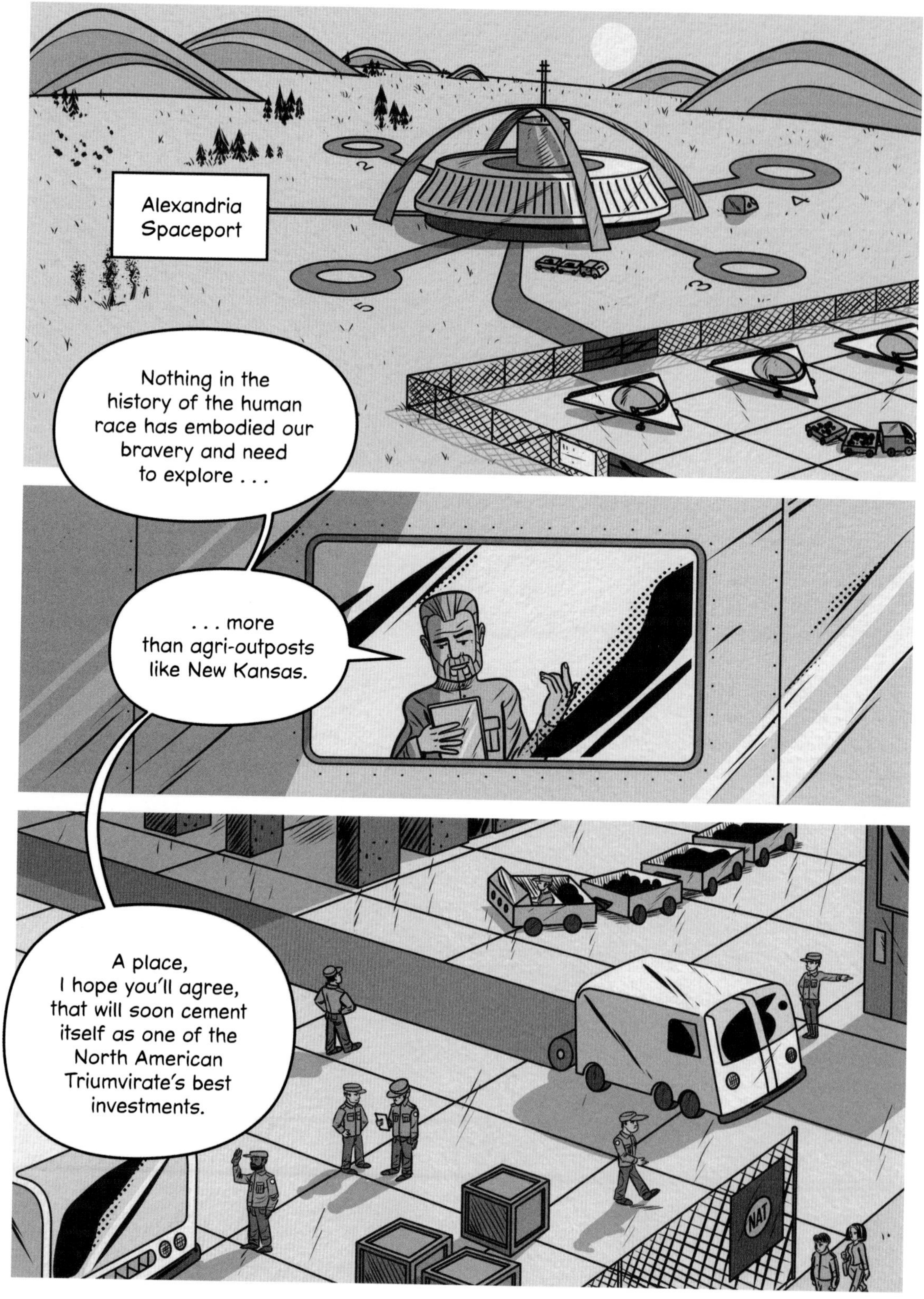
Alexandria Spaceport
Nothing in the history of the human race has embodied our bravery and need to explore . . .
. . . more than agri-outposts like New Kansas.
A place, I hope you'll agree, that will soon cement itself as one of the North American Triumvirate's best investments.
NAT

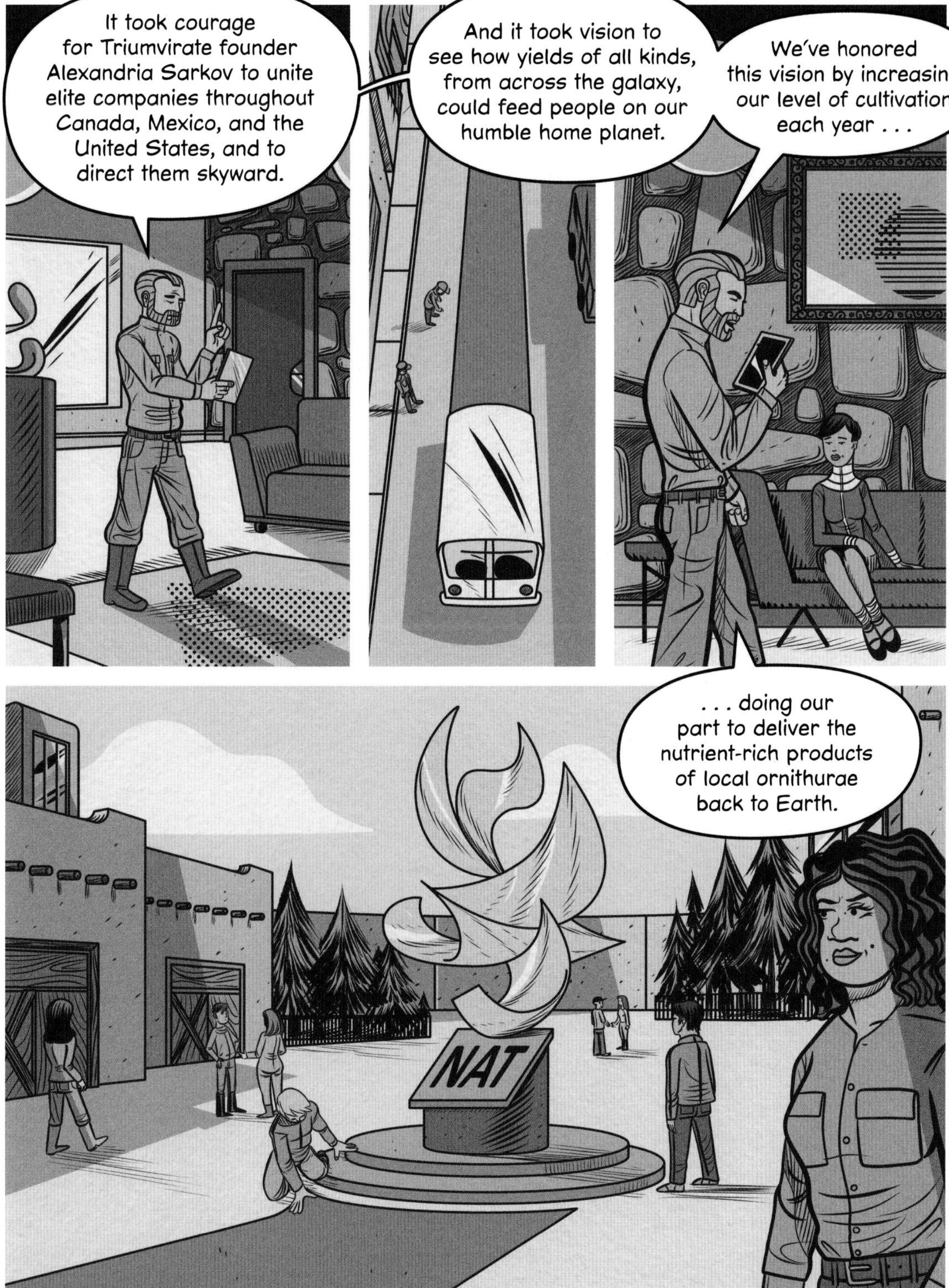
It took courage for Triumvirate founder Alexandria Sarkov to unite elite companies throughout Canada, Mexico, and the United States, and to direct them skyward.
And it took vision to see how yields of all kinds, from across the galaxy, could feed people on our humble home planet.
We've honored this vision by increasing our level of cultivation each year . . .
. . . doing our part to deliver the nutrient-rich products of local ornithurae back to Earth.
NAT

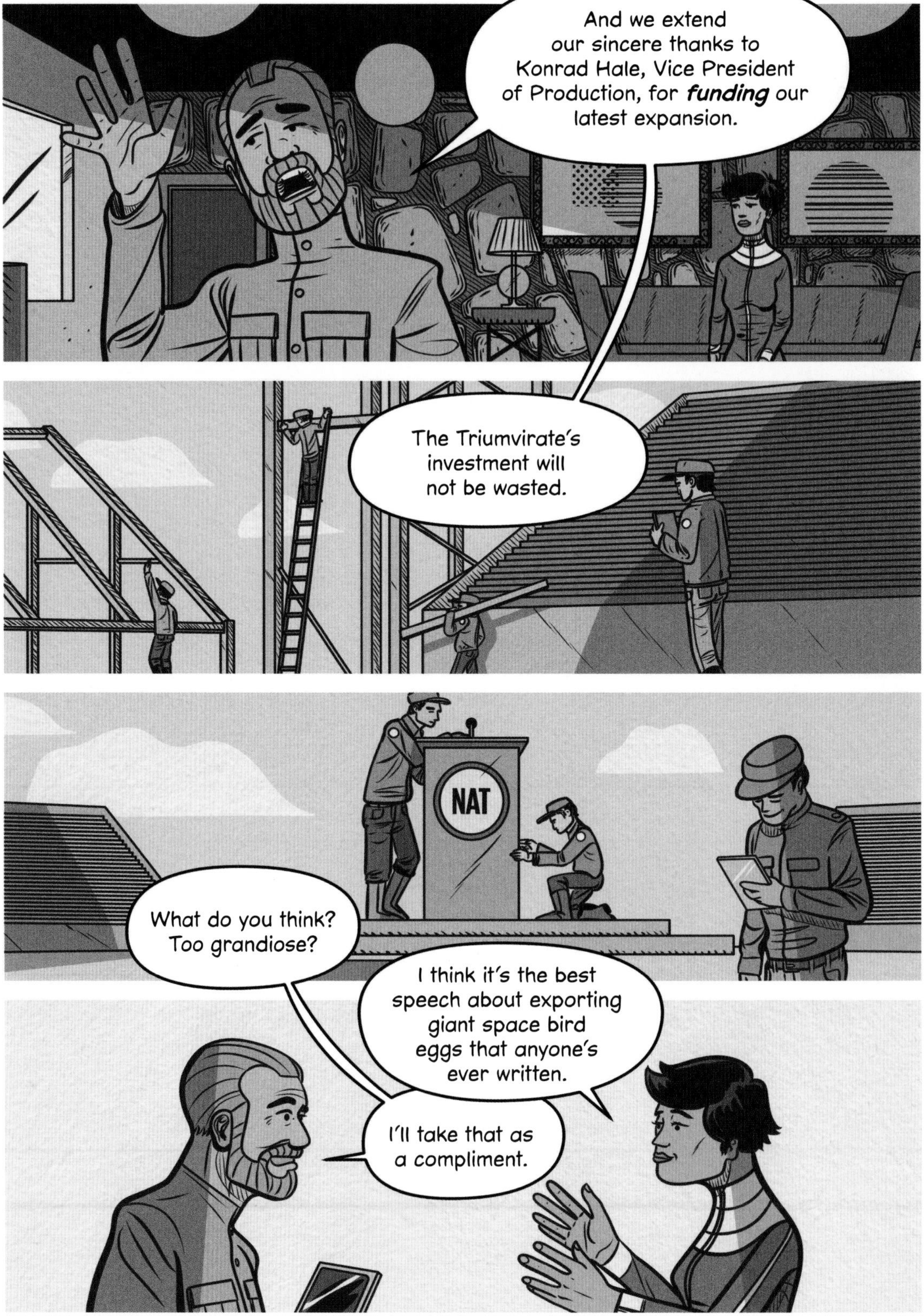
And we extend our sincere thanks to Konrad Hale, Vice President of Production, for ***funding*** our latest expansion.
The Triumvirate's investment will not be wasted.
NAT
What do you think? Too grandiose?
I think it's the best speech about exporting giant space bird eggs that anyone's ever written.
I'll take that as a compliment.

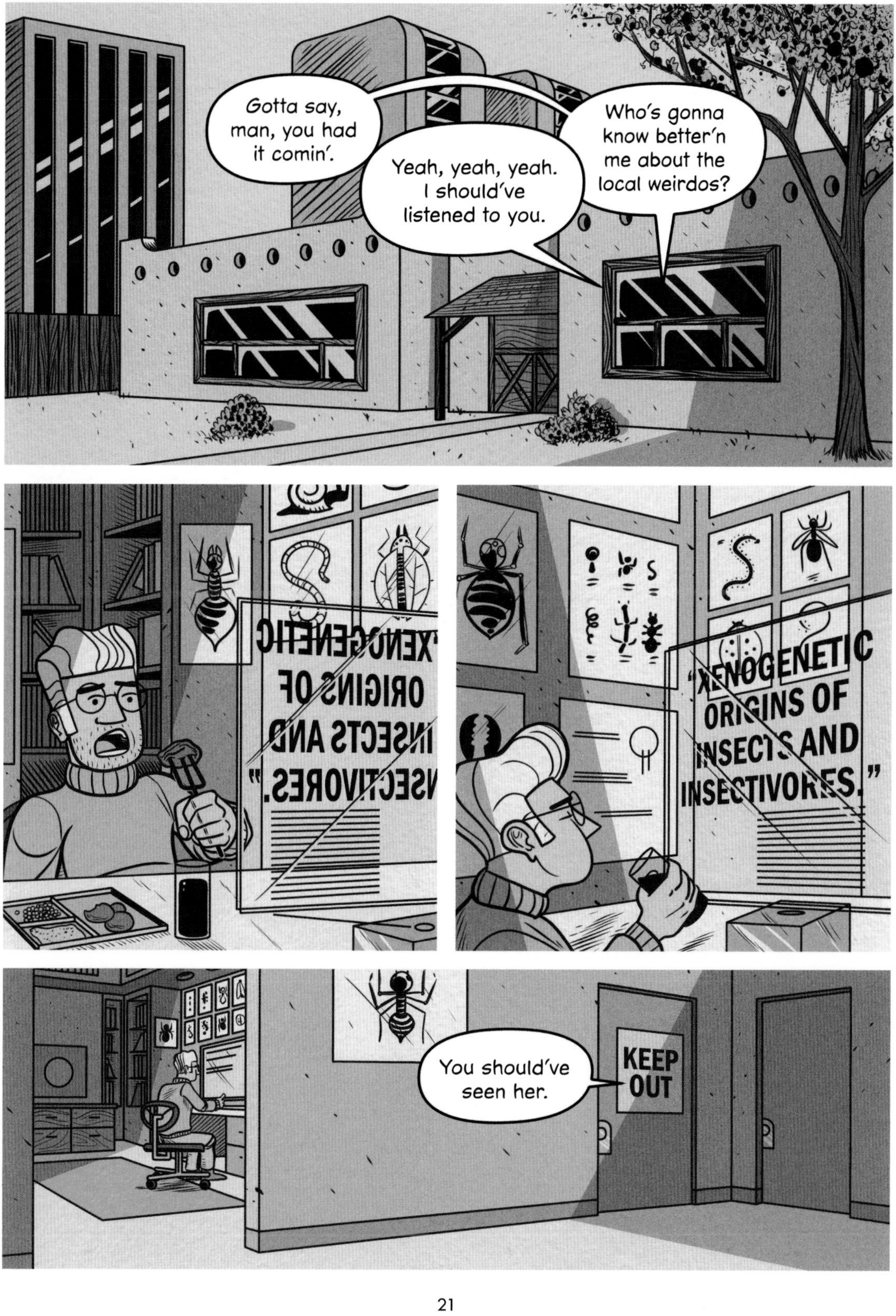
Gotta say, man, you had it comin'.
Yeah, yeah, yeah. I should've listened to you.
Who's gonna know better'n me about the local weirdos?
"XENOGENETIC ORIGINS OF INSECTS AND INSECTIVORES."
You should've seen her.
KEEP OUT

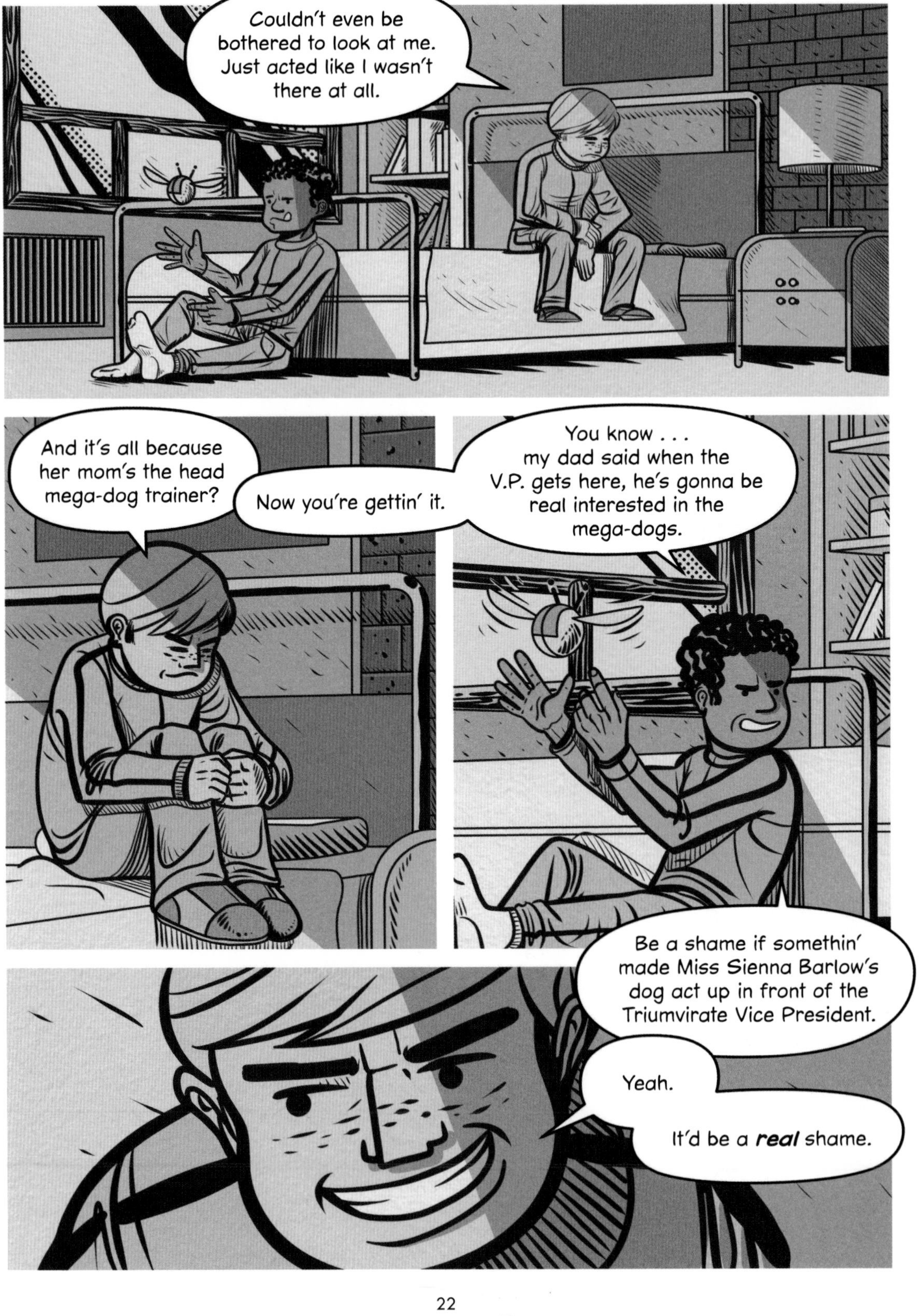

Couldn't even be bothered to look at me. Just acted like I wasn't there at all.
And it's all because her mom's the head mega-dog trainer?
Now you're gettin' it.
You know . . . my dad said when the V.P. gets here, he's gonna be real interested in the mega-dogs.
Be a shame if somethin' made Miss Sienna Barlow's dog act up in front of the Triumvirate Vice President.
Yeah.
It'd be a ***real*** shame.

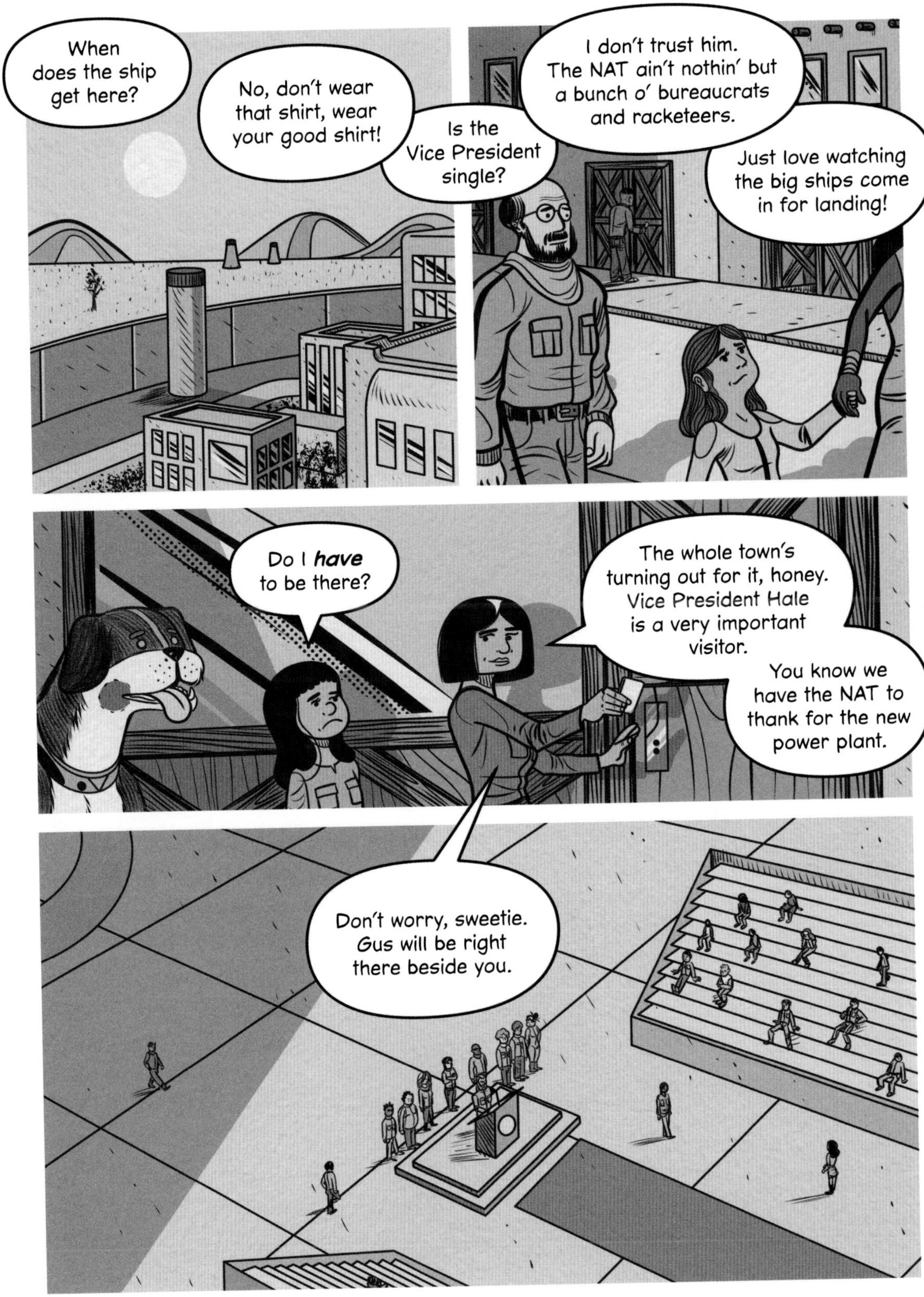
When does the ship get here?
No, don't wear that shirt, wear your good shirt!
Is the Vice President single?
I don't trust him. The NAT ain't nothin' but a bunch o' bureaucrats and racketeers.
Just love watching the big ships come in for landing!
Do I *have* to be there?
The whole town's turning out for it, honey. Vice President Hale is a very important visitor.
You know we have the NAT to thank for the new power plant.
Don't worry, sweetie. Gus will be right there beside you.

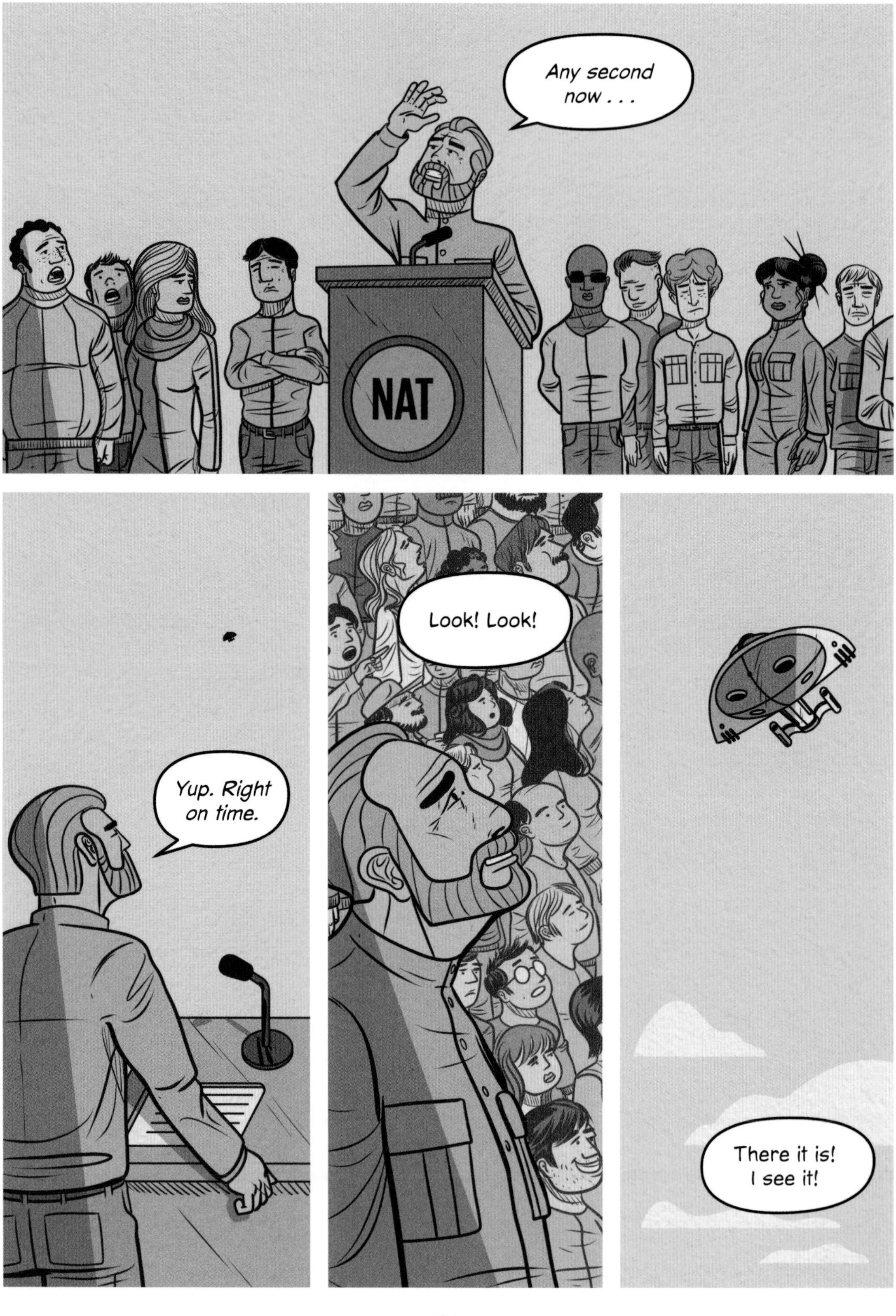
Any second now . . .
NAT
Yup. Right on time.
Look! Look!
There it is! I see it!

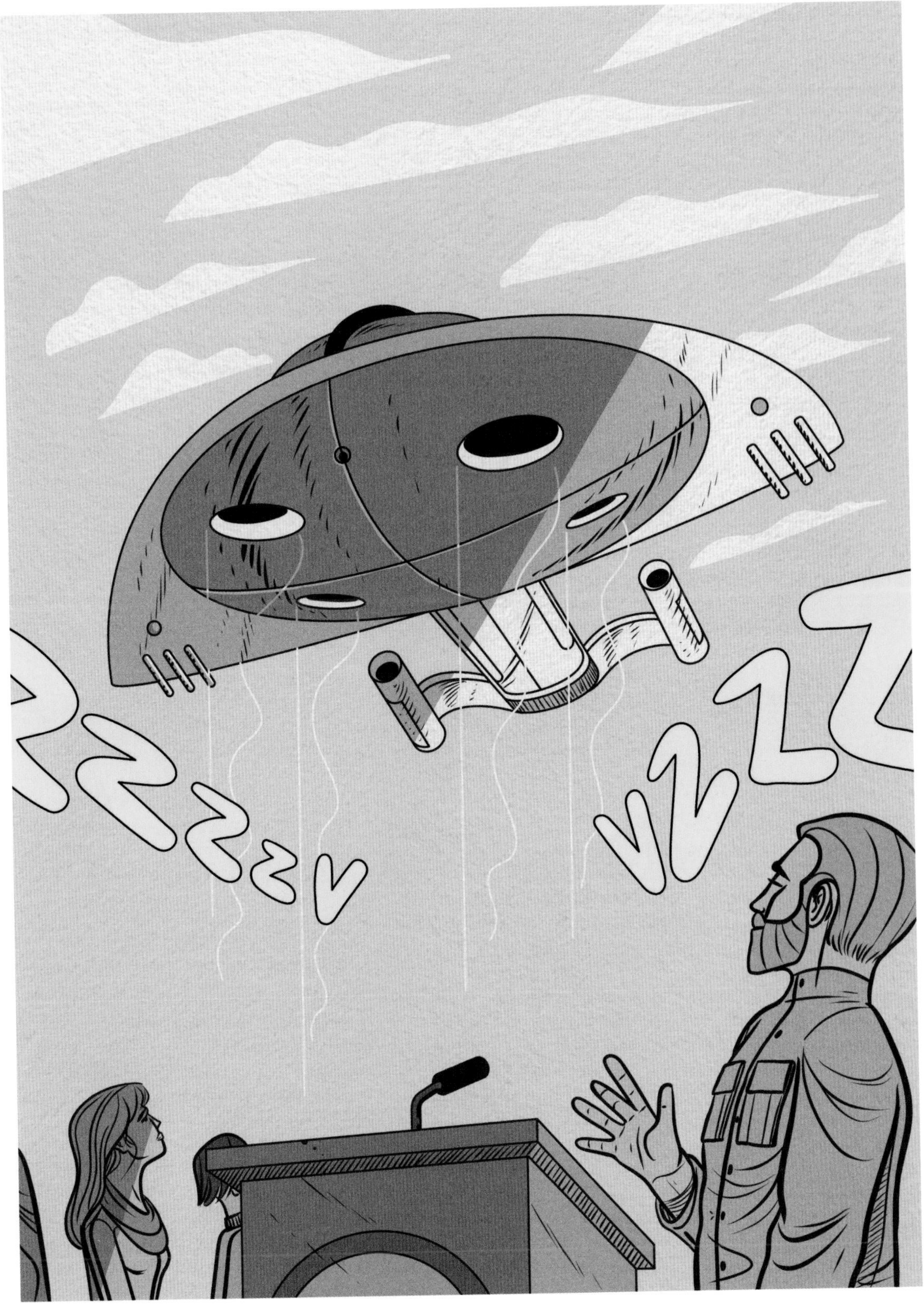
ZZZZV
VZZZ

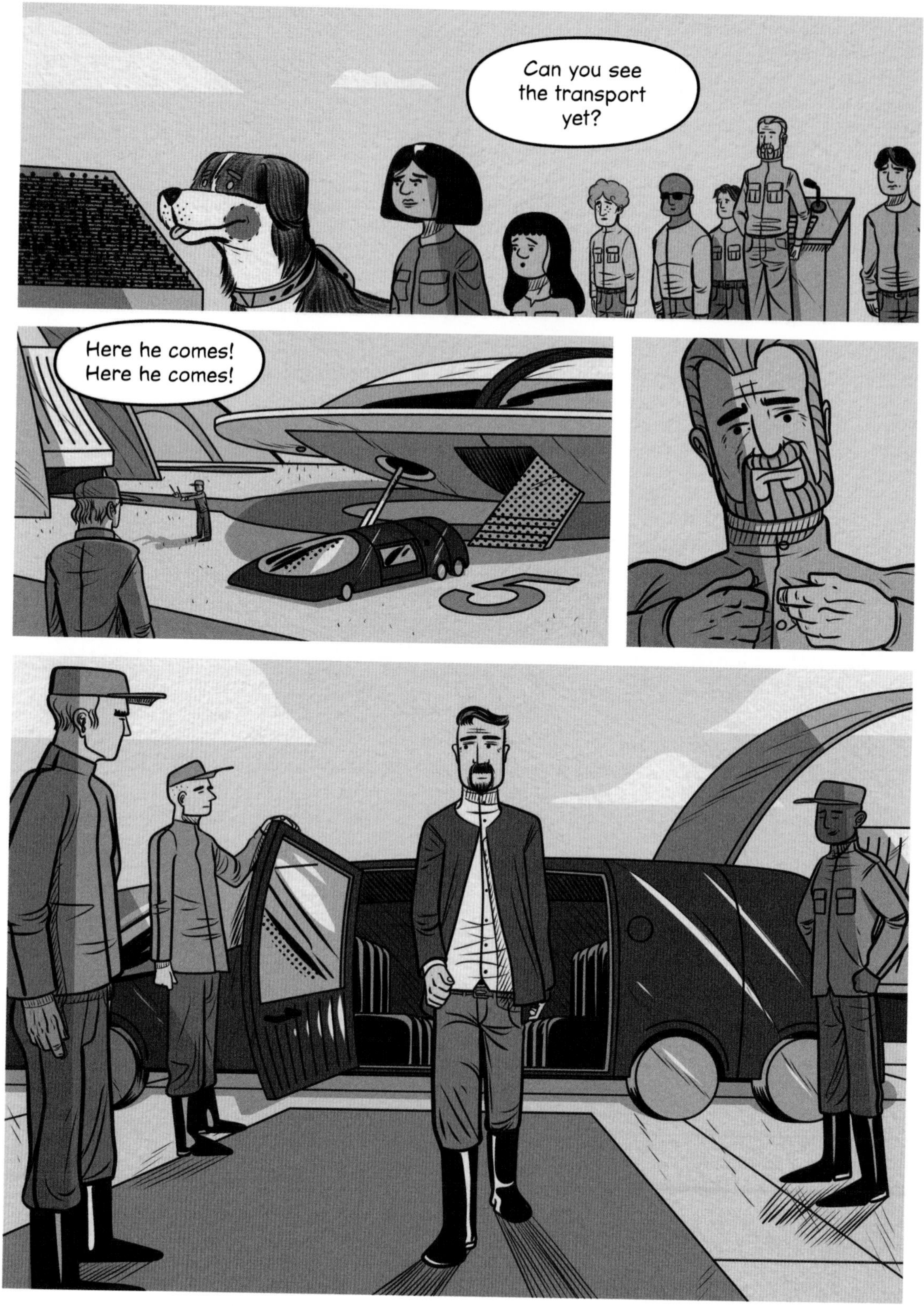

Can you see the transport yet?
Here he comes! Here he comes!

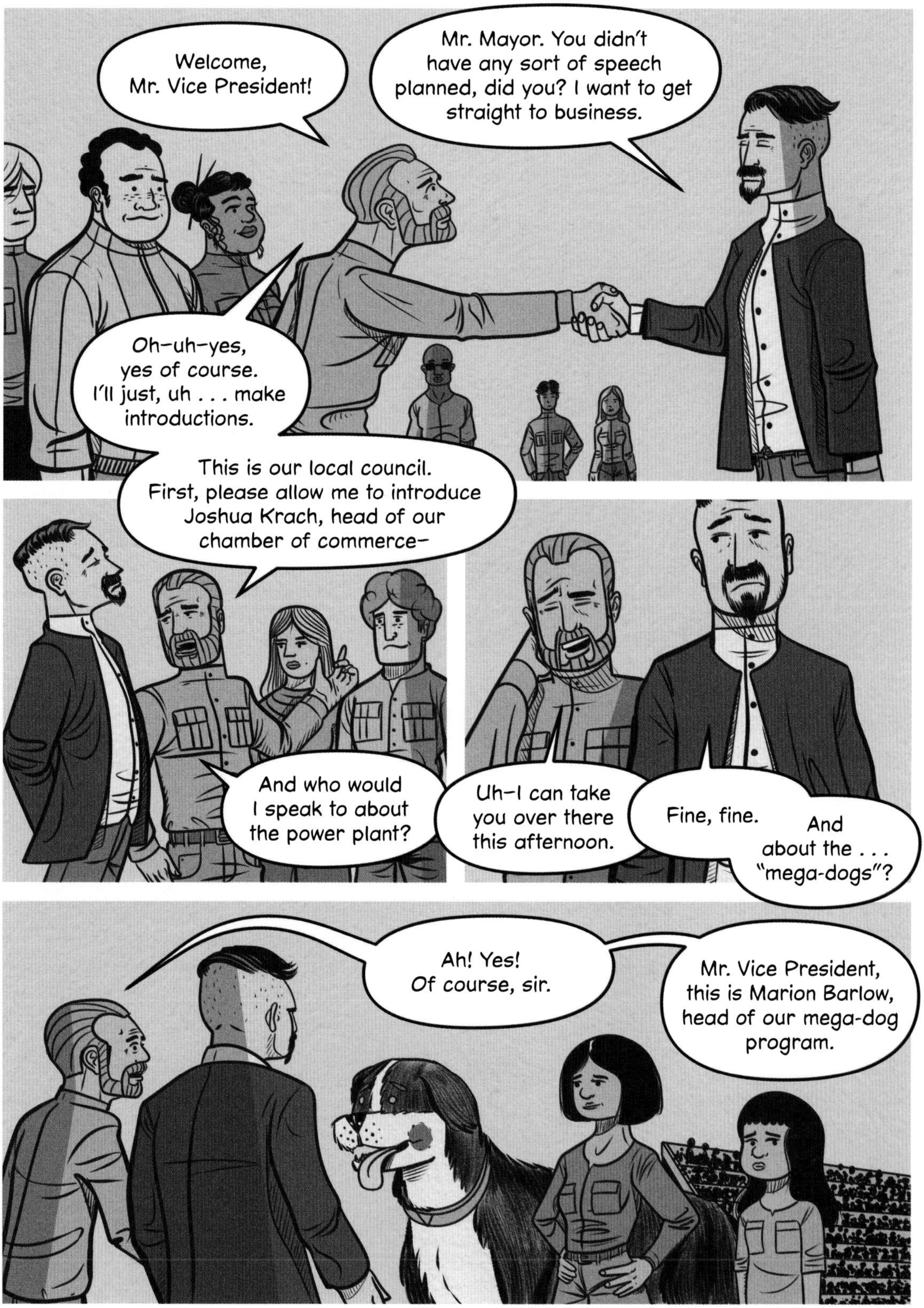

Welcome, Mr. Vice President!
Mr. Mayor. You didn't have any sort of speech planned, did you? I want to get straight to business.
Oh–uh–yes, yes of course. I'll just, uh . . . make introductions.
This is our local council. First, please allow me to introduce Joshua Krach, head of our chamber of commerce–
And who would I speak to about the power plant?
Uh–I can take you over there this afternoon.
Fine, fine.
And about the . . . "mega-dogs"?
Ah! Yes! Of course, sir.
Mr. Vice President, this is Marion Barlow, head of our mega-dog program.

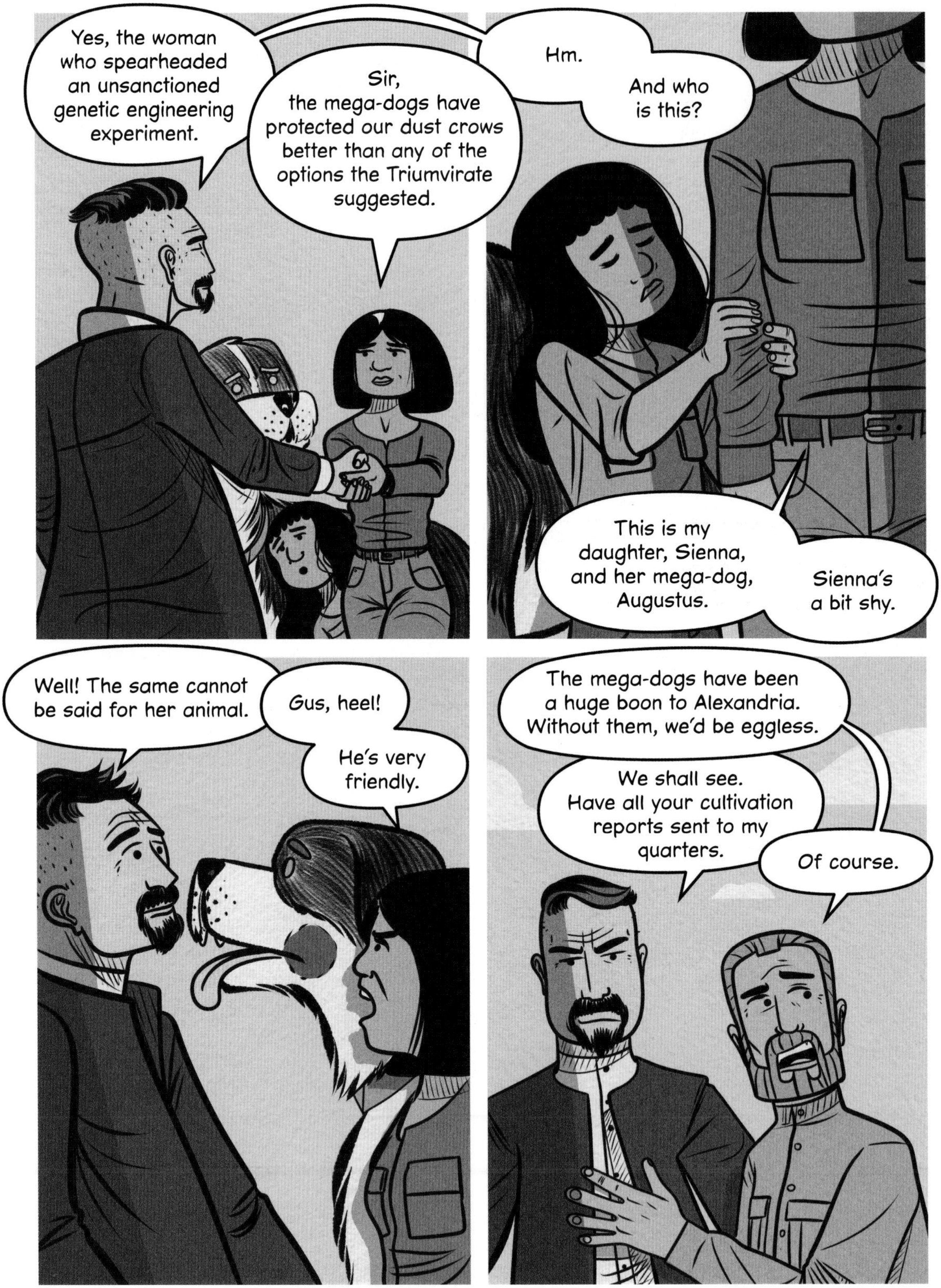
Yes, the woman who spearheaded an unsanctioned genetic engineering experiment.
Sir, the mega-dogs have protected our dust crows better than any of the options the Triumvirate suggested.
Hm.
And who is this?
This is my daughter, Sienna, and her mega-dog, Augustus.
Sienna's a bit shy.
Well! The same cannot be said for her animal.
Gus, heel!
He's very friendly.
The mega-dogs have been a huge boon to Alexandria. Without them, we'd be eggless.
We shall see. Have all your cultivation reports sent to my quarters.
Of course.

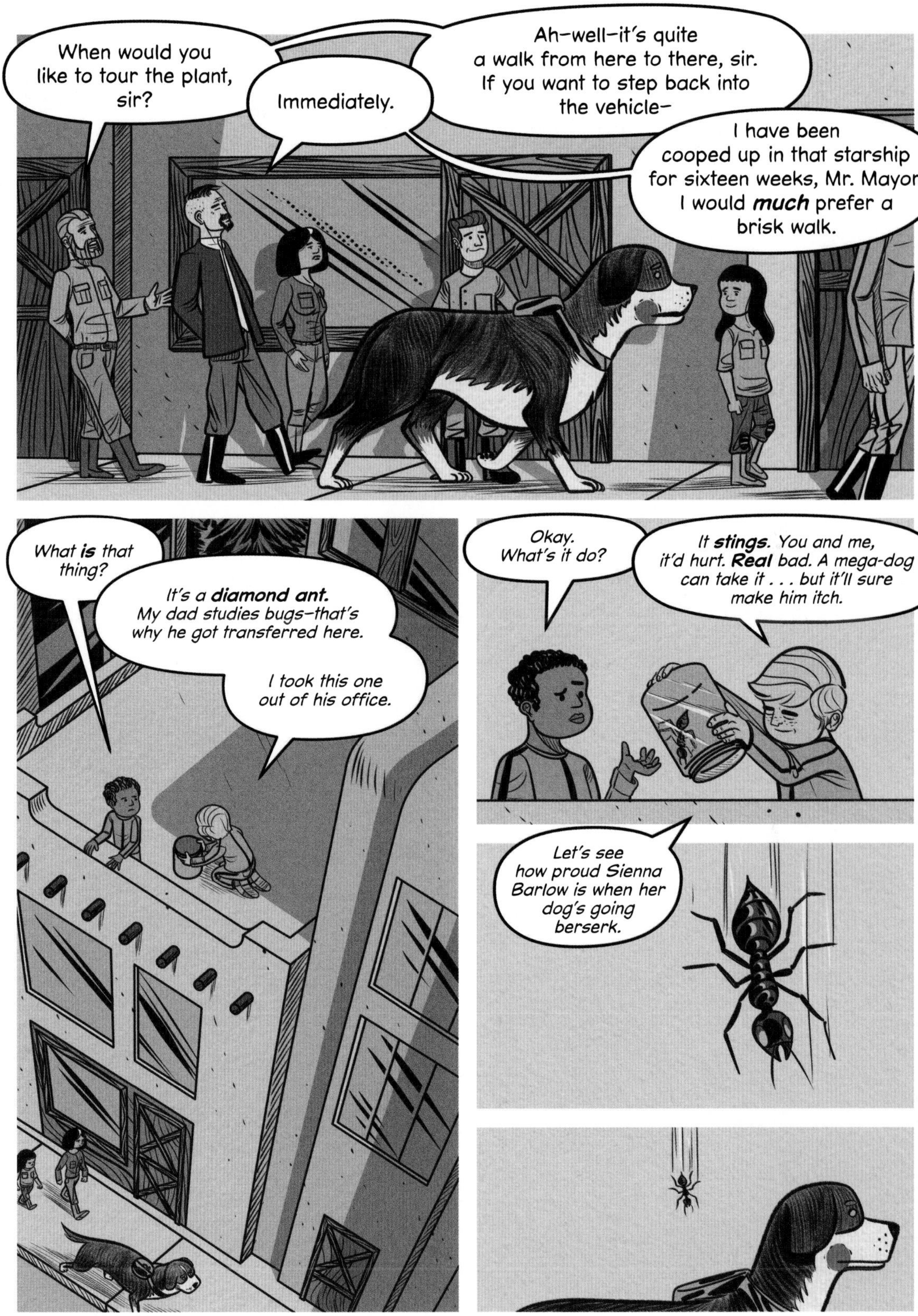

When would you like to tour the plant, sir?
Immediately.
Ah–well–it's quite a walk from here to there, sir. If you want to step back into the vehicle–
I have been cooped up in that starship for sixteen weeks, Mr. Mayor. I would **much** prefer a brisk walk.
What **is** that thing?
It's a **diamond ant.** My dad studies bugs–that's why he got transferred here.
I took this one out of his office.
Okay. What's it do?
It **stings**. You and me, it'd hurt. **Real** bad. A mega-dog can take it . . . but it'll sure make him itch.
Let's see how proud Sienna Barlow is when her dog's going berserk.

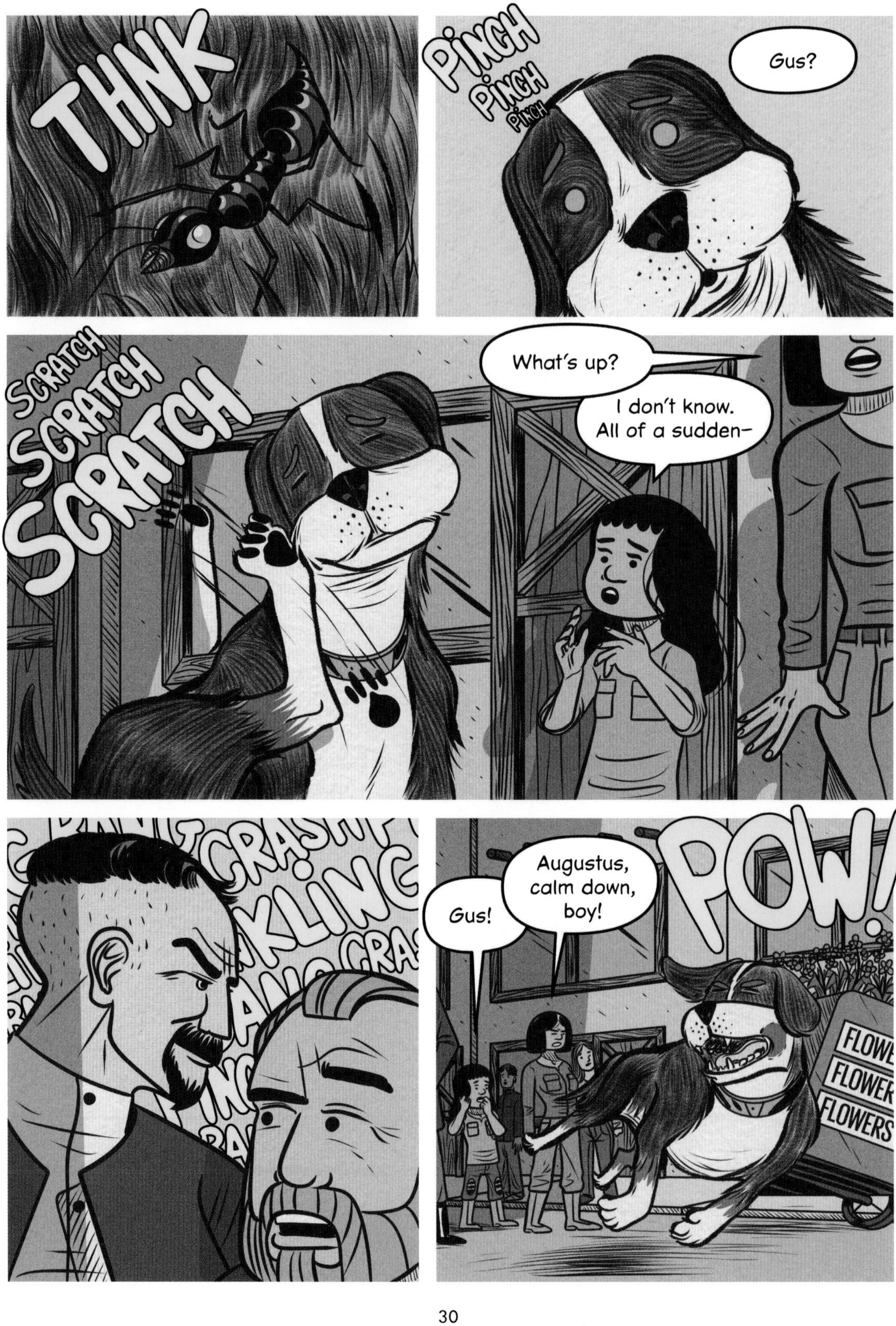
THNK
PINCH
PINCH
PINCH
Gus?
SCRATCH
SCRATCH
SCRATCH
What's up?
I don't know. All of a sudden–
CRASH
KLING
Gus!
Augustus, calm down, boy!
POW!
FLOWERS
FLOWERS
FLOWERS

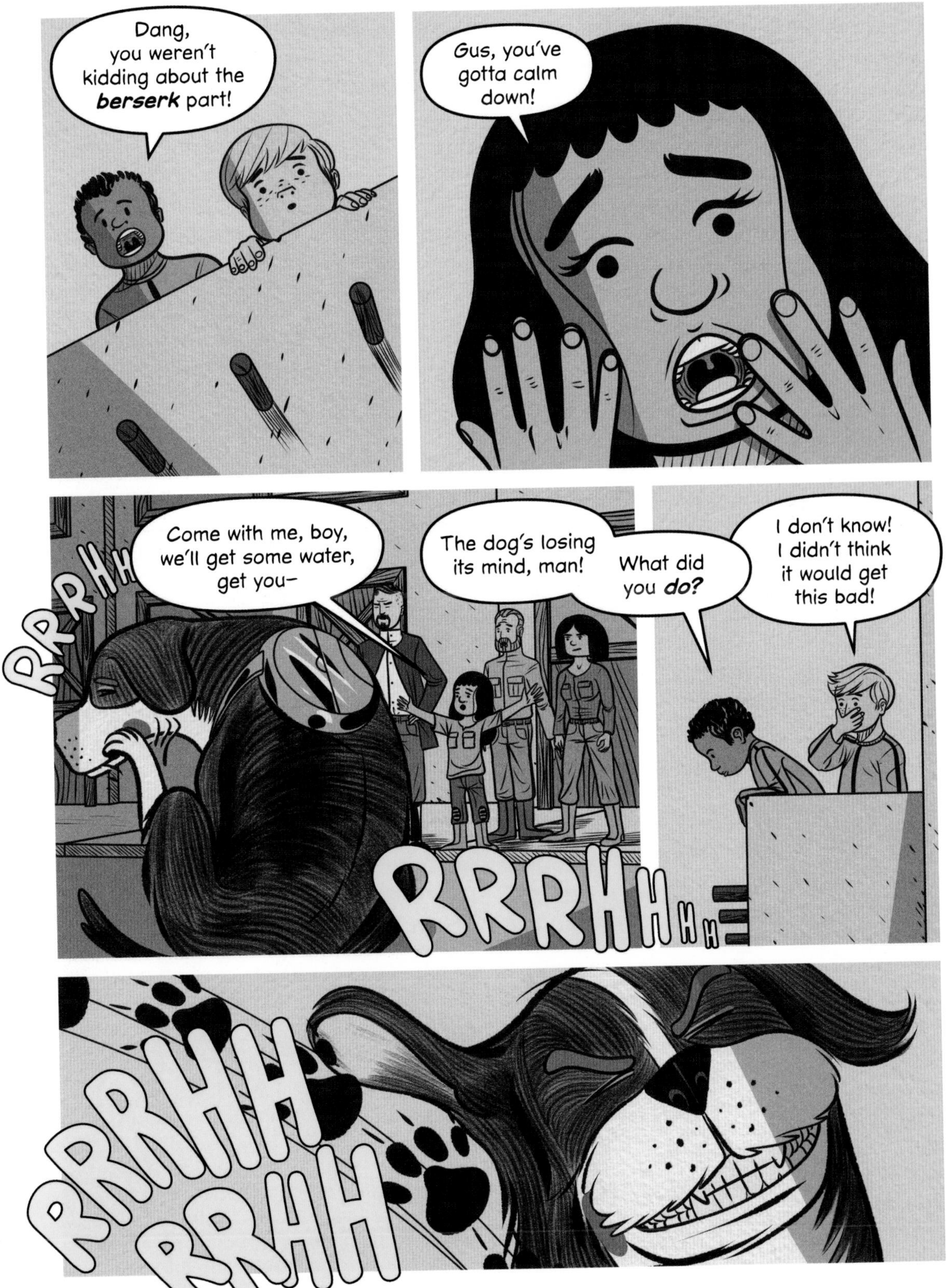

Dang, you weren't kidding about the **berserk** part!
Gus, you've gotta calm down!
RRRHHH
Come with me, boy, we'll get some water, get you–
The dog's losing its mind, man!
What did you **do?**
I don't know! I didn't think it would get this bad!
RRRHHHHH
RRHH RRHH

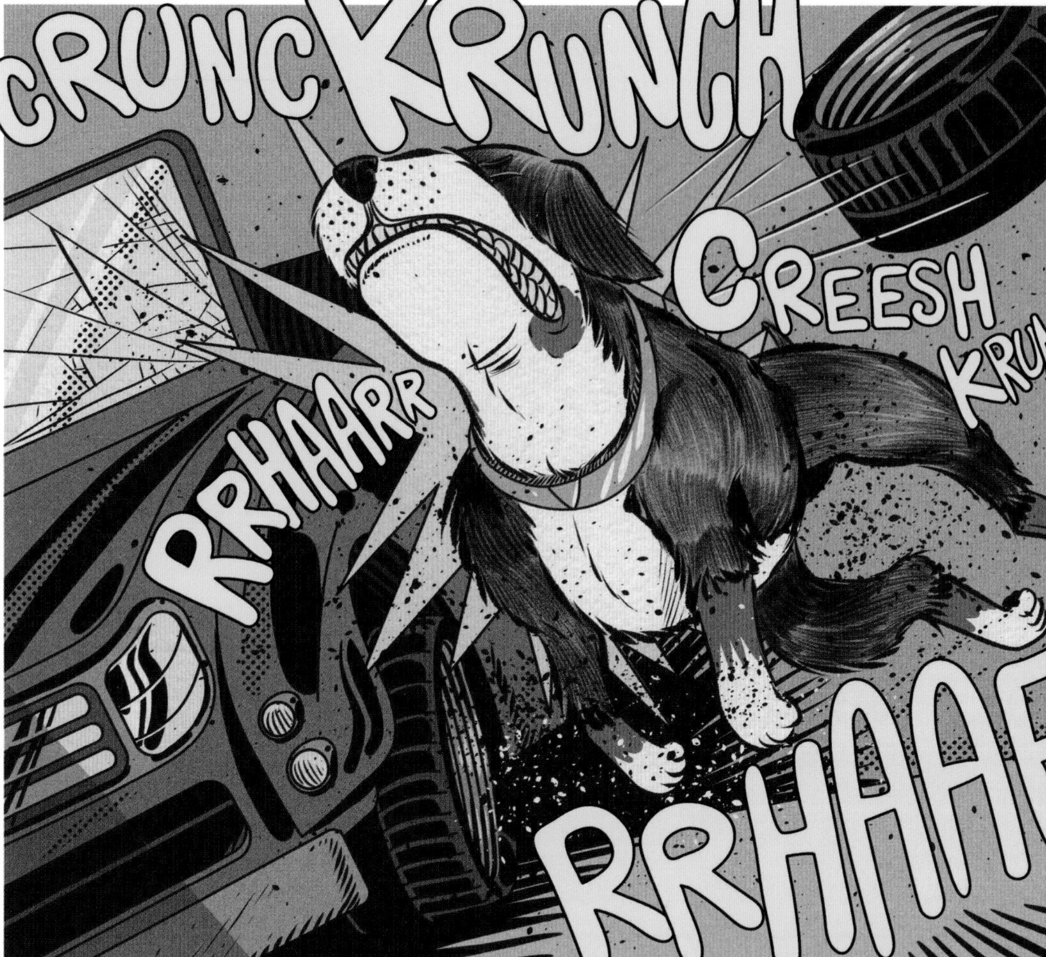
CRUNCKRUNCH
CREESH
KRUMPP
RRHAARR
RRHAAFF

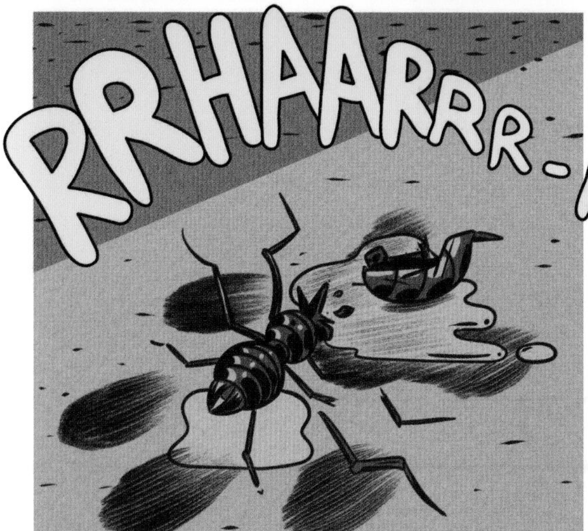
RRHAARRR-ARR-ARR!

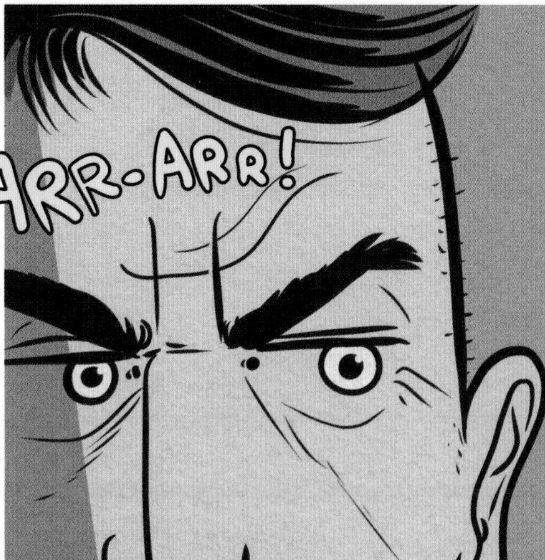

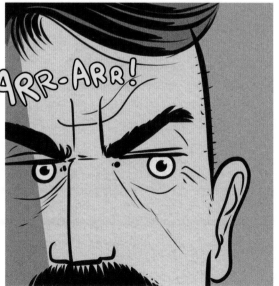

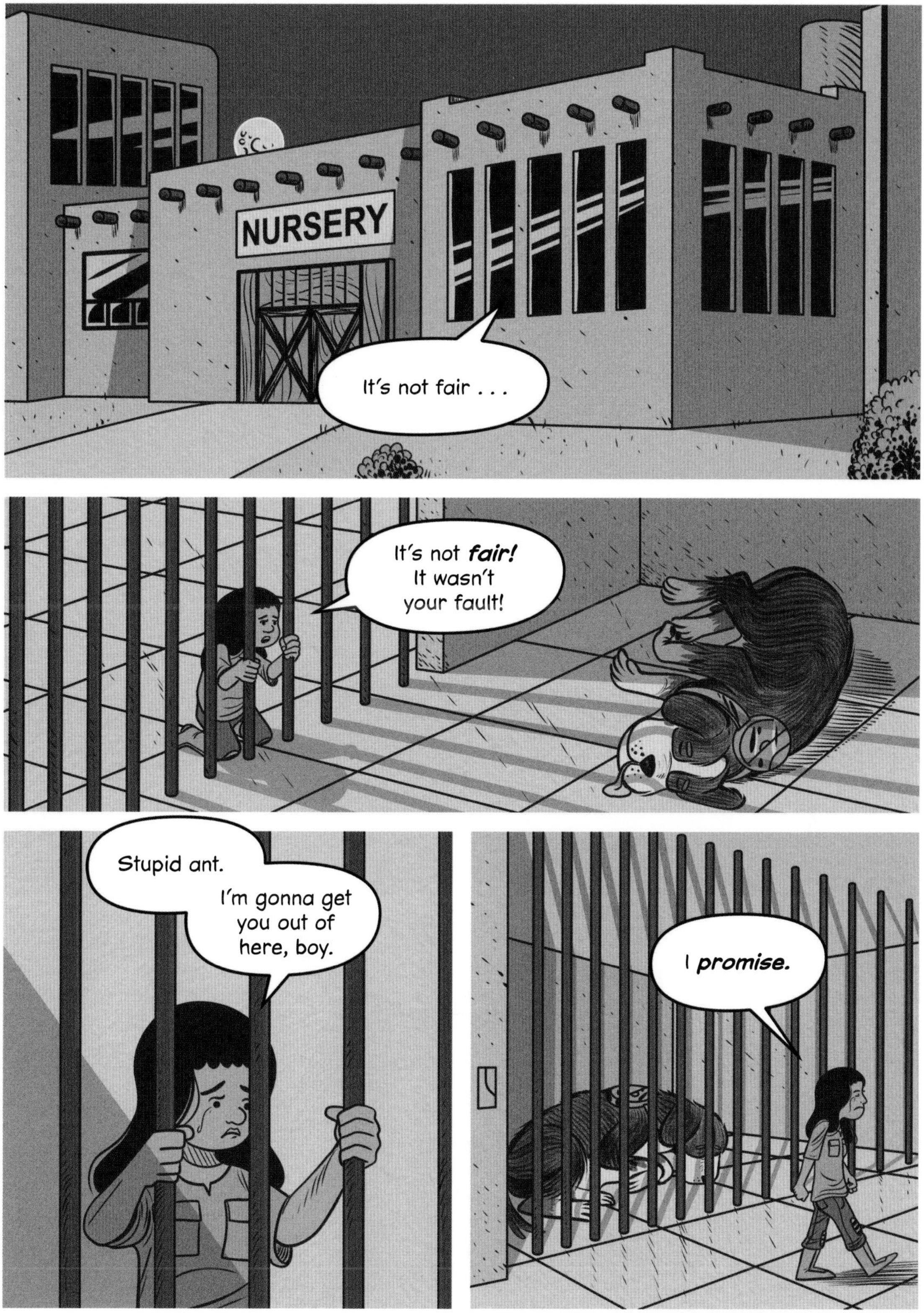
It's not fair . . .
It's not ***fair!*** It wasn't your fault!
Stupid ant.
I'm gonna get you out of here, boy.
I ***promise.***

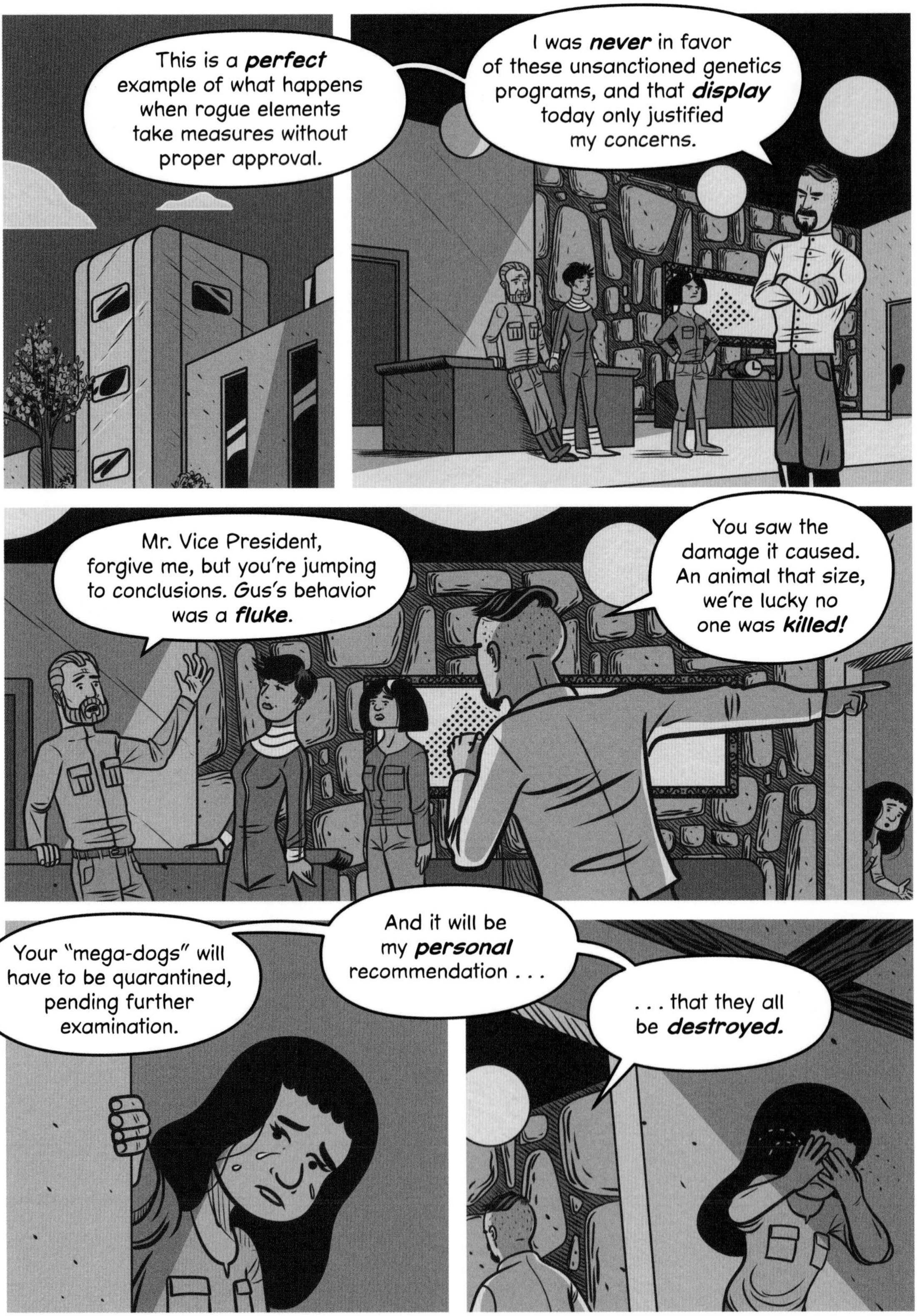
This is a ***perfect*** example of what happens when rogue elements take measures without proper approval.
I was ***never*** in favor of these unsanctioned genetics programs, and that ***display*** today only justified my concerns.
Mr. Vice President, forgive me, but you're jumping to conclusions. *Gus's* behavior was a ***fluke***.
You saw the damage it caused. An animal that size, we're lucky no one was ***killed!***
Your "mega-dogs" will have to be quarantined, pending further examination.
And it will be my ***personal*** recommendation . . .
. . . that they all be ***destroyed.***

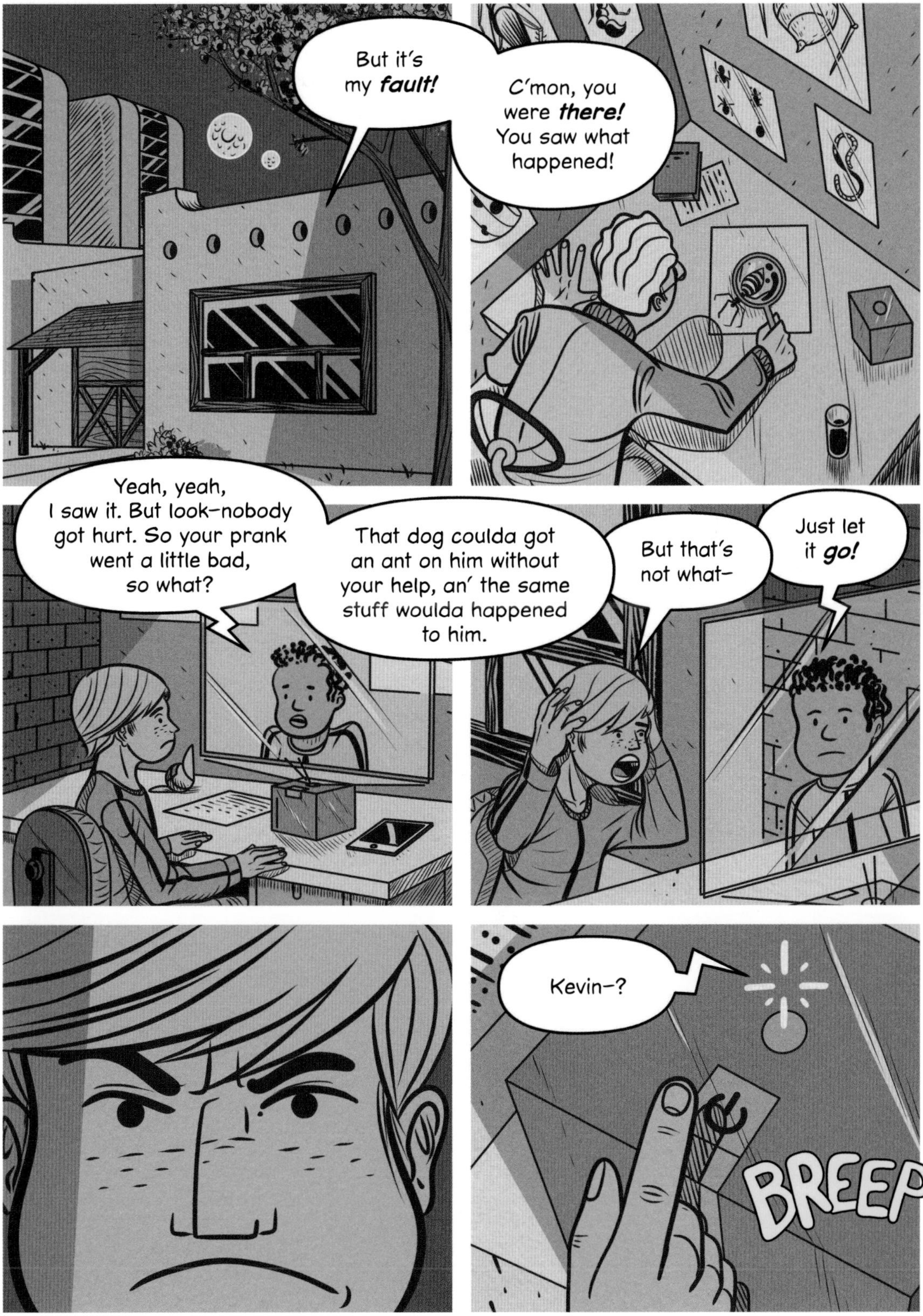
But it's my *fault!*
C'mon, you were *there!* You saw what happened!
Yeah, yeah, I saw it. But look–nobody got hurt. So your prank went a little bad, so what?
That dog coulda got an ant on him without your help, an' the same stuff woulda happened to him.
But that's not what–
Just let it *go!*
Kevin–?
BREEP

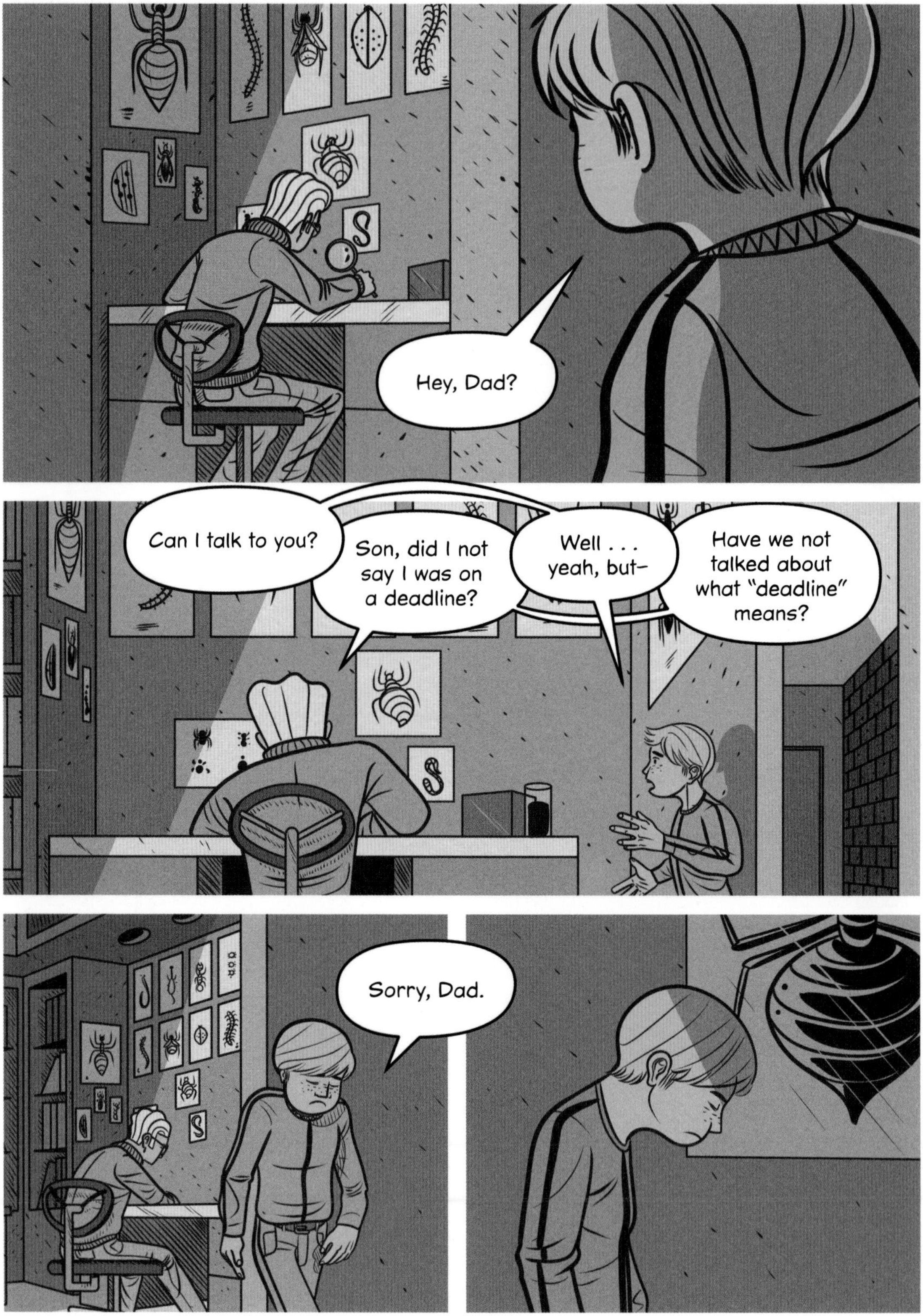
Hey, Dad?
Can I talk to you?
Son, did I not say I was on a deadline?
Well . . . yeah, but-
Have we not talked about what "deadline" means?
Sorry, Dad.

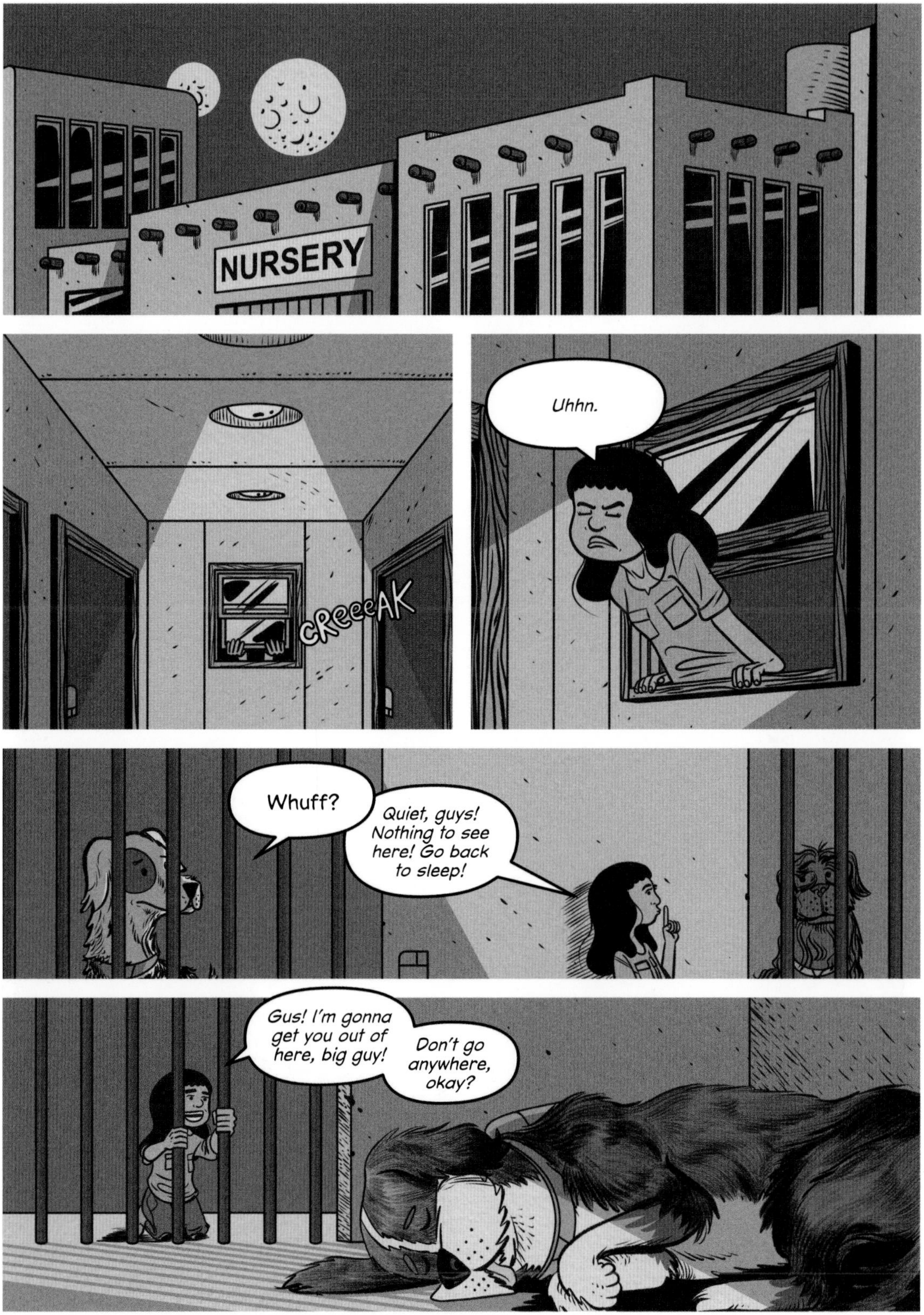
NURSERY
CREEEAK
Uhhn.
Whuff?
Quiet, guys! Nothing to see here! Go back to sleep!
Gus! I'm gonna get you out of here, big guy!
Don't go anywhere, okay?

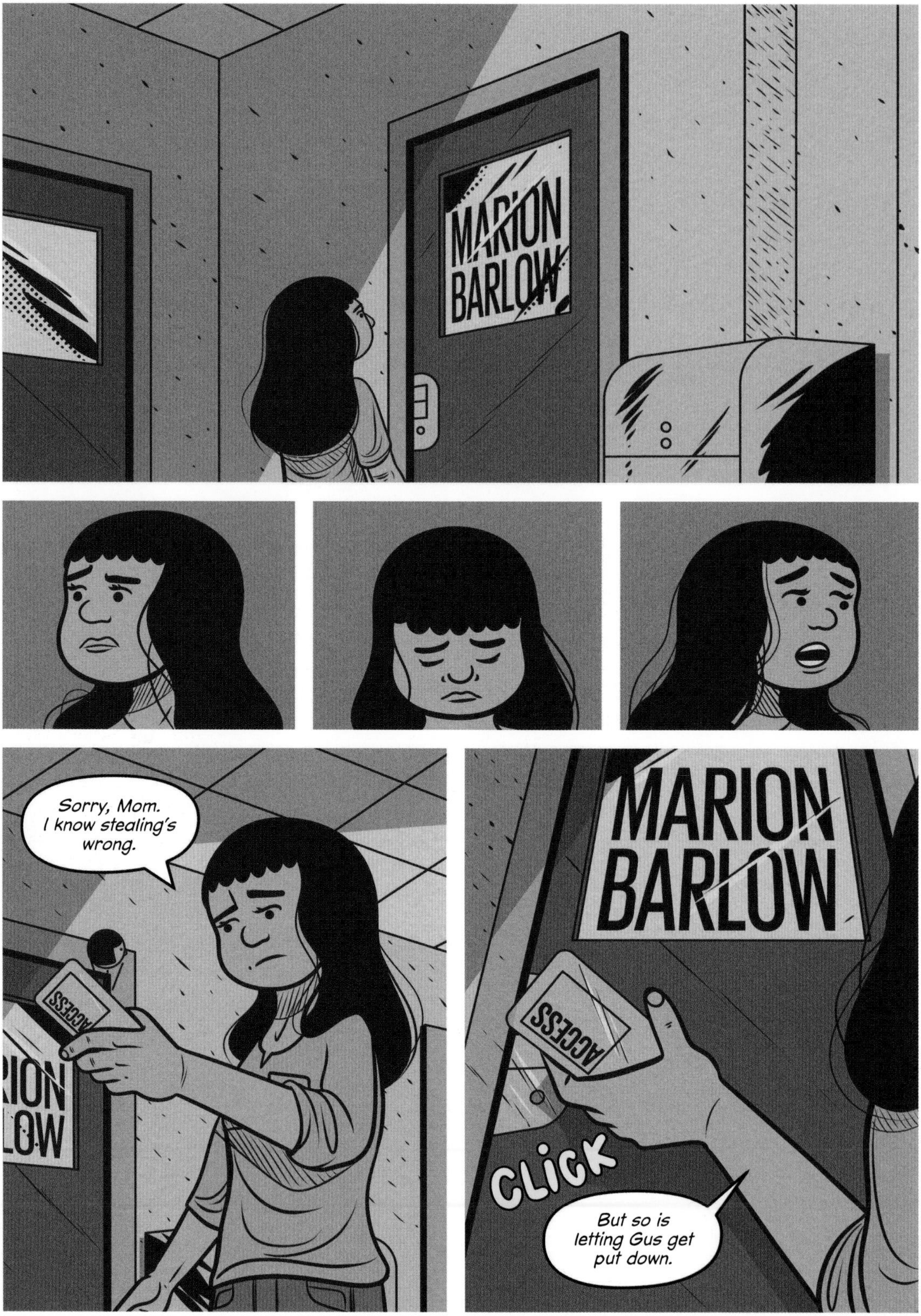
MARION BARLOW
Sorry, Mom. I know stealing's wrong.
ACCESS
MARION BARLOW
ACCESS
CLICK
But so is letting Gus get put down.

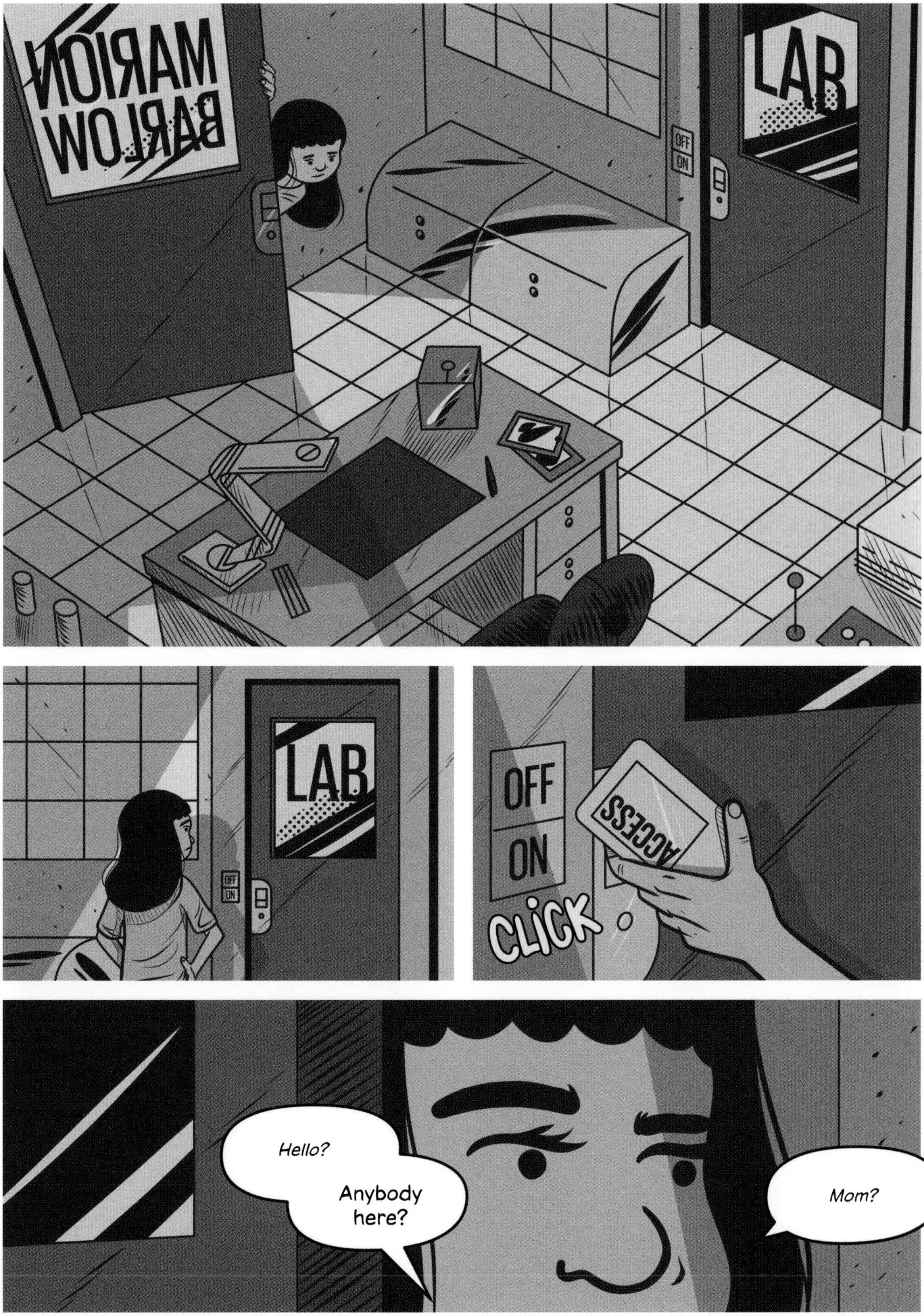
MARION BARLOW
LAB
OFF
ON
LAB
OFF
ON
OFF
ON
ACCESS
CLICK
Hello?
Anybody here?
Mom?

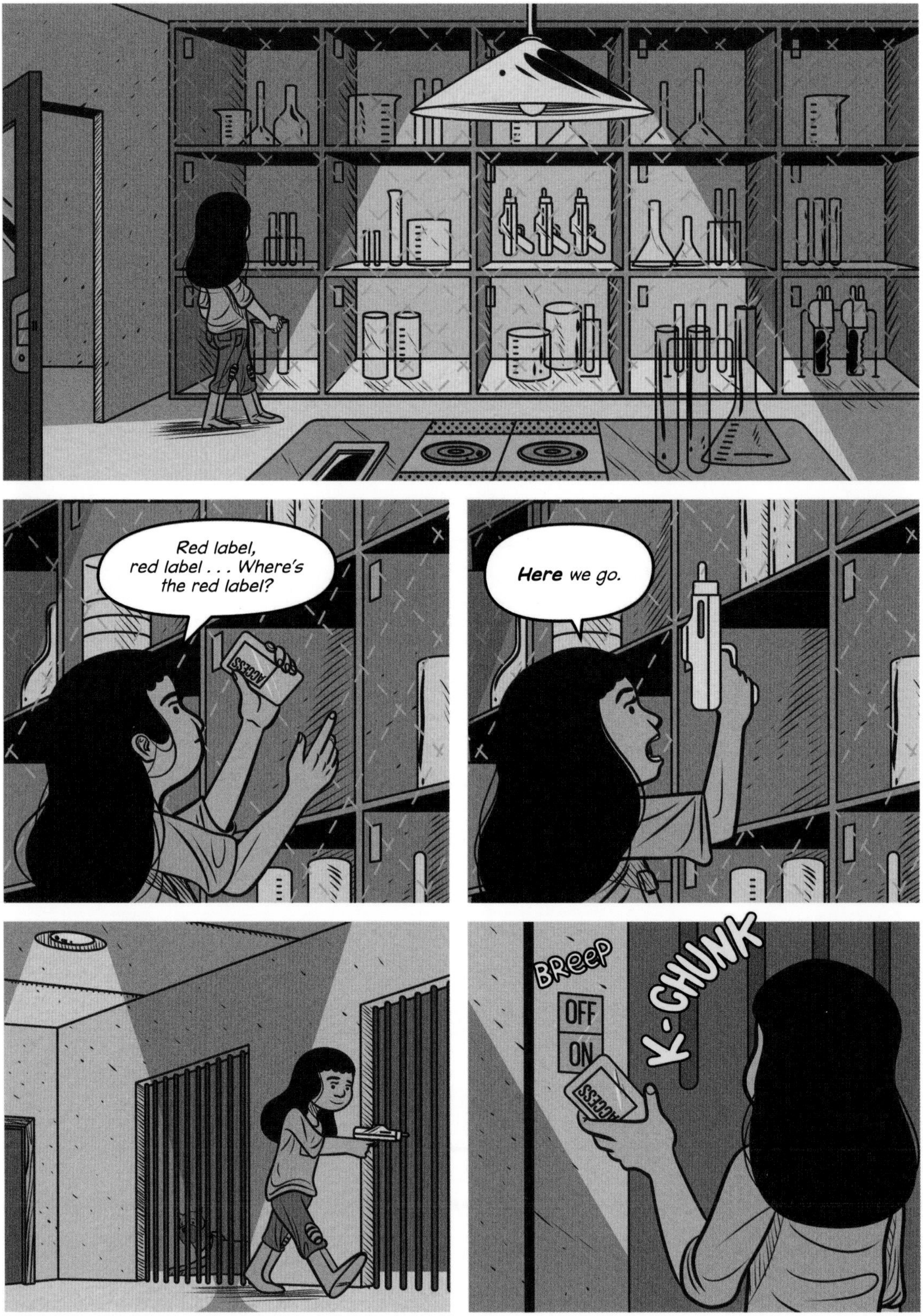
Red label, red label . . . Where's the red label?
ACCESS
Here we go.
BREEP
K-CHUNK
OFF
ON
ACCESS

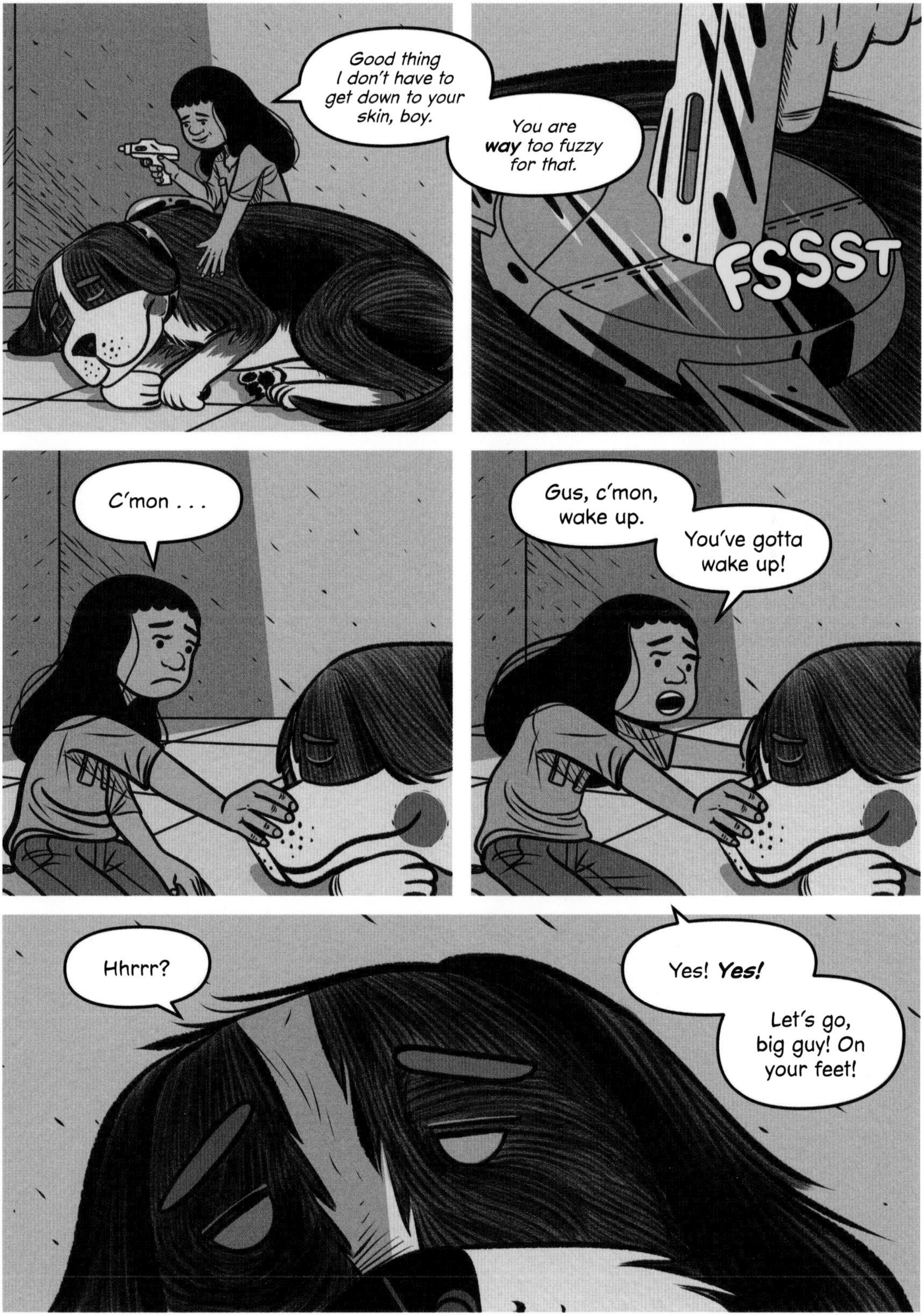
Good thing I don't have to get down to your skin, boy.
You are **way** too fuzzy for that.
FSSST
C'mon . . .
Gus, c'mon, wake up.
You've gotta wake up!
Hhrrr?
Yes! ***Yes!***
Let's go, big guy! On your feet!

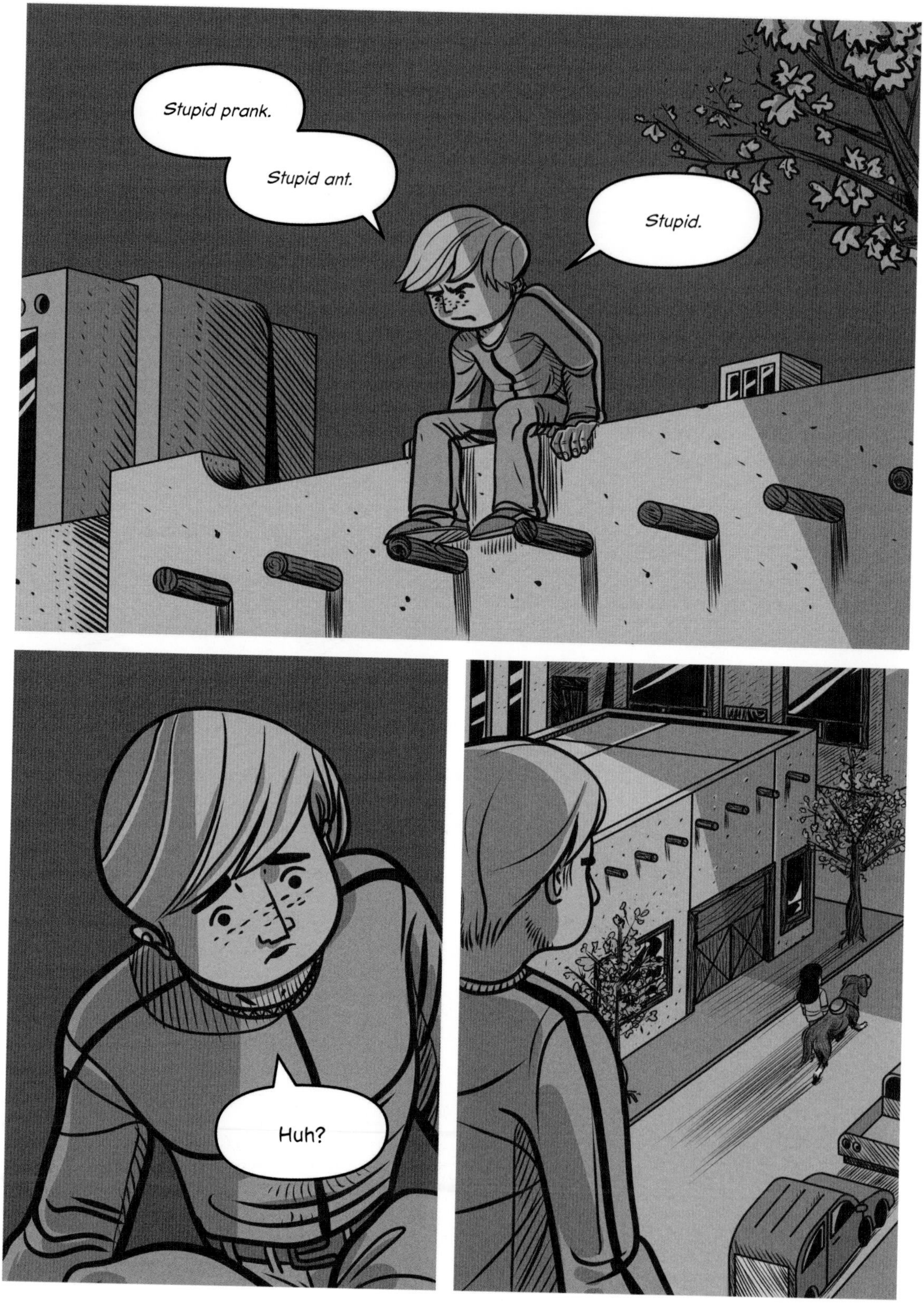
Stupid prank.
Stupid ant.
Stupid.
Huh?

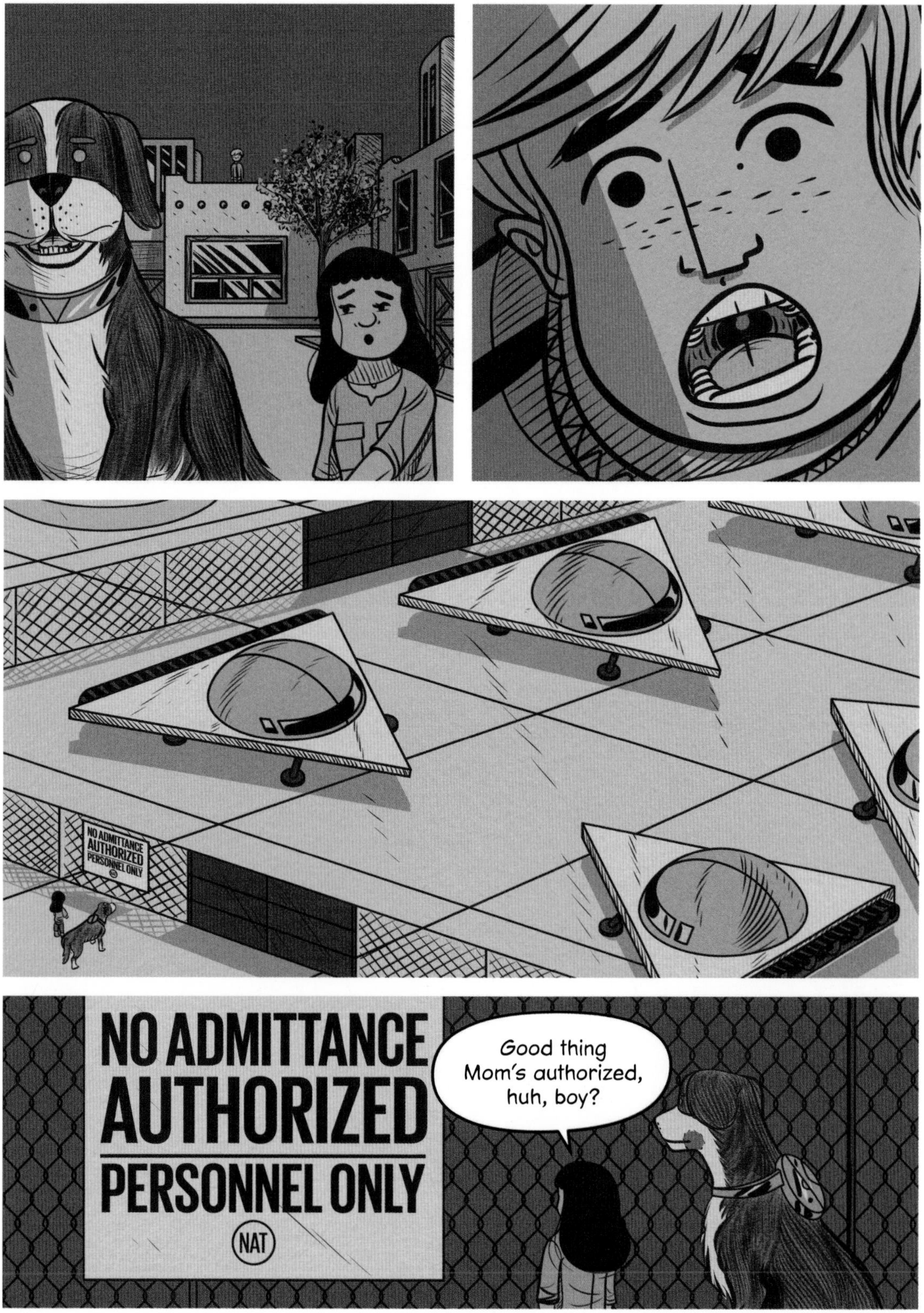
NO ADMITTANCE
AUTHORIZED
PERSONNEL ONLY
NO ADMITTANCE
AUTHORIZED
PERSONNEL ONLY
NAT
Good thing Mom's authorized, huh, boy?

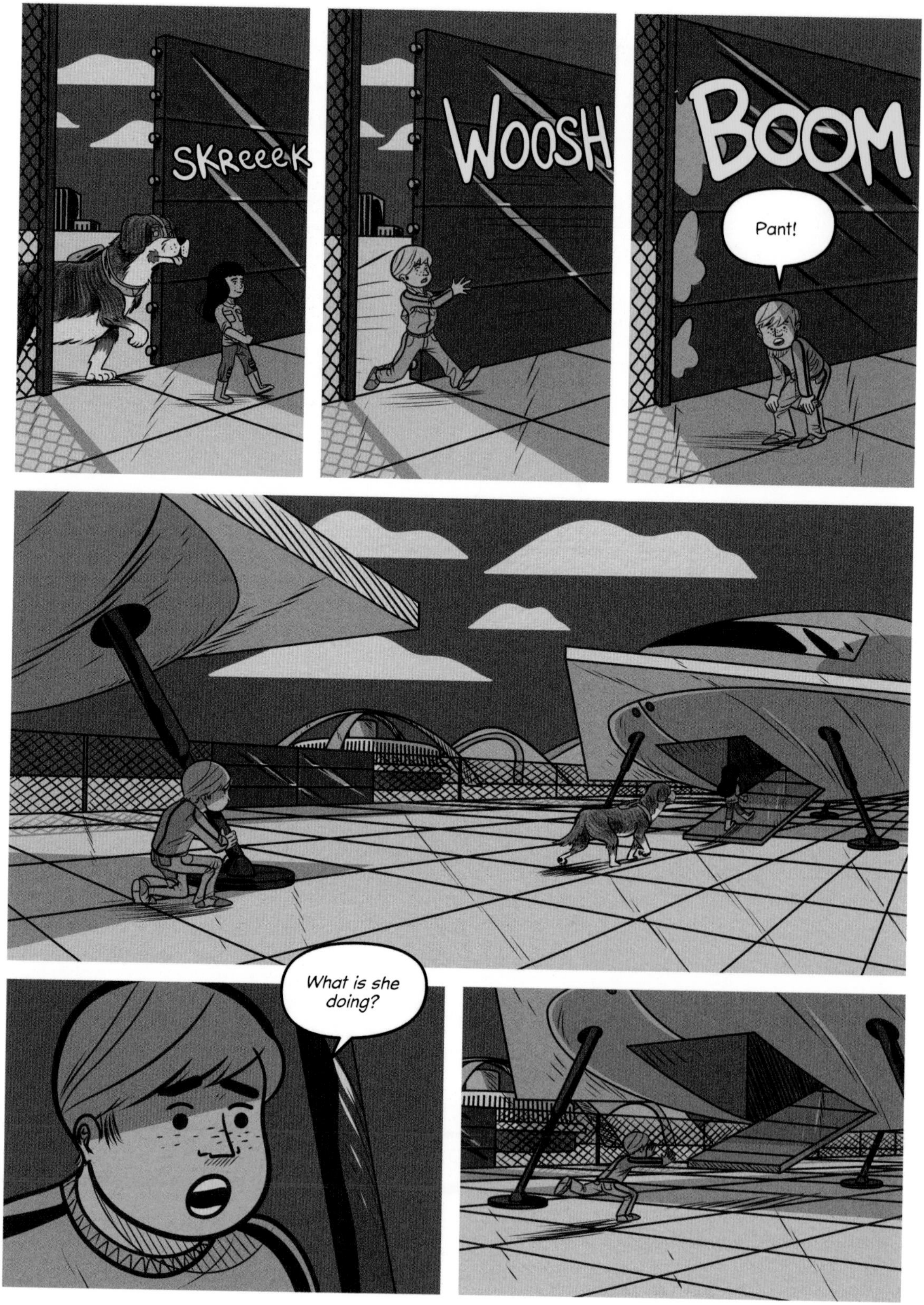
SKREEEK
WOOSH
BOOM
Pant!
What is she doing?

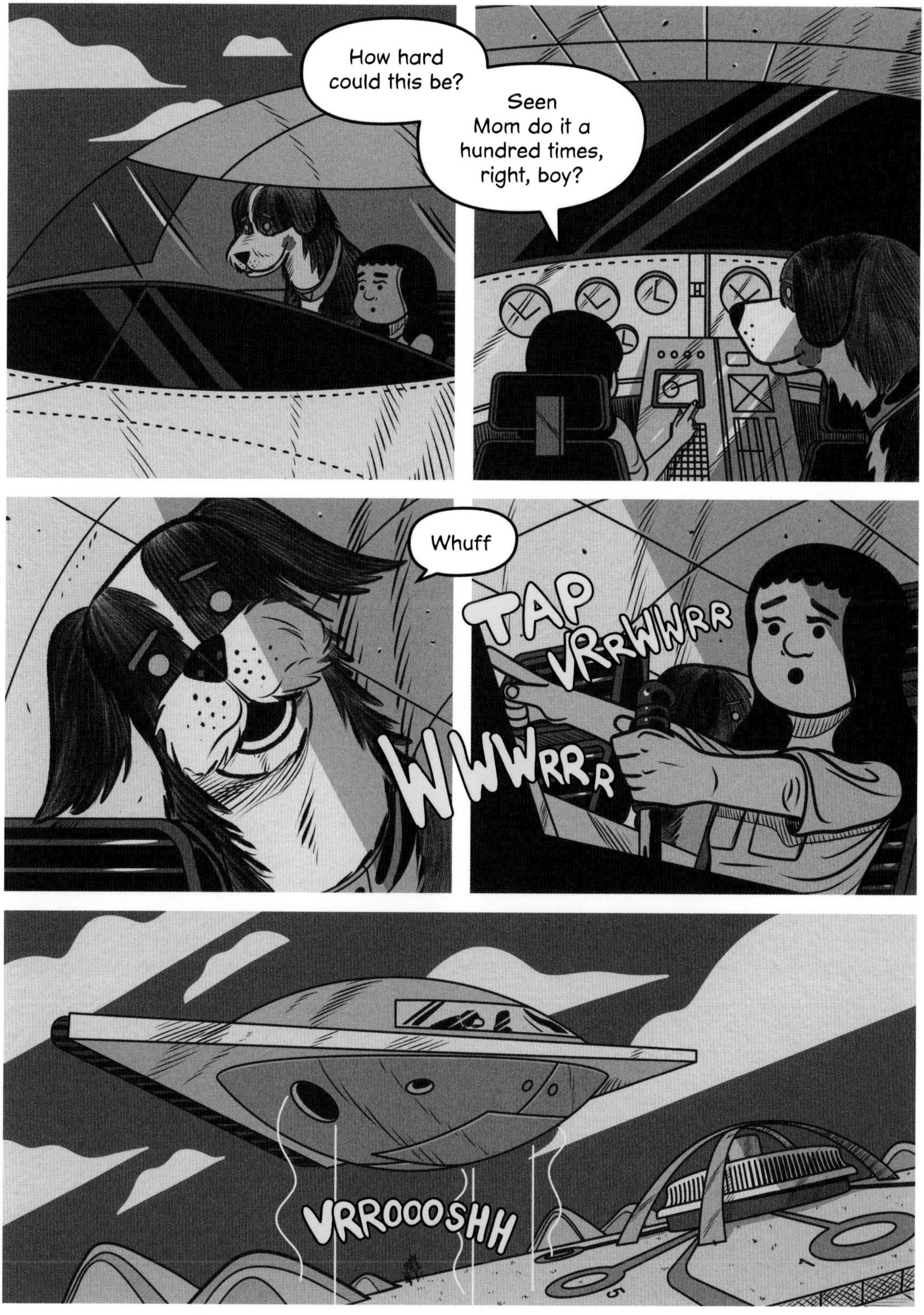
How hard could this be?
Seen Mom do it a hundred times, right, boy?
Whuff
TAP
VRRWWRR
WWWRRR
VRROOOSHH

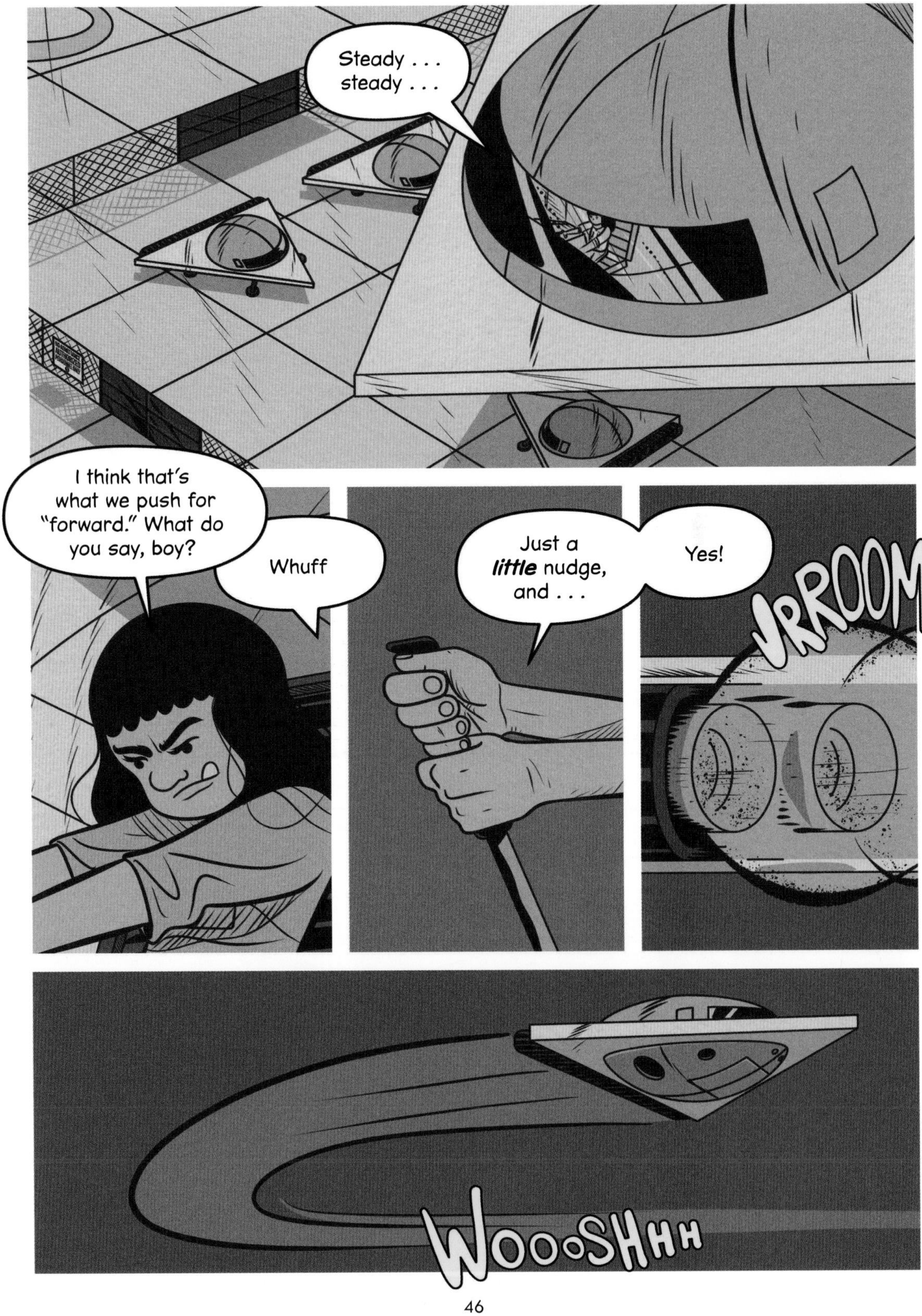
Steady . . .
steady . . .
I think that's what we push for "forward." What do you say, boy?
Whuff
Just a *little* nudge, and . . .
Yes!
VRROOM
WOOOSHHH

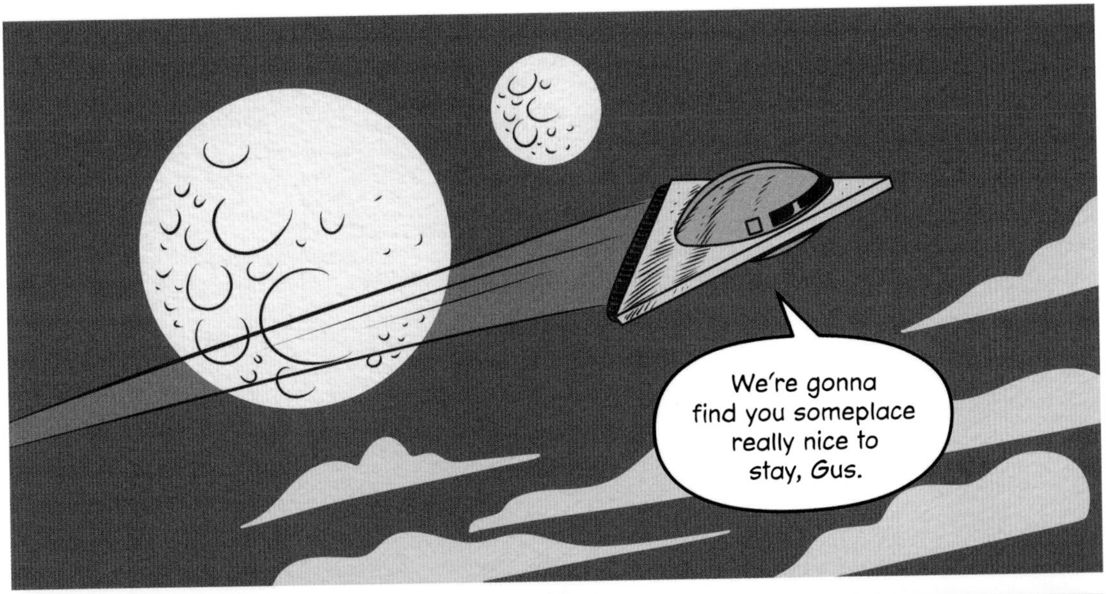
We're gonna find you someplace really nice to stay, Gus.

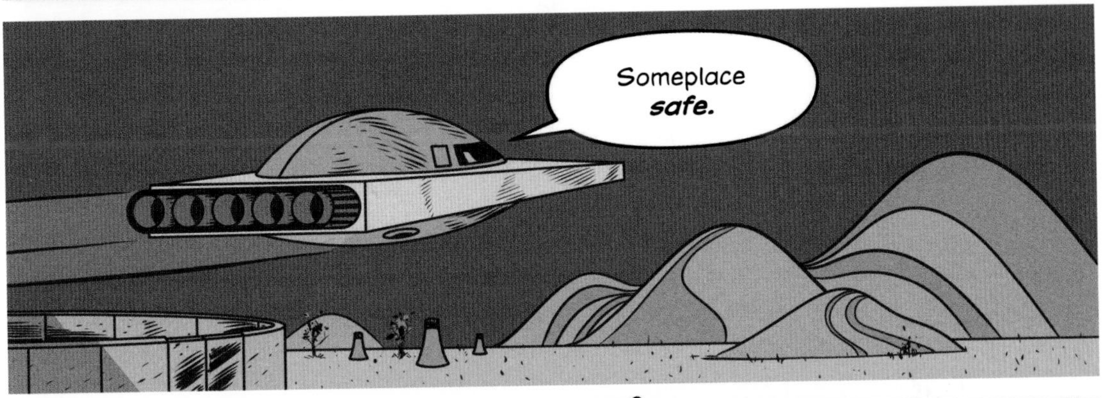
Someplace **safe.**

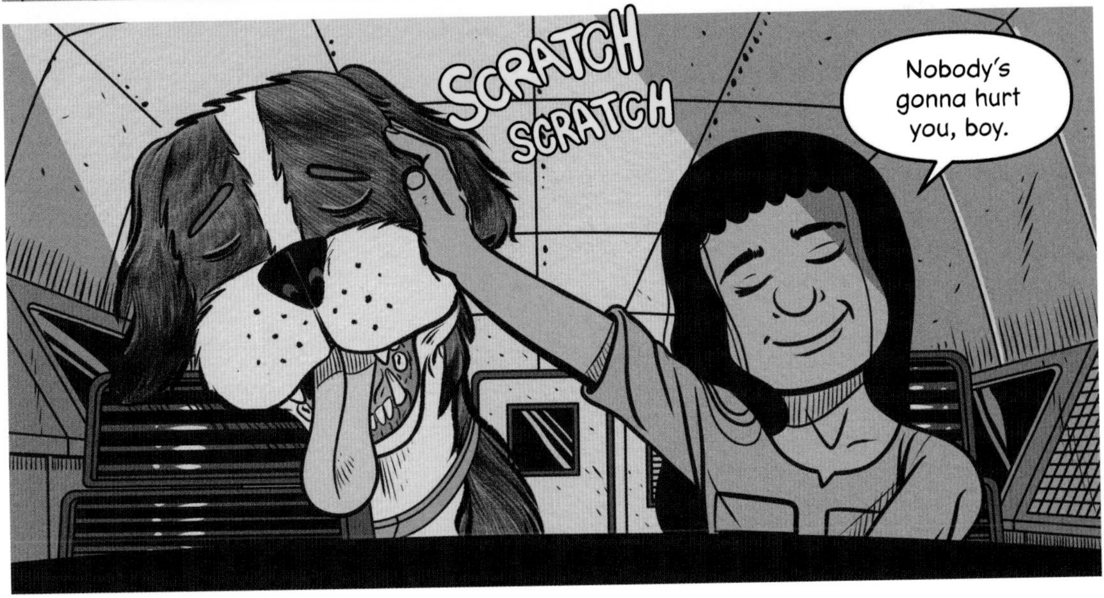
SCRATCH
SCRATCH
Nobody's gonna hurt you, boy.

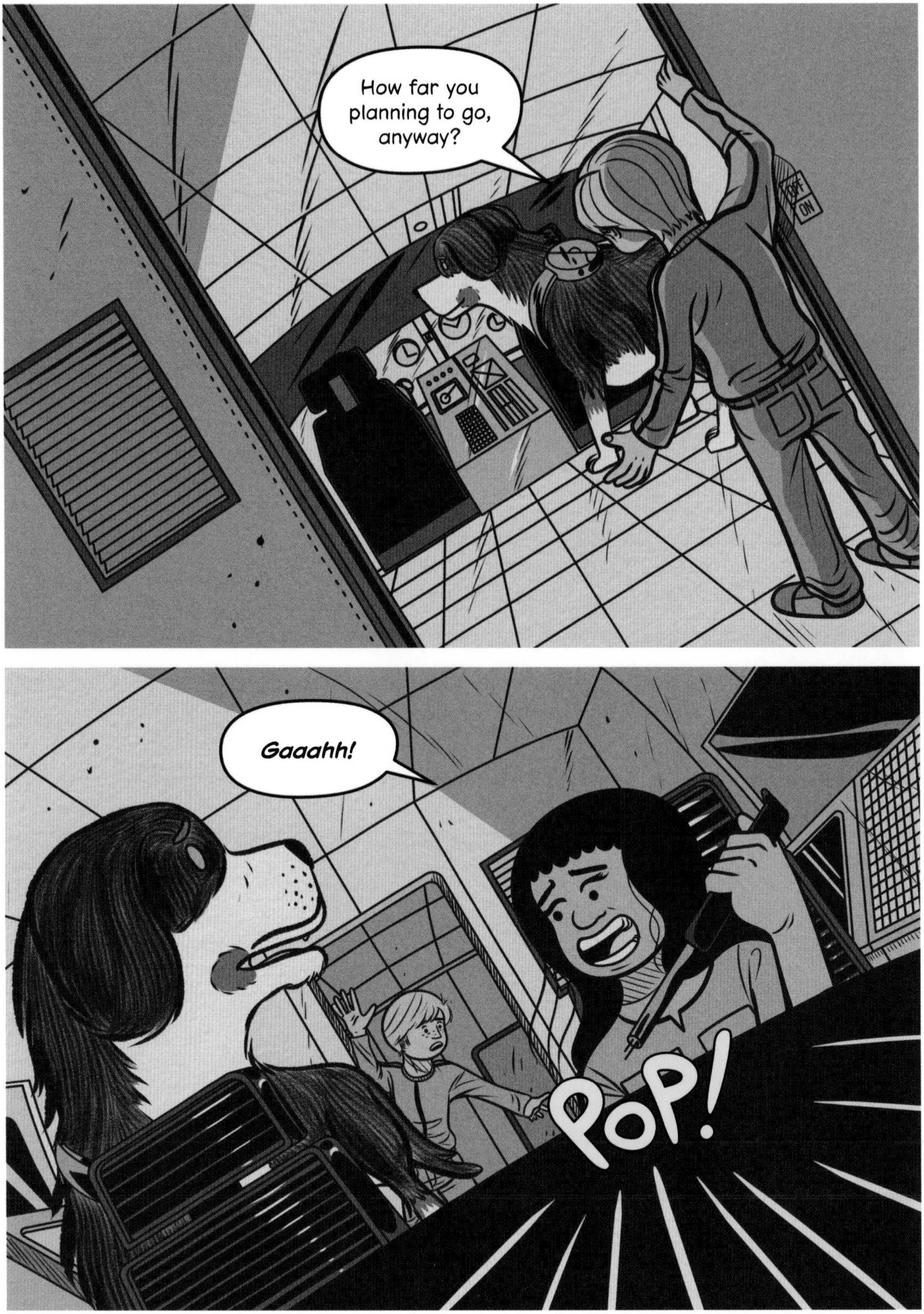
How far you planning to go, anyway?
Gaaahh!
POP!

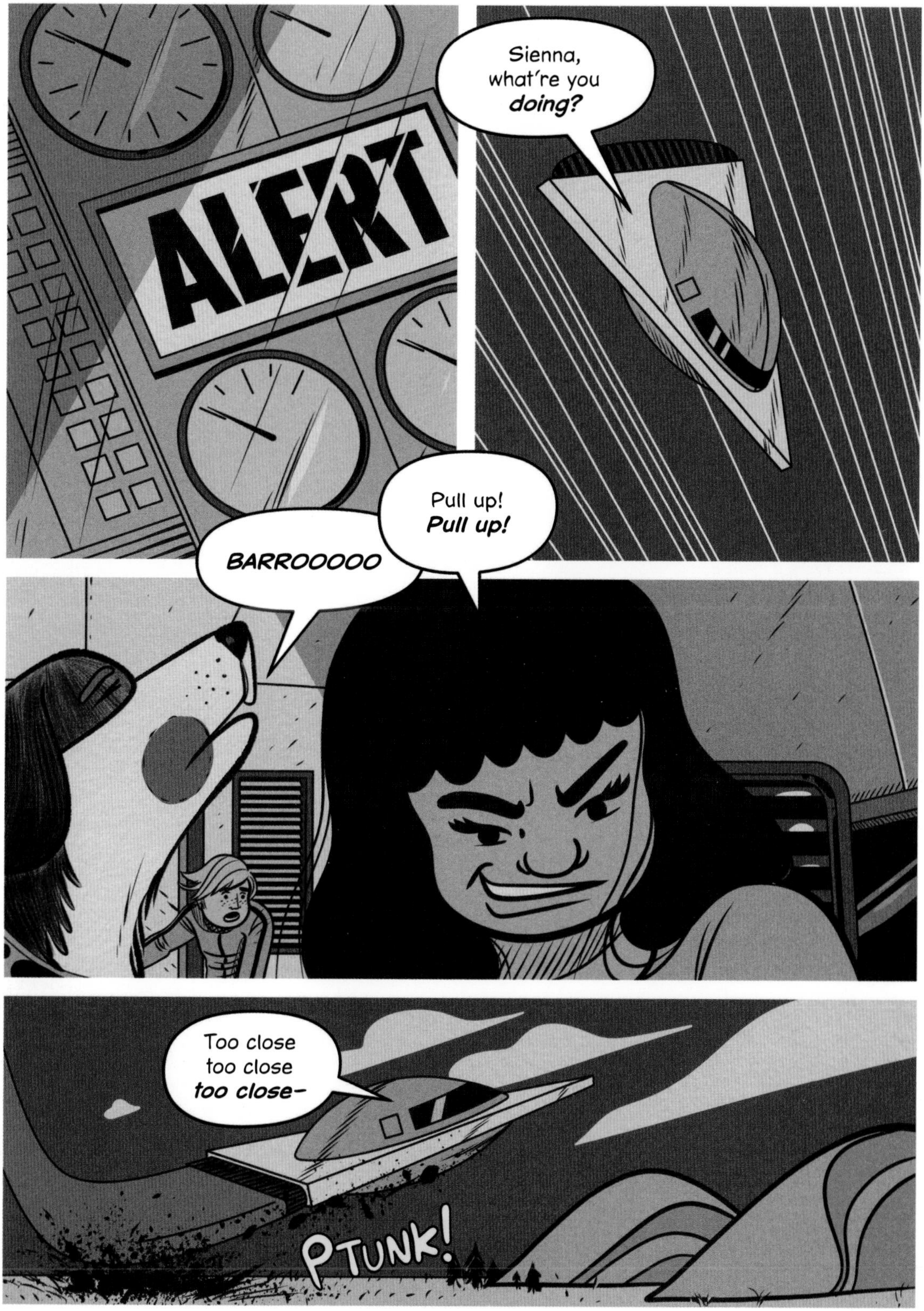
ALERT
Sienna, what're you *doing?*
BARROOOOO
Pull up! *Pull up!*
Too close too close *too close-*
PTUNK!

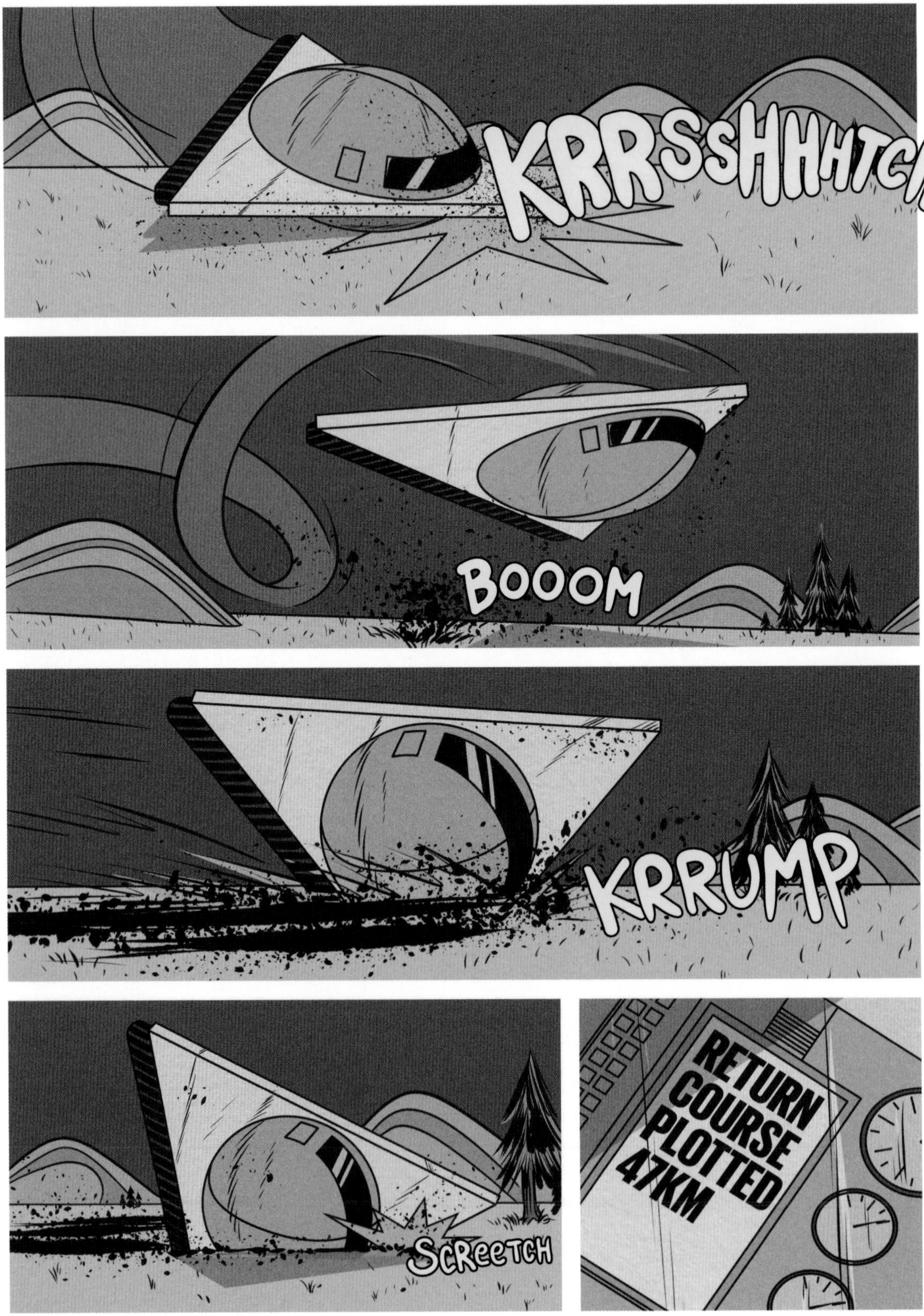
KRRSSHHHTCH
BOOOM
KRRUMP
SCREETCH
RETURN COURSE PLOTTED 47KM

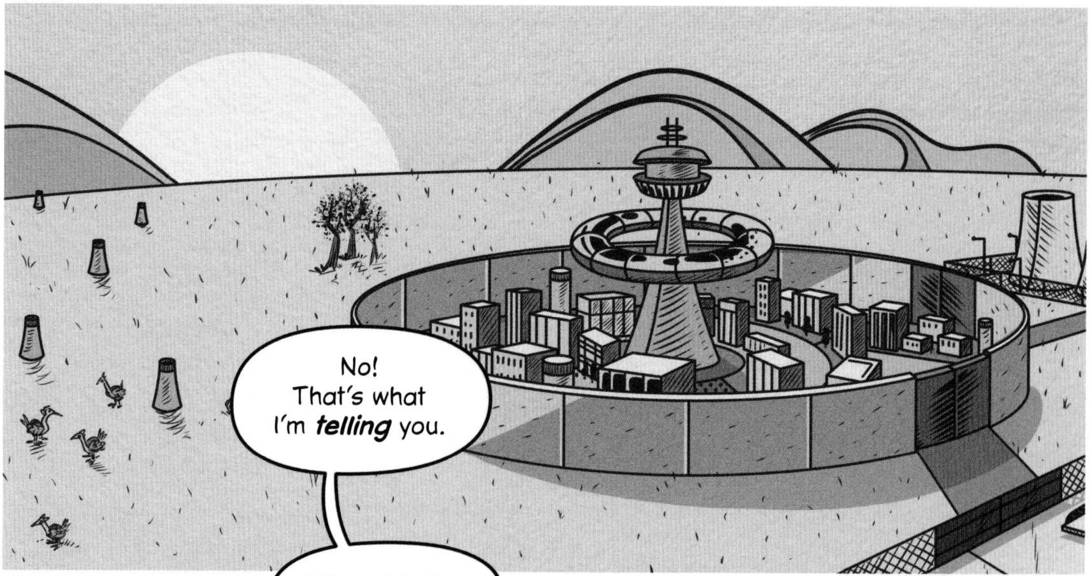
No! That's what I'm *telling* you.

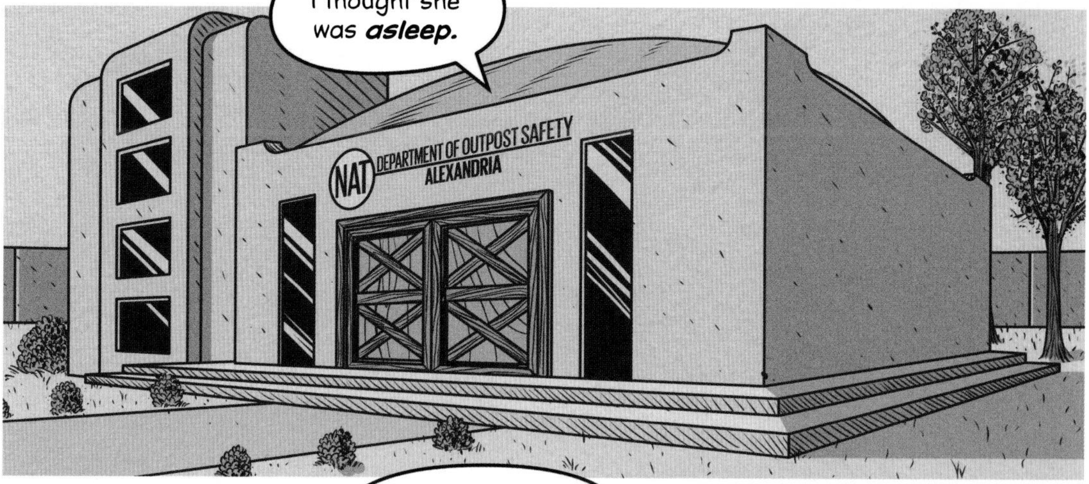
I thought she was *asleep.*
NAT
DEPARTMENT OF OUTPOST SAFETY
ALEXANDRIA

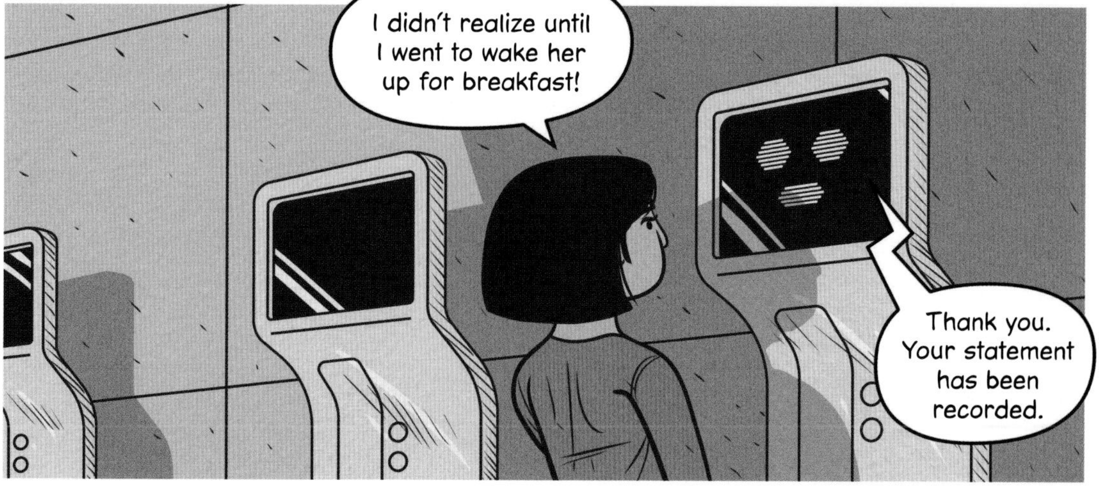
I didn't realize until I went to wake her up for breakfast!
Thank you. Your statement has been recorded.

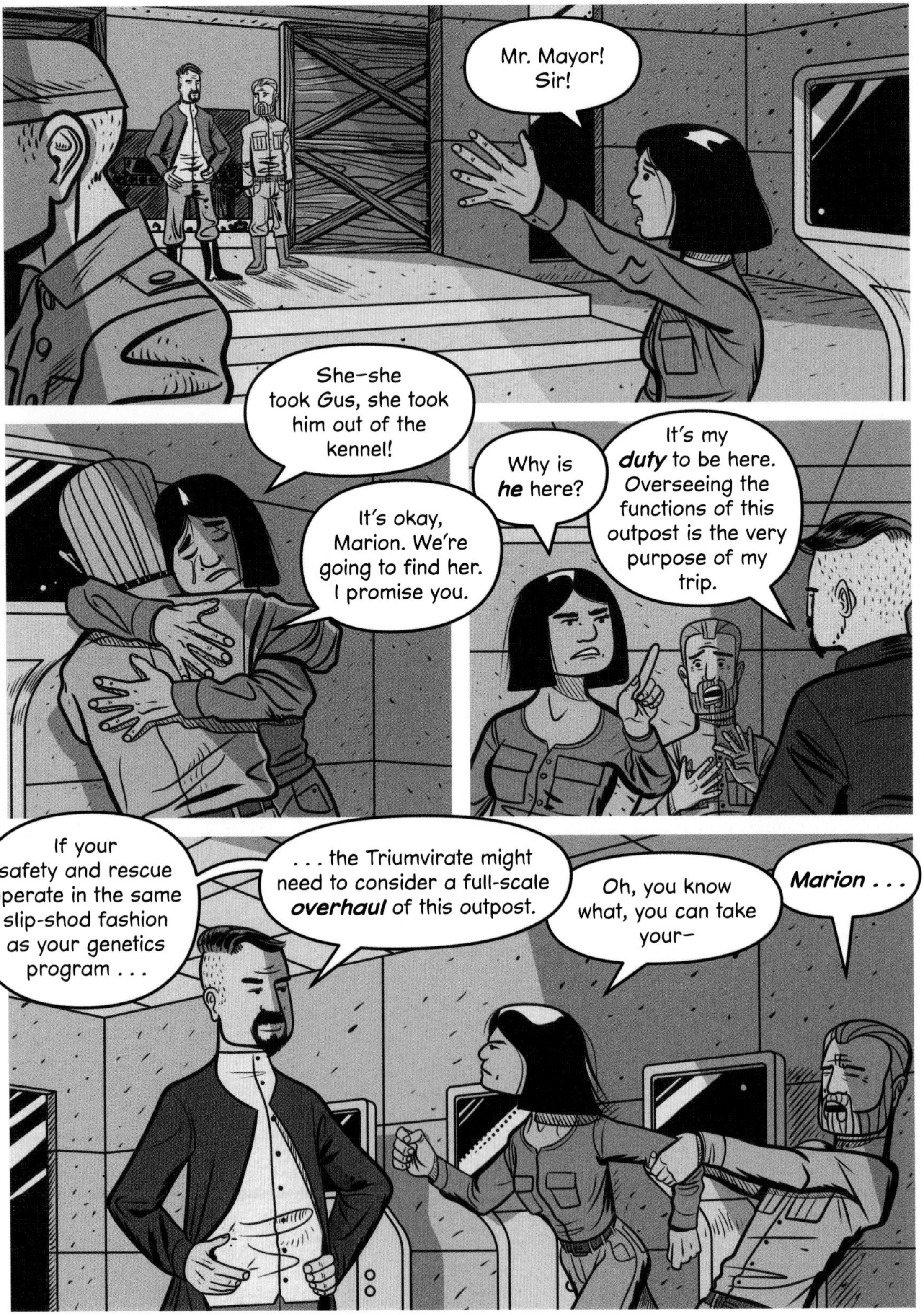
Mr. Mayor! Sir!
She–she took Gus, she took him out of the kennel!
It's okay, Marion. We're going to find her. I promise you.
Why is **he** here?
It's my **duty** to be here. Overseeing the functions of this outpost is the very purpose of my trip.
If your safety and rescue operate in the same slip-shod fashion as your genetics program . . .
. . . the Triumvirate might need to consider a full-scale **overhaul** of this outpost.
Oh, you know what, you can take your–
Marion . . .

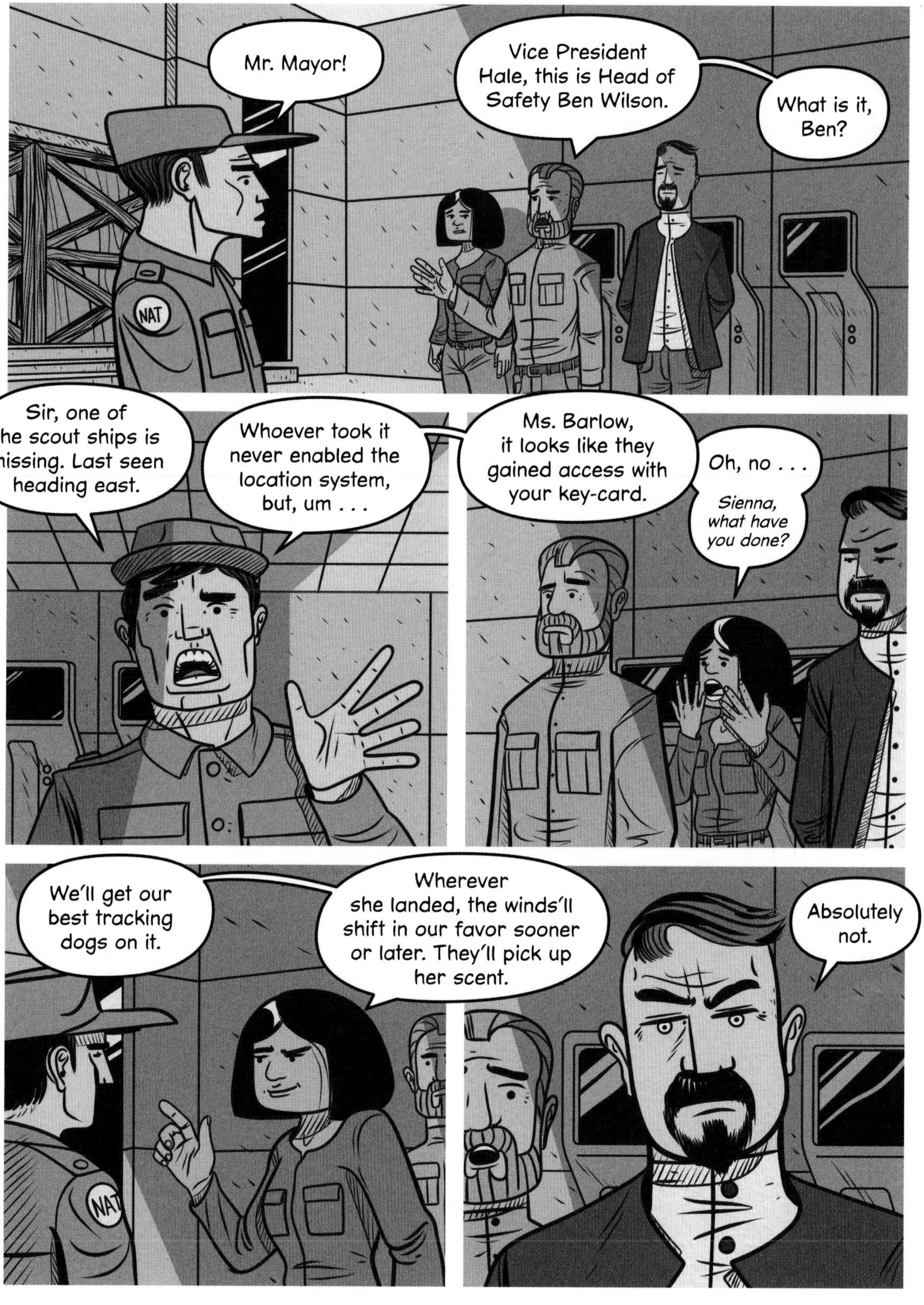
Mr. Mayor!
Vice President Hale, this is Head of Safety Ben Wilson.
What is it, Ben?
Sir, one of the scout ships is missing. Last seen heading east.
Whoever took it never enabled the location system, but, um . . .
Ms. Barlow, it looks like they gained access with your key-card.
Oh, no . . .
Sienna, what have you done?
NAT
We'll get our best tracking dogs on it.
Wherever she landed, the winds'll shift in our favor sooner or later. They'll pick up her scent.
Absolutely not.

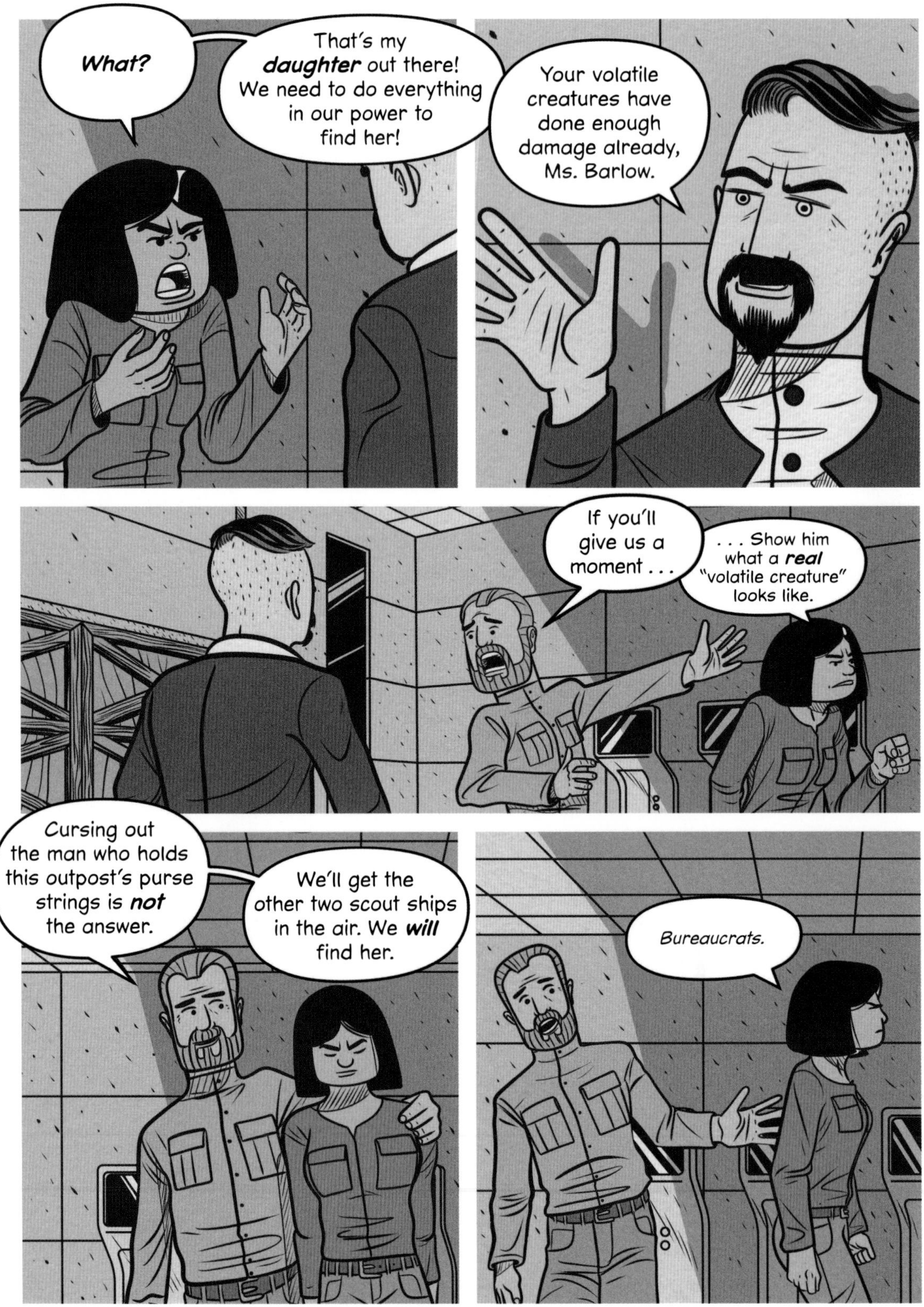

What?
That's my **daughter** out there! We need to do everything in our power to find her!
Your volatile creatures have done enough damage already, Ms. Barlow.
If you'll give us a moment . . .
. . . Show him what a ***real*** "volatile creature" looks like.
Cursing out the man who holds this outpost's purse strings is ***not*** the answer.
We'll get the other two scout ships in the air. We ***will*** find her.
Bureaucrats.

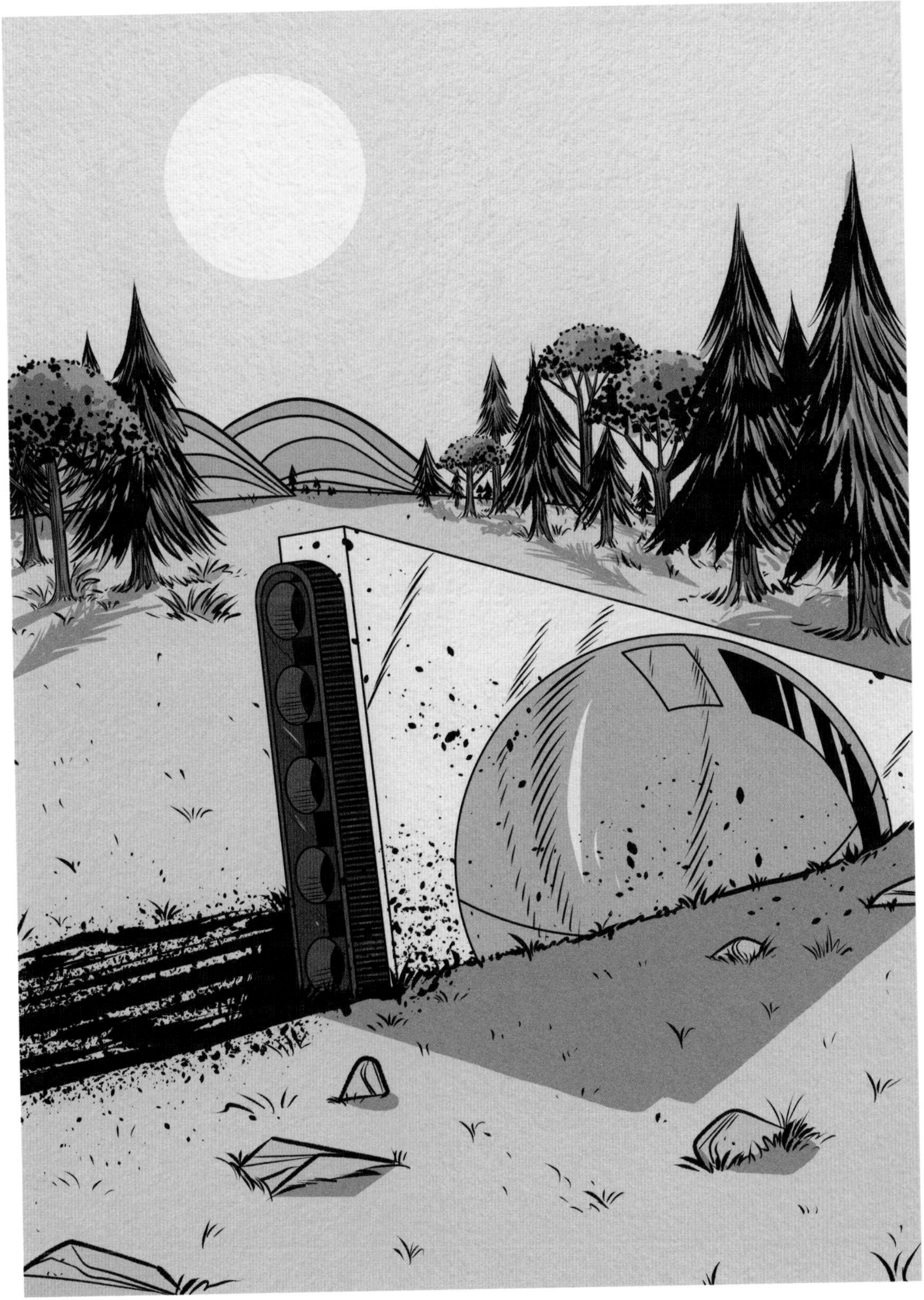

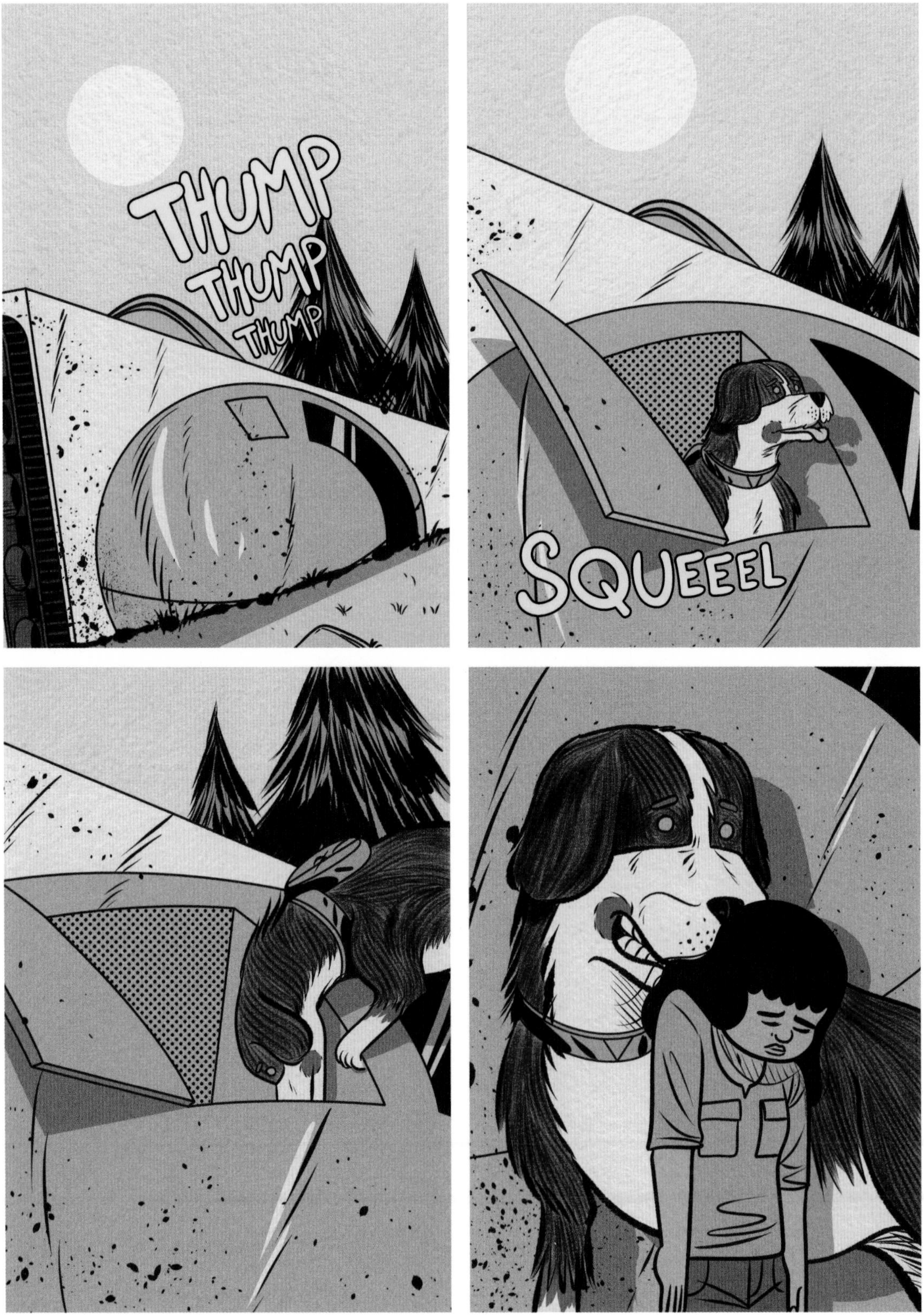
THUMP
THUMP
THUMP
SQUEEEL

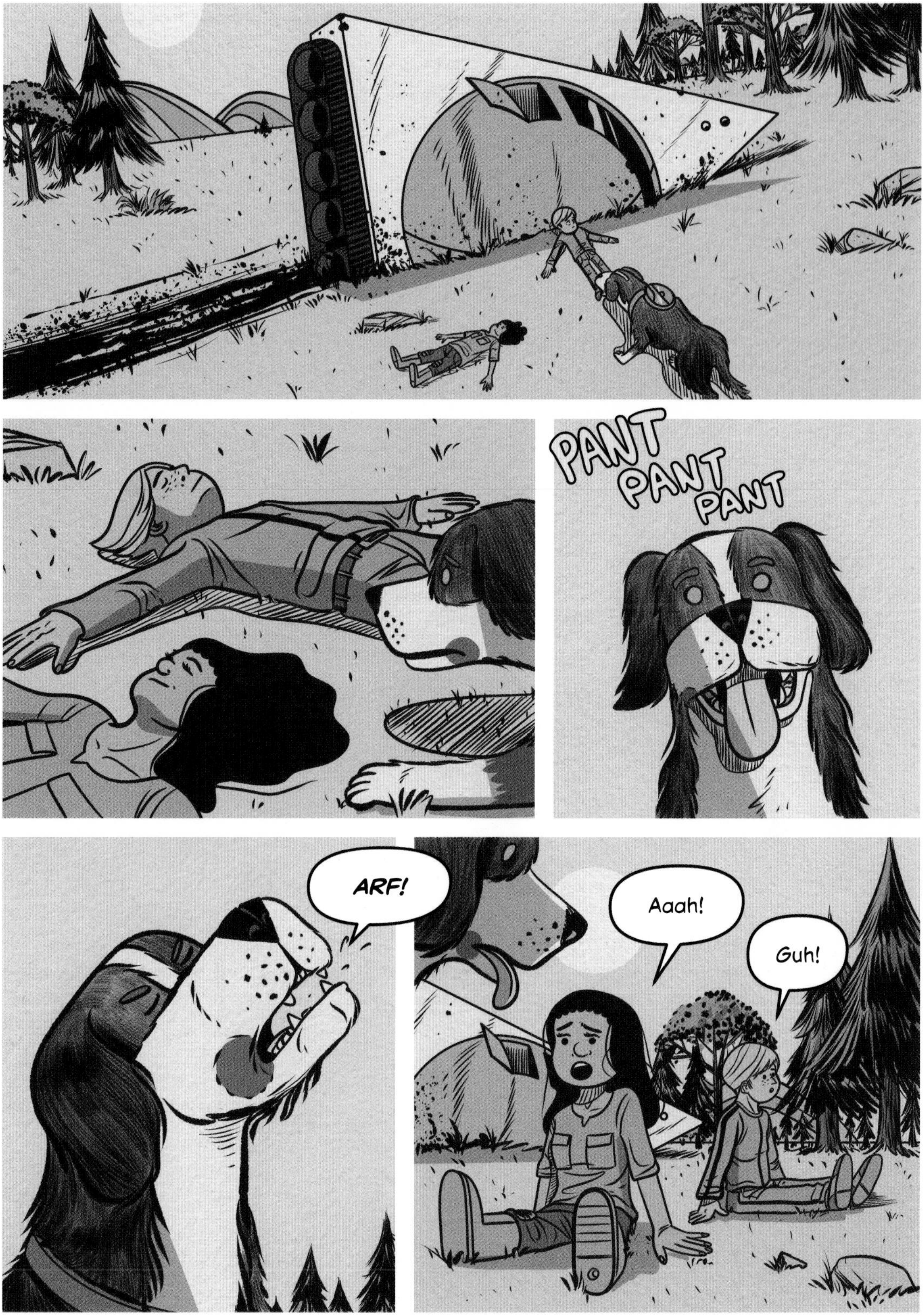
PANT
PANT
PANT
ARF!
Aaah!
Guh!

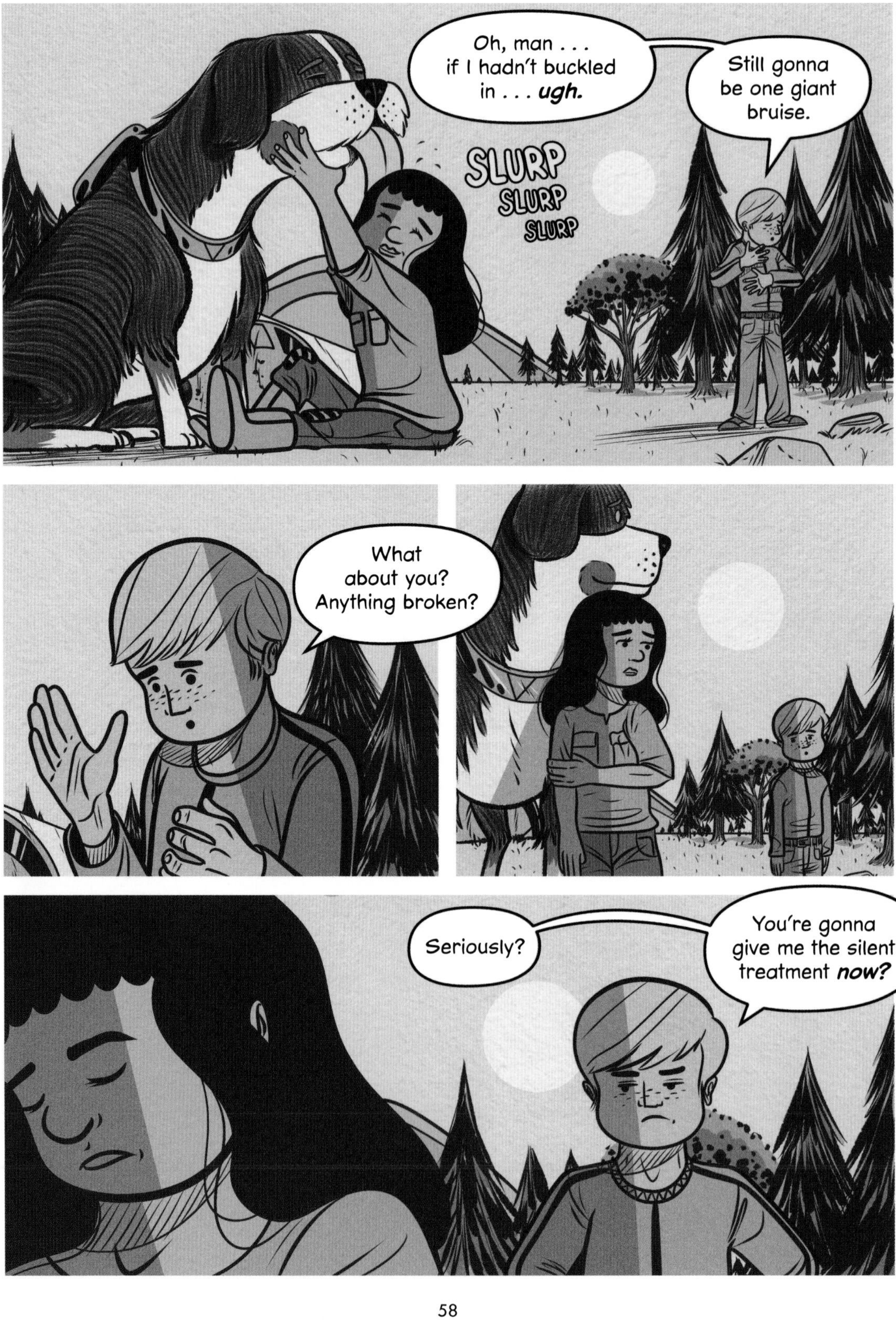
Oh, man . . . if I hadn't buckled in . . . ***ugh.***
Still gonna be one giant bruise.
SLURP
SLURP
SLURP
What about you? Anything broken?
Seriously?
You're gonna give me the silent treatment ***now?***

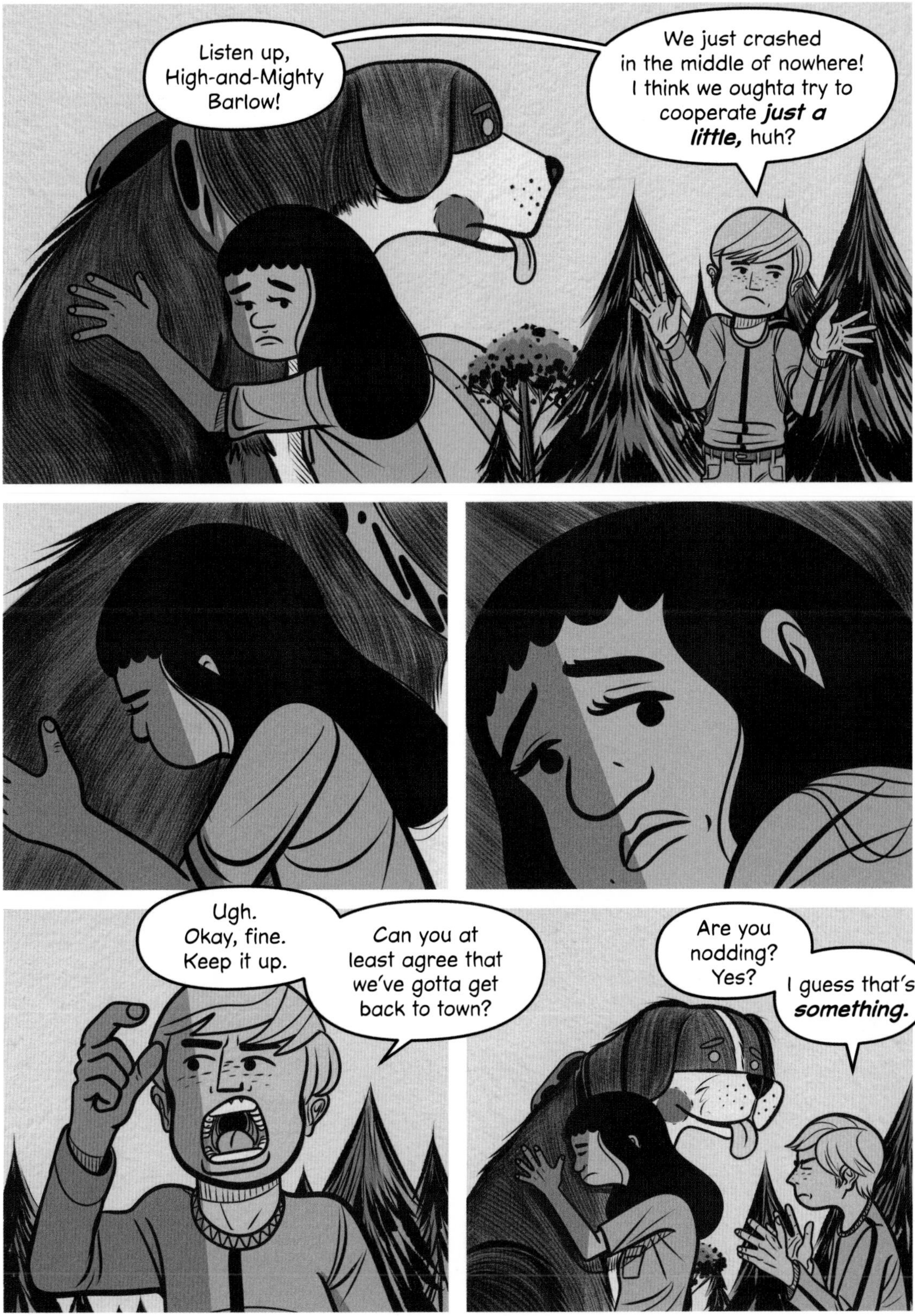
Listen up, High-and-Mighty Barlow!
We just crashed in the middle of nowhere! I think we oughta try to cooperate ***just a little,*** huh?
Ugh. Okay, fine. Keep it up.
Can you at least agree that we've gotta get back to town?
Are you nodding? Yes?
I guess that's ***something.***

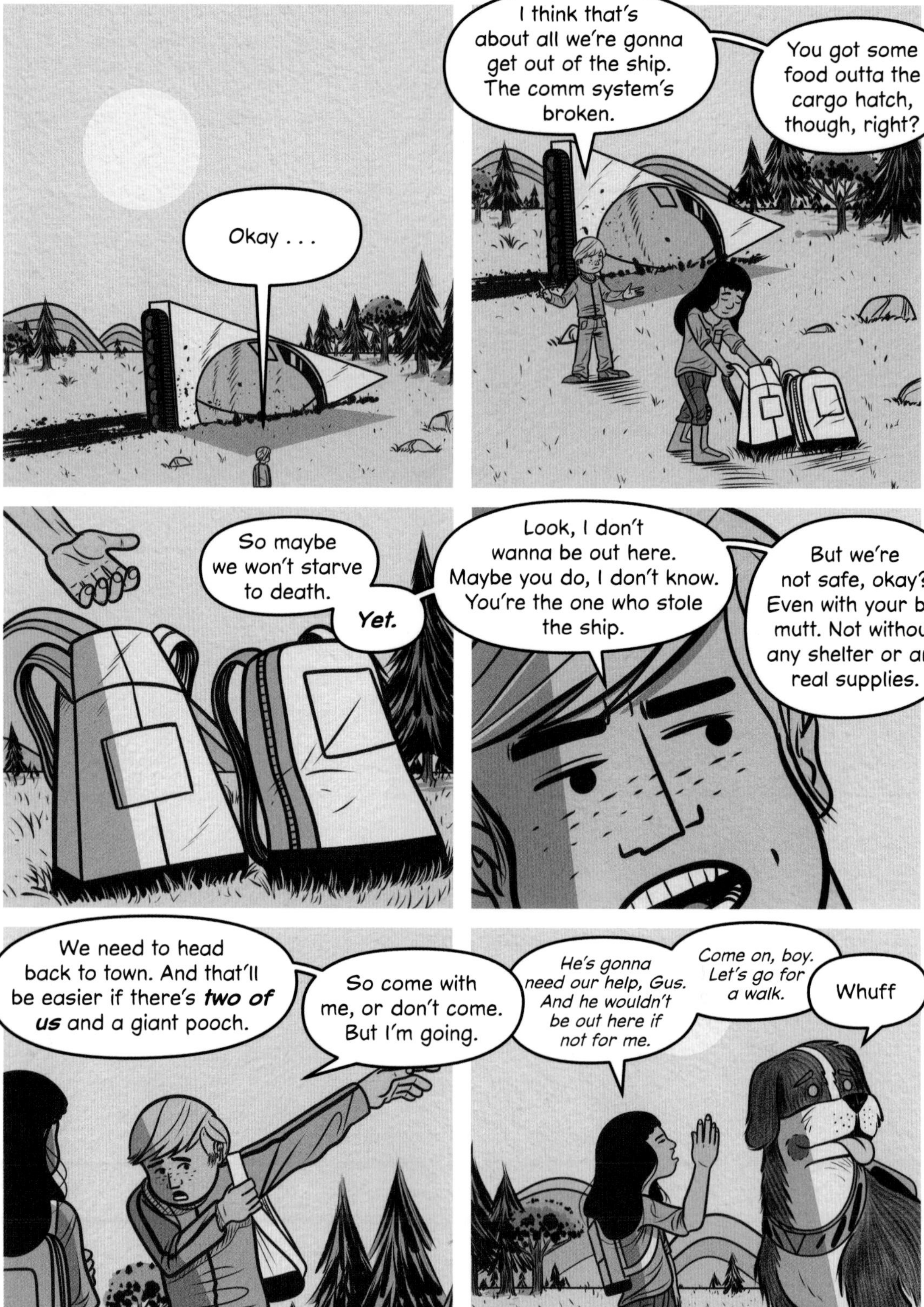
Okay . . .
I think that's about all we're gonna get out of the ship. The comm system's broken.
You got some food outta the cargo hatch, though, right?
So maybe we won't starve to death.
Yet.
Look, I don't wanna be out here. Maybe you do, I don't know. You're the one who stole the ship.
But we're not safe, okay? Even with your big mutt. Not without any shelter or any real supplies.
We need to head back to town. And that'll be easier if there's two of us and a giant pooch.
So come with me, or don't come. But I'm going.
He's gonna need our help, Gus. And he wouldn't be out here if not for me.
Come on, boy. Let's go for a walk.
Whuff

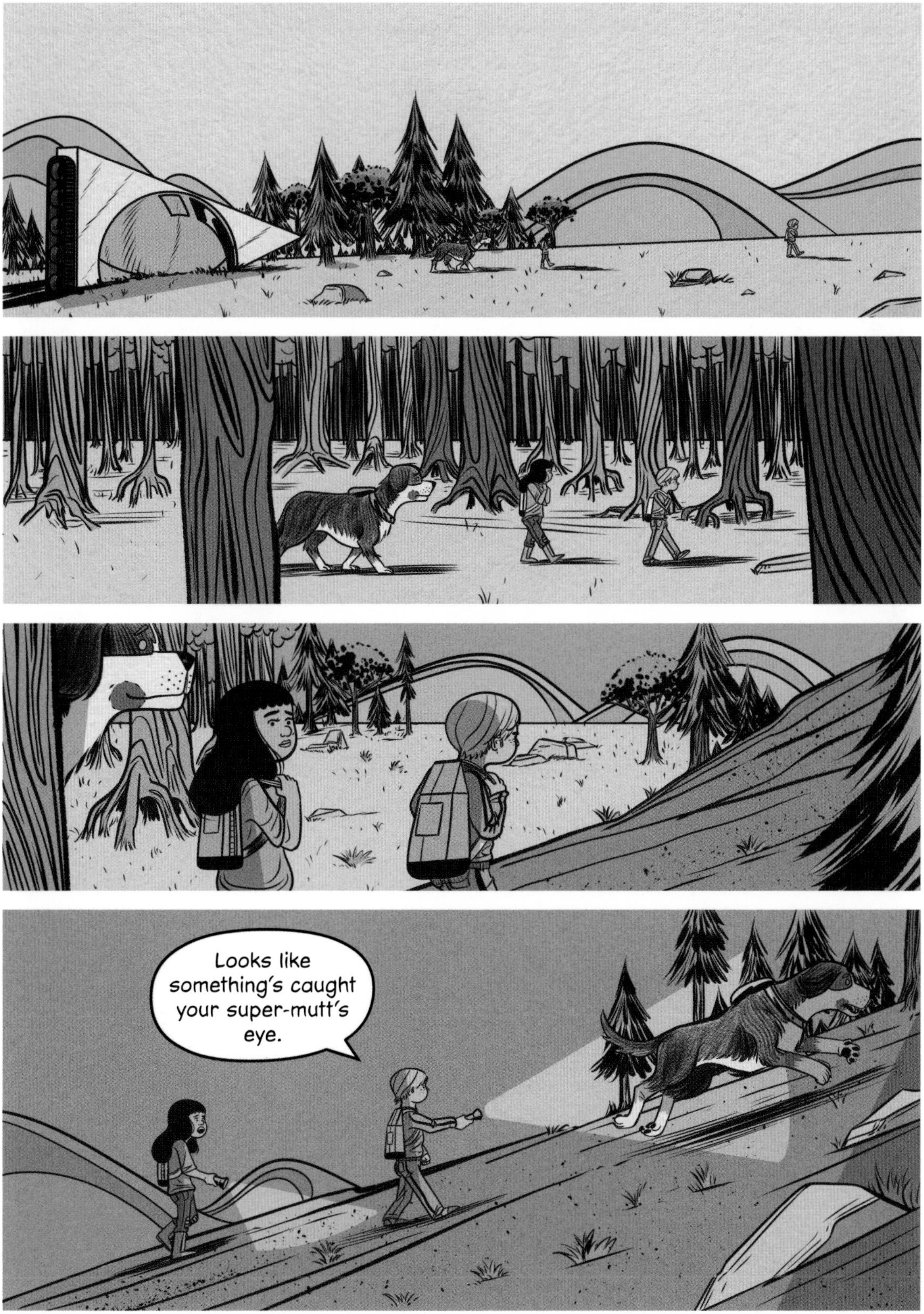
Looks like something's caught your super-mutt's eye.

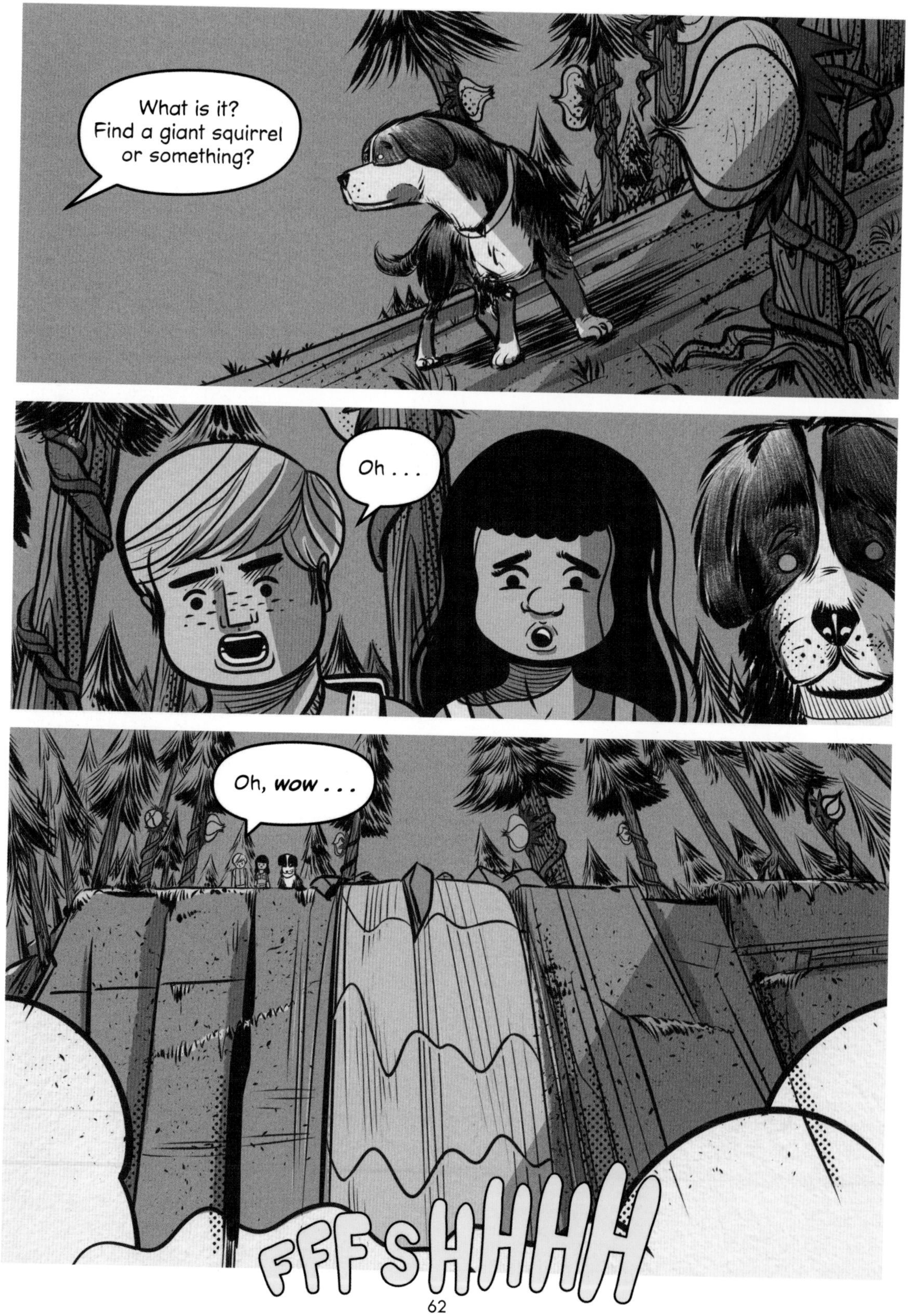
What is it? Find a giant squirrel or something?
Oh . . .
Oh, **wow** . . .
FFFSHHHH

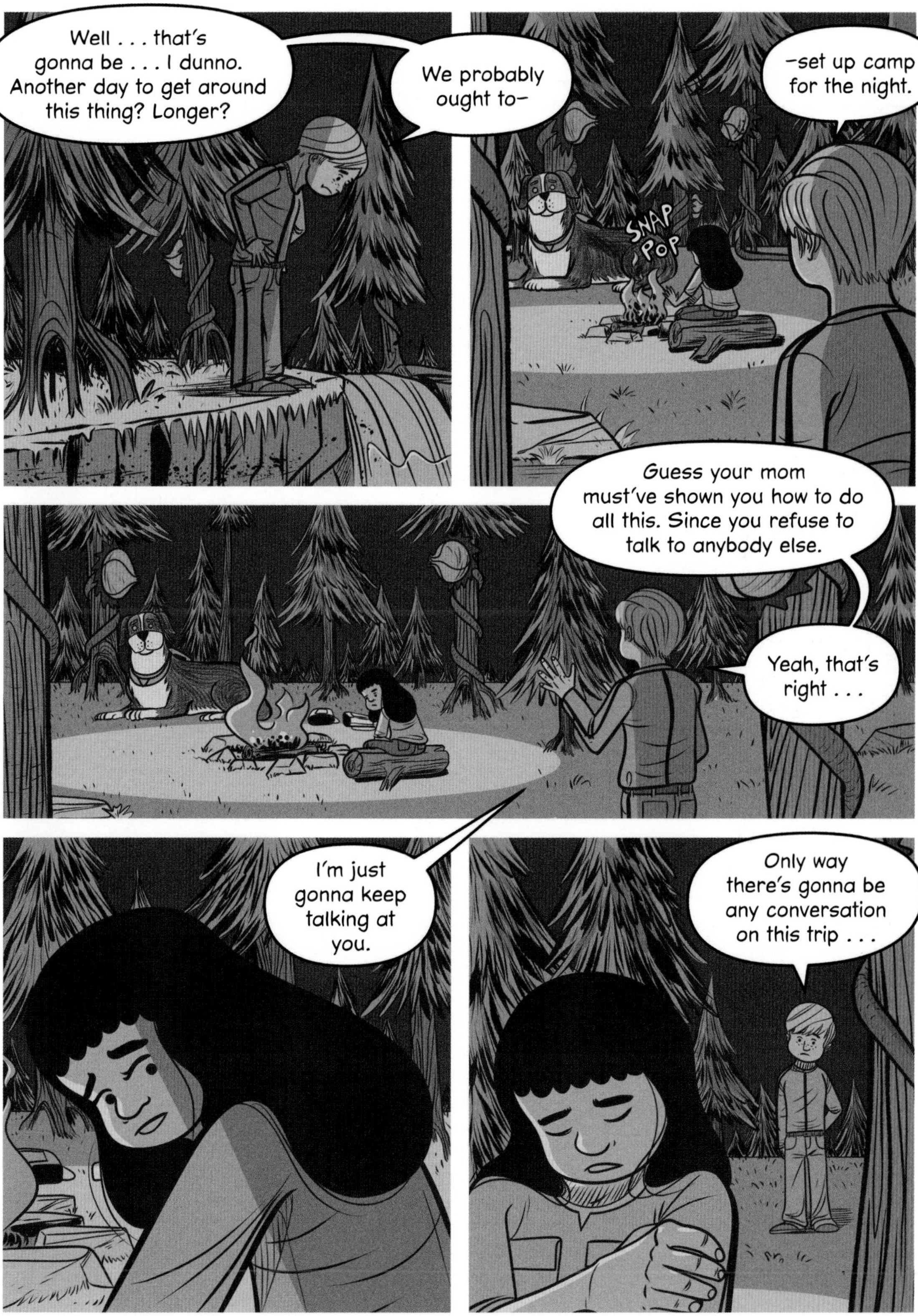
Well . . . that's gonna be . . . I dunno. Another day to get around this thing? Longer?
We probably ought to–
–set up camp for the night.
SNAP
POP
Guess your mom must've shown you how to do all this. Since you refuse to talk to anybody else.
Yeah, that's right . . .
I'm just gonna keep talking at you.
Only way there's gonna be any conversation on this trip . . .

So why were you sneaking the pooch out of town?

Why'd you need to steal a scout ship?

Near as I can tell, you didn't even have a *plan.*

What were you going to do? Dump your dog off in the middle of nowhere? Hang around till people brought you **both** back?

I'm just gonna keep asking you this stuff.

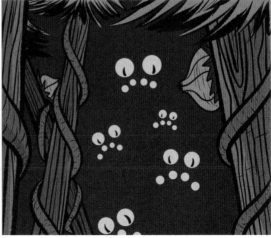

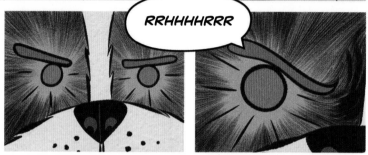

RRHHHHRRR

Hmm?
Whuzzit?

SPLICK
-CHUK

RRRHHHHRRRR

Gaaahh!

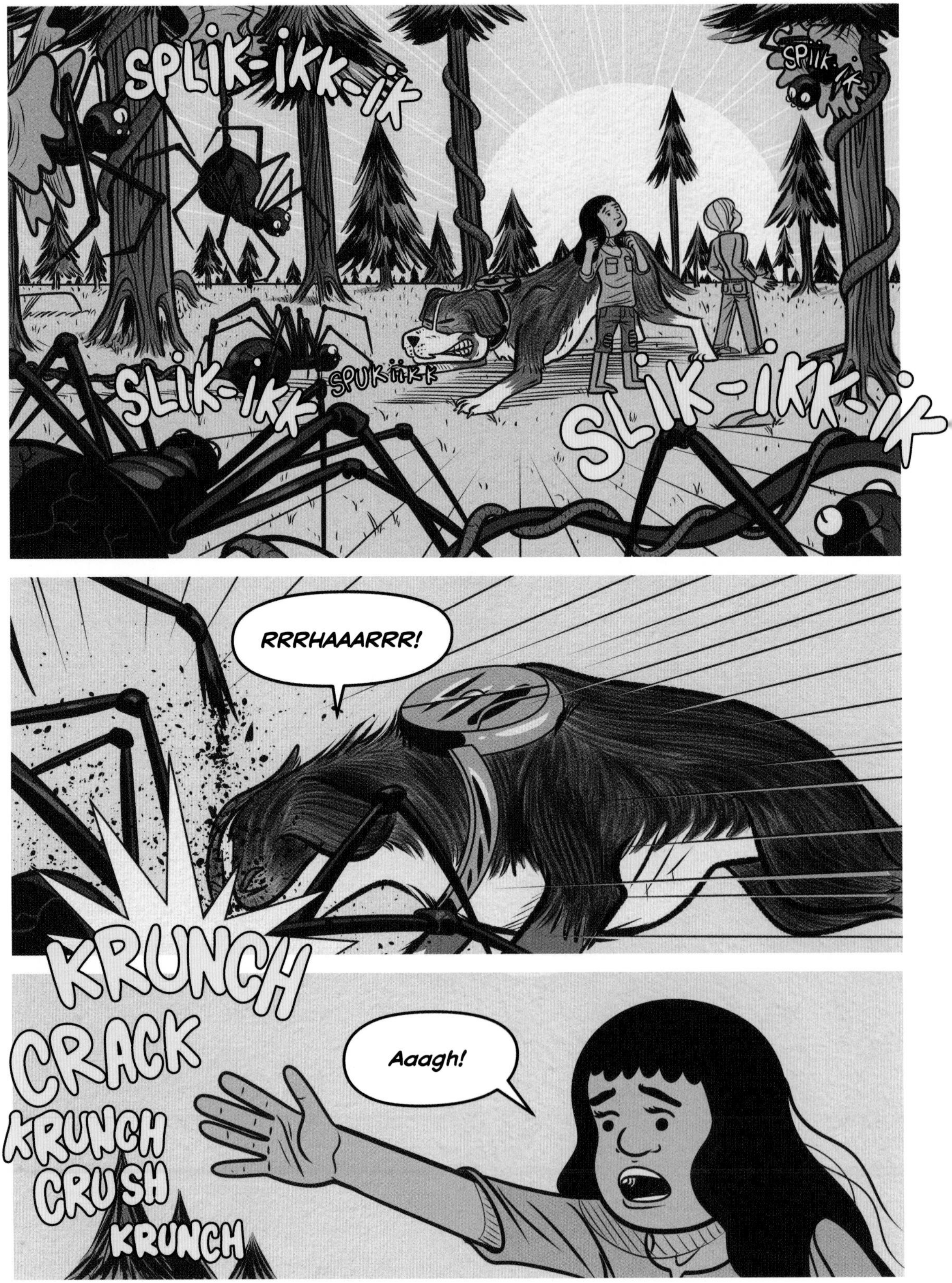
SPLIK-IKK-IK
SPIIK-IK
SLIK-IKK
SPUK-IKK
SLIK-IKK-IK
RRRHAAARRR!
KRUNCH
CRACK
Aaagh!
KRUNCH
CRUSH
KRUNCH

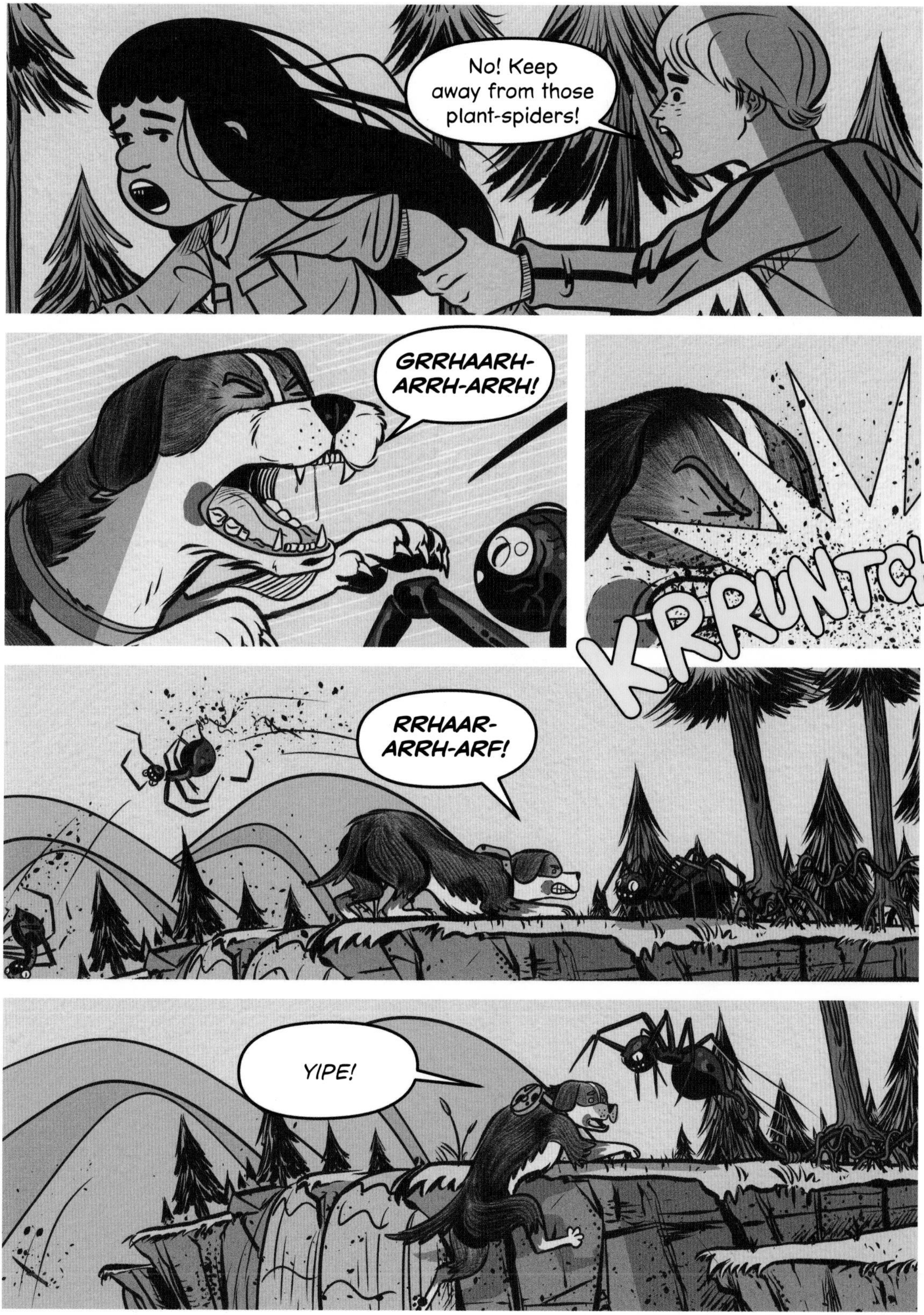
No! Keep away from those plant-spiders!
GRRHAARH-ARRH-ARRH!
KRRUNTCH
RRHAAR-ARRH-ARF!
YIPE!

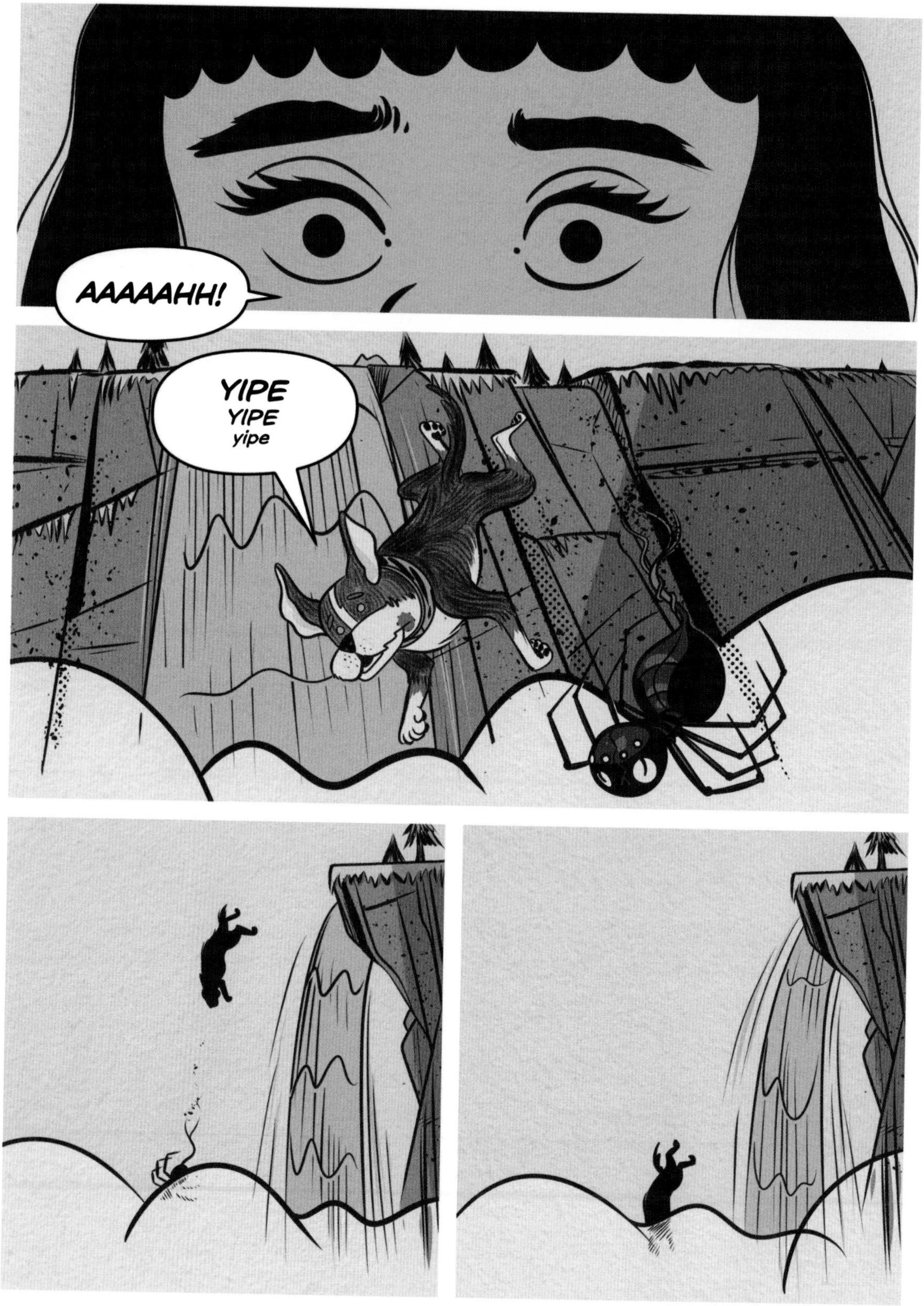
AAAAAHH!
YIPE
YIPE
yipe

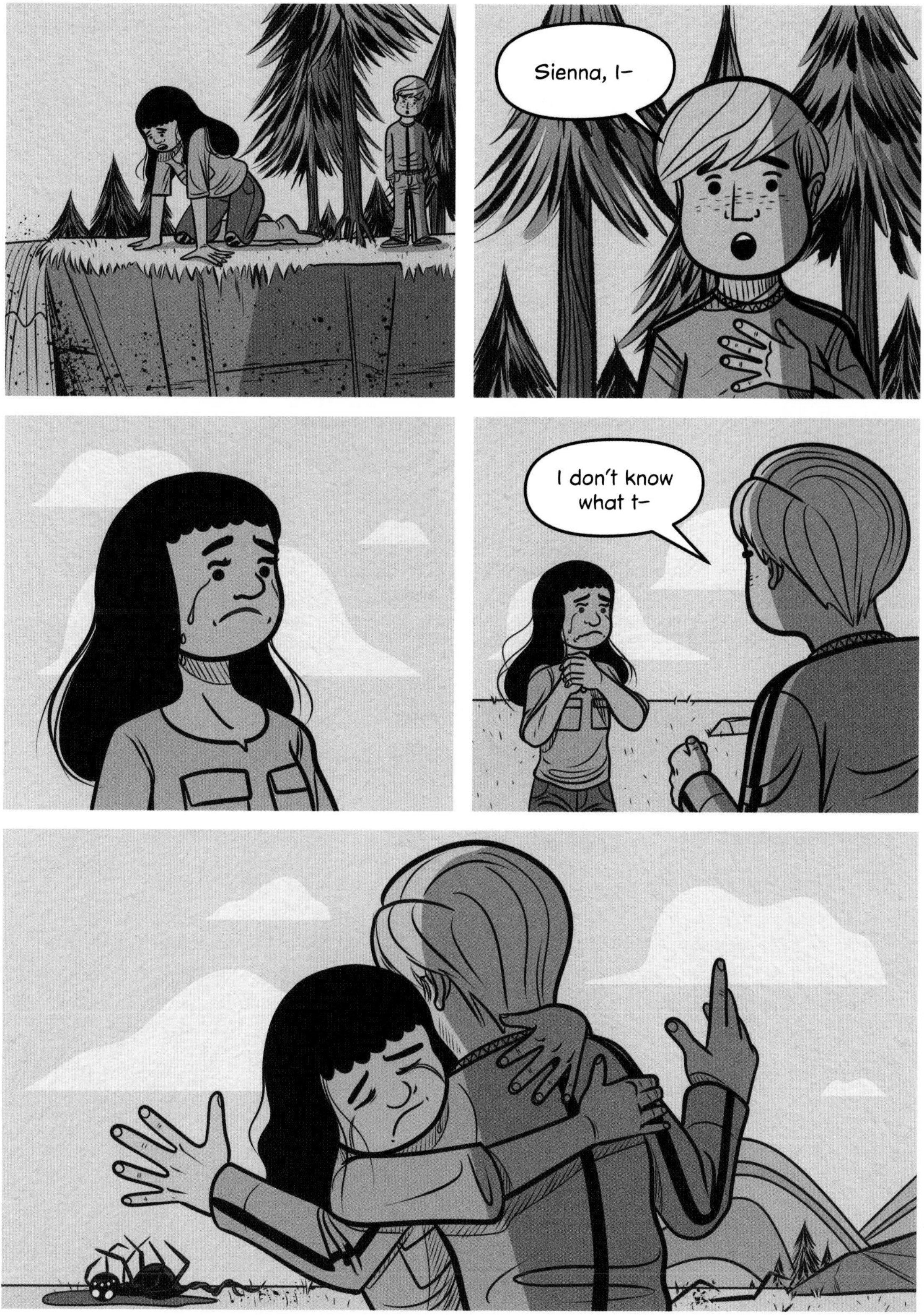
Sienna, I-
I don't know what t-

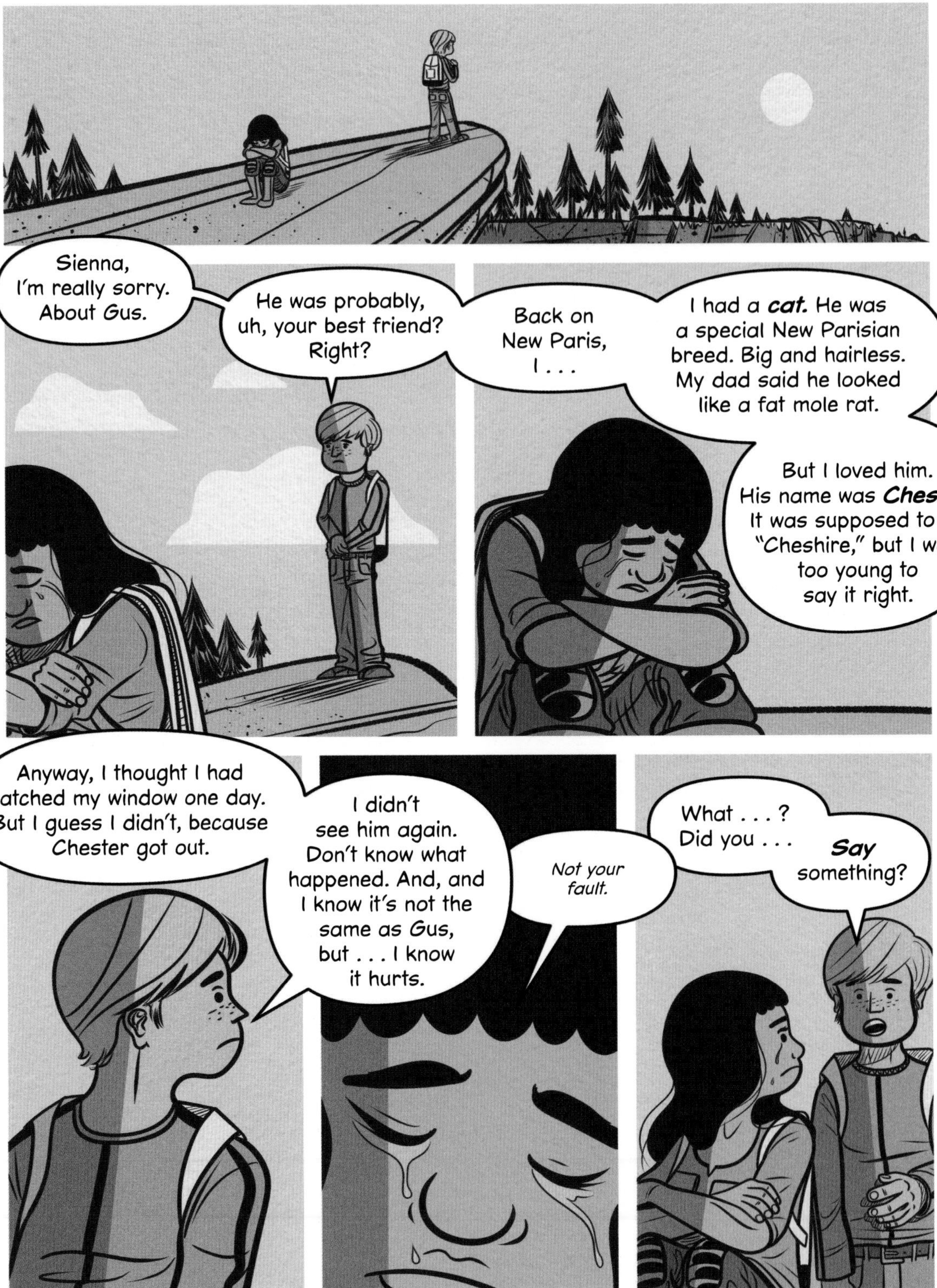

Sienna, I'm really sorry. About Gus.
He was probably, uh, your best friend? Right?
Back on New Paris, I . . .
I had a ***cat.*** He was a special New Parisian breed. Big and hairless. My dad said he looked like a fat mole rat.
But I loved him. His name was ***Chester.*** It was supposed to be "Cheshire," but I was too young to say it right.
Anyway, I thought I had latched my window one day. But I guess I didn't, because Chester got out.
I didn't see him again. Don't know what happened. And, and I know it's not the same as Gus, but . . . I know it hurts.
Not your fault.
What . . . ? Did you . . .
Say something?

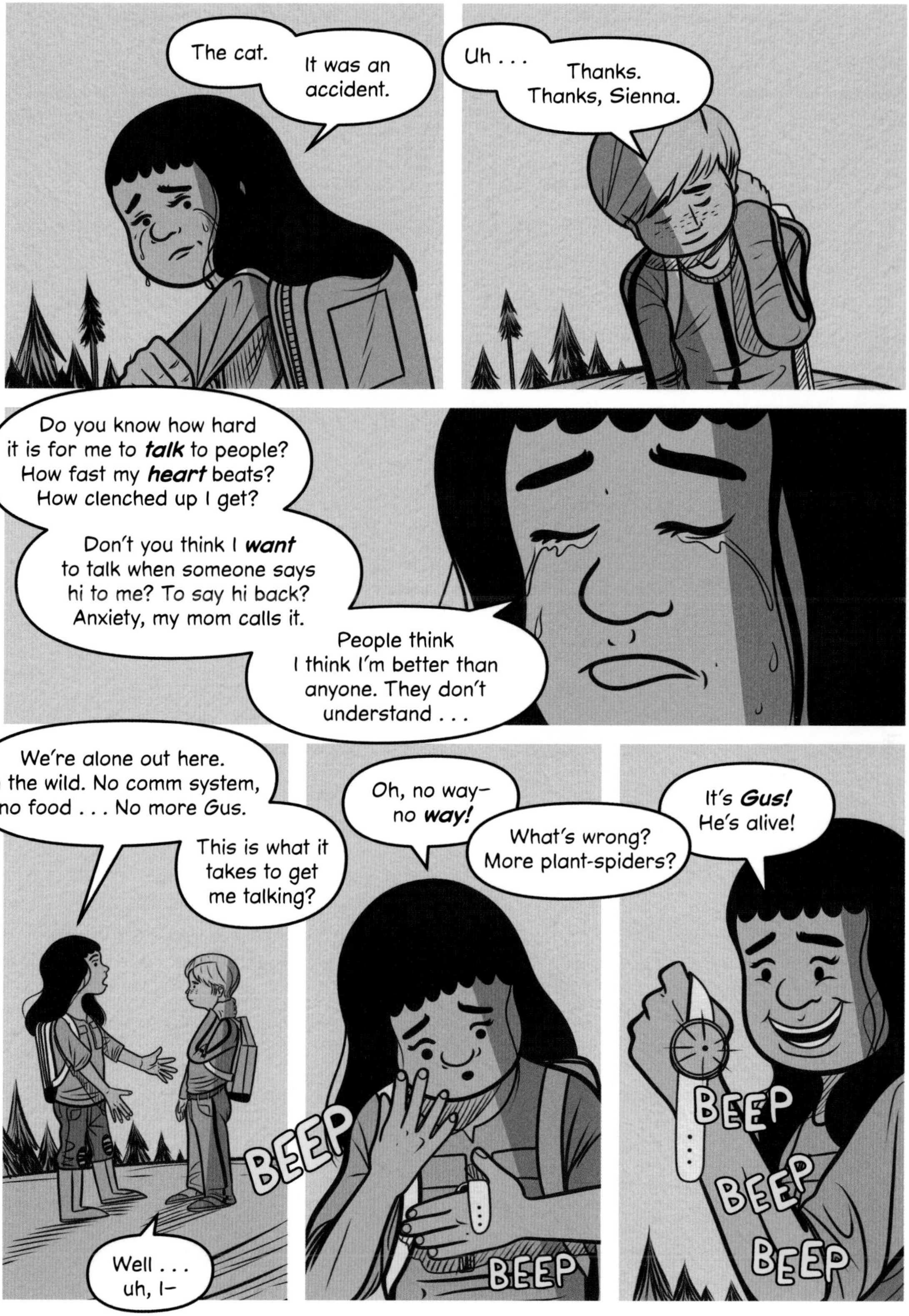
The cat.
It was an accident.
Uh . . .
Thanks. Thanks, Sienna.
Do you know how hard it is for me to **talk** to people? How fast my **heart** beats? How clenched up I get?
Don't you think I **want** to talk when someone says hi to me? To say hi back? Anxiety, my mom calls it.
People think I think I'm better than anyone. They don't understand . . .
We're alone out here. In the wild. No comm system, no food . . . No more Gus.
This is what it takes to get me talking?
Well . . . uh, I–
BEEP
Oh, no way– no **way!**
BEEP
What's wrong? More plant-spiders?
It's **Gus!** He's alive!
BEEP
BEEP
BEEP

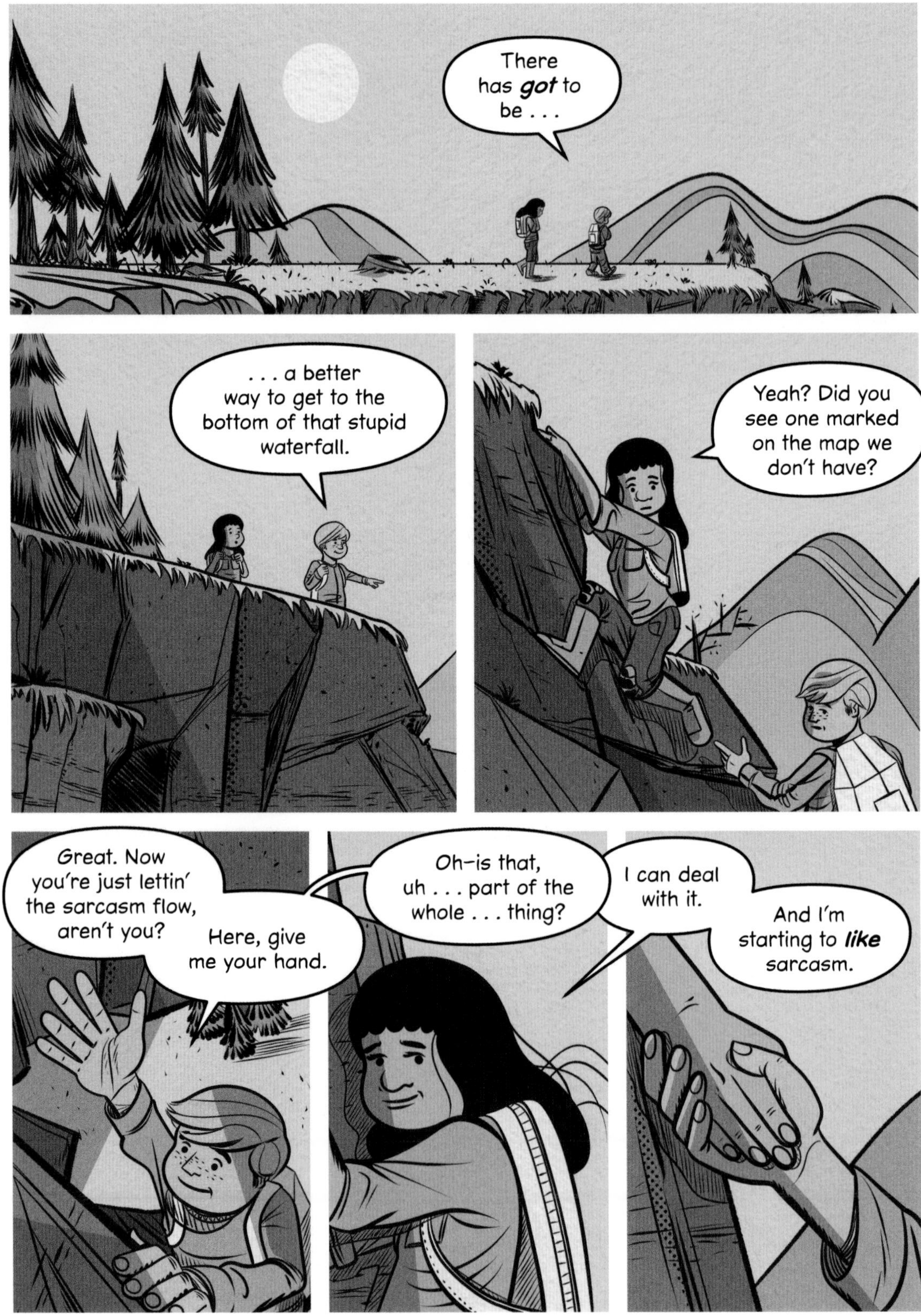

There has *got* to be . . .
. . . a better way to get to the bottom of that stupid waterfall.
Yeah? Did you see one marked on the map we don't have?
Great. Now you're just lettin' the sarcasm flow, aren't you?
Here, give me your hand.
Oh—is that, uh . . . part of the whole . . . thing?
I can deal with it.
And I'm starting to *like* sarcasm.

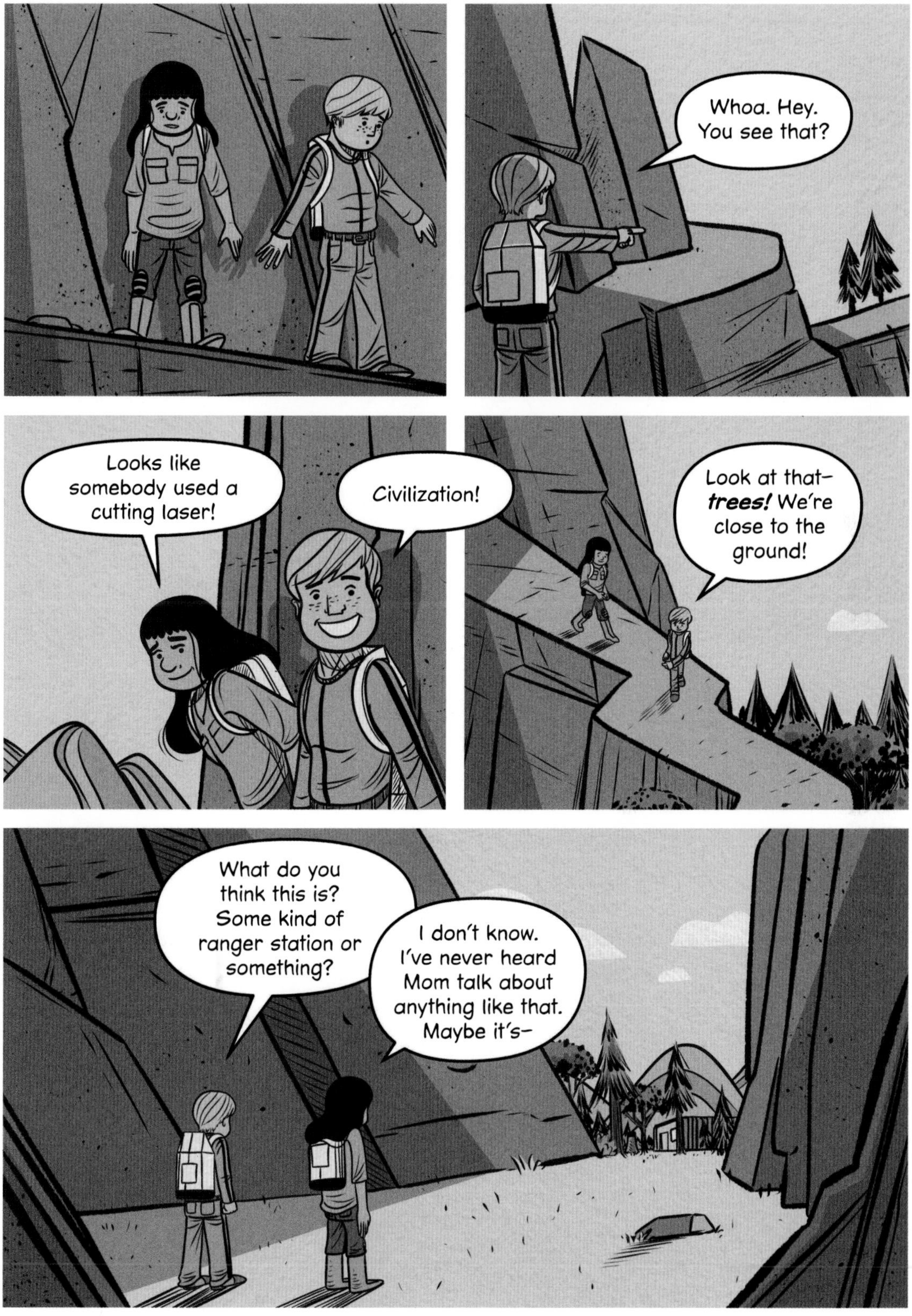

Whoa. Hey. You see that?
Looks like somebody used a cutting laser!
Civilization!
Look at that—*trees!* We're close to the ground!
What do you think this is? Some kind of ranger station or something?
I don't know. I've never heard Mom talk about anything like that. Maybe it's—

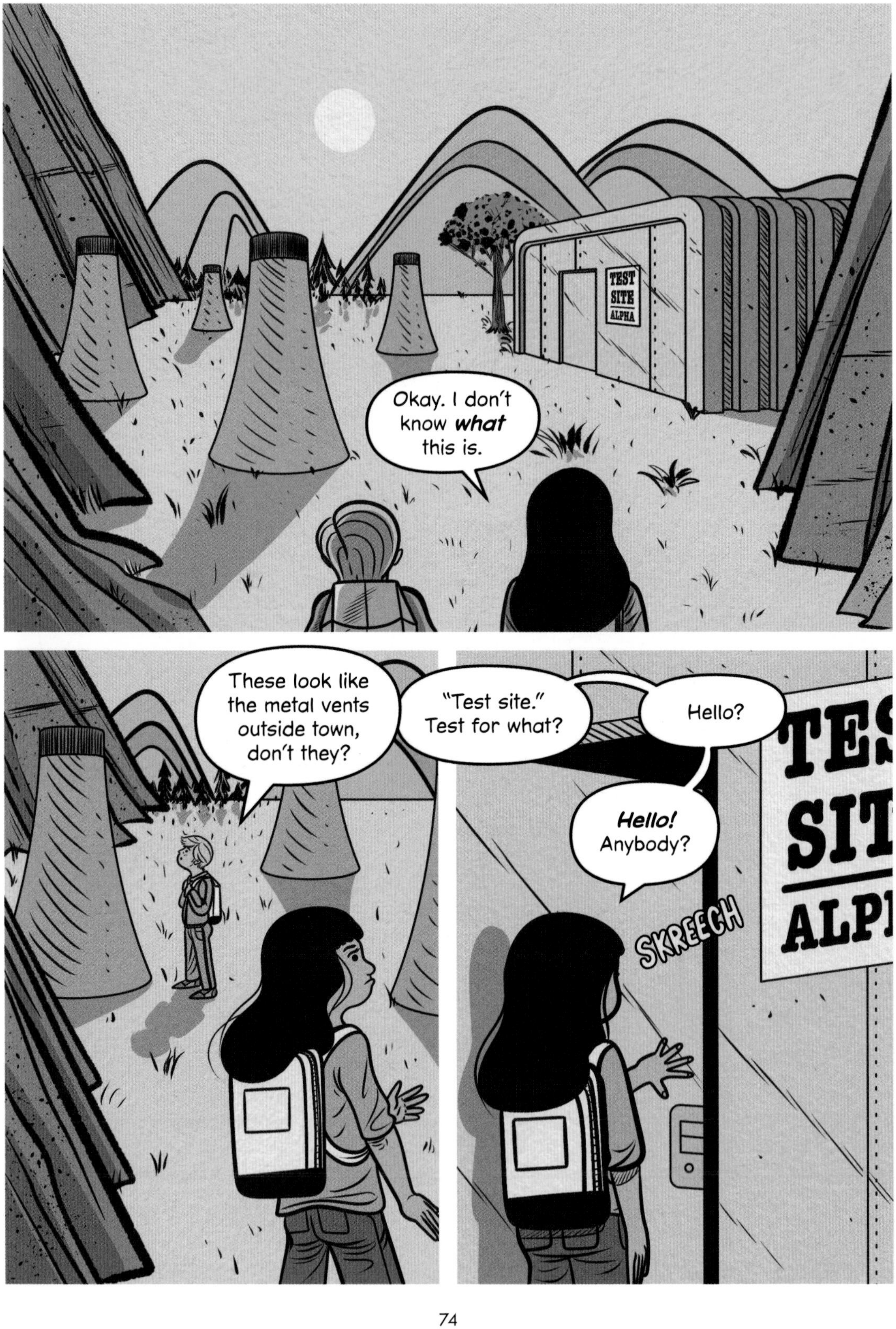
TEST SITE ALPHA
Okay. I don't know ***what*** this is.
These look like the metal vents outside town, don't they?
"Test site." Test for what?
Hello?
Hello! Anybody?
SKREECH
TES SIT ALP

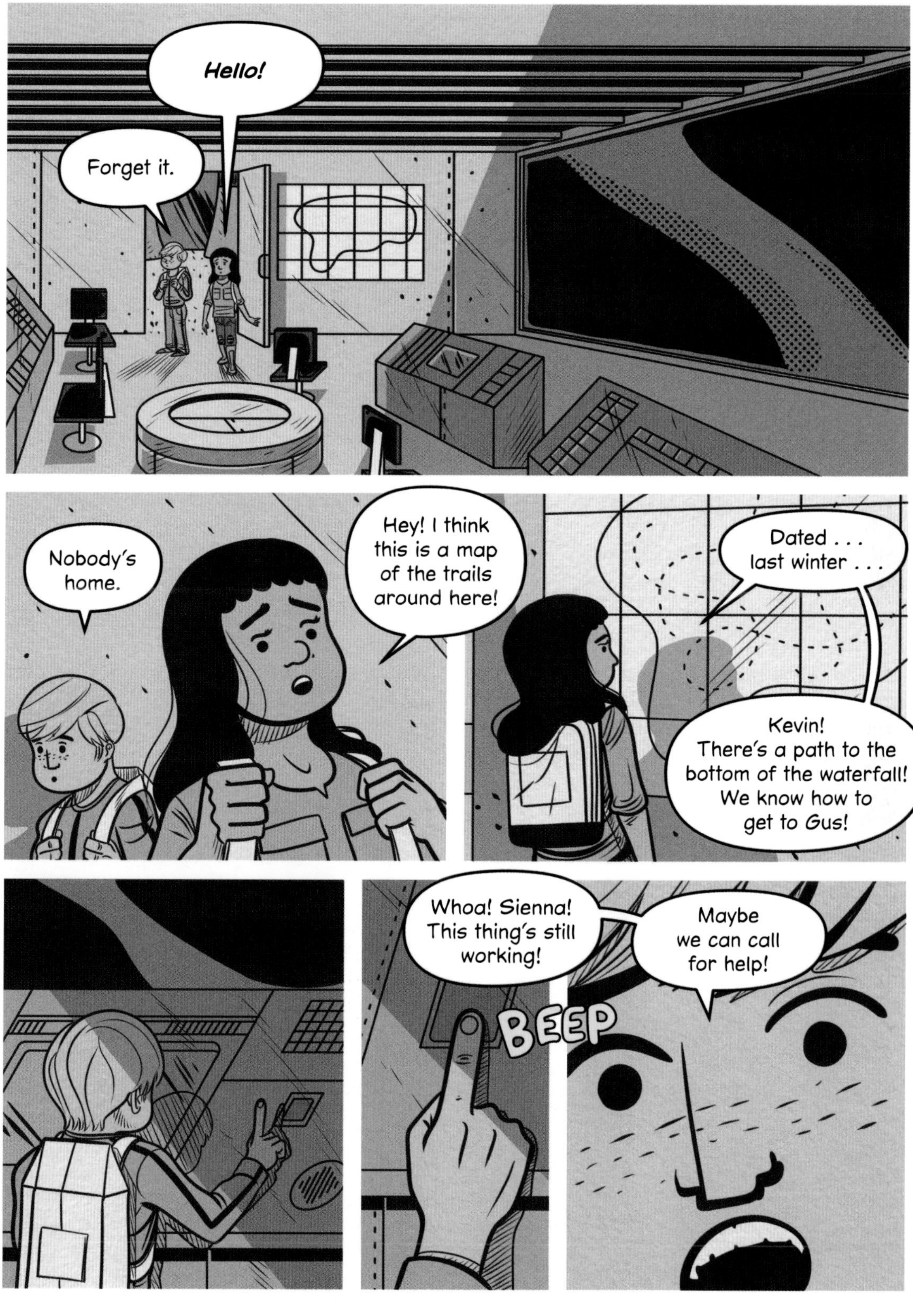
Hello!
Forget it.
Nobody's home.
Hey! I think this is a map of the trails around here!
Dated . . . last winter . . .
Kevin! There's a path to the bottom of the waterfall! We know how to get to Gus!
Whoa! Sienna! This thing's still working!
Maybe we can call for help!
BEEP

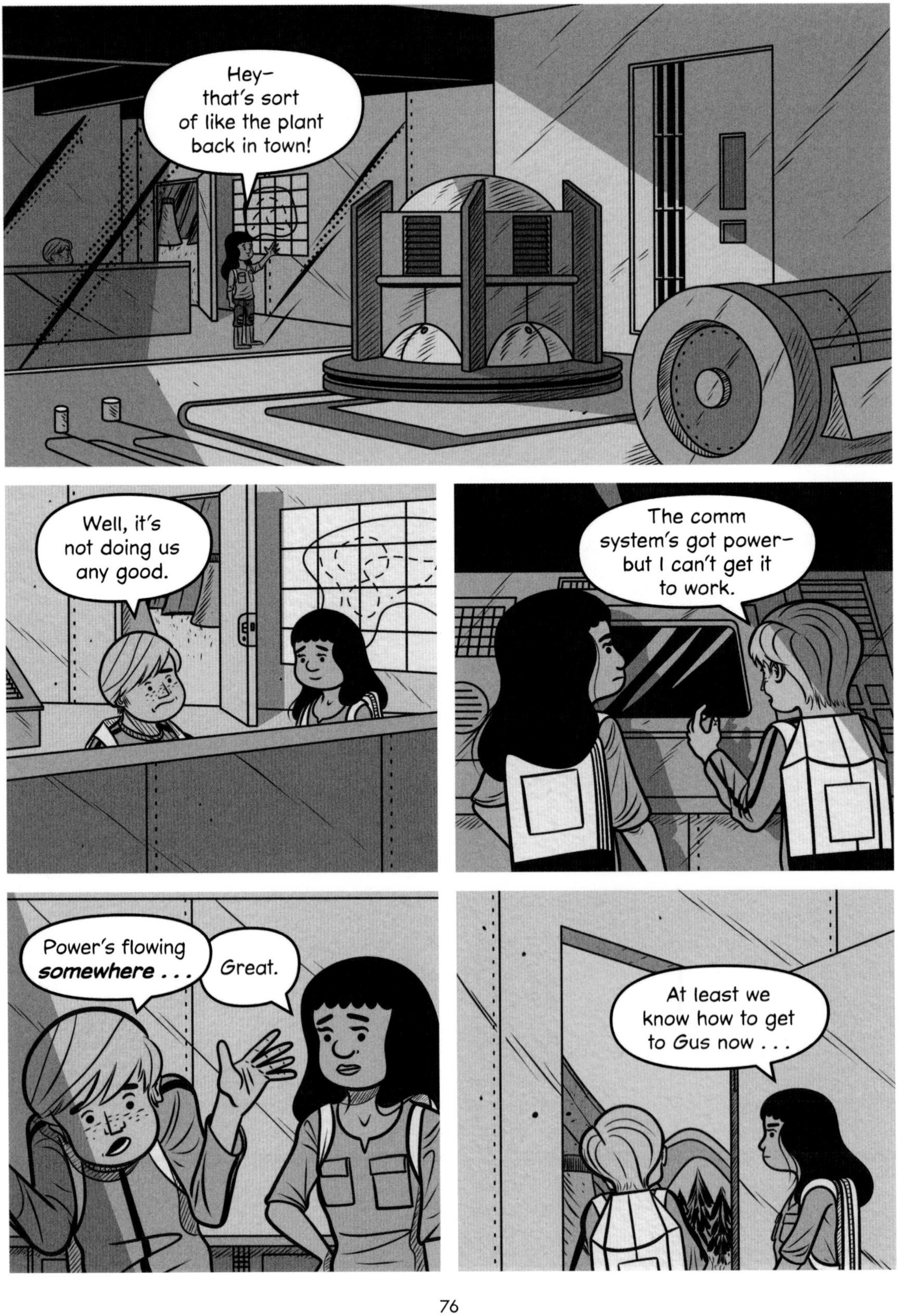
Hey—that's sort of like the plant back in town!
Well, it's not doing us any good.
The comm system's got power—but I can't get it to work.
Power's flowing ***somewhere . . .***
Great.
At least we know how to get to Gus now . . .

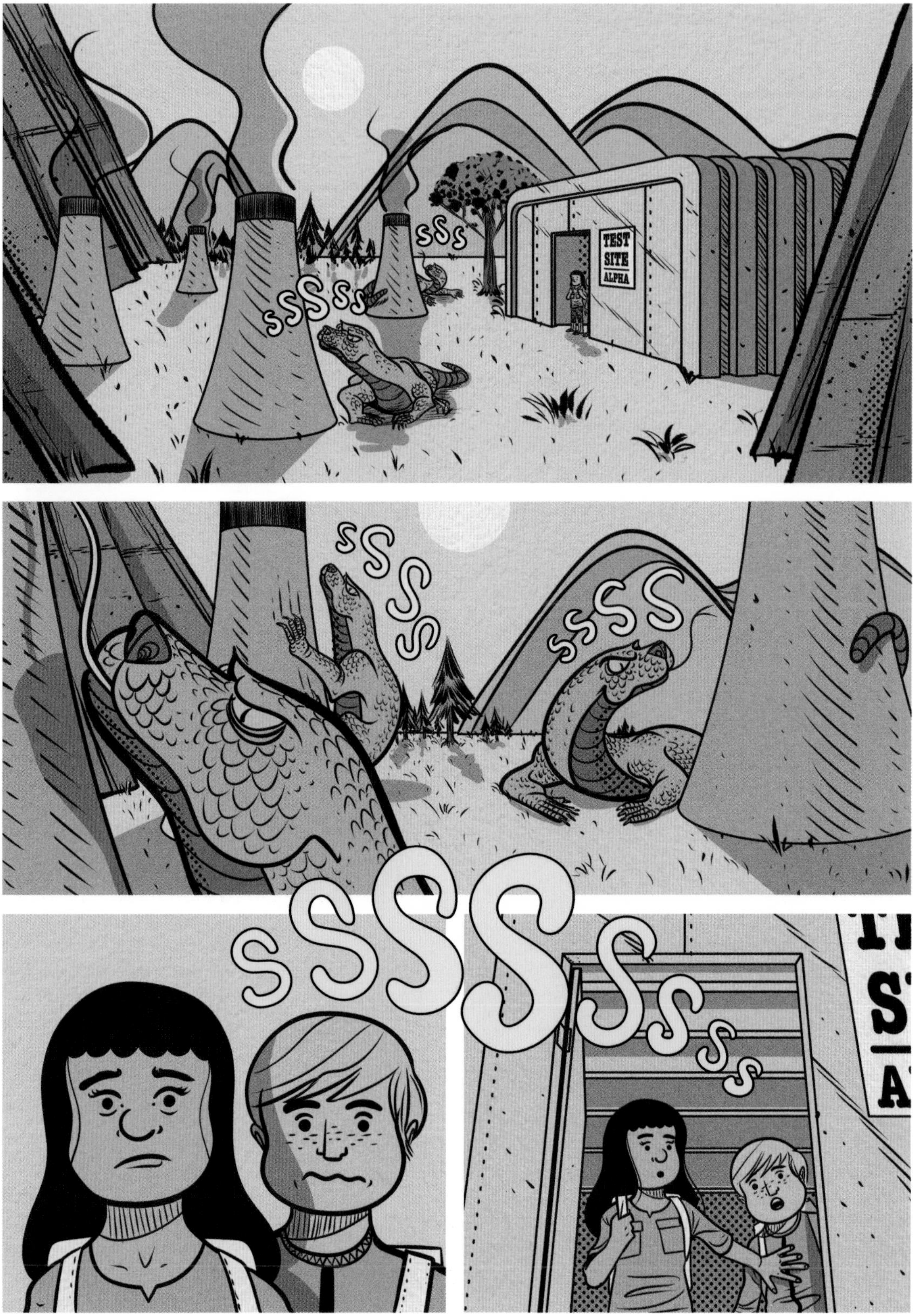
TEST SITE ALPHA
sSSss
sSSss
sSSSS
ssSS
sSSSSSSsss

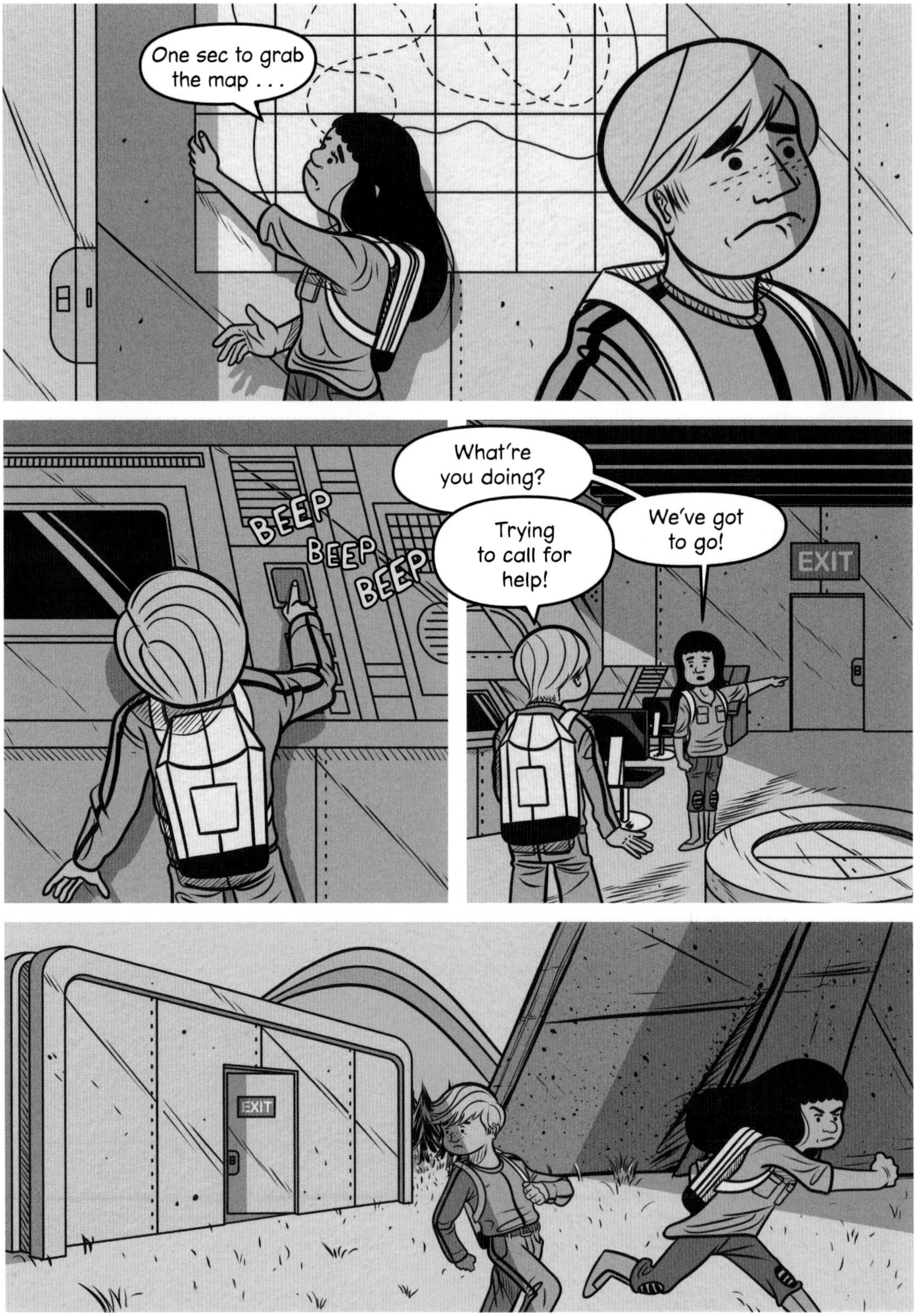
One sec to grab the map . . .
BEEP
BEEP
BEEP
What're you doing?
Trying to call for help!
We've got to go!
EXIT
EXIT

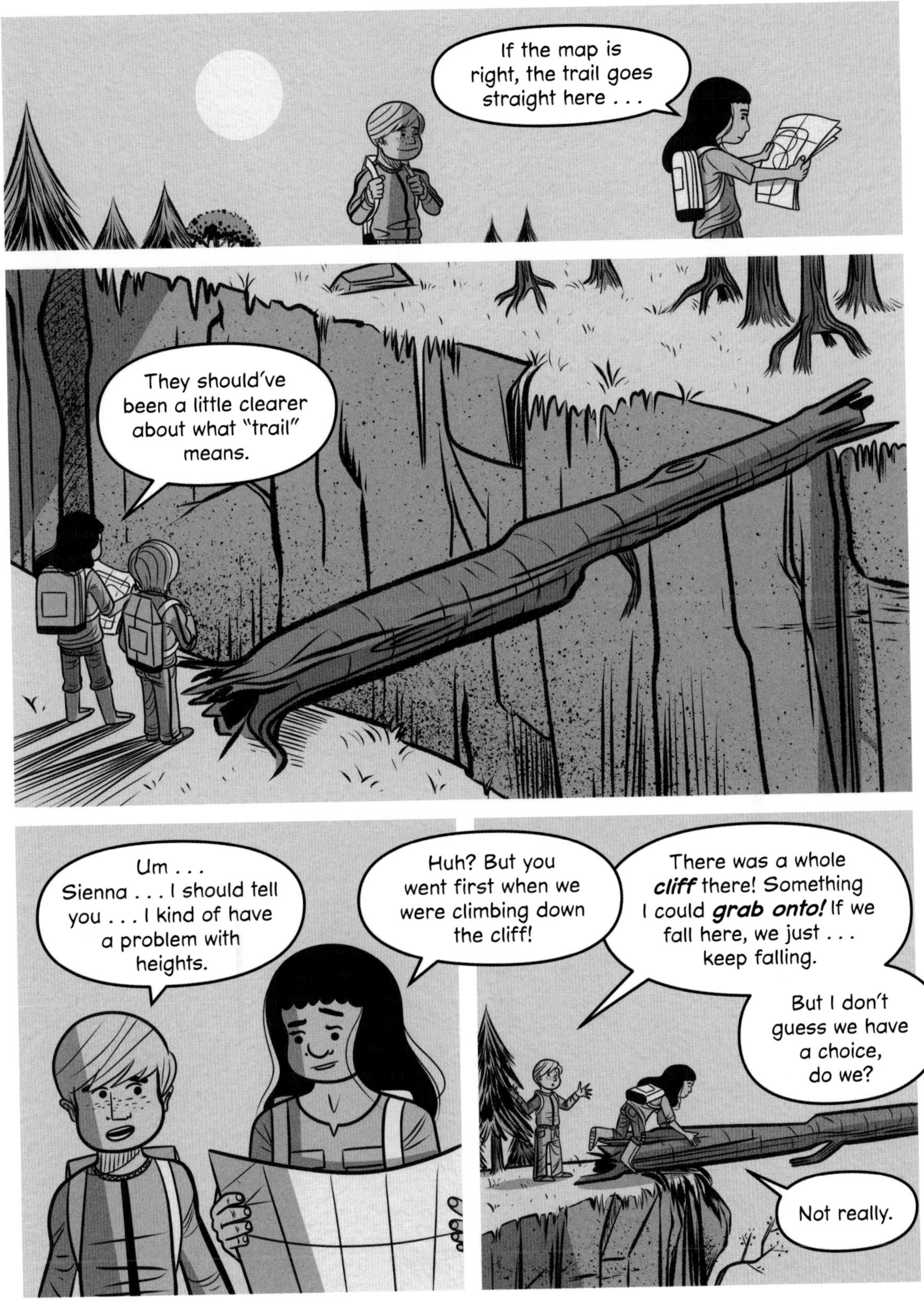

If the map is right, the trail goes straight here . . .
They should've been a little clearer about what "trail" means.
Um . . . Sienna . . . I should tell you . . . I kind of have a problem with heights.
Huh? But you went first when we were climbing down the cliff!
There was a whole ***cliff*** there! Something I could ***grab onto!*** If we fall here, we just . . . keep falling.
But I don't guess we have a choice, do we?
Not really.

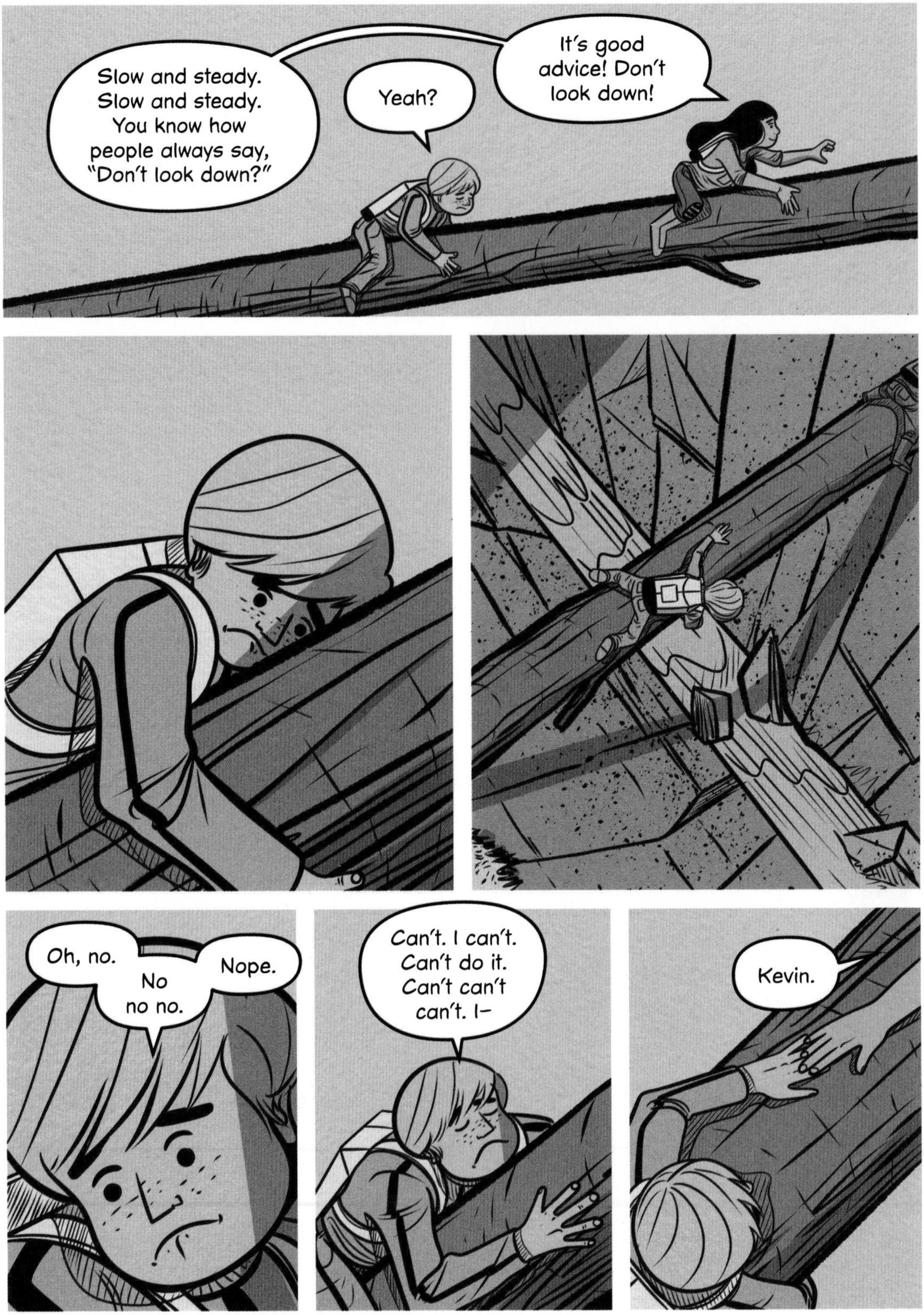
Slow and steady. Slow and steady. You know how people always say, "Don't look down?"
Yeah?
It's good advice! Don't look down!
Oh, no.
No no no.
Nope.
Can't. I can't. Can't do it. Can't can't can't. I–
Kevin.

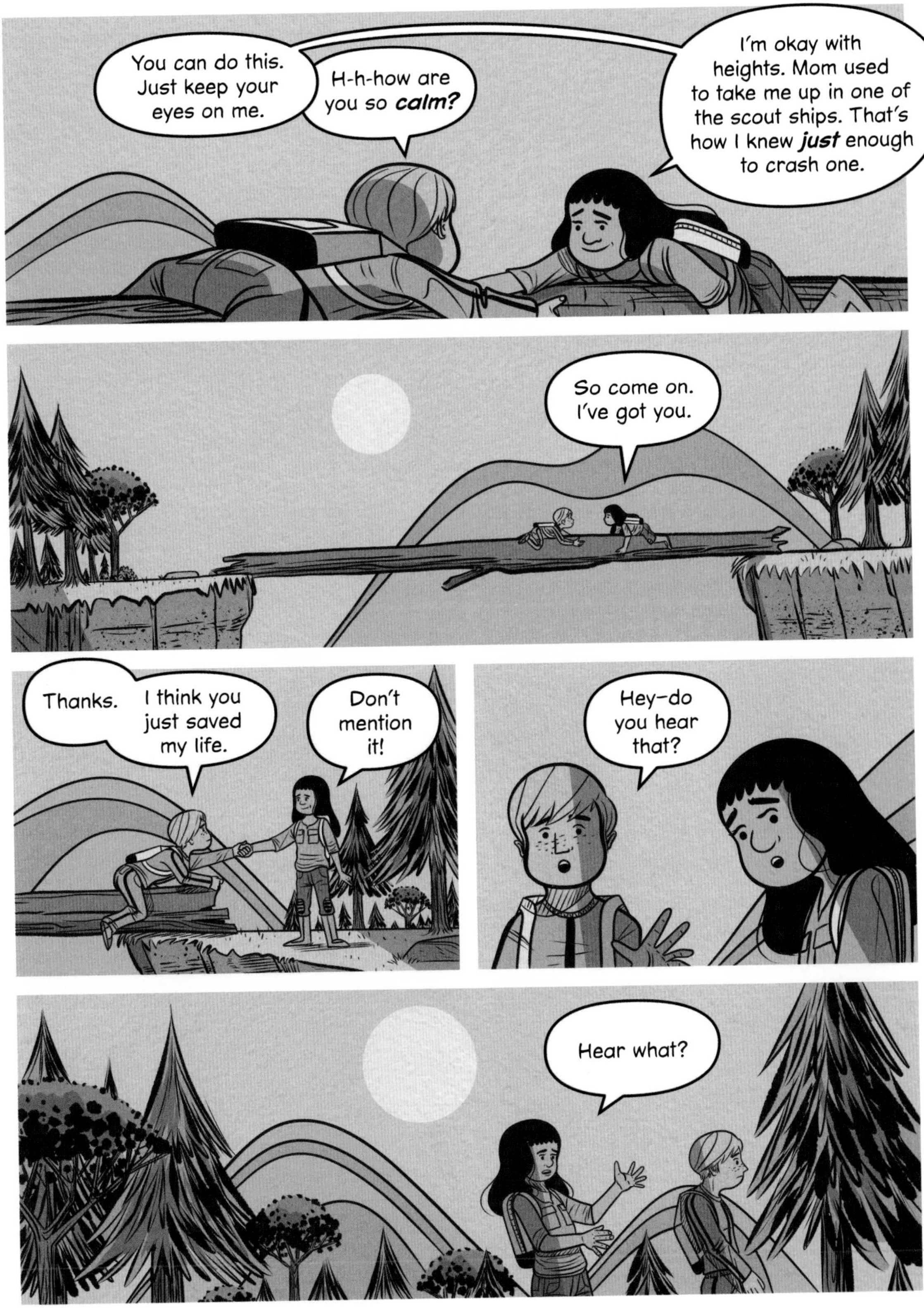
You can do this. Just keep your eyes on me.
H-h-how are you so *calm?*
I'm okay with heights. Mom used to take me up in one of the scout ships. That's how I knew ***just*** enough to crash one.
So come on. I've got you.
Thanks.
I think you just saved my life.
Don't mention it!
Hey—do you hear that?
Hear what?

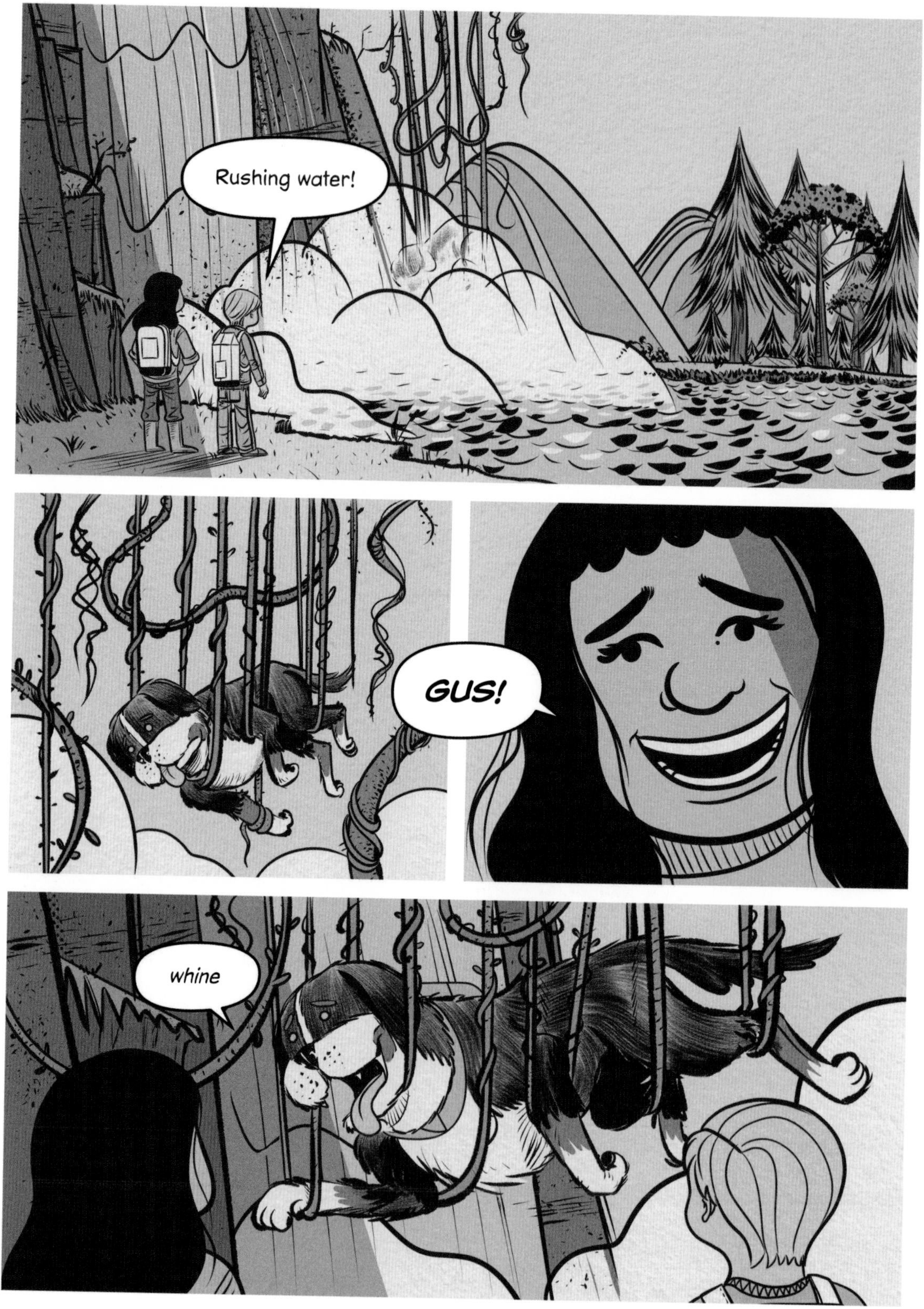

Rushing water!
GUS!
whine

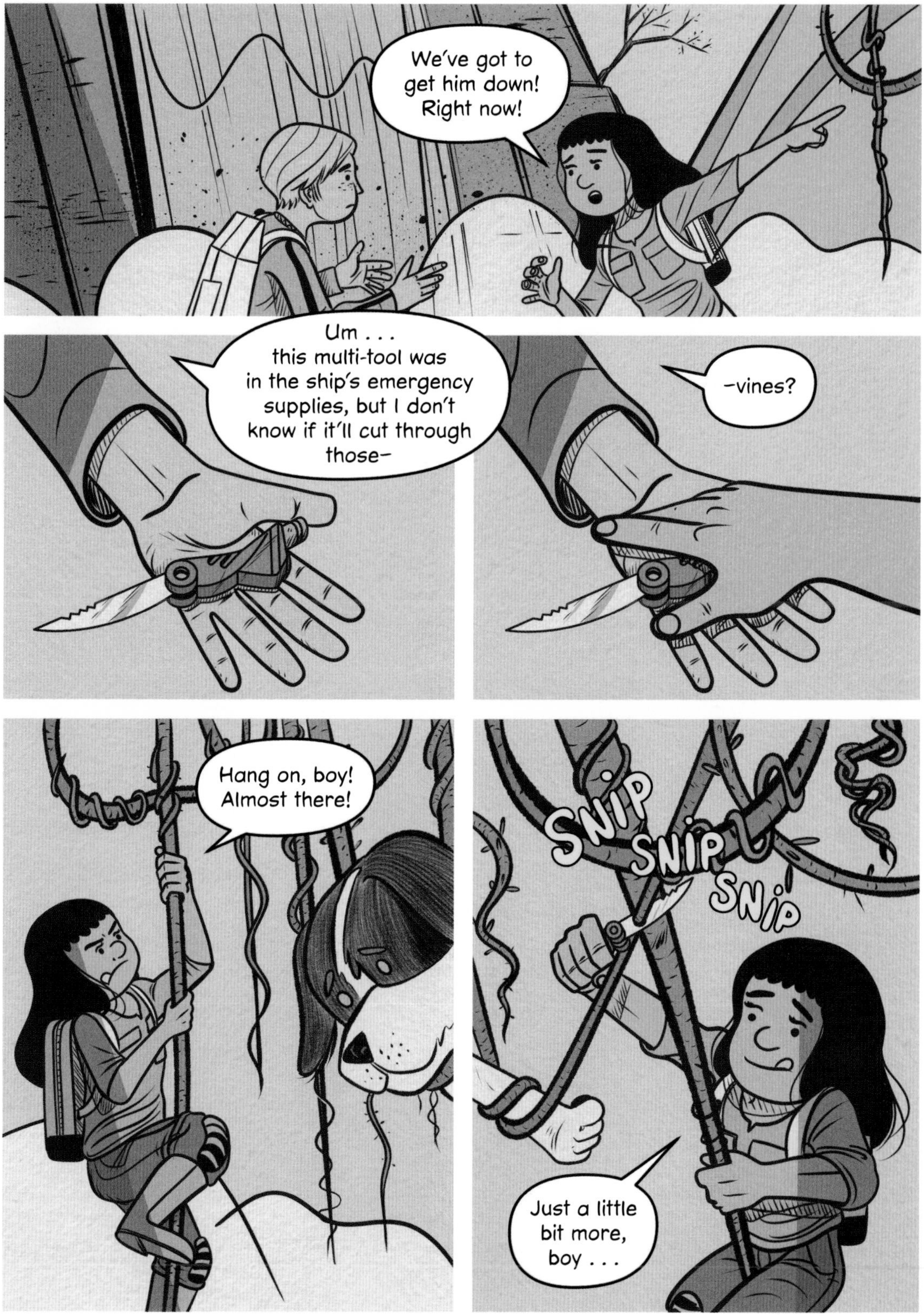
We've got to get him down! Right now!
Um . . . this multi-tool was in the ship's emergency supplies, but I don't know if it'll cut through those-
-vines?
Hang on, boy! Almost there!
SNIP SNIP SNIP
Just a little bit more, boy . . .

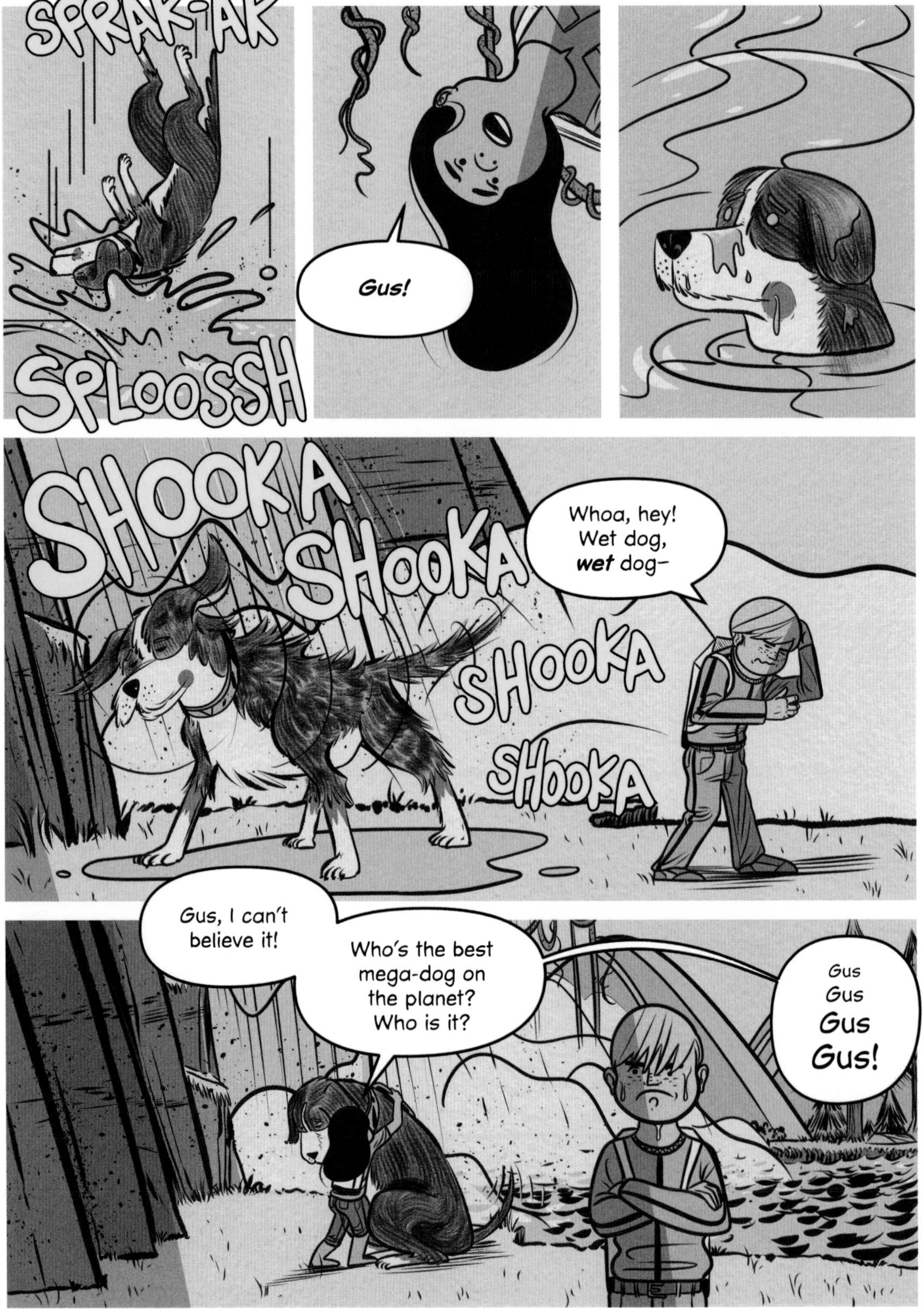
SPRAK-AK
SPLOOSSH
Gus!
SHOOKA
SHOOKA
Whoa, hey! Wet dog, **wet** dog–
SHOOKA
SHOOKA
Gus, I can't believe it!
Who's the best mega-dog on the planet? Who is it?
Gus Gus Gus Gus!

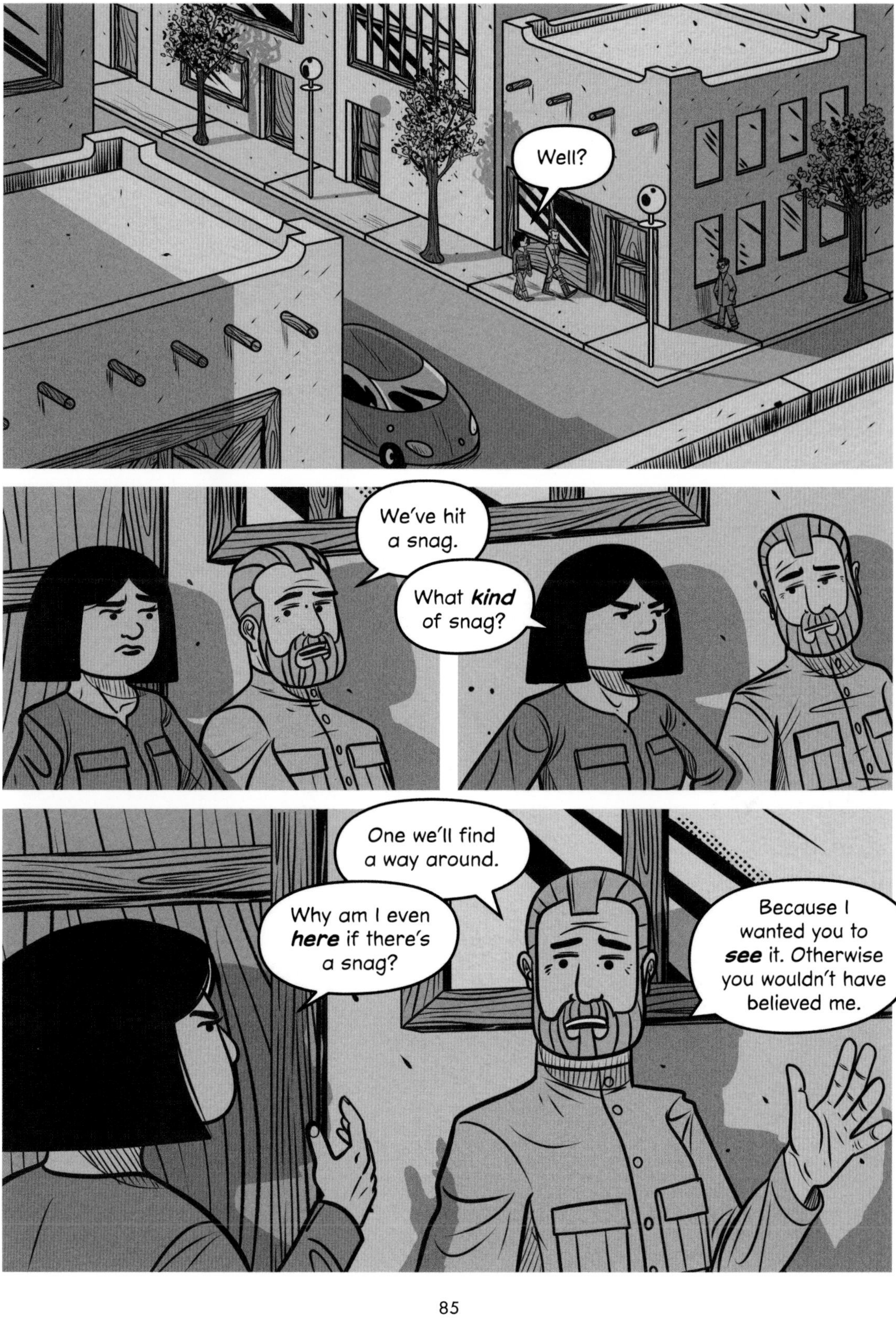
Well?
We've hit a snag.
What *kind* of snag?
One we'll find a way around.
Why am I even *here* if there's a snag?
Because I wanted you to *see* it. Otherwise you wouldn't have believed me.

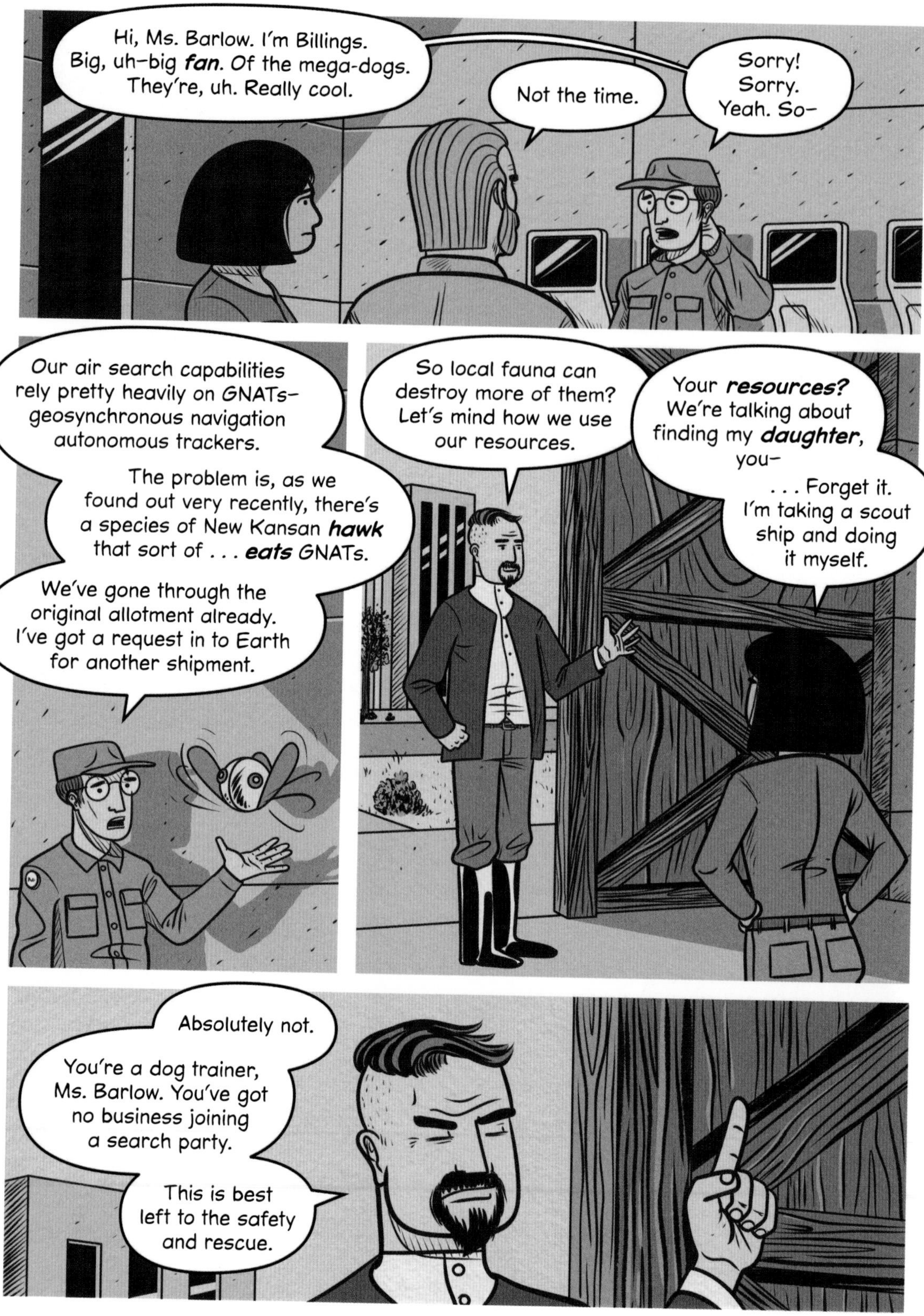
Hi, Ms. Barlow. I'm Billings. Big, uh–big **fan**. Of the mega-dogs. They're, uh. Really cool.
Not the time.
Sorry! Sorry. Yeah. So–
Our air search capabilities rely pretty heavily on GNATs– geosynchronous navigation autonomous trackers.
The problem is, as we found out very recently, there's a species of New Kansan **hawk** that sort of . . . **eats** GNATs.
We've gone through the original allotment already. I've got a request in to Earth for another shipment.
So local fauna can destroy more of them? Let's mind how we use our resources.
Your **resources?** We're talking about finding my **daughter**, you–
. . . Forget it. I'm taking a scout ship and doing it myself.
Absolutely not.
You're a dog trainer, Ms. Barlow. You've got no business joining a search party.
This is best left to the safety and rescue.

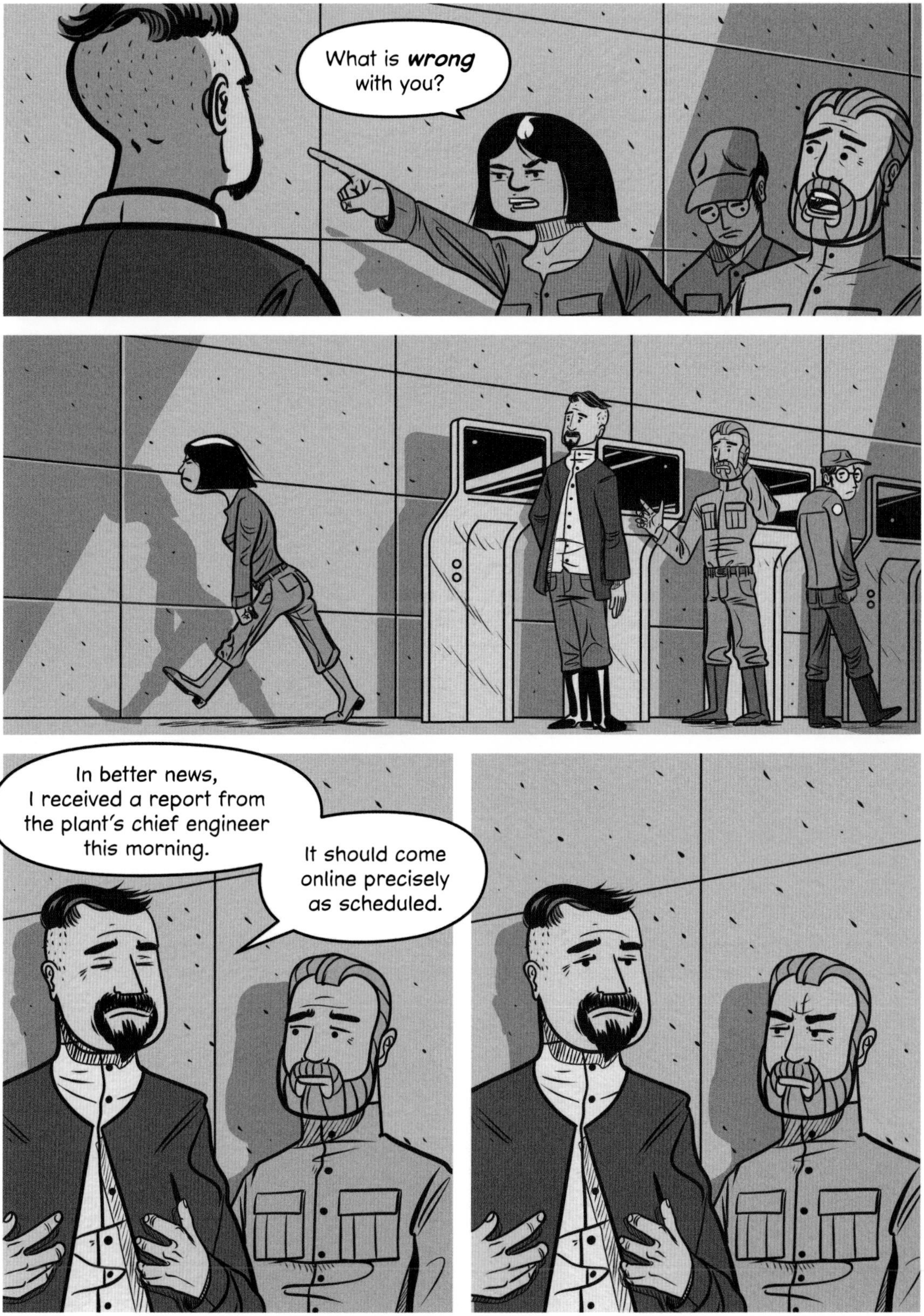
What is **wrong** with you?
In better news, I received a report from the plant's chief engineer this morning.
It should come online precisely as scheduled.

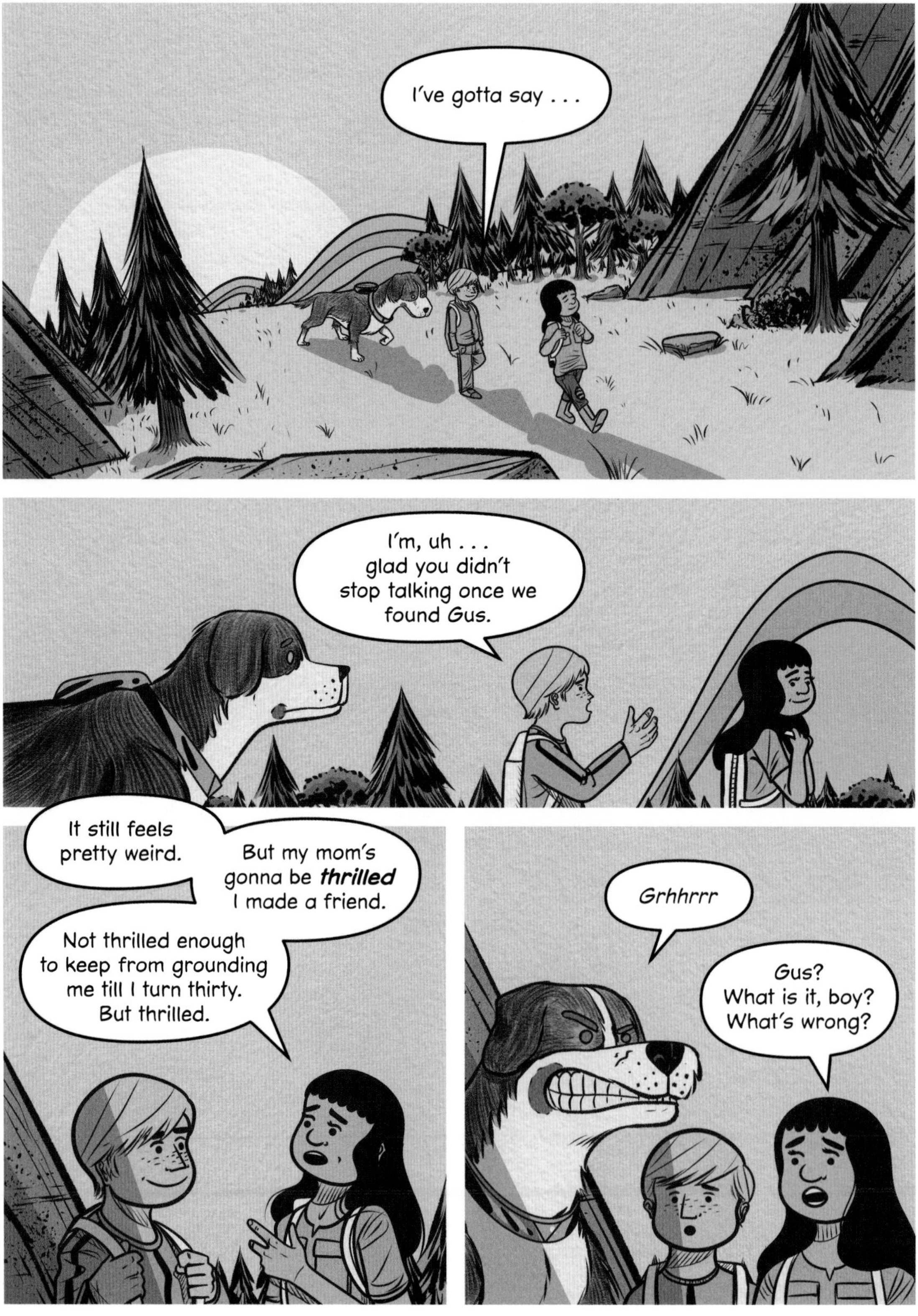
I've gotta say . . .
I'm, uh . . . glad you didn't stop talking once we found Gus.
It still feels pretty weird.
But my mom's gonna be ***thrilled*** I made a friend.
Not thrilled enough to keep from grounding me till I turn thirty. But thrilled.
Grhhrrr
Gus? What is it, boy? What's wrong?

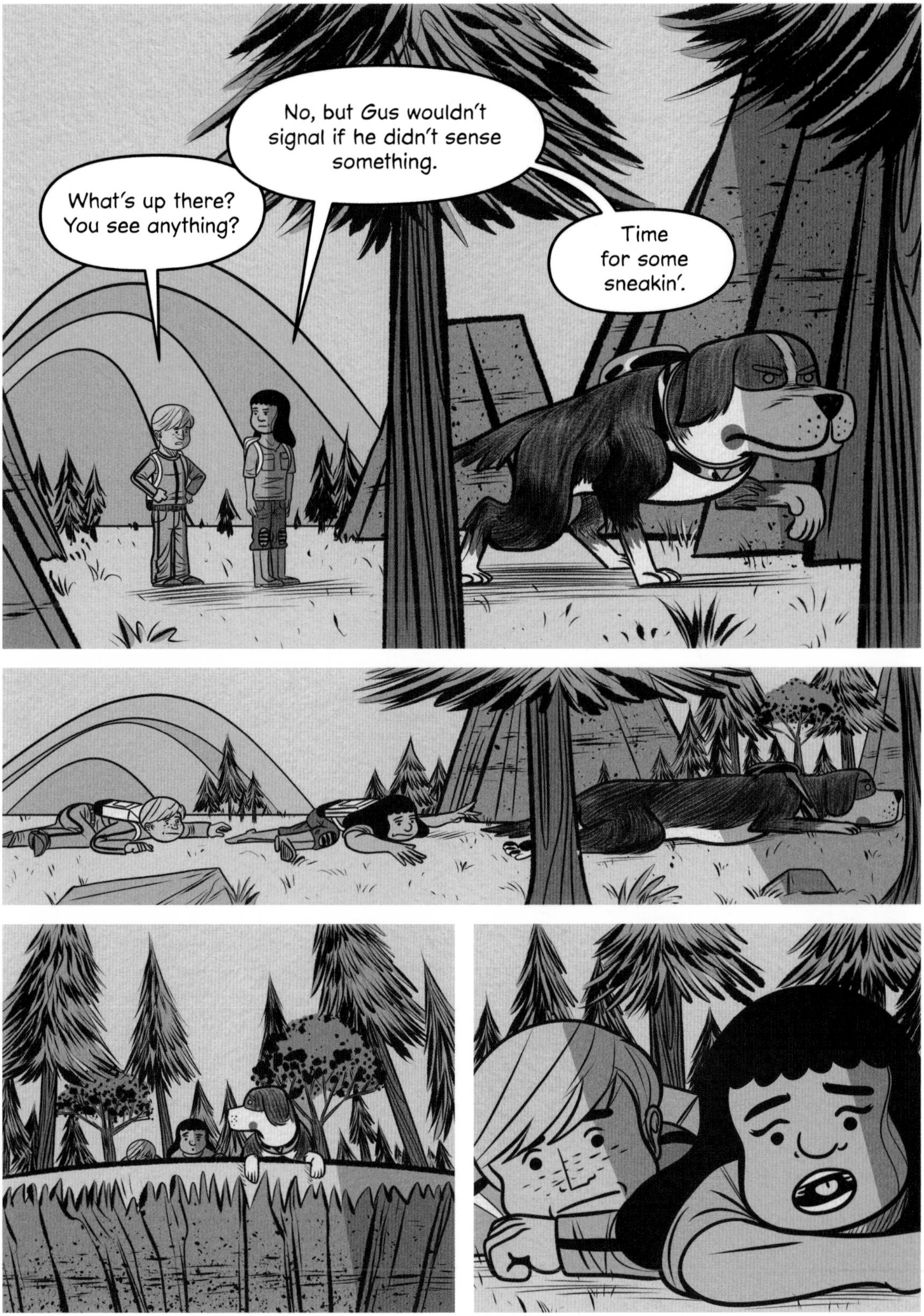
What's up there? You see anything?
No, but Gus wouldn't signal if he didn't sense something.
Time for some sneakin'.

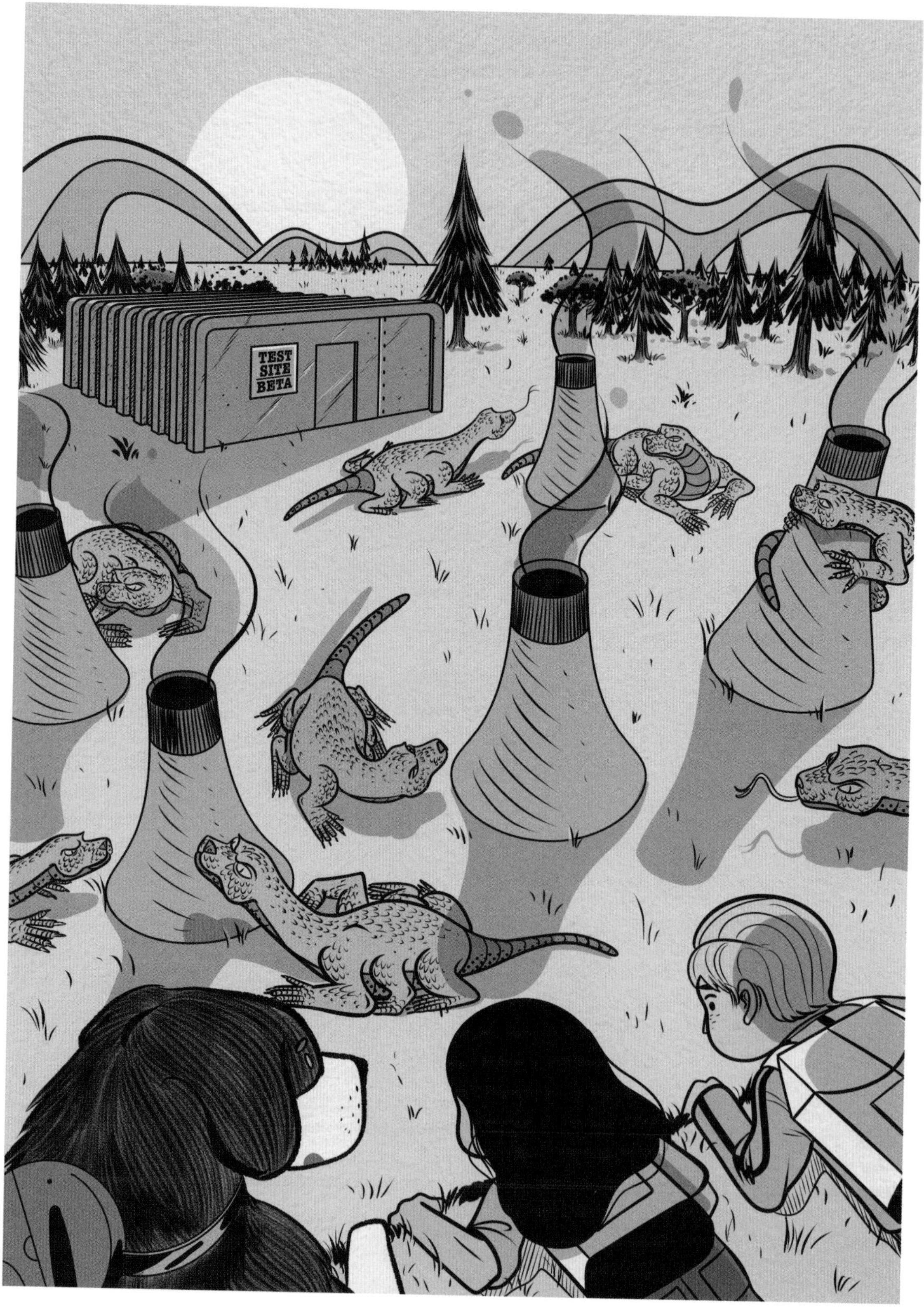
TEST SITE BETA

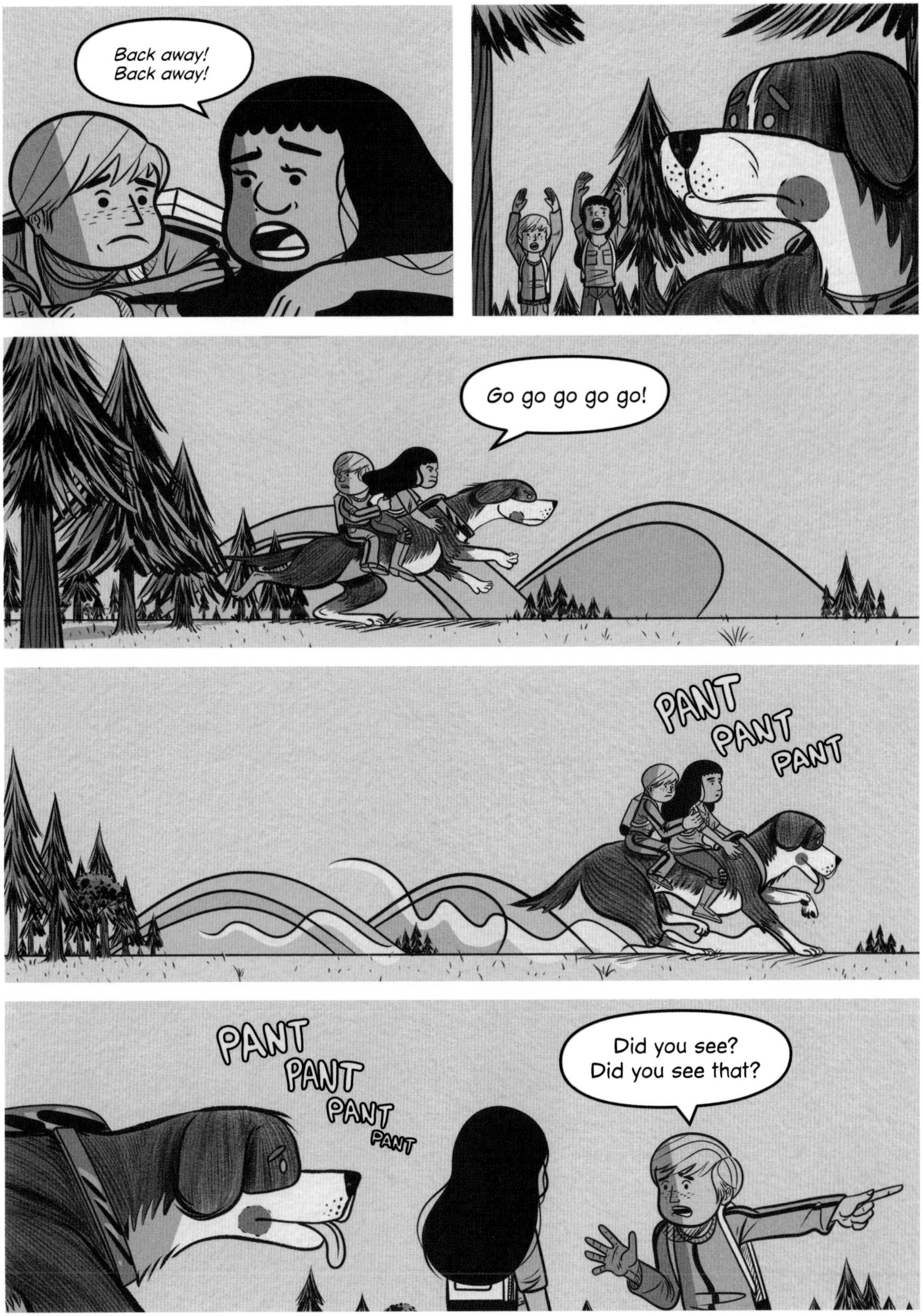
Back away! Back away!
Go go go go go!
PANT PANT PANT
PANT PANT PANT PANT
Did you see? Did you see that?

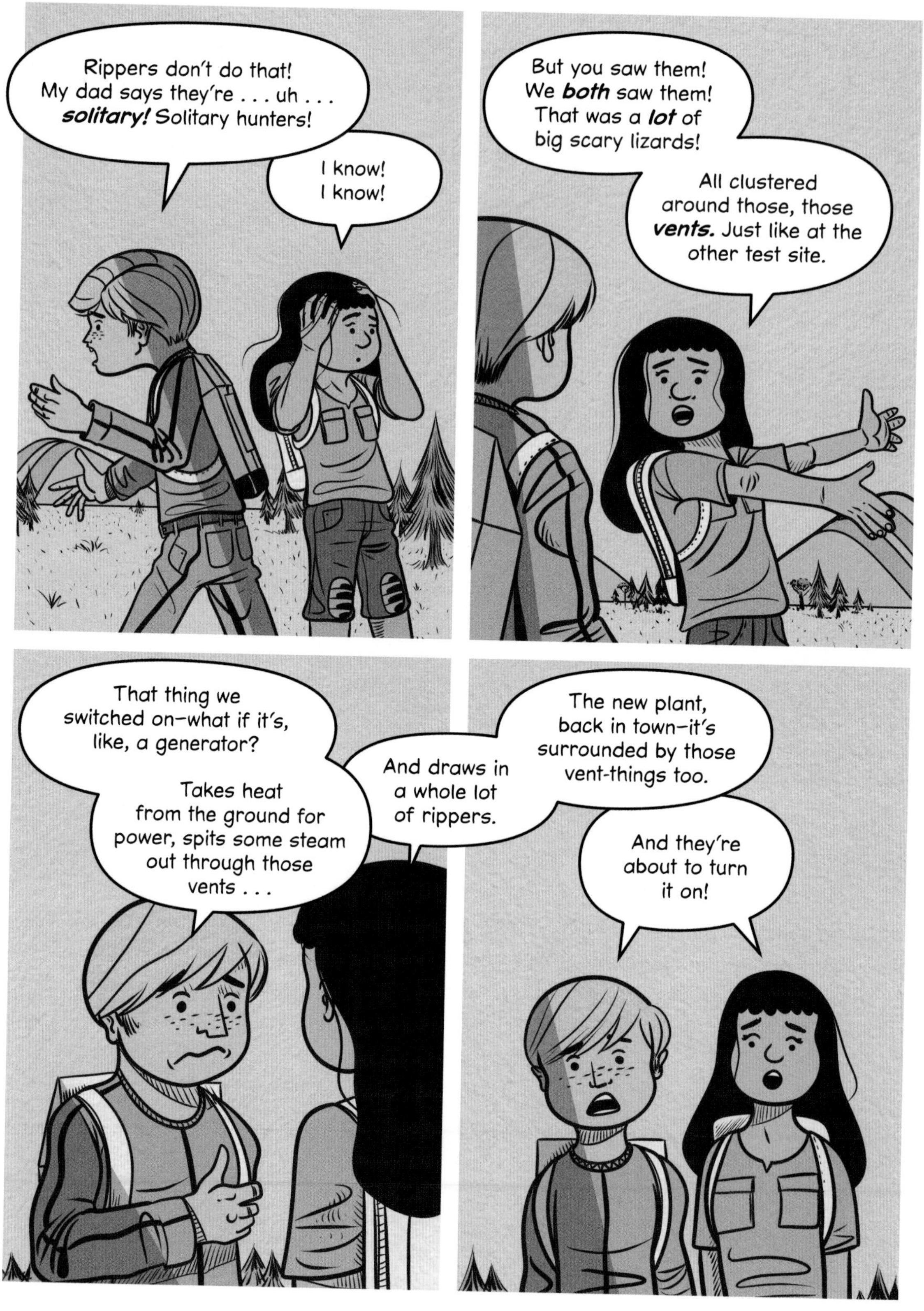

Rippers don't do that! My dad says they're . . . uh . . . ***solitary!*** Solitary hunters!
I know! I know!
But you saw them! We ***both*** saw them! That was a ***lot*** of big scary lizards!
All clustered around those, those ***vents.*** Just like at the other test site.
That thing we switched on—what if it's, like, a generator?
Takes heat from the ground for power, spits some steam out through those vents . . .
And draws in a whole lot of rippers.
The new plant, back in town—it's surrounded by those vent-things too.
And they're about to turn it on!

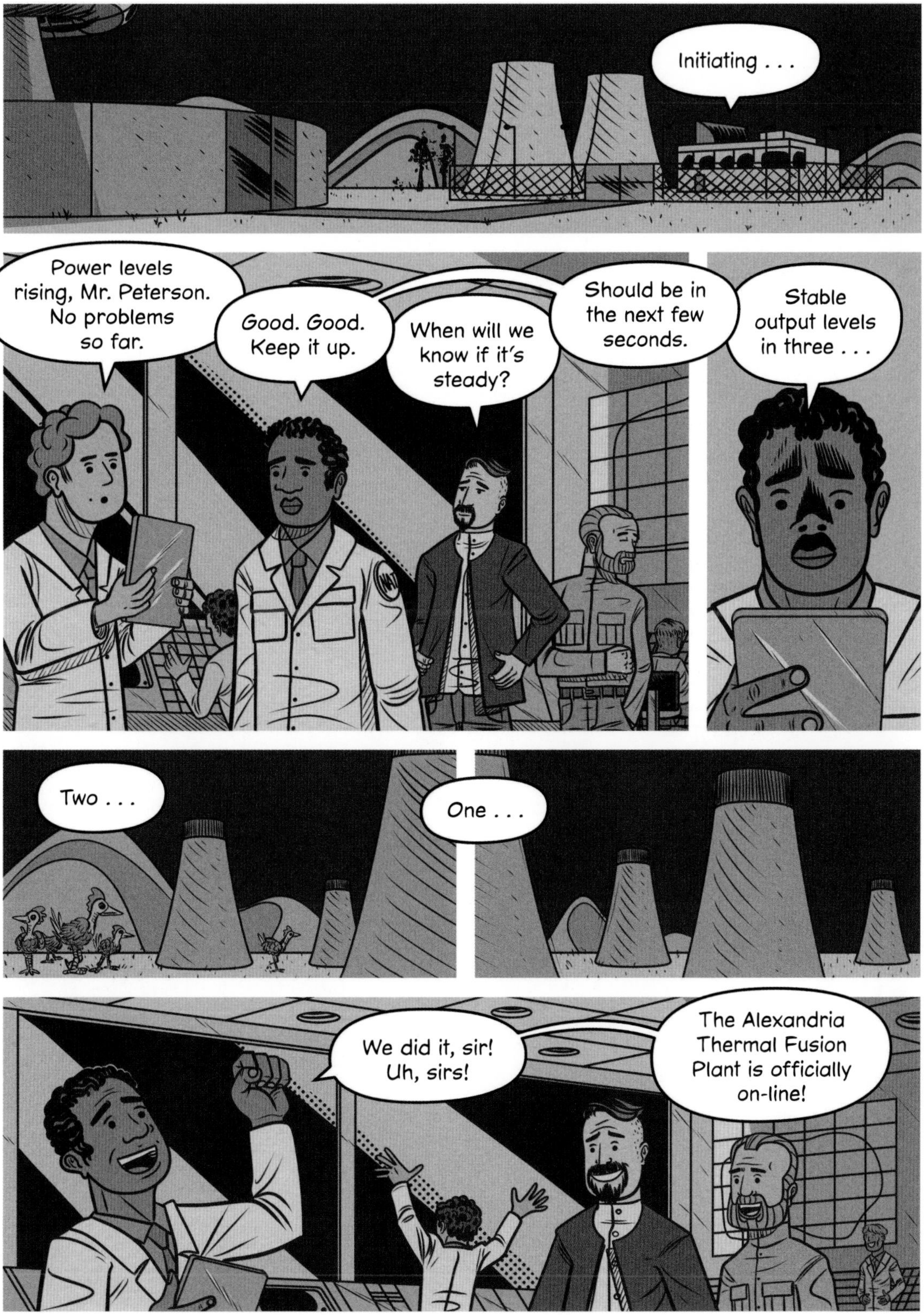
Initiating . . .
Power levels rising, Mr. Peterson. No problems so far.
Good. Good. Keep it up.
When will we know if it's steady?
Should be in the next few seconds.
Stable output levels in three . . .
Two . . .
One . . .
We did it, sir! Uh, sirs!
The Alexandria Thermal Fusion Plant is officially on-line!

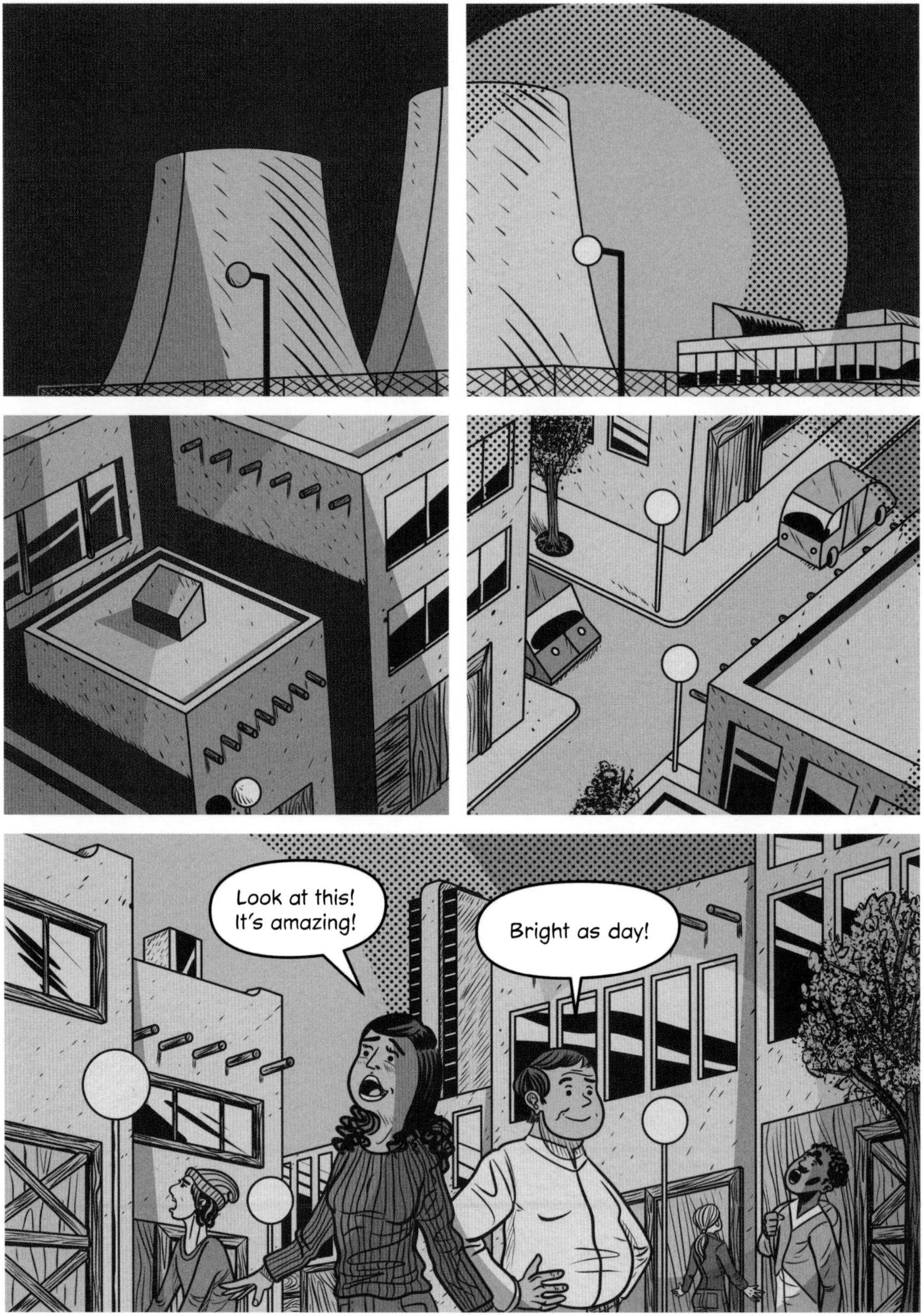
Look at this! It's amazing!
Bright as day!

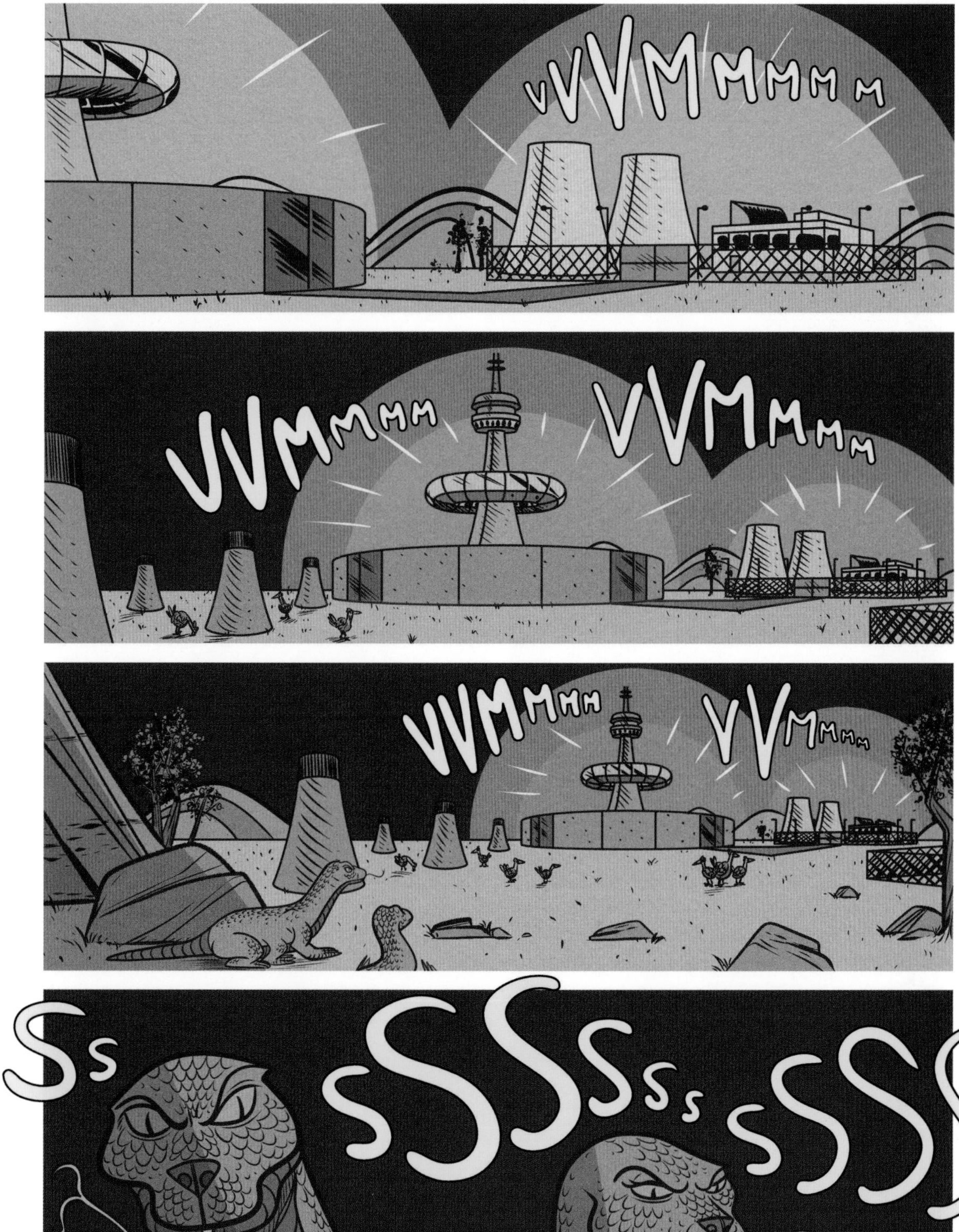
vVVMMMMM
VVMMMM
VVMMMM
VVMMMM
VVMMMM
Ss
sSSSsssSSS

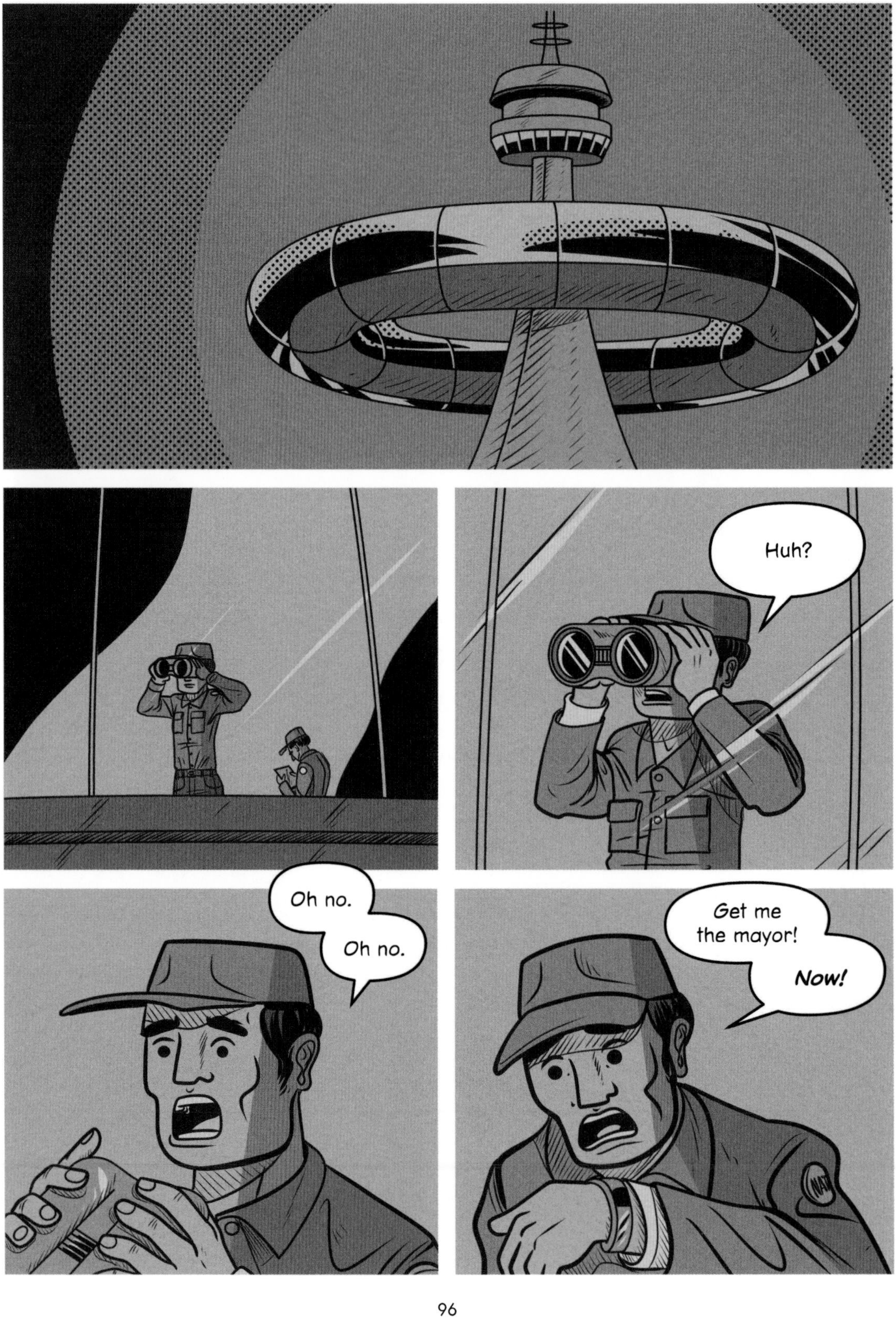
Huh?
Oh no.
Oh no.
Get me the mayor!
Now!

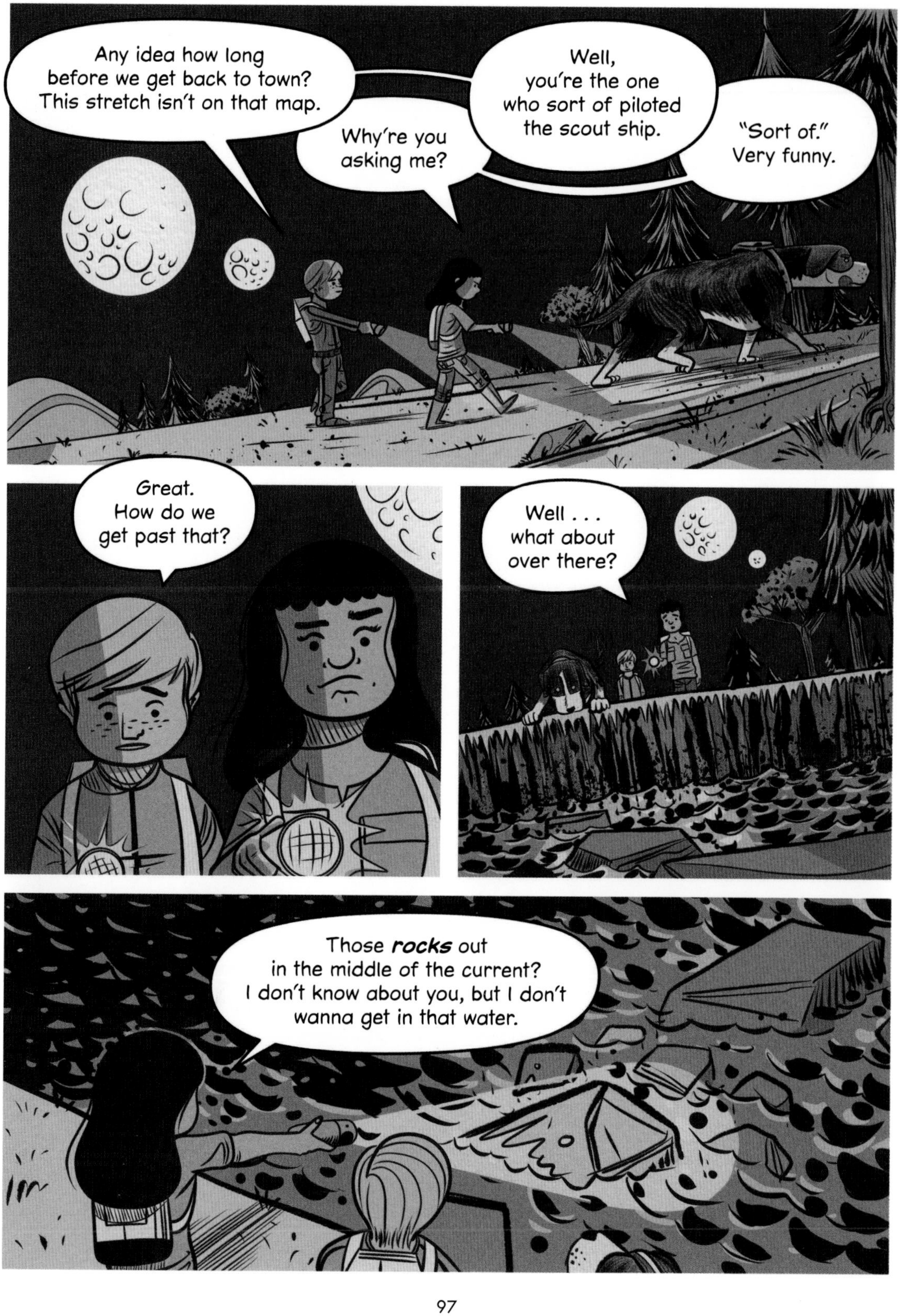
Any idea how long before we get back to town? This stretch isn't on that map.
Why're you asking me?
Well, you're the one who sort of piloted the scout ship.
"Sort of." Very funny.
Great. How do we get past that?
Well . . . what about over there?
Those ***rocks*** out in the middle of the current? I don't know about you, but I don't wanna get in that water.

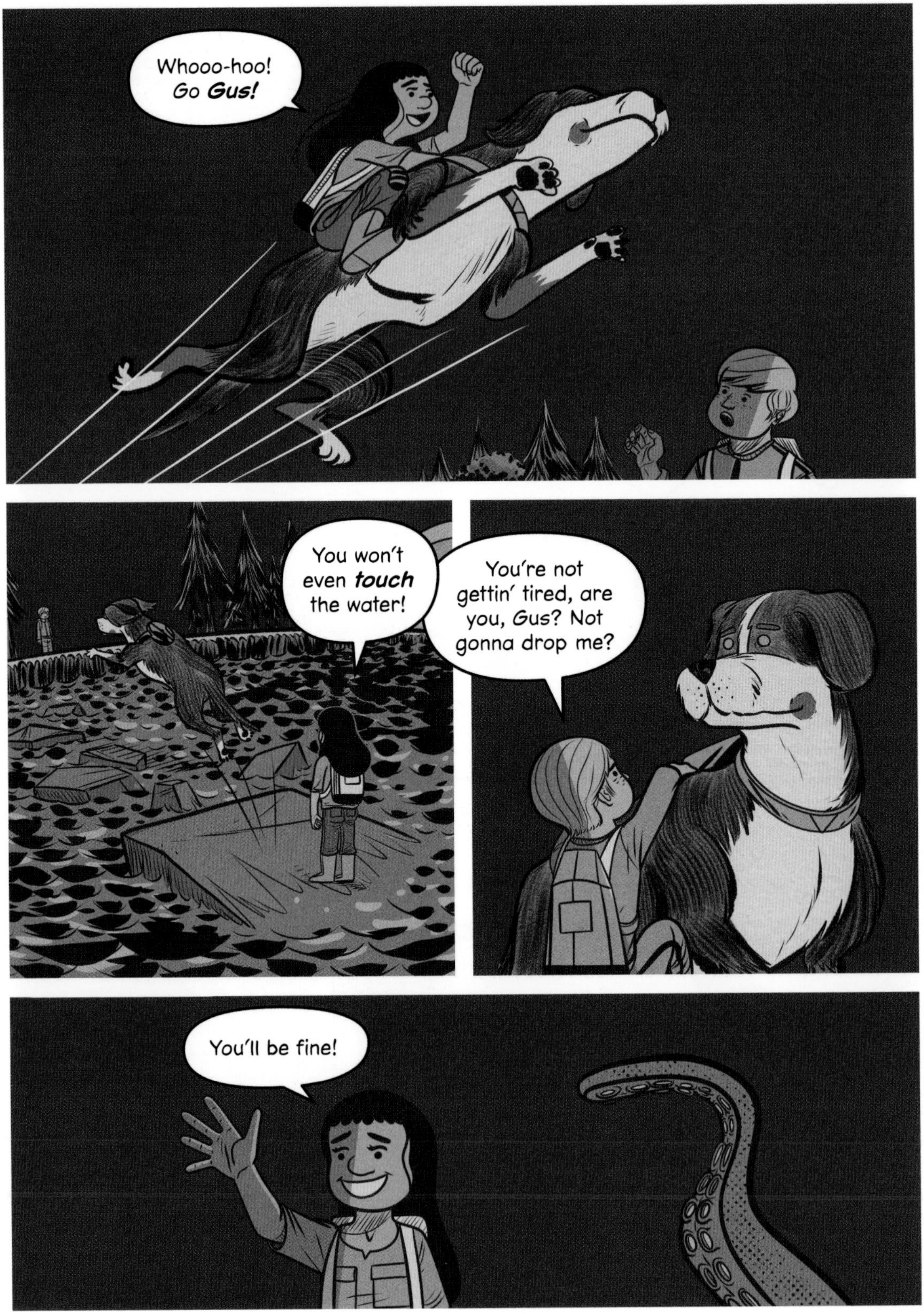
Whooo-hoo! Go Gus!
You won't even touch the water!
You're not gettin' tired, are you, Gus? Not gonna drop me?
You'll be fine!

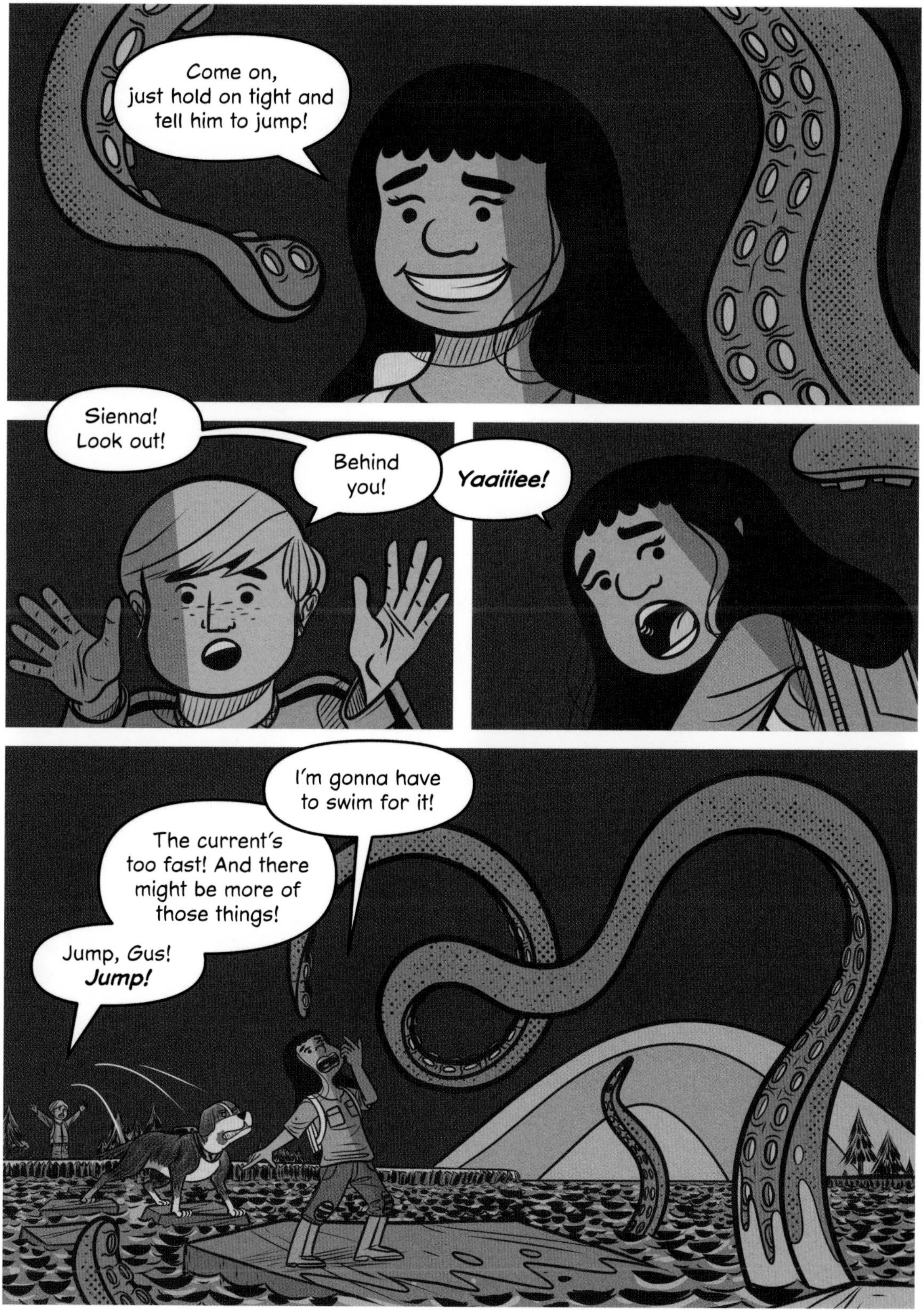
Come on, just hold on tight and tell him to jump!
Sienna! Look out!
Behind you!
Yaaiiiee!
I'm gonna have to swim for it!
The current's too fast! And there might be more of those things!
Jump, Gus! ***Jump!***

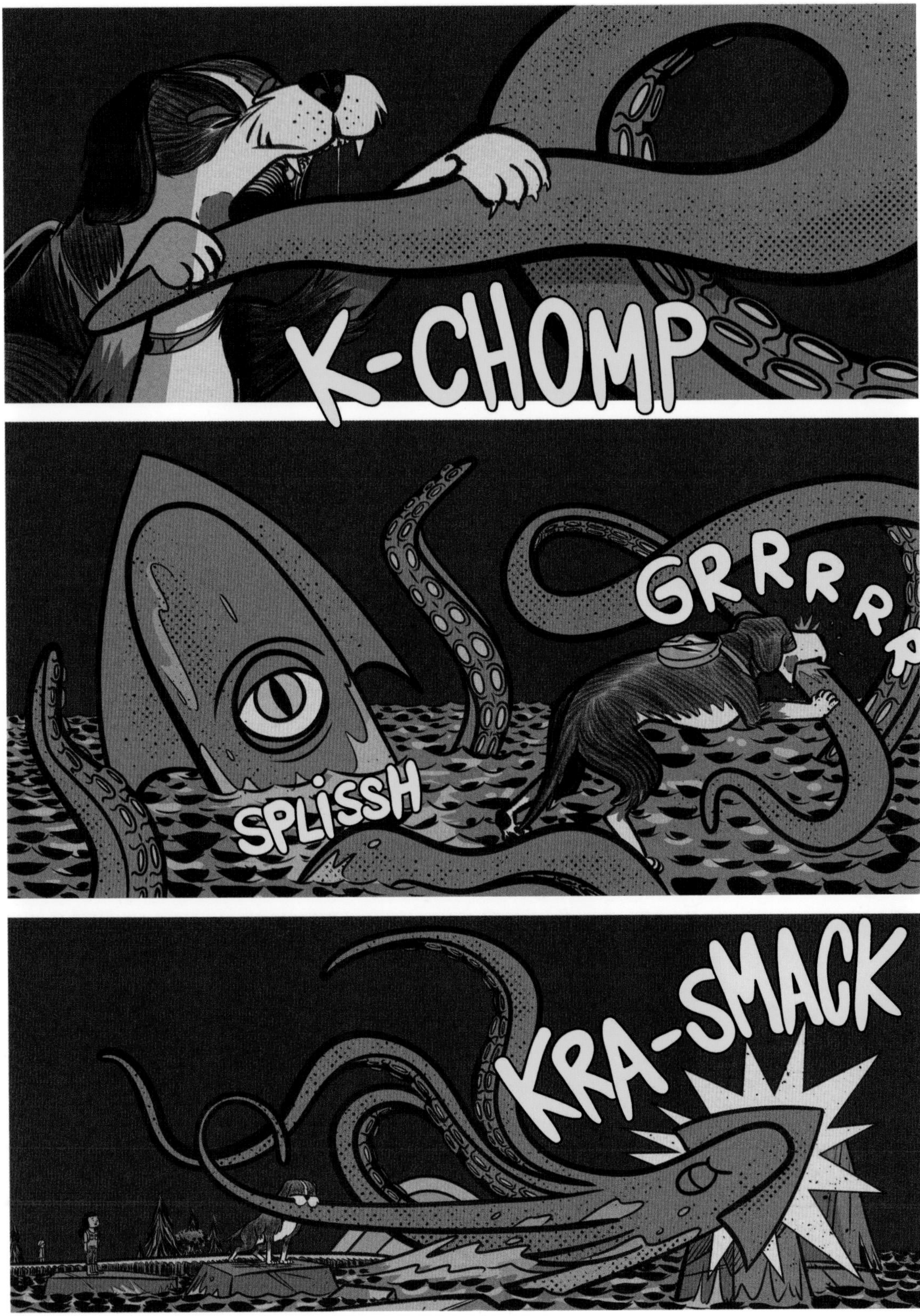
K-CHOMP
GRRRRRR
SPLISSH
KRA-SMACK

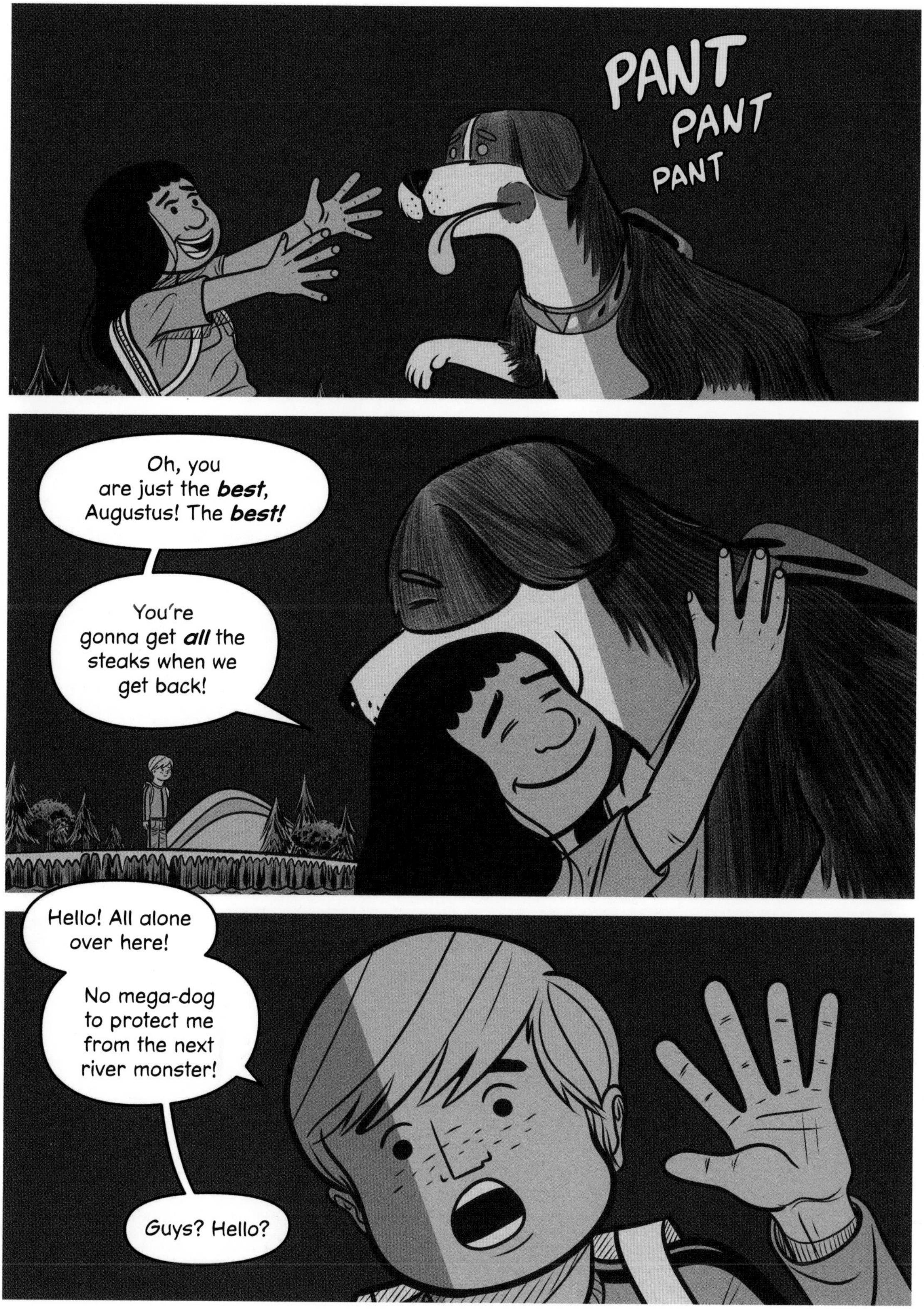
PANT
PANT
PANT
Oh, you are just the *best*, Augustus! The *best!*
You're gonna get *all* the steaks when we get back!
Hello! All alone over here!
No mega-dog to protect me from the next river monster!
Guys? Hello?

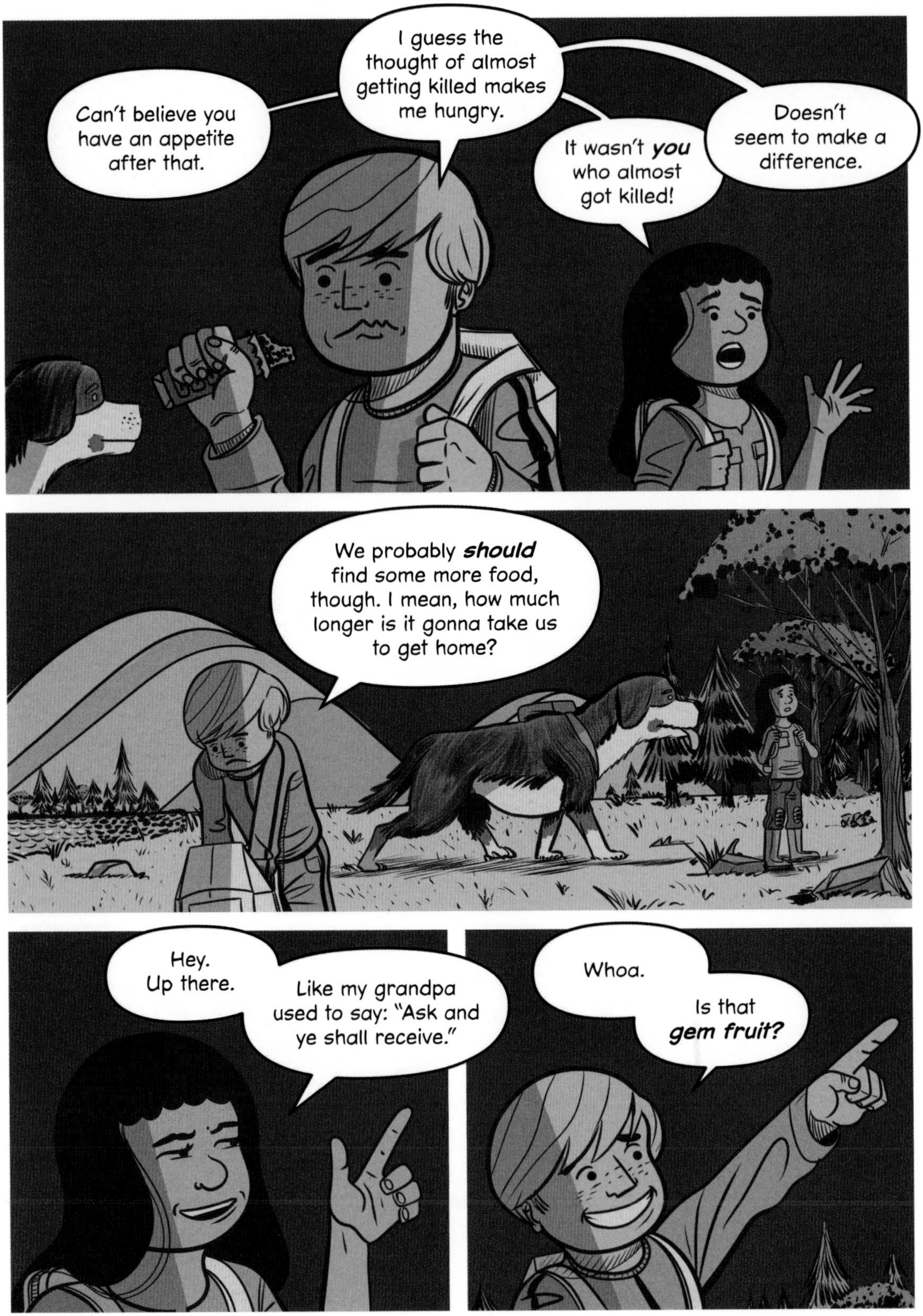
Can't believe you have an appetite after that.
I guess the thought of almost getting killed makes me hungry.
It wasn't *you* who almost got killed!
Doesn't seem to make a difference.
We probably ***should*** find some more food, though. I mean, how much longer is it gonna take us to get home?
Hey. Up there.
Like my grandpa used to say: "Ask and ye shall receive."
Whoa.
Is that ***gem fruit?***

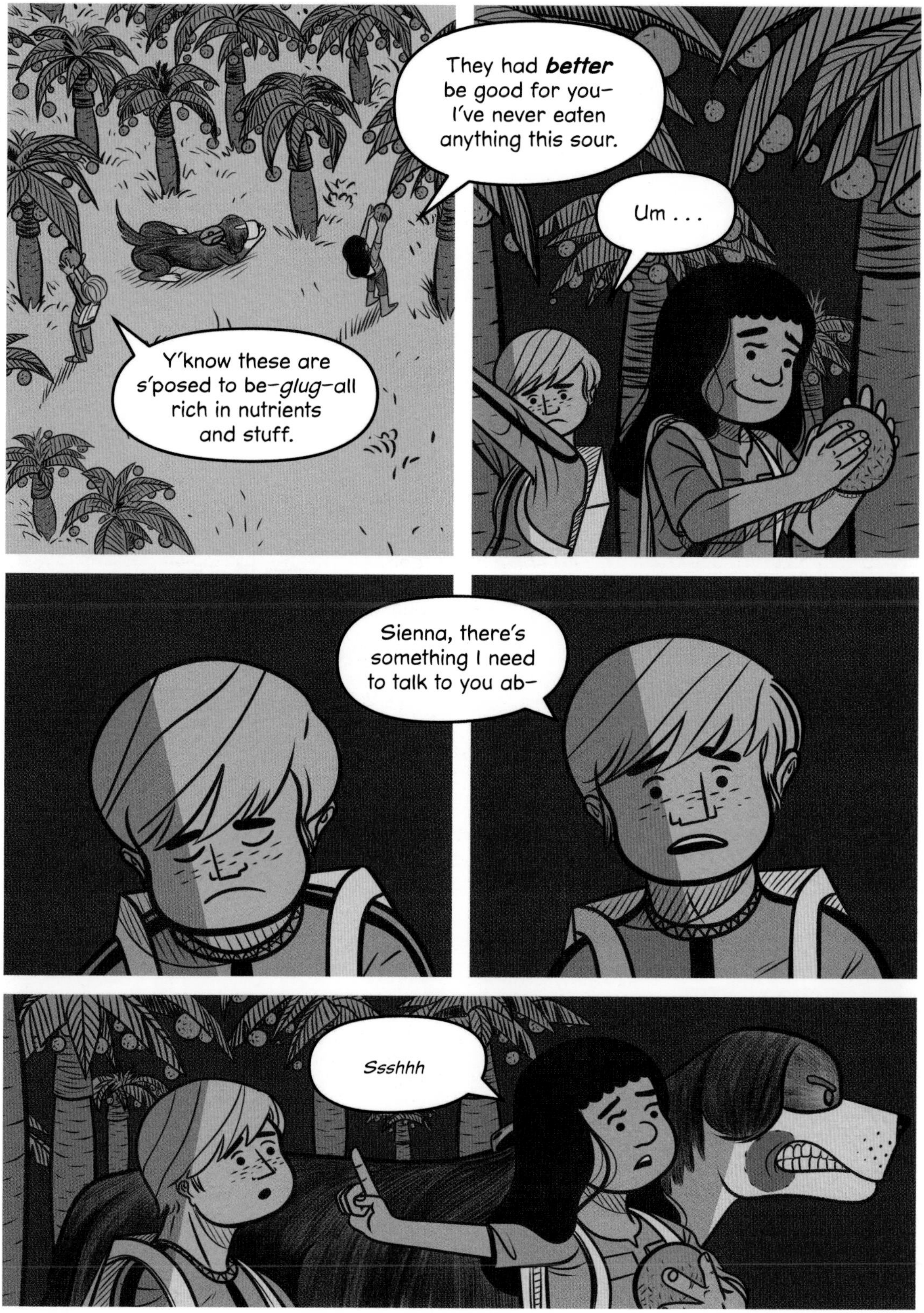
They had **better** be good for you- I've never eaten anything this sour.
Y'know these are s'posed to be-*glug*-all rich in nutrients and stuff.
Um . . .
Sienna, there's something I need to talk to you ab-
Ssshhh

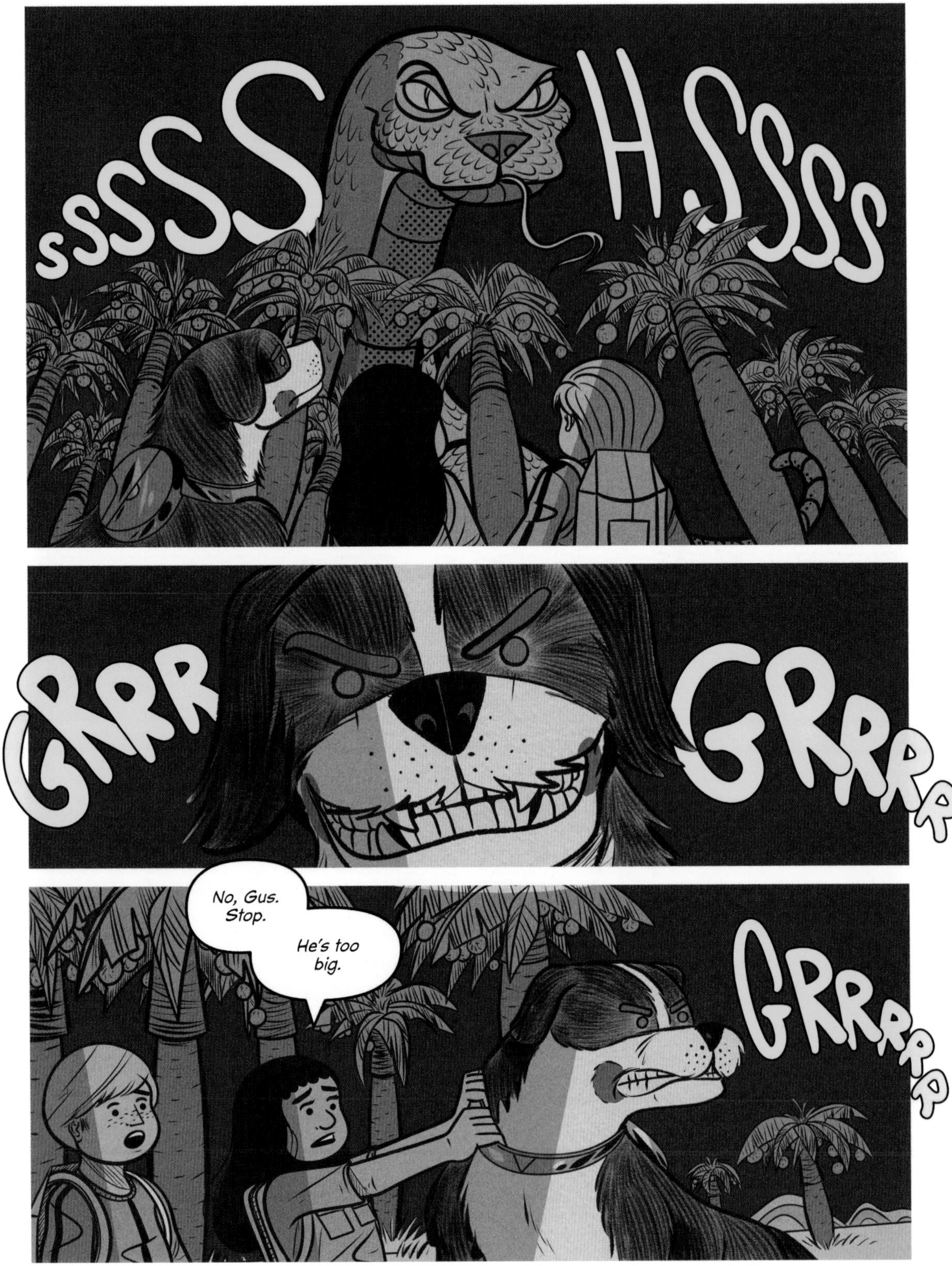

sSSSS
HSSSSS
GRRR
GRRRRR
No, Gus. Stop.
He's too big.
GRRRRRR

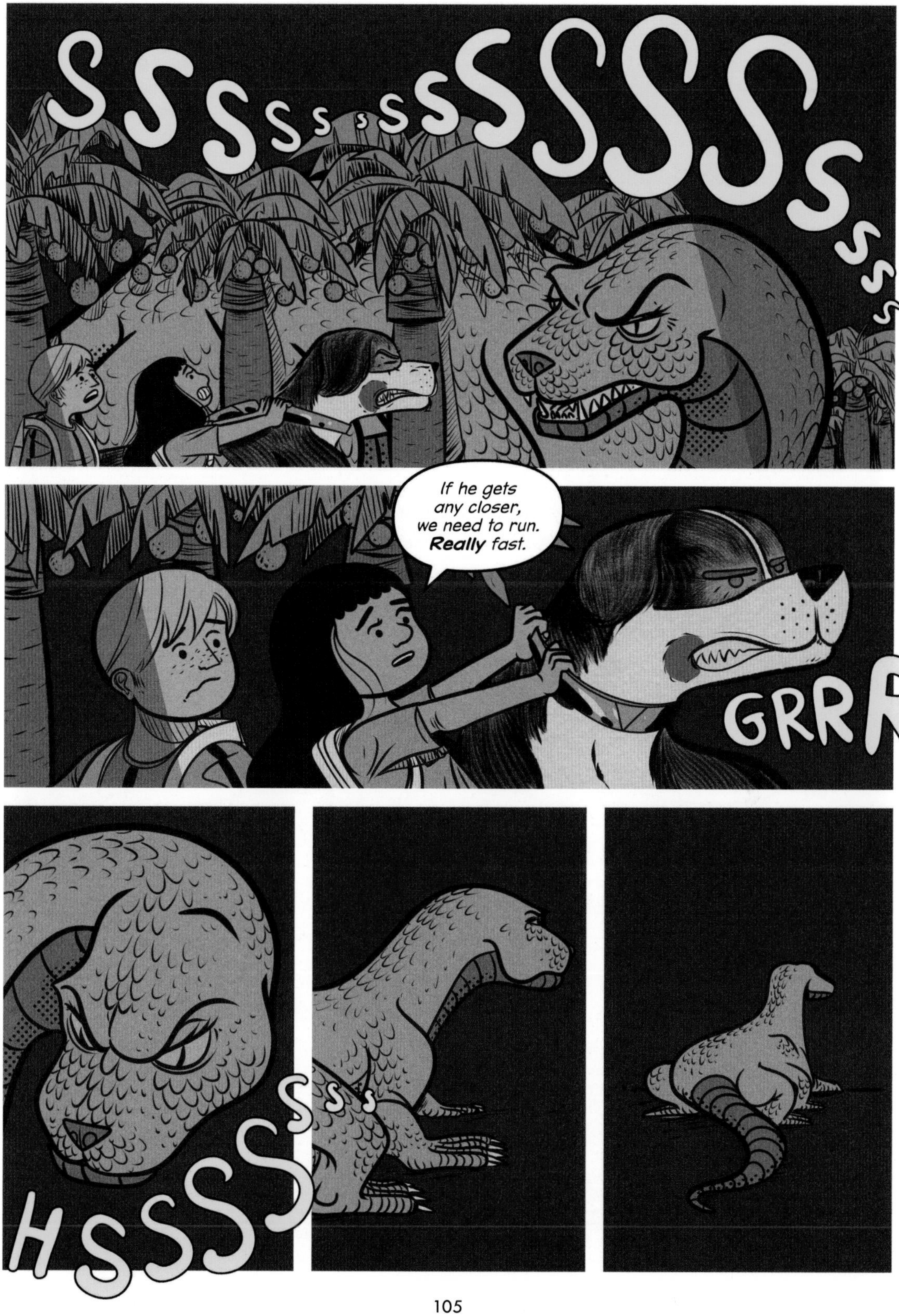
SSSSSSSSSSSSSSSSSS
If he gets any closer, we need to run. **Really** fast.
GRRR
HSSSSSS

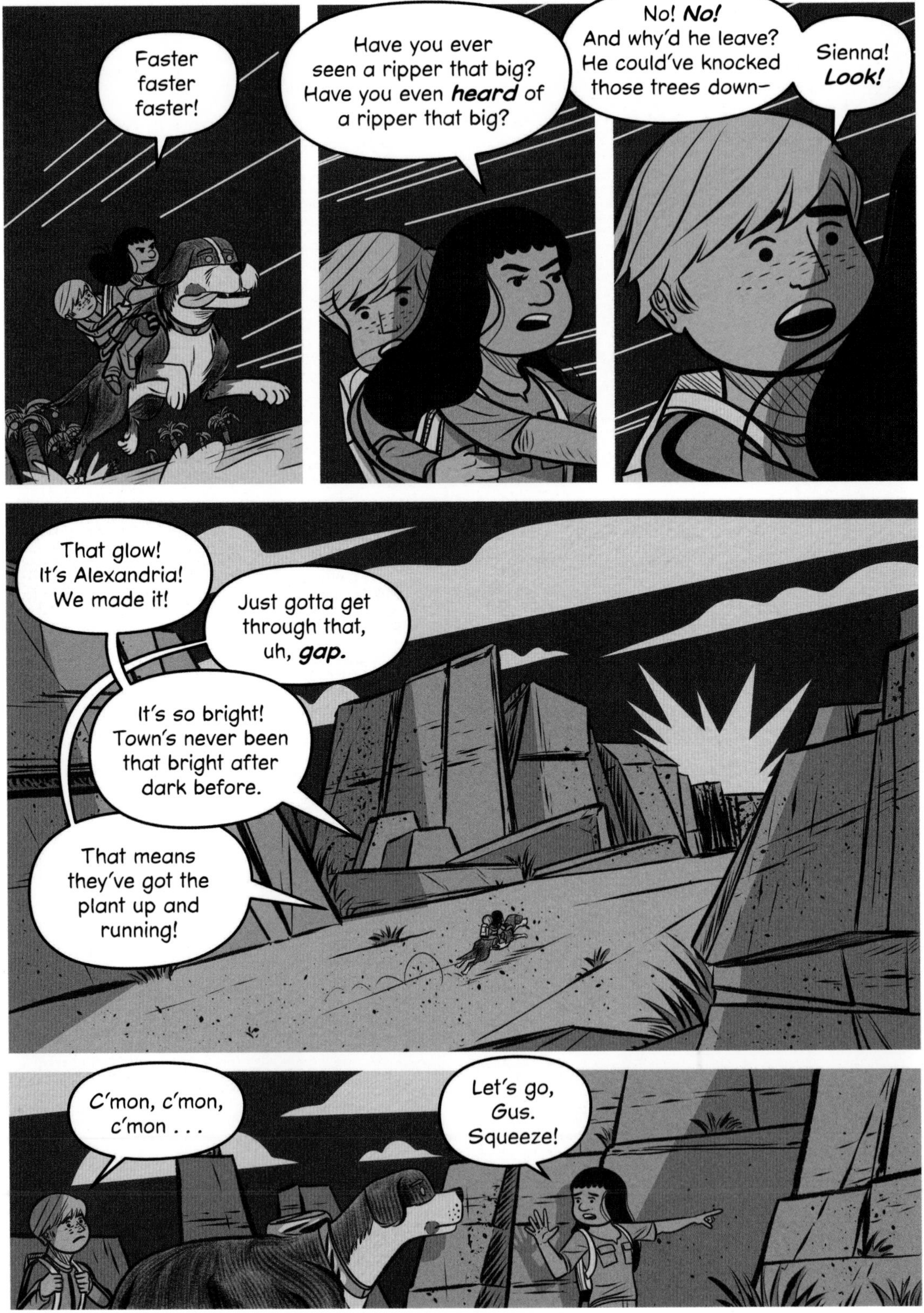

Faster faster faster!
Have you ever seen a ripper that big? Have you even **heard** of a ripper that big?
No! ***No!*** And why'd he leave? He could've knocked those trees down–
Sienna! ***Look!***
That glow! It's Alexandria! We made it!
Just gotta get through that, uh, ***gap.***
It's so bright! Town's never been that bright after dark before.
That means they've got the plant up and running!
C'mon, c'mon, c'mon . . .
Let's go, Gus. Squeeze!

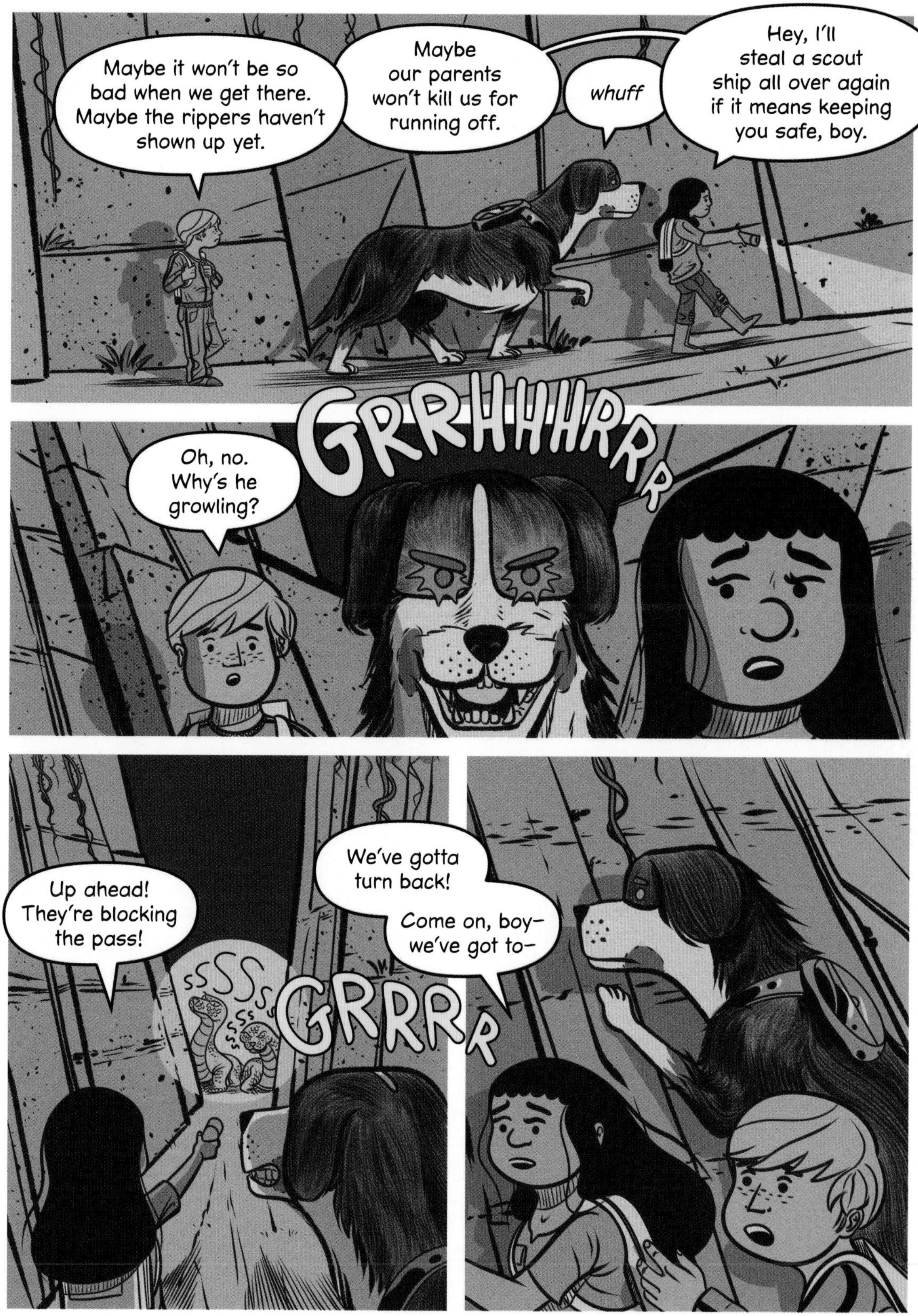
Maybe it won't be so bad when we get there. Maybe the rippers haven't shown up yet.
Maybe our parents won't kill us for running off.
whuff
Hey, I'll steal a scout ship all over again if it means keeping you safe, boy.
GRRHHHRRR
Oh, no. Why's he growling?
Up ahead! They're blocking the pass!
sSSSss
sss
GRRRR
We've gotta turn back!
Come on, boy— we've got to—

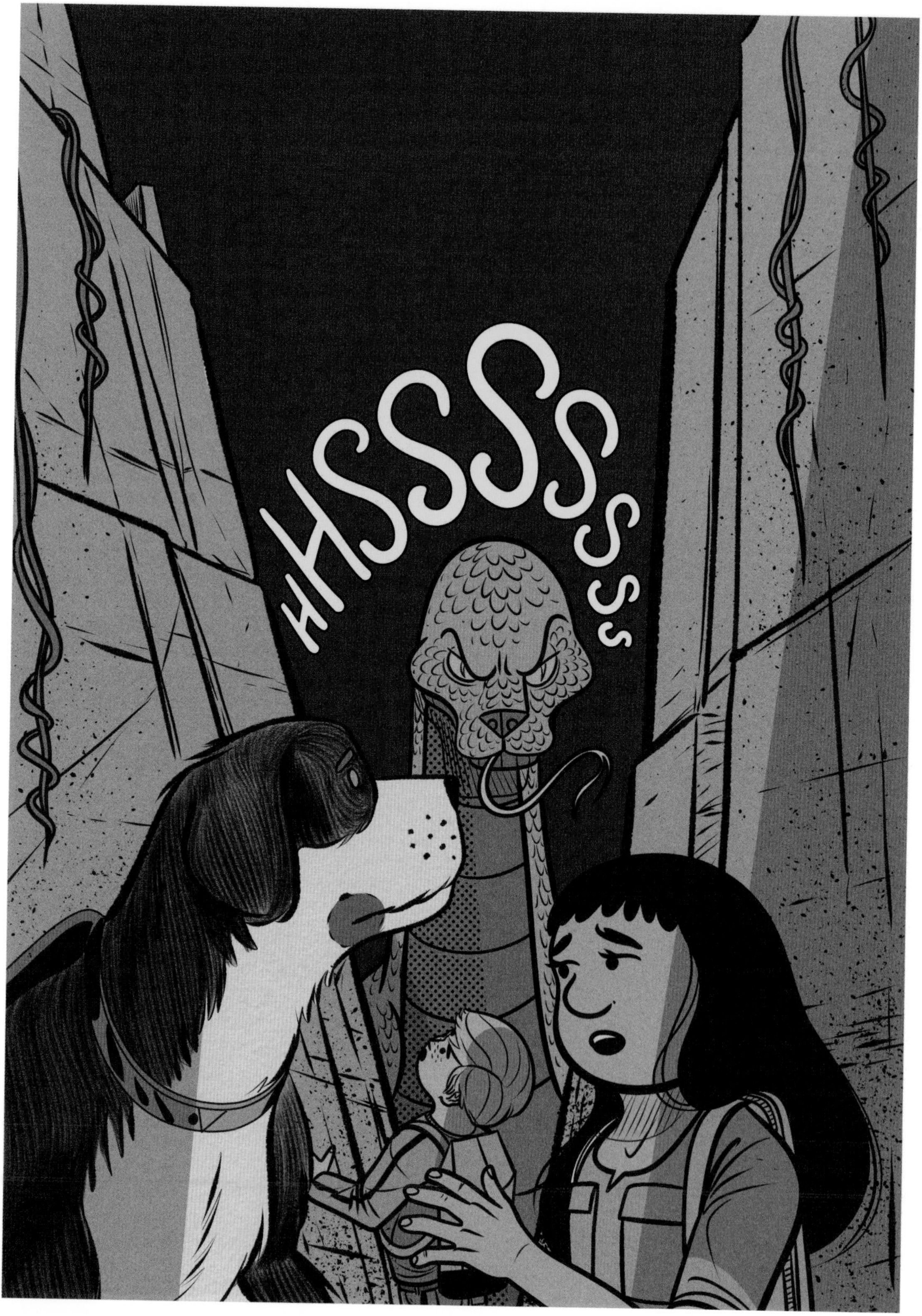
HSSSSsss

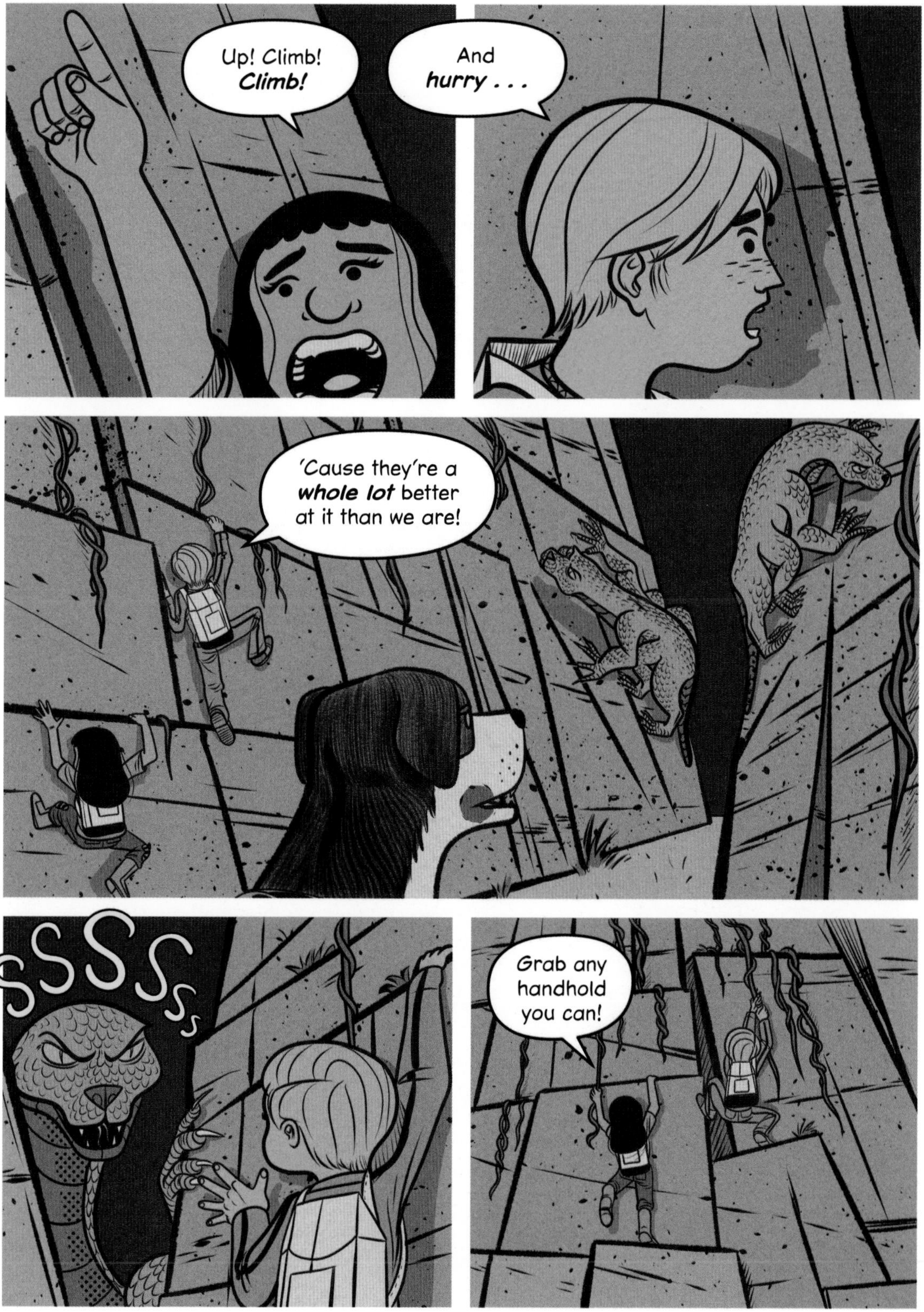
Up! Climb! **Climb!**
And **hurry . . .**
'Cause they're a **whole lot** better at it than we are!
SSSSSss
Grab any handhold you can!

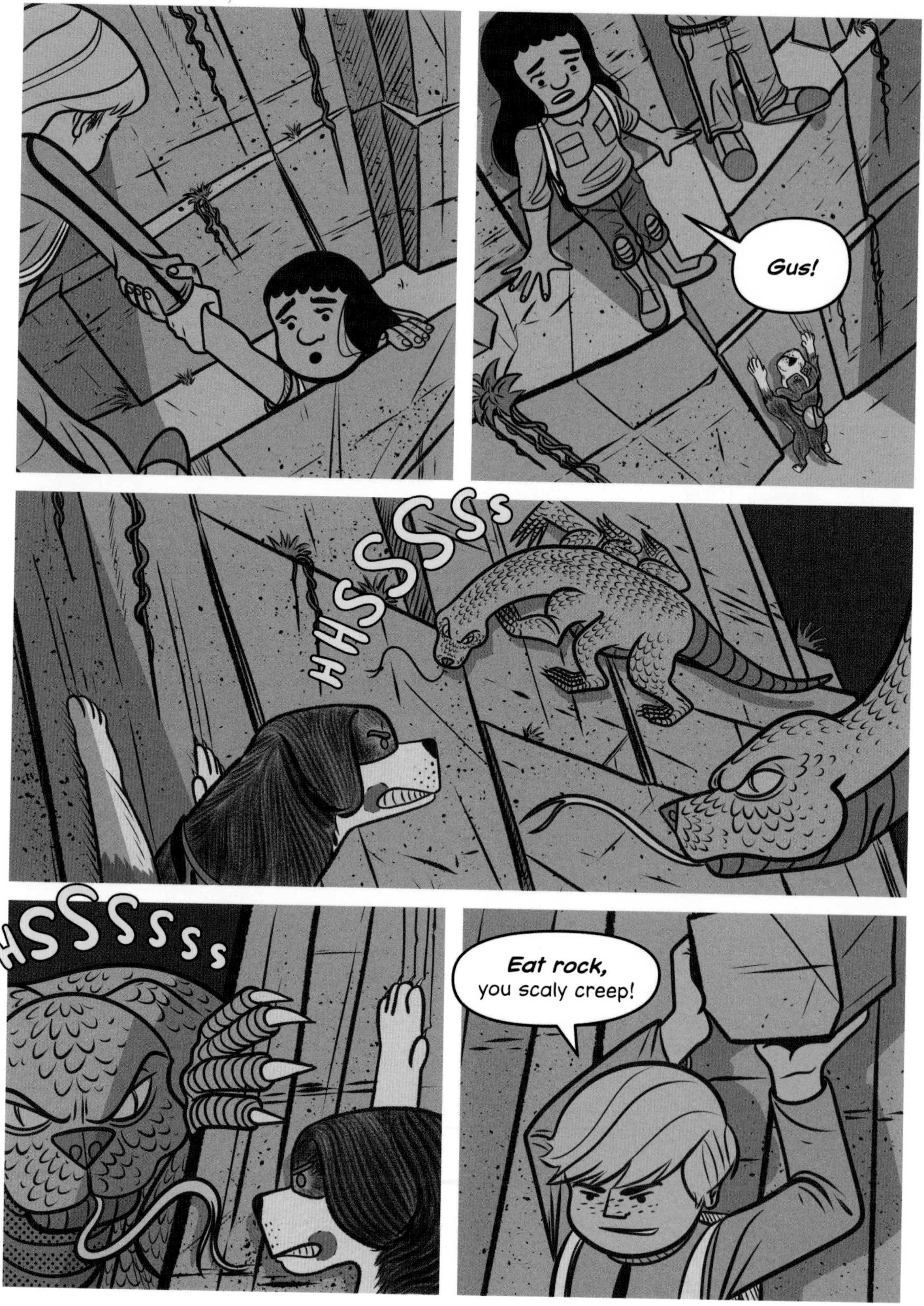
Gus!
HHSSSSs
HSSSSSs
Eat rock, you scaly creep!

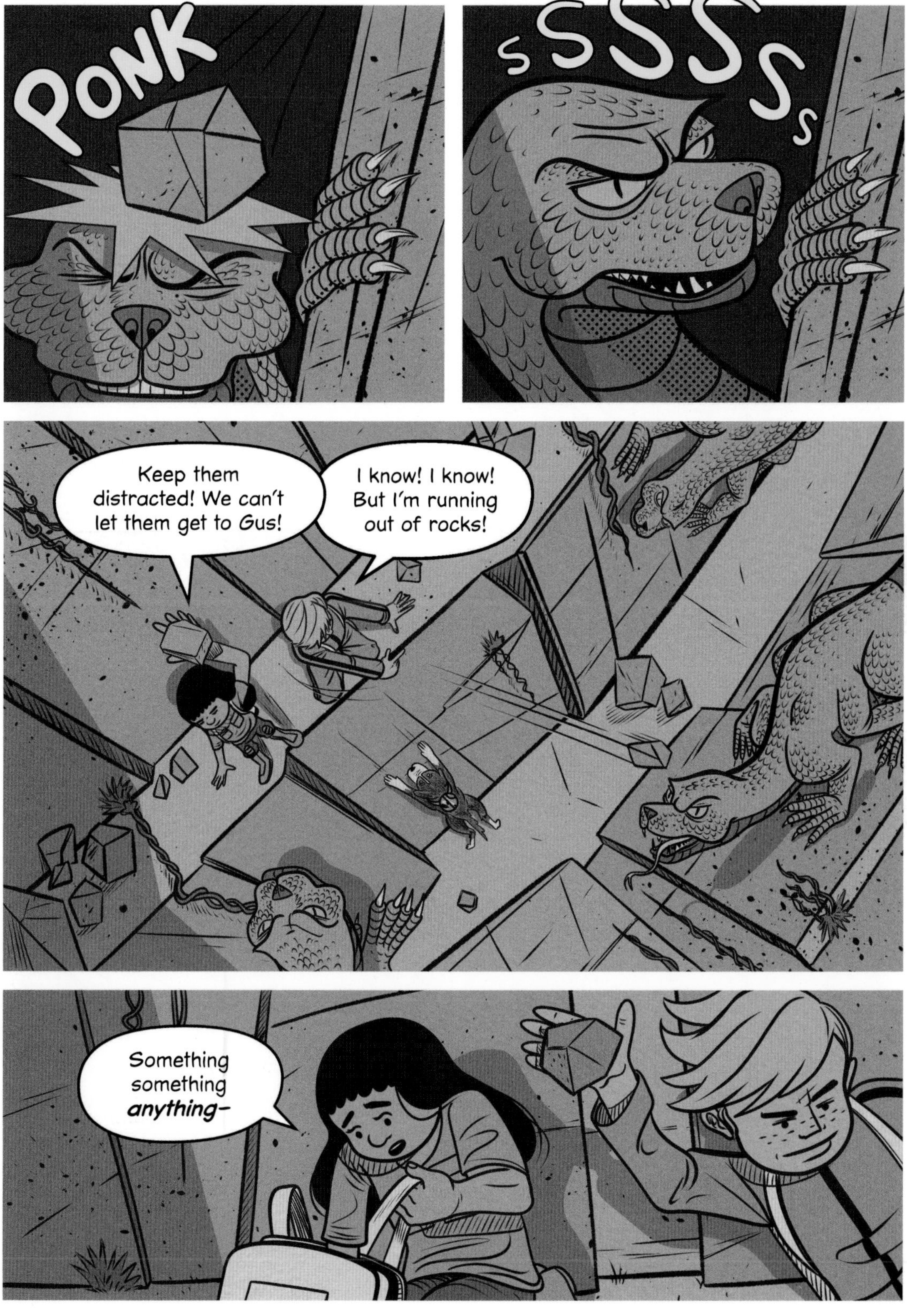

PONK
sSSSSs
Keep them distracted! We can't let them get to Gus!
I know! I know! But I'm running out of rocks!
Something something ***anything***–

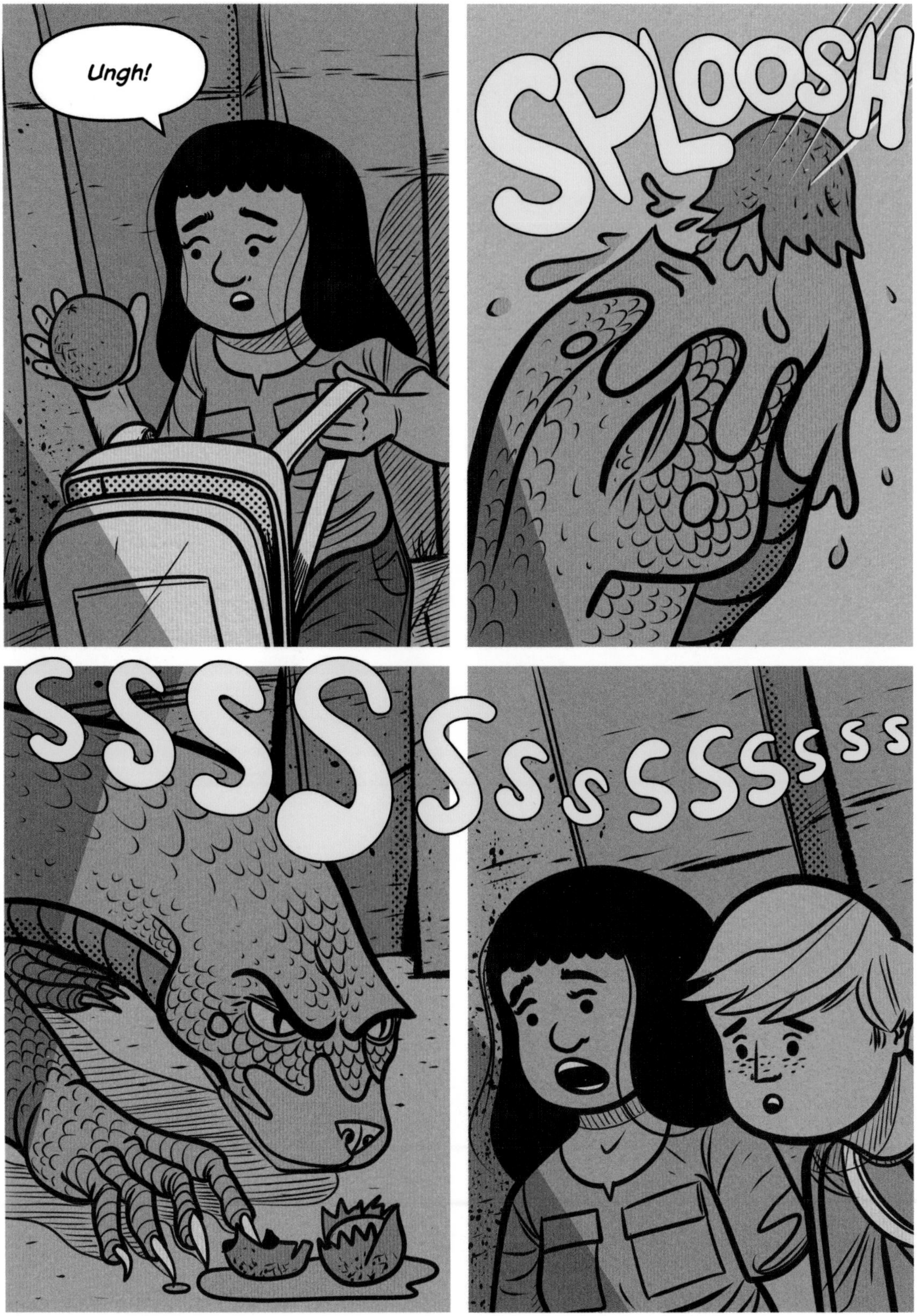
Ungh!
SPLOOSH
SSSSSSSSSSSSSS

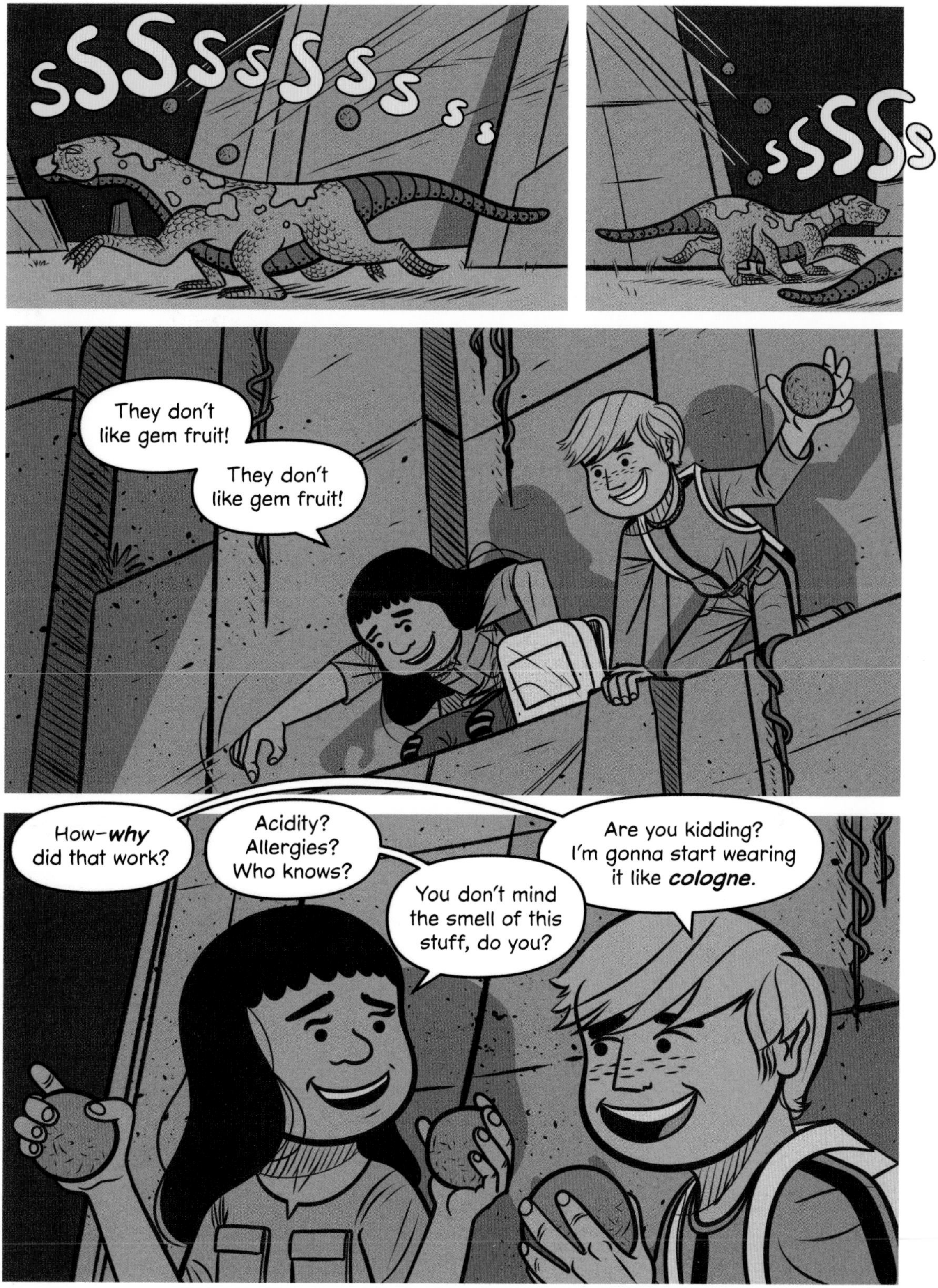

sSSSsSSSsss
sSSSs
They don't like gem fruit!
They don't like gem fruit!
How-**why** did that work?
Acidity? Allergies? Who knows?
You don't mind the smell of this stuff, do you?
Are you kidding? I'm gonna start wearing it like **cologne**.

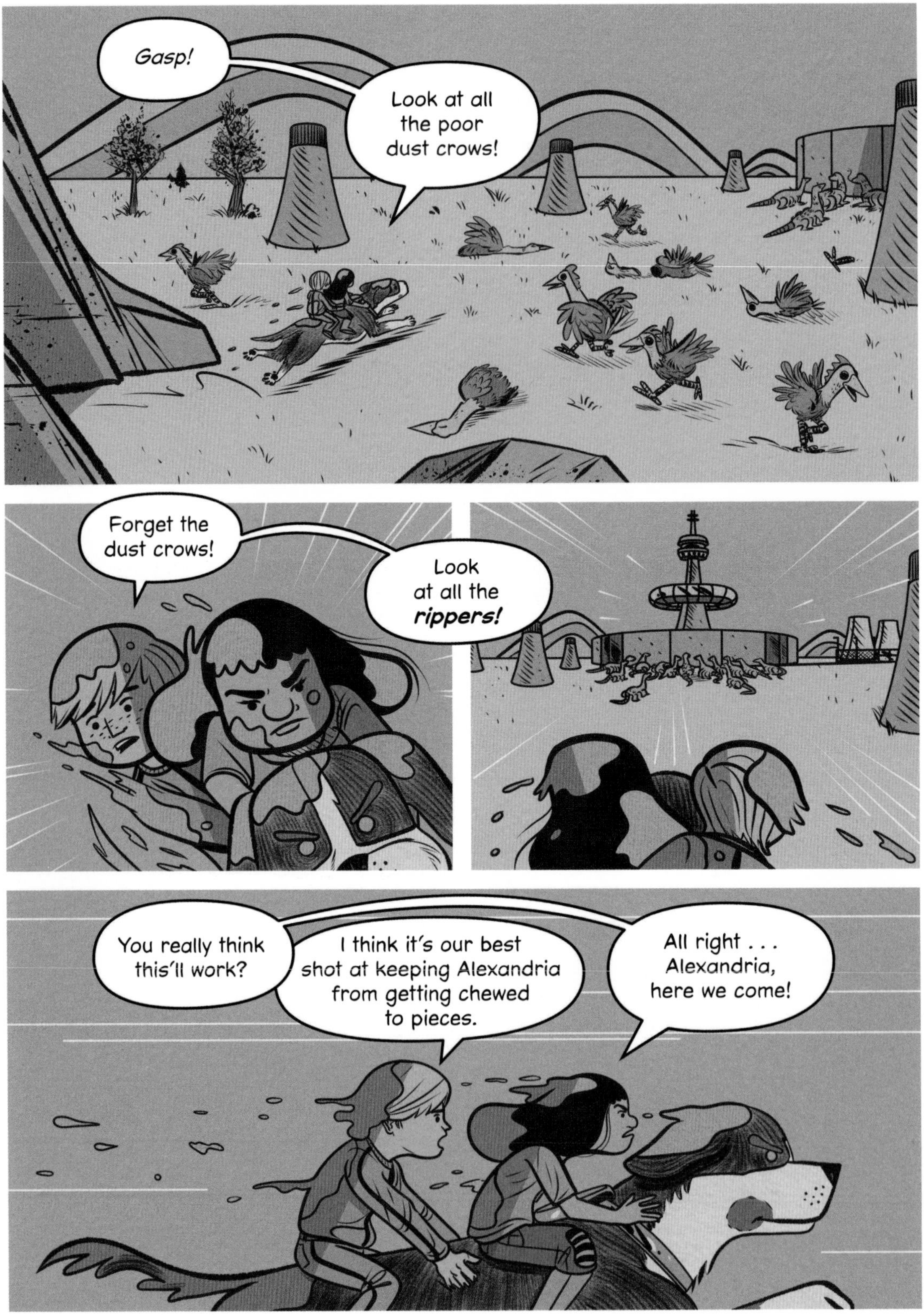

Gasp!
Look at all the poor dust crows!
Forget the dust crows!
Look at all the ***rippers!***
You really think this'll work?
I think it's our best shot at keeping Alexandria from getting chewed to pieces.
All right . . . Alexandria, here we come!

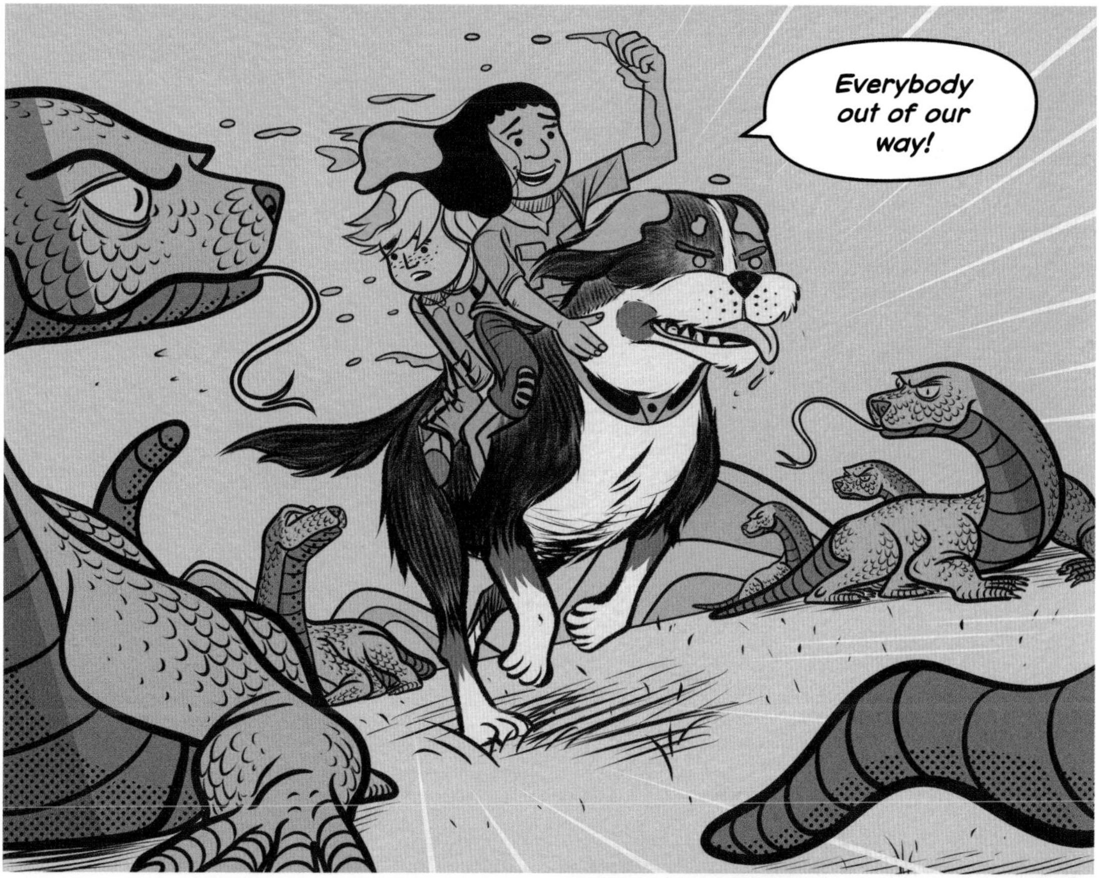
Everybody out of our way!

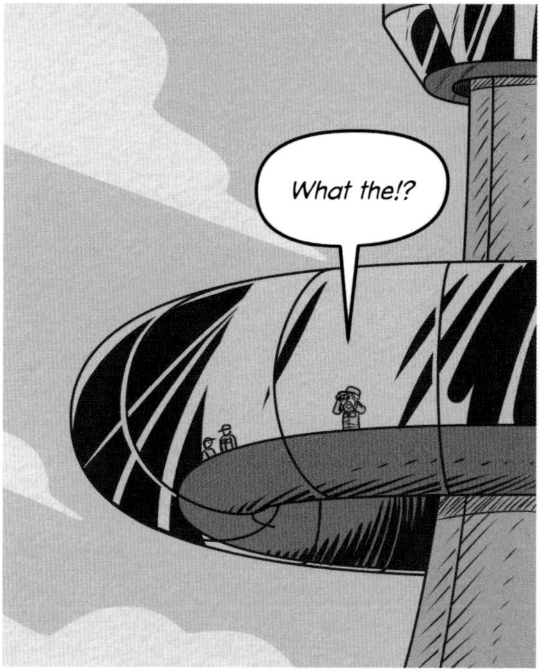
What the!?

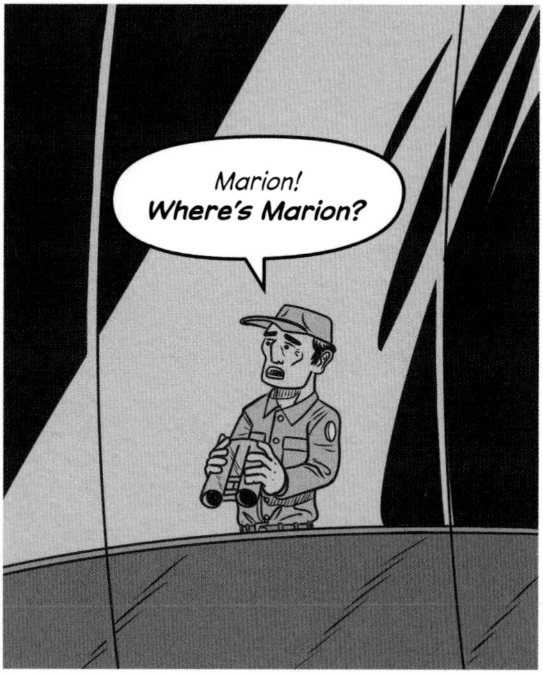
Marion!
Where's Marion?

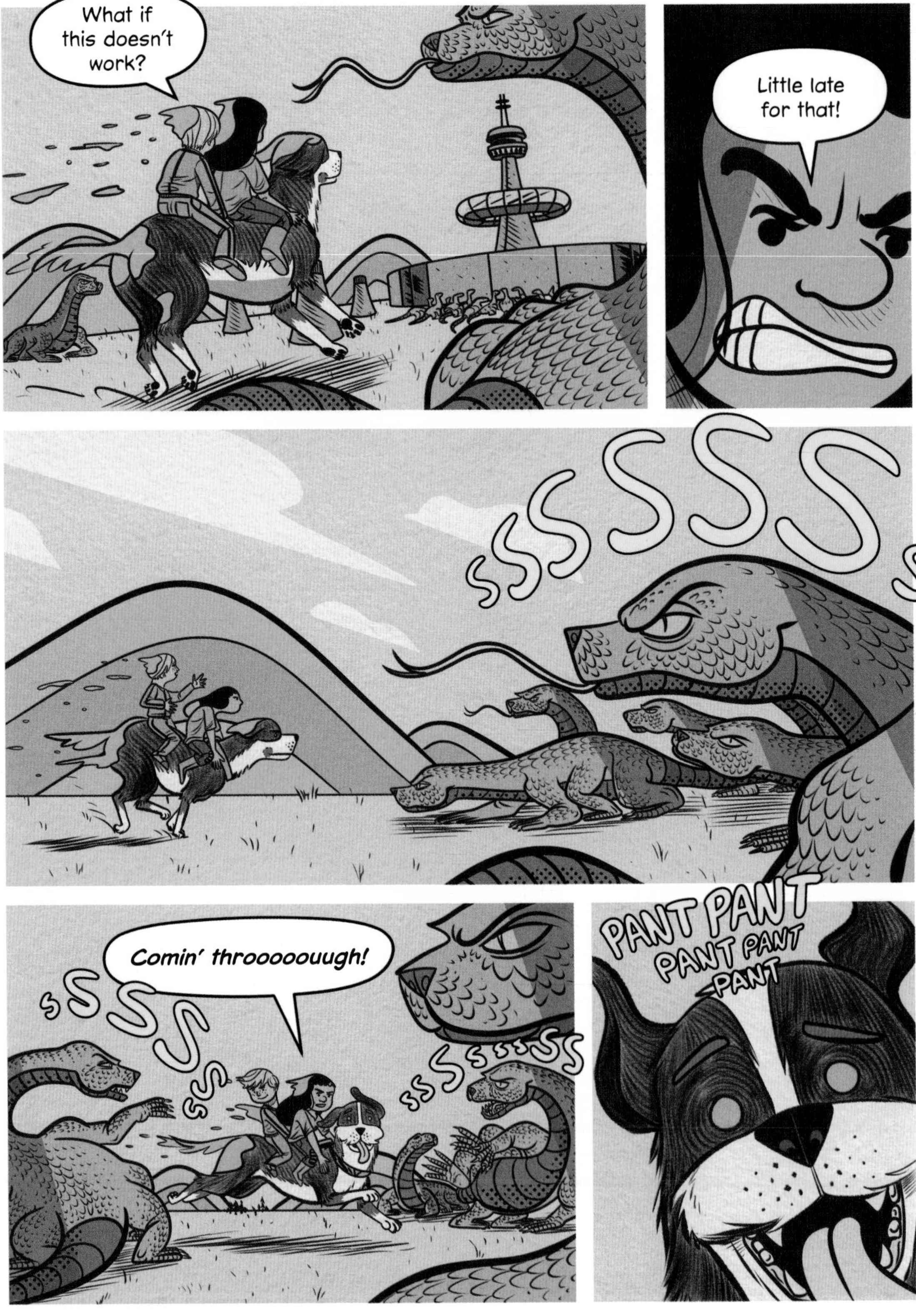
What if this doesn't work?
Little late for that!
sSSSSSs
Comin' throoooouugh!
sSSSss
ssSsssSS
PANT PANT
PANT PANT
PANT

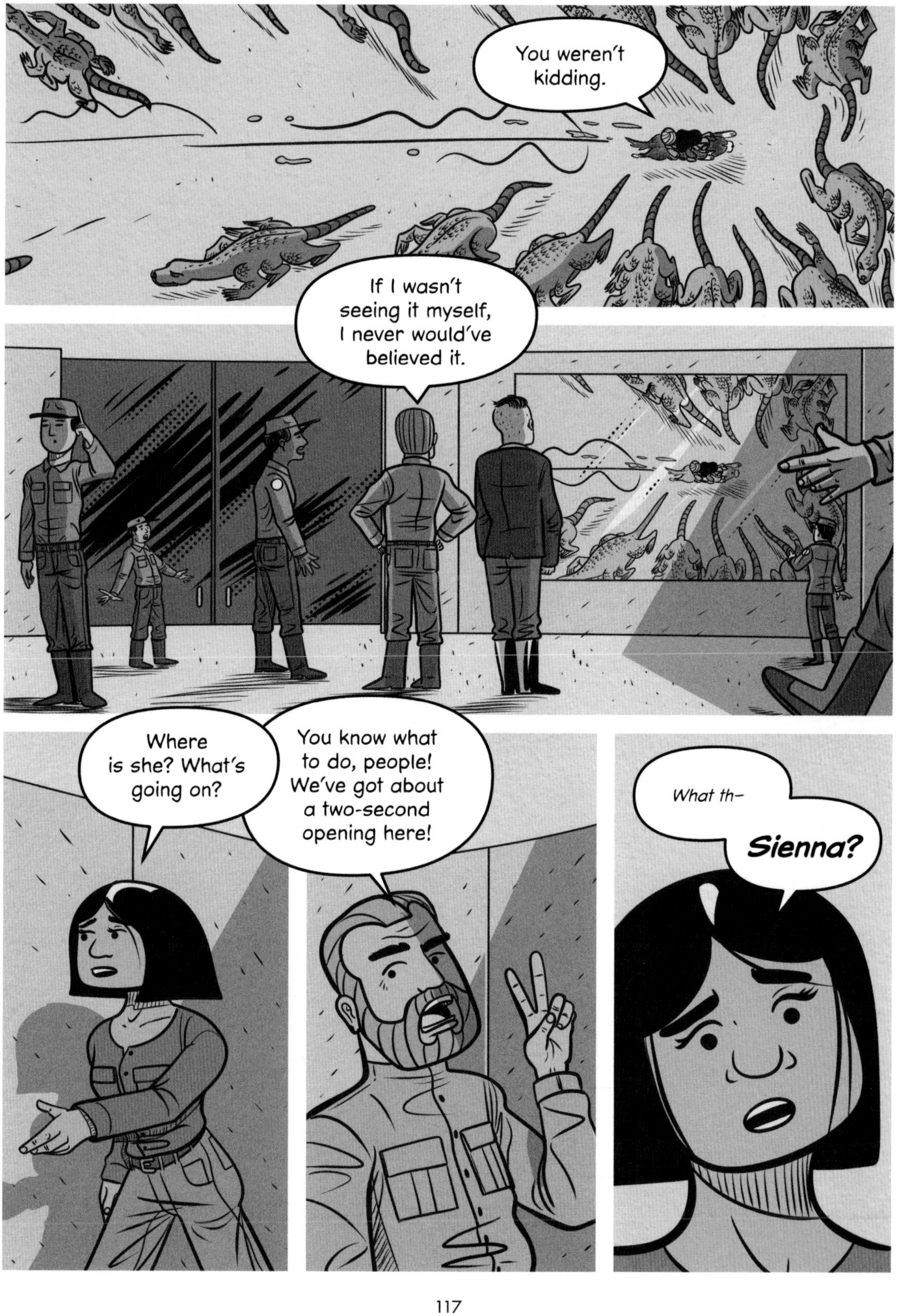

You weren't kidding.
If I wasn't seeing it myself, I never would've believed it.
Where is she? What's going on?
You know what to do, people! We've got about a two-second opening here!
What th–
Sienna?

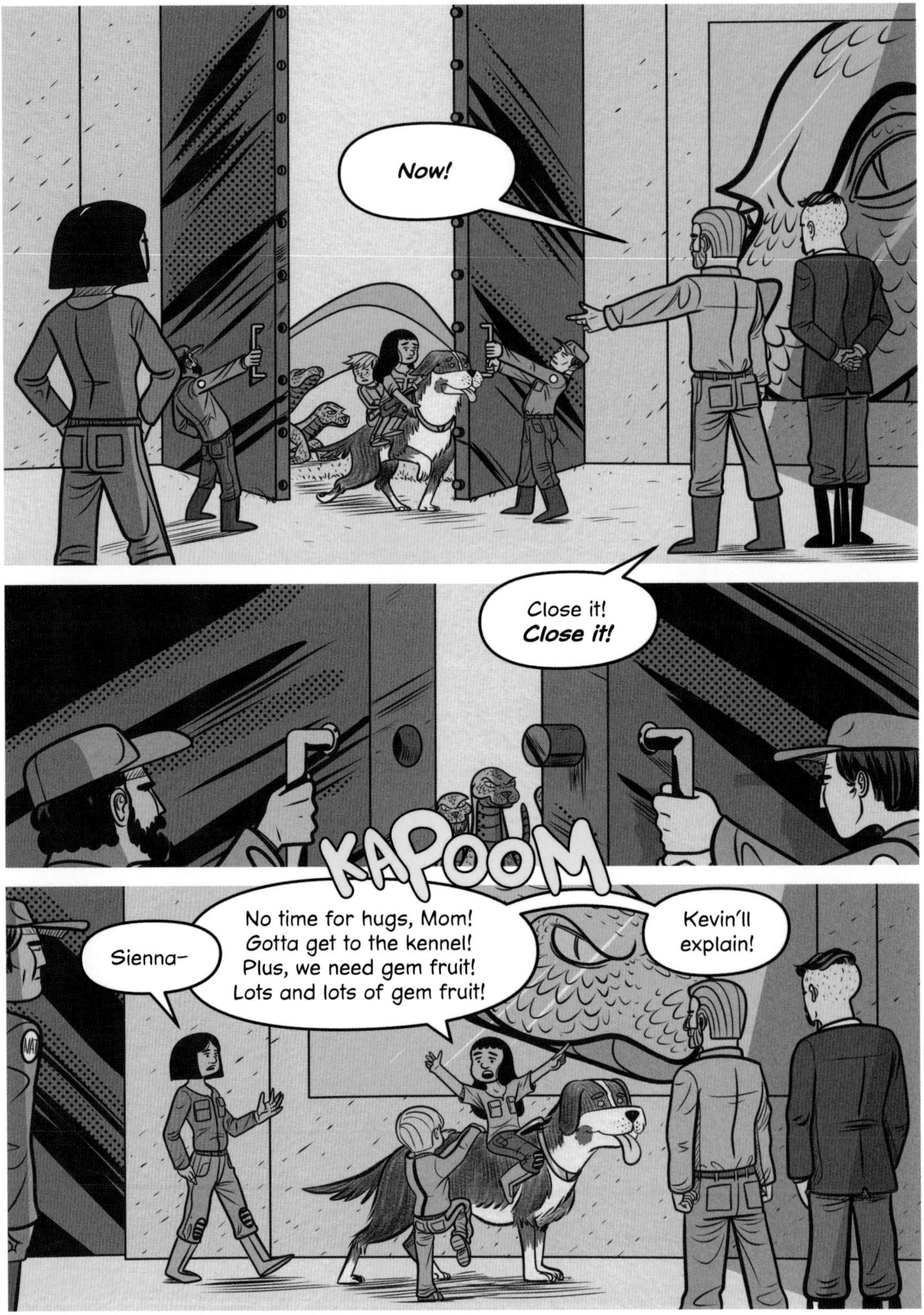
Now!
Close it!
Close it!
KAPOOM
Sienna–
No time for hugs, Mom! Gotta get to the kennel! Plus, we need gem fruit! Lots and lots of gem fruit!
Kevin'll explain!

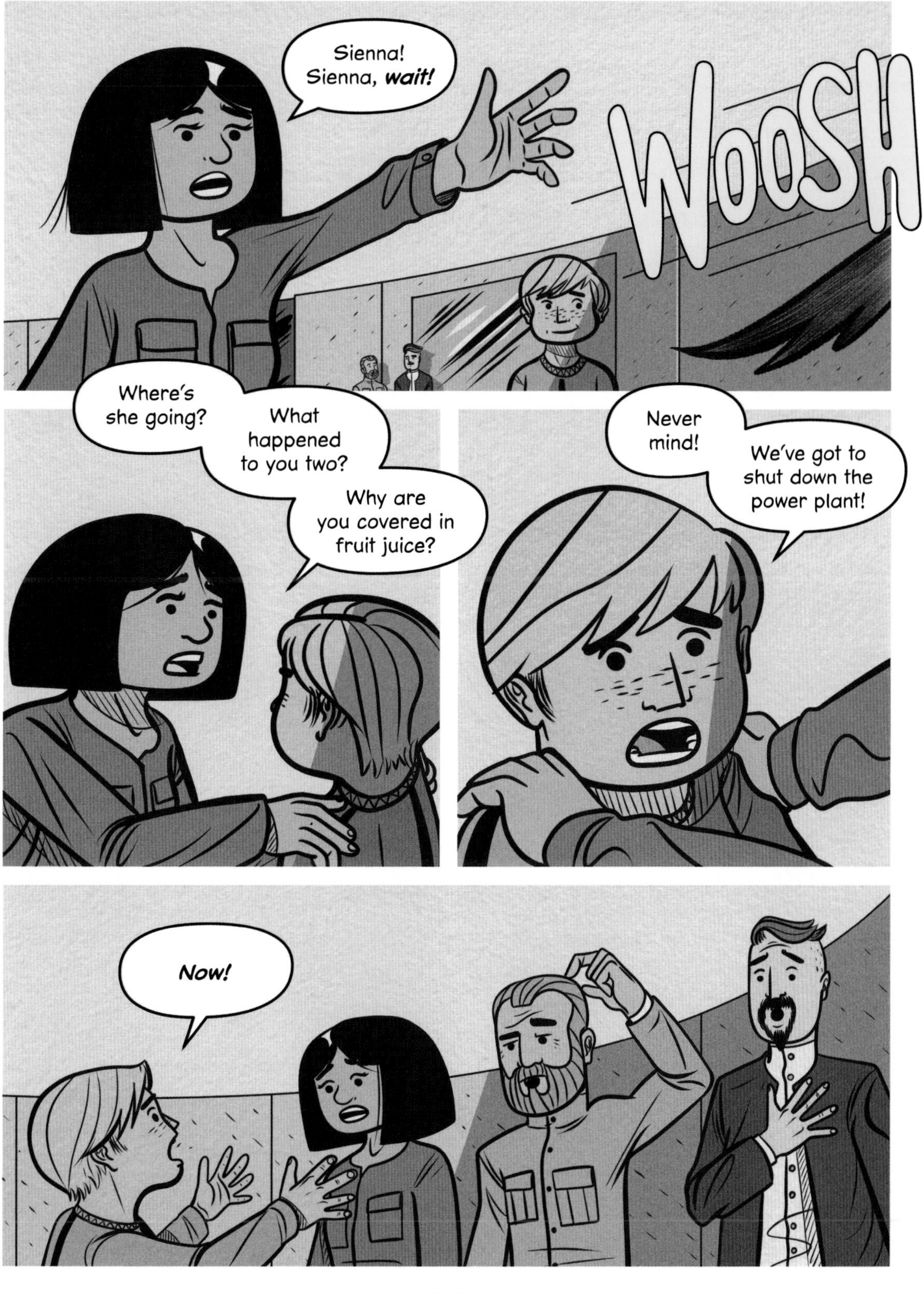
Sienna! Sienna, *wait!*
WOOSH
Where's she going?
What happened to you two?
Why are you covered in fruit juice?
Never mind!
We've got to shut down the power plant!
Now!

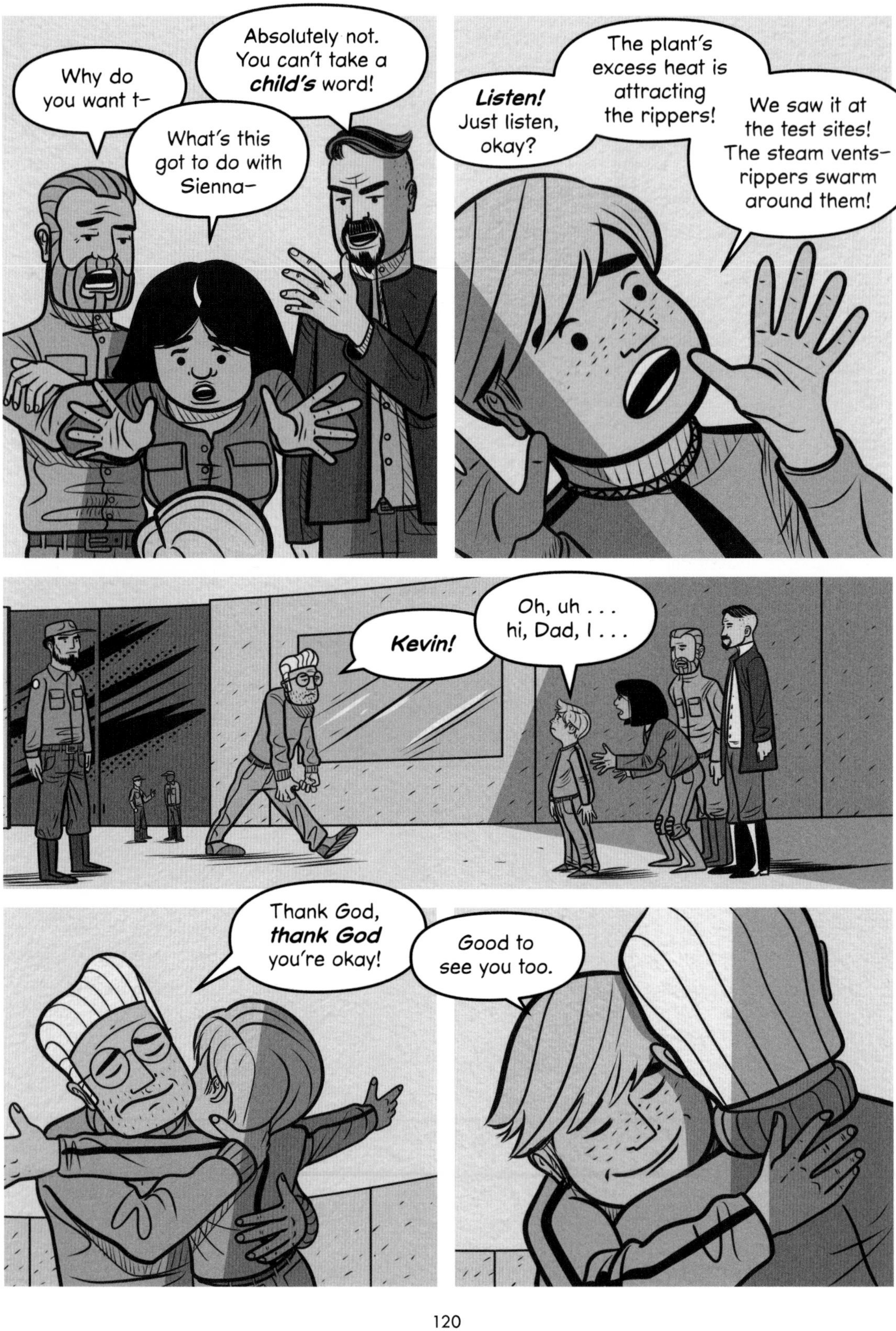
Why do you want t-
Absolutely not. You can't take a ***child's*** word!
What's this got to do with Sienna-
Listen! Just listen, okay?
The plant's excess heat is attracting the rippers!
We saw it at the test sites! The steam vents- rippers swarm around them!
Kevin!
Oh, uh . . . hi, Dad, I . . .
Thank God, ***thank God*** you're okay!
Good to see you too.

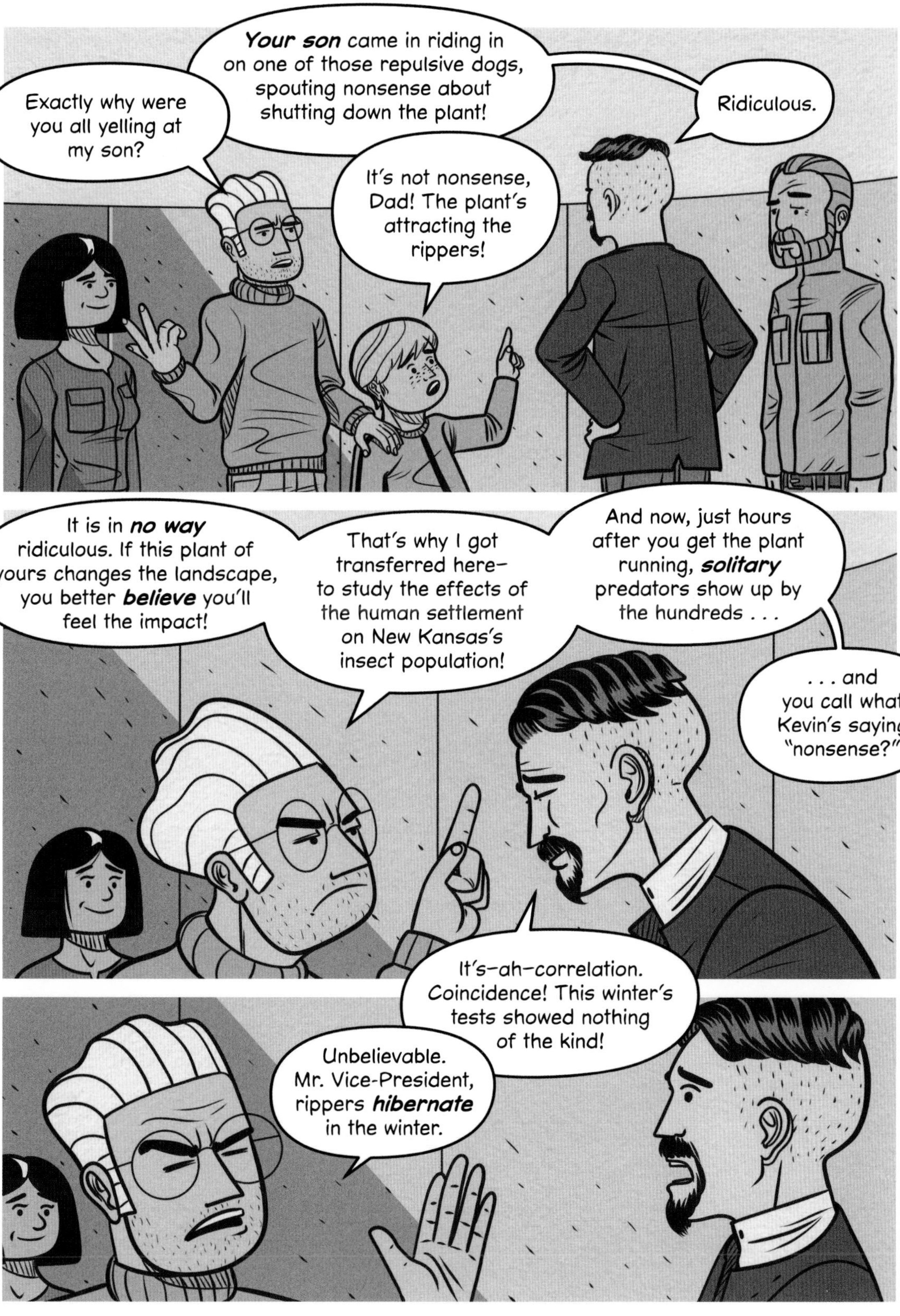
Exactly why were you all yelling at my son?
Your son came in riding in on one of those repulsive dogs, spouting nonsense about shutting down the plant!
Ridiculous.
It's not nonsense, Dad! The plant's attracting the rippers!
It is in no way ridiculous. If this plant of yours changes the landscape, you better believe you'll feel the impact!
That's why I got transferred here— to study the effects of the human settlement on New Kansas's insect population!
And now, just hours after you get the plant running, solitary predators show up by the hundreds . . .
. . . and you call what Kevin's saying "nonsense?"
It's—ah—correlation. Coincidence! This winter's tests showed nothing of the kind!
Unbelievable. Mr. Vice-President, rippers hibernate in the winter.

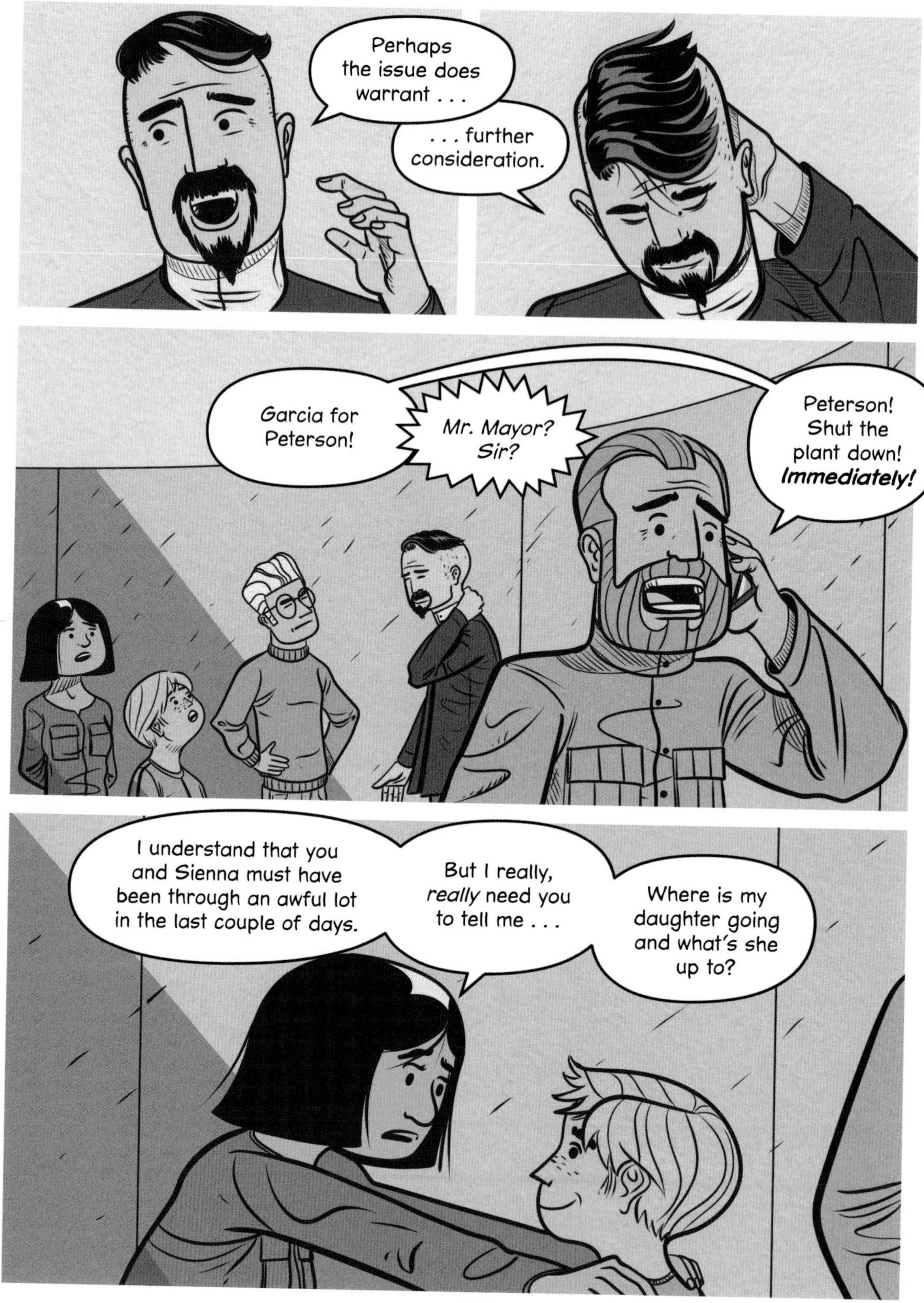

Perhaps the issue does warrant . . .
. . . further consideration.
Garcia for Peterson!
Mr. Mayor? Sir?
Peterson! Shut the plant down! ***Immediately!***
I understand that you and Sienna must have been through an awful lot in the last couple of days.
But I really, *really* need you to tell me . . .
Where is my daughter going and what's she up to?

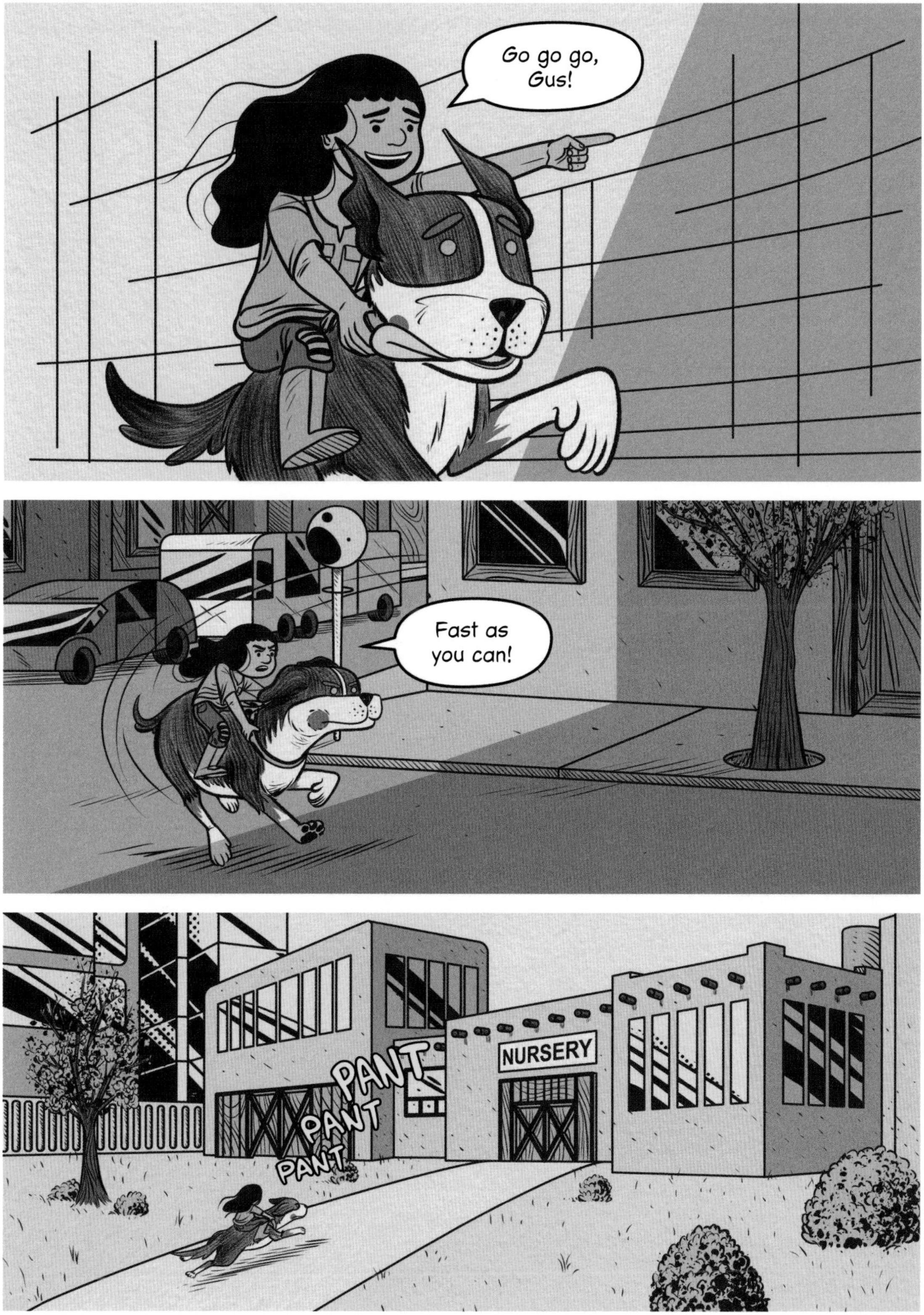
Go go go, Gus!
Fast as you can!
NURSERY
PANT
PANT
PANT

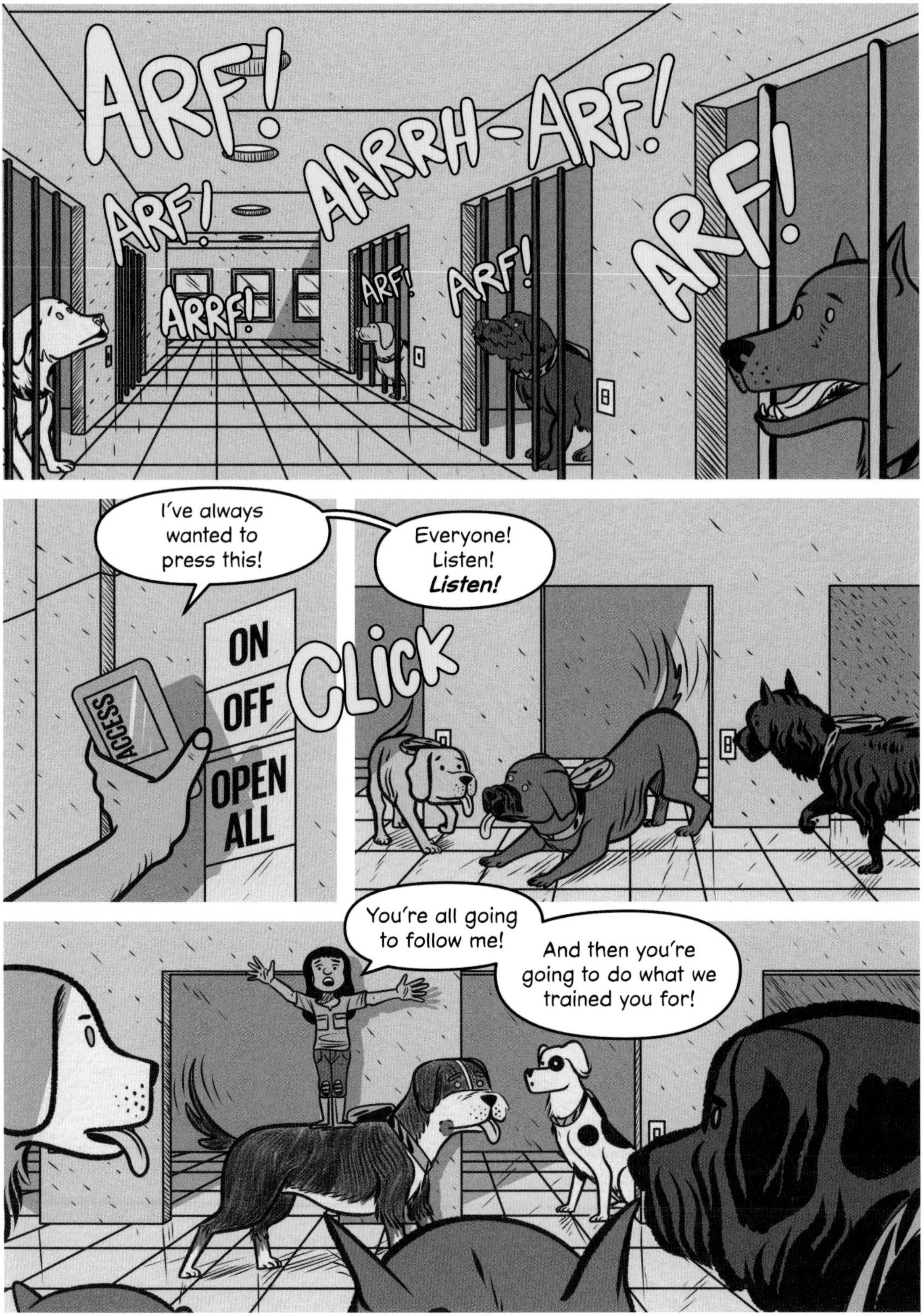
ARF!
AARRH-ARF!
ARF!
ARF!
ARRF!
ARF!
ARF!
I've always wanted to press this!
ON
OFF
OPEN ALL
ACCESS
CLICK
Everyone! Listen! ***Listen!***
You're all going to follow me!
And then you're going to do what we trained you for!

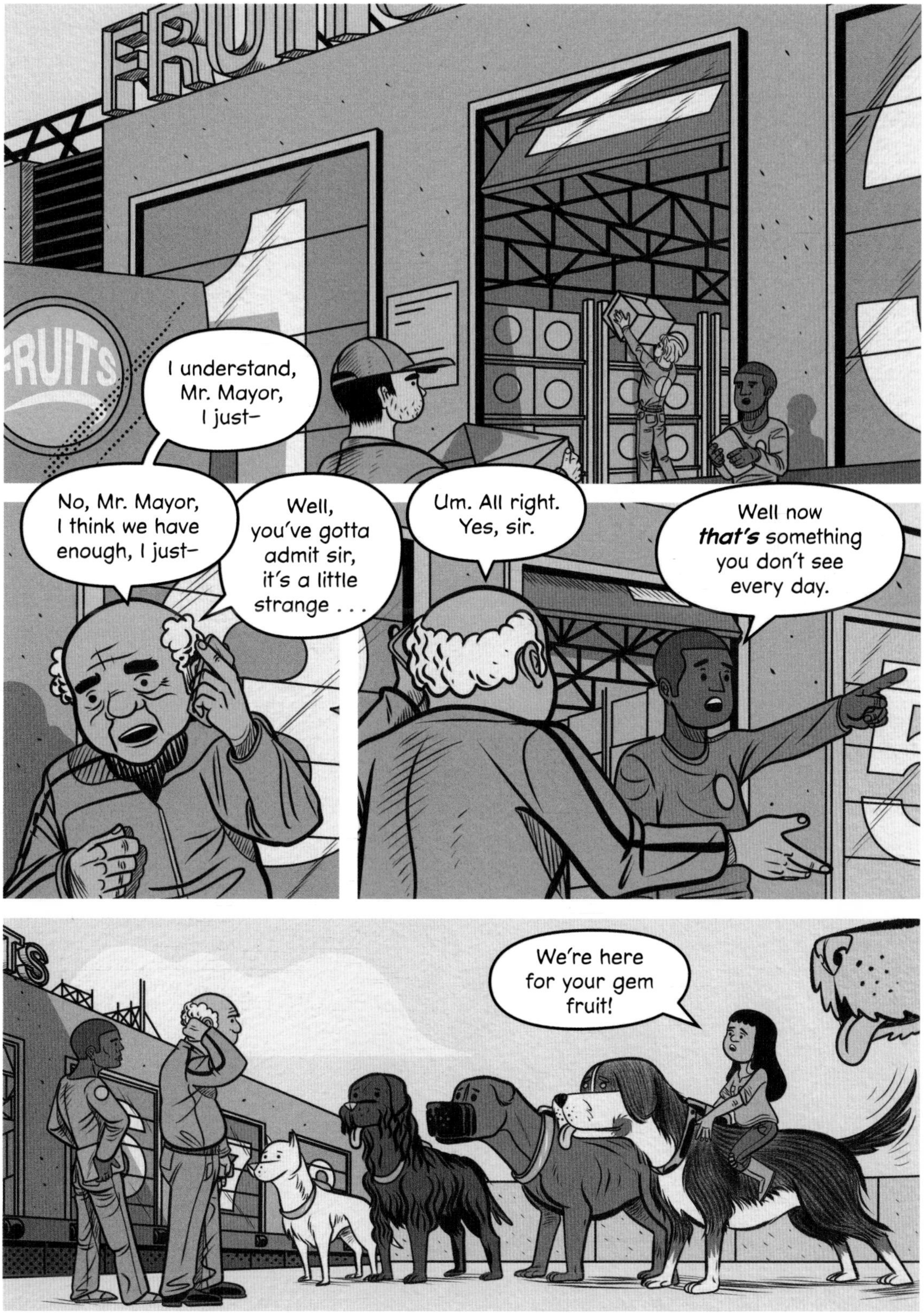
FRUITS
FRUITS
I understand, Mr. Mayor, I just–
No, Mr. Mayor, I think we have enough, I just–
Well, you've gotta admit sir, it's a little strange . . .
Um. All right. Yes, sir.
Well now ***that's*** something you don't see every day.
We're here for your gem fruit!

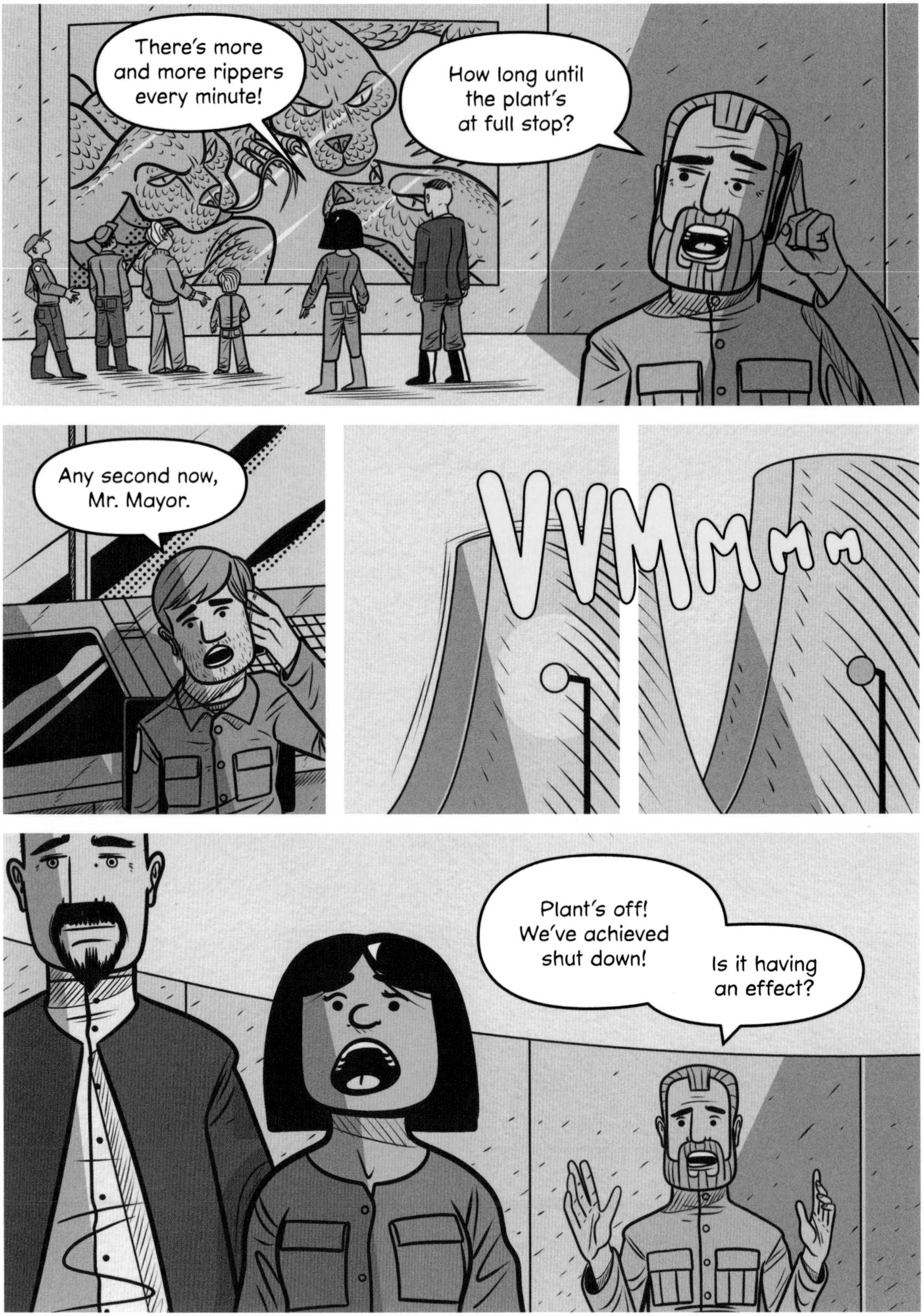
There's more and more rippers every minute!
How long until the plant's at full stop?
Any second now, Mr. Mayor.
VVMMMMM
Plant's off! We've achieved shut down!
Is it having an effect?

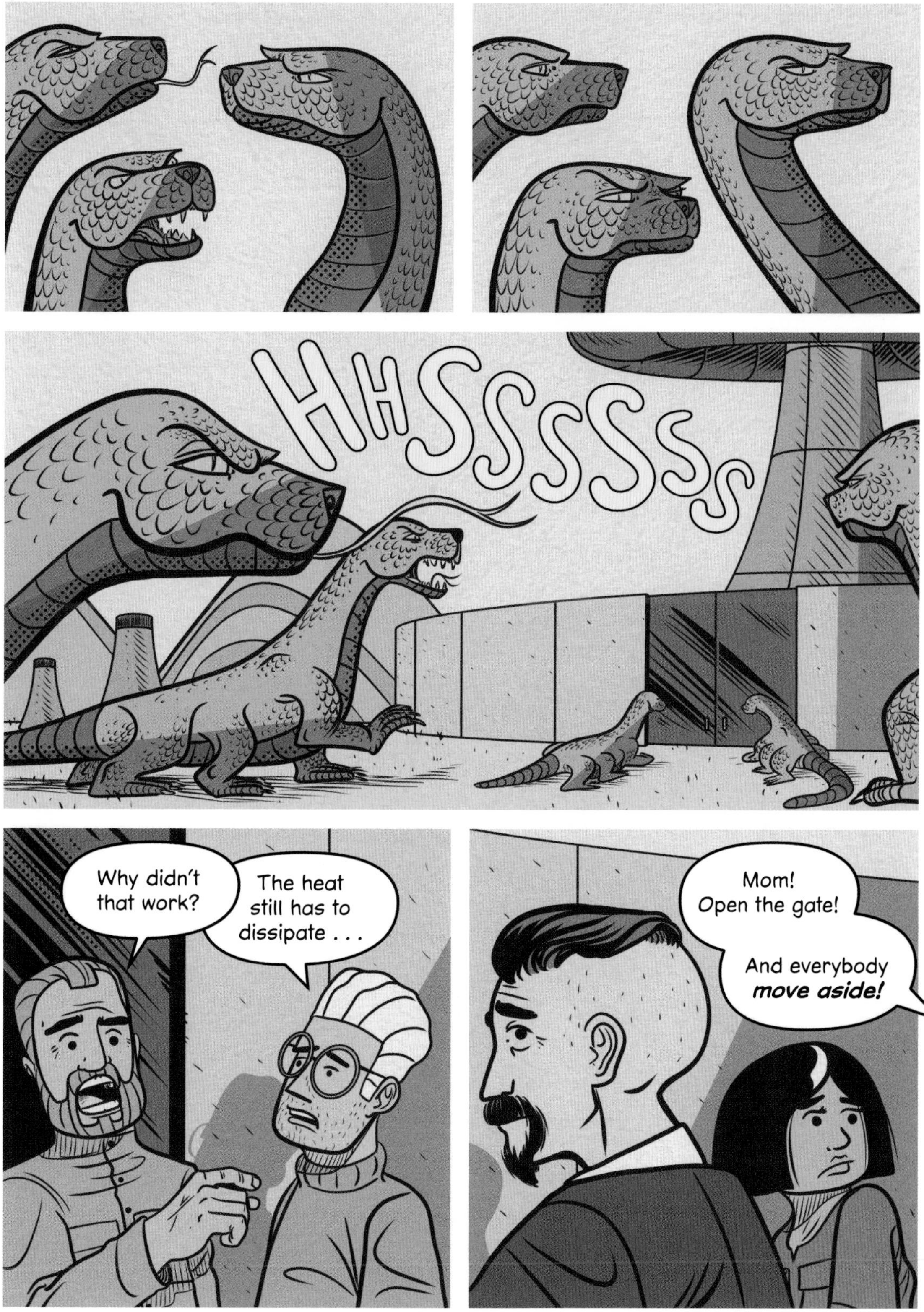
HHSSSSSS
Why didn't that work?
The heat still has to dissipate . . .
Mom! Open the gate!
And everybody ***move aside!***

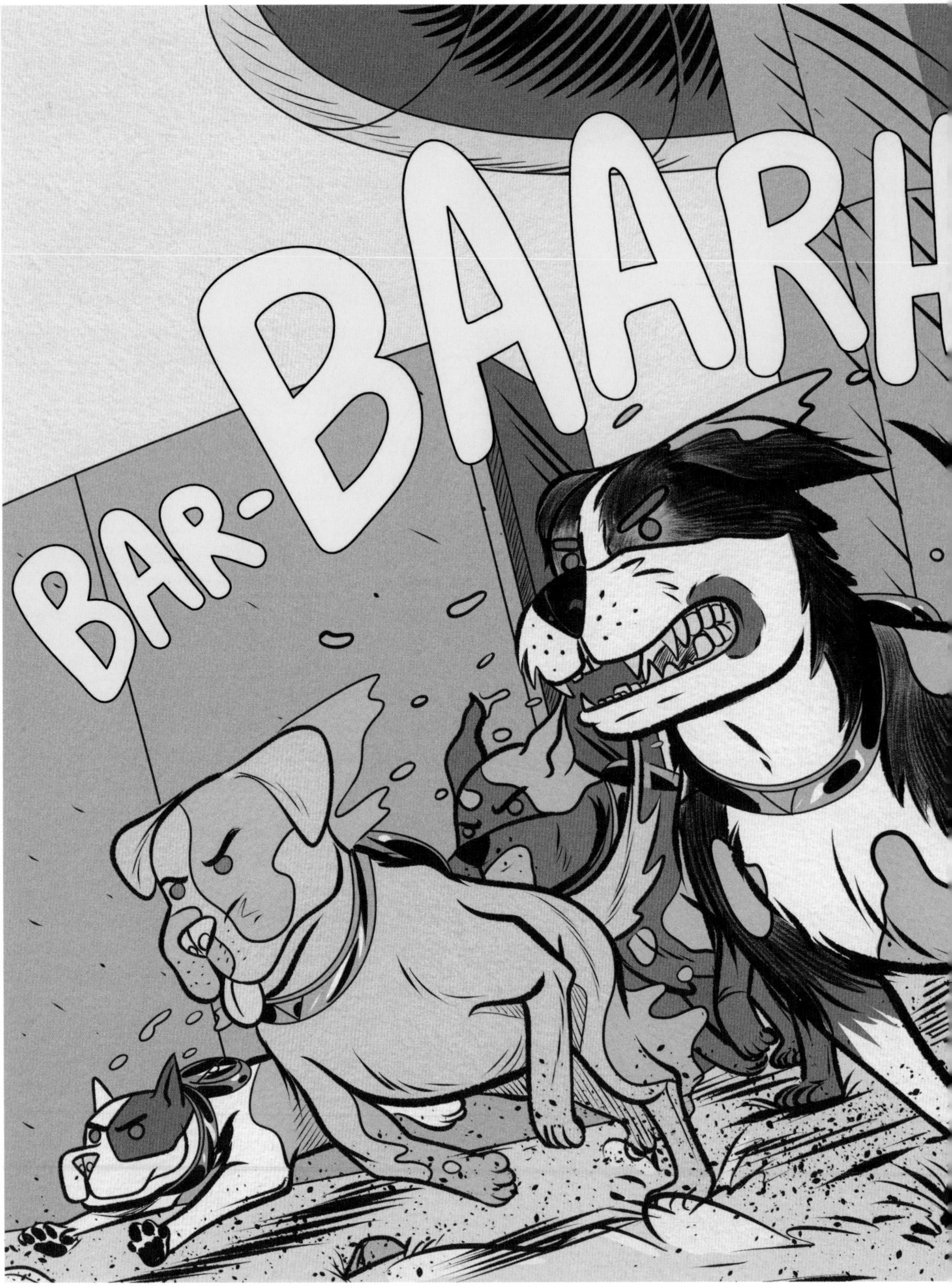
BAR-BAARH

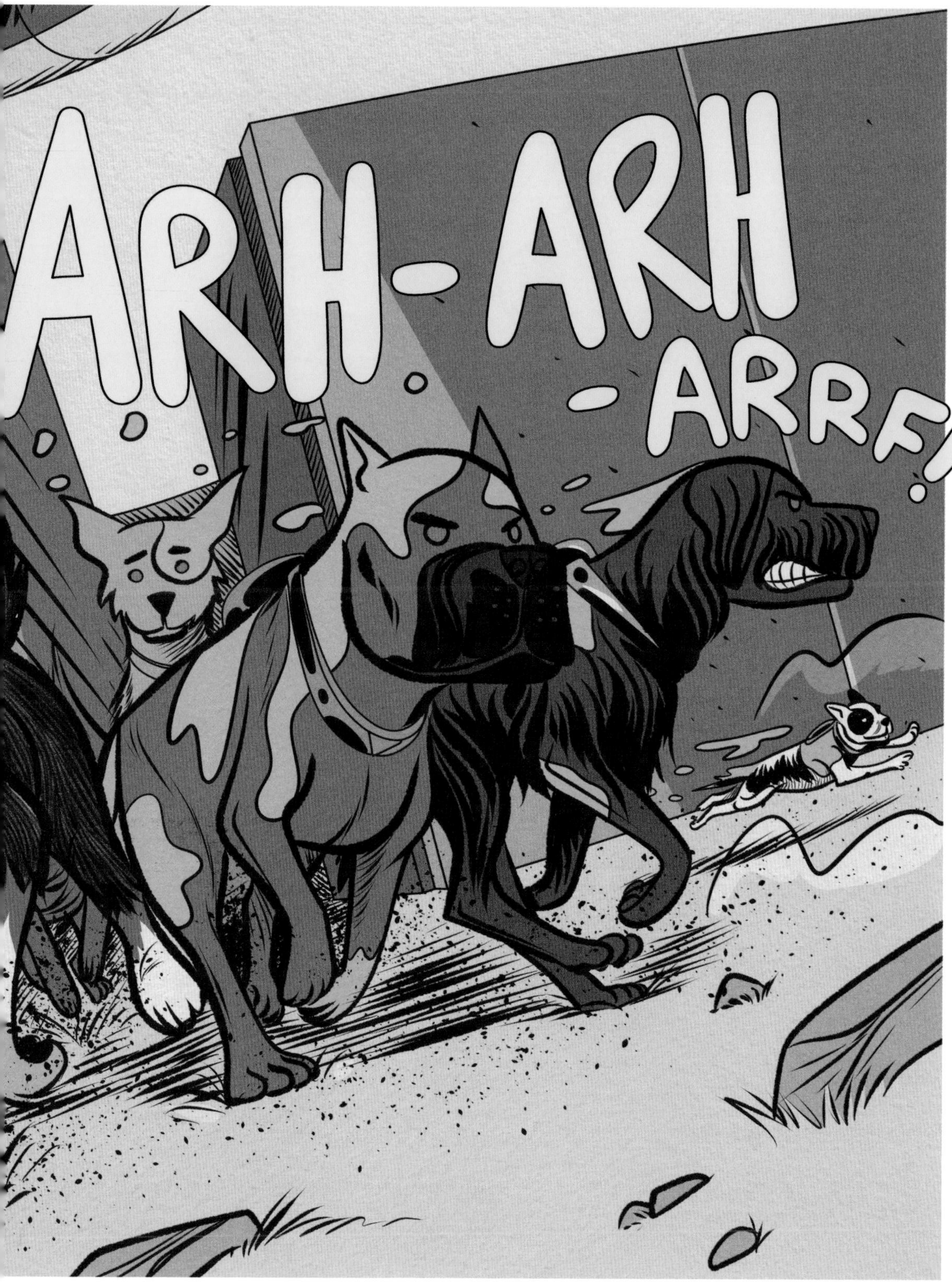
ARH-ARH
-ARRF!

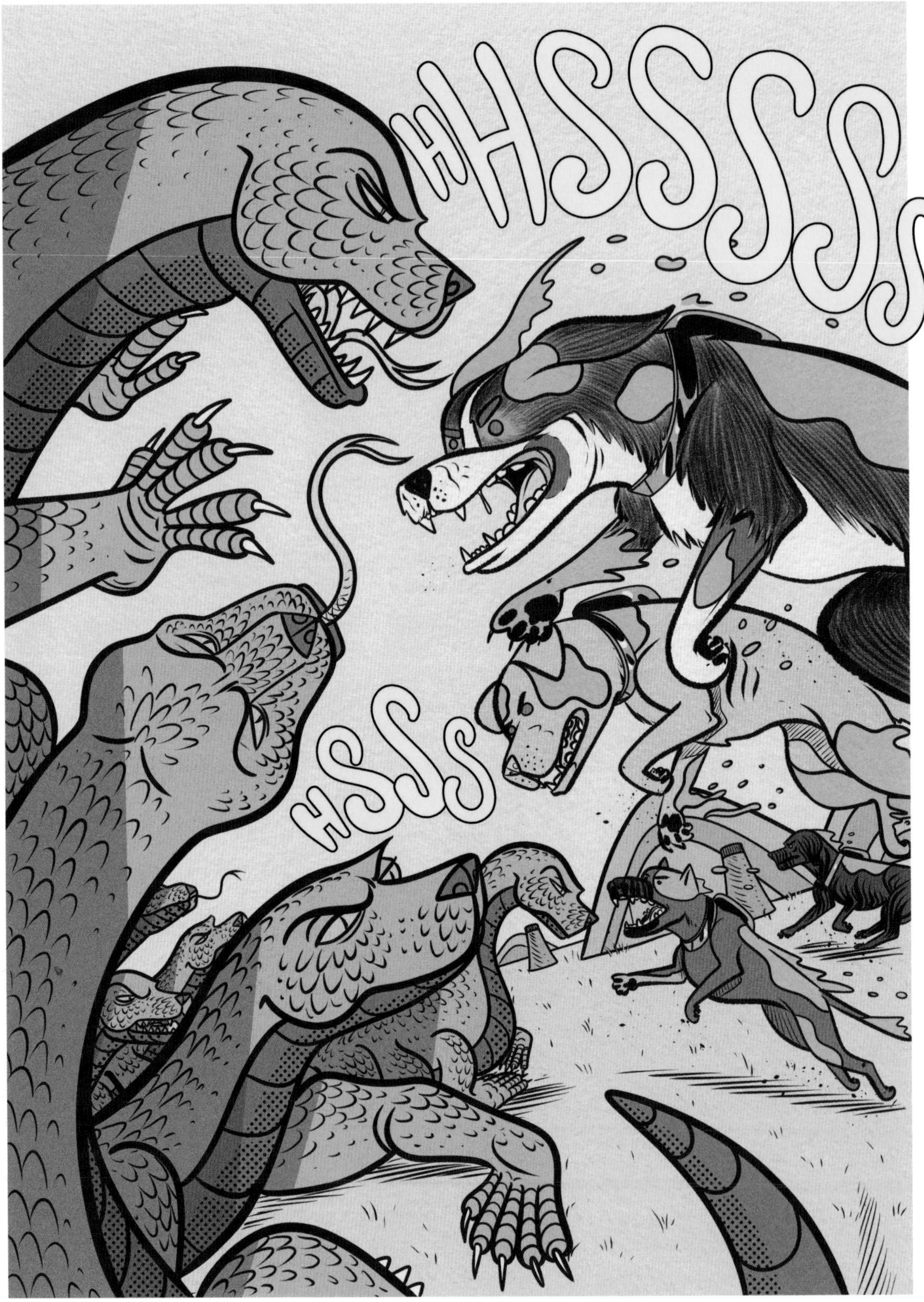
HHSSSSSS
HSSS

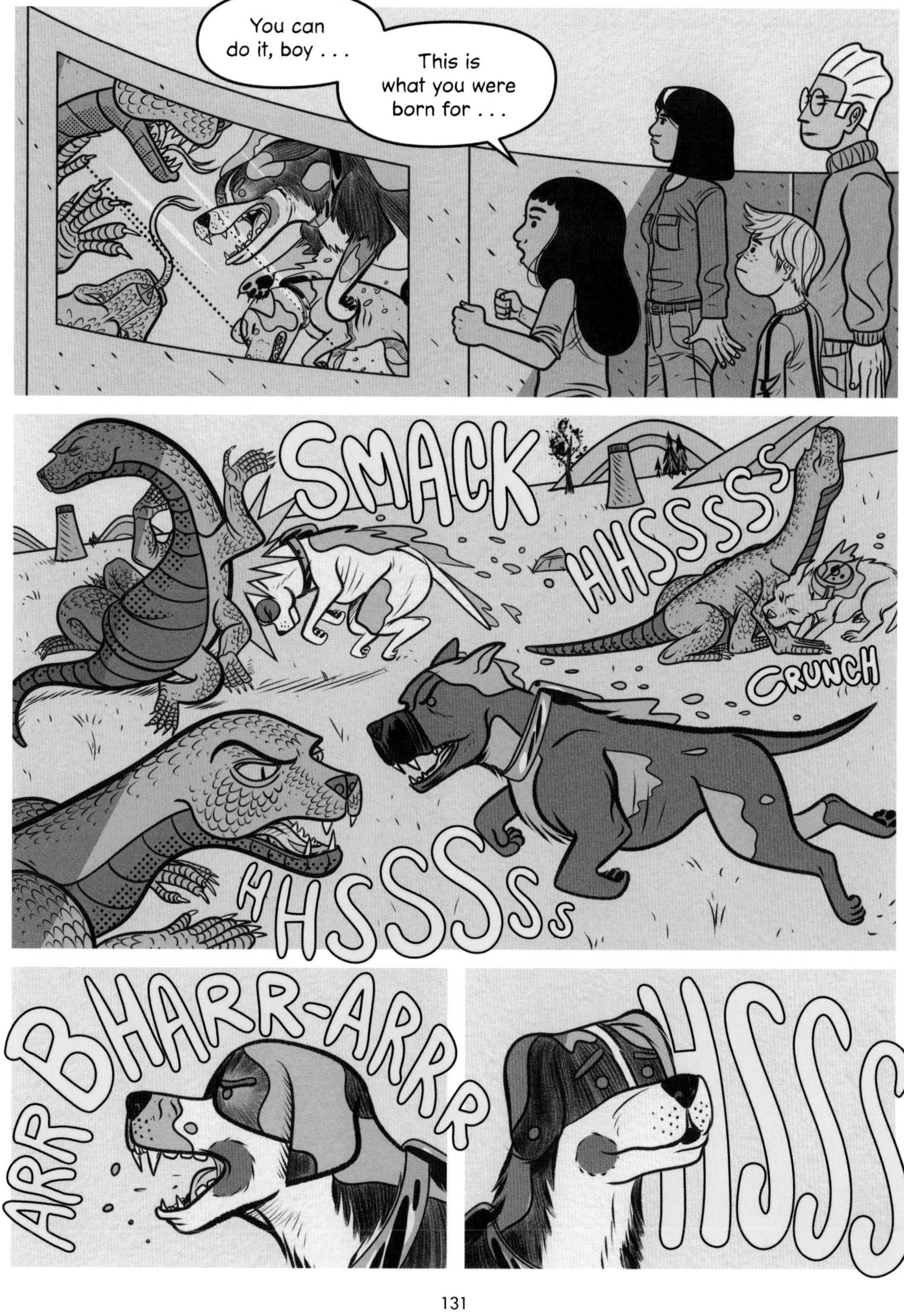

You can do it, boy . . .
This is what you were born for . . .
SMACK
HHSSSSS
CRUNCH
HHSSSSs
ARRBHARR-ARRRR
HSSS

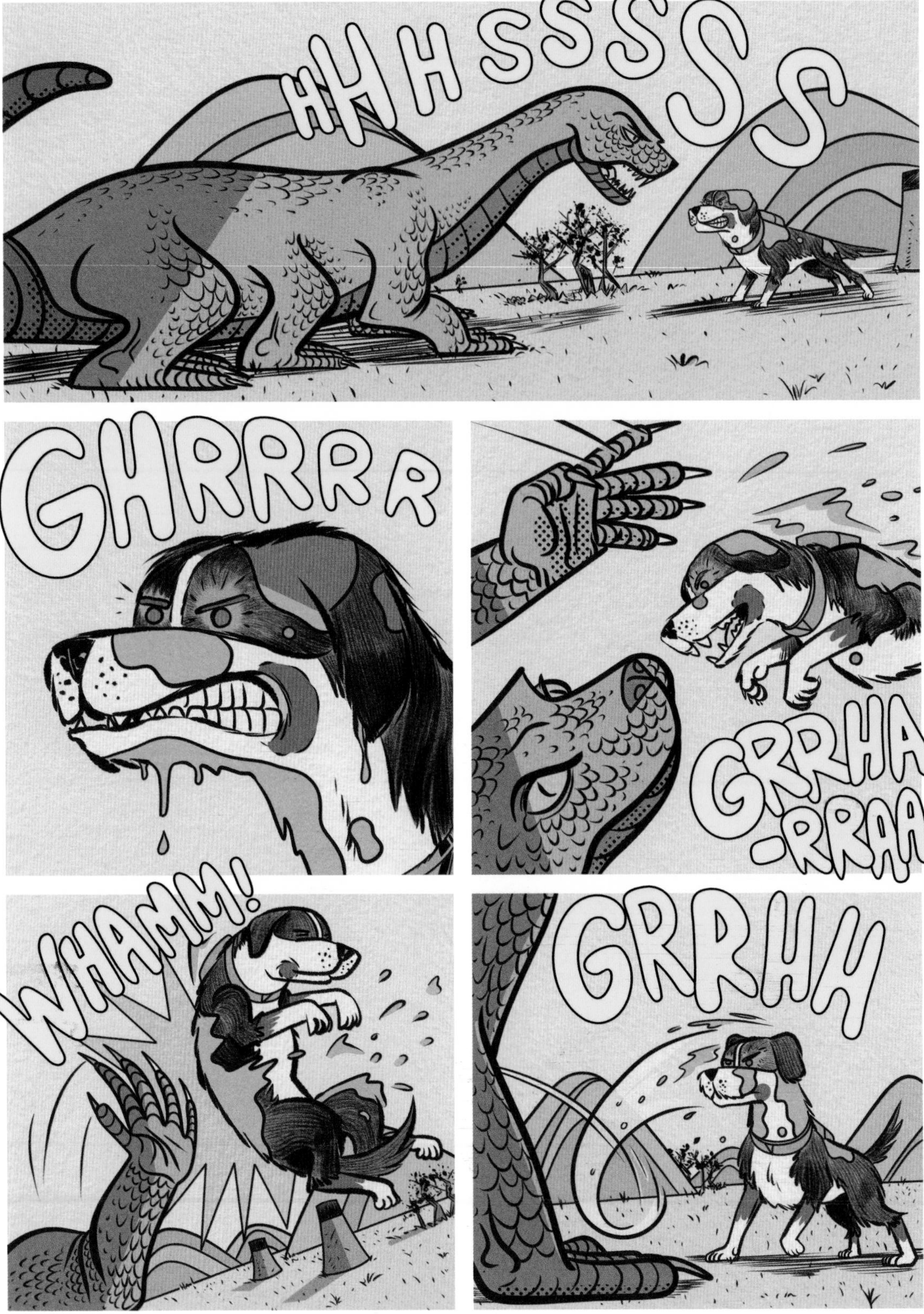
HHHSSSSS
GHRRRR
GRRHA-RRAA!
WHAMM!
GRRHH

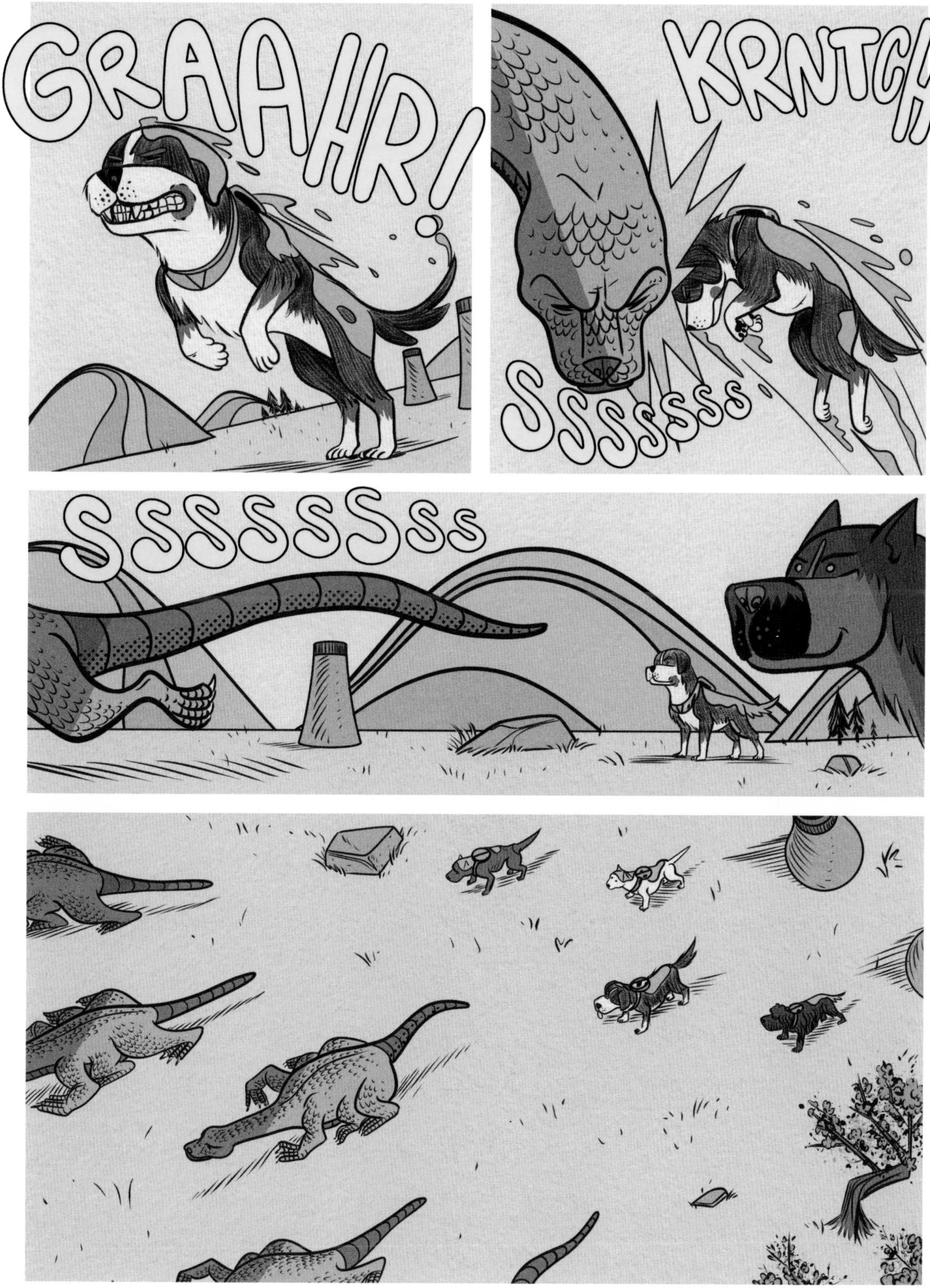
GRAAHR!
KRNTCH
SSSSSSS
SSSSSSSSS

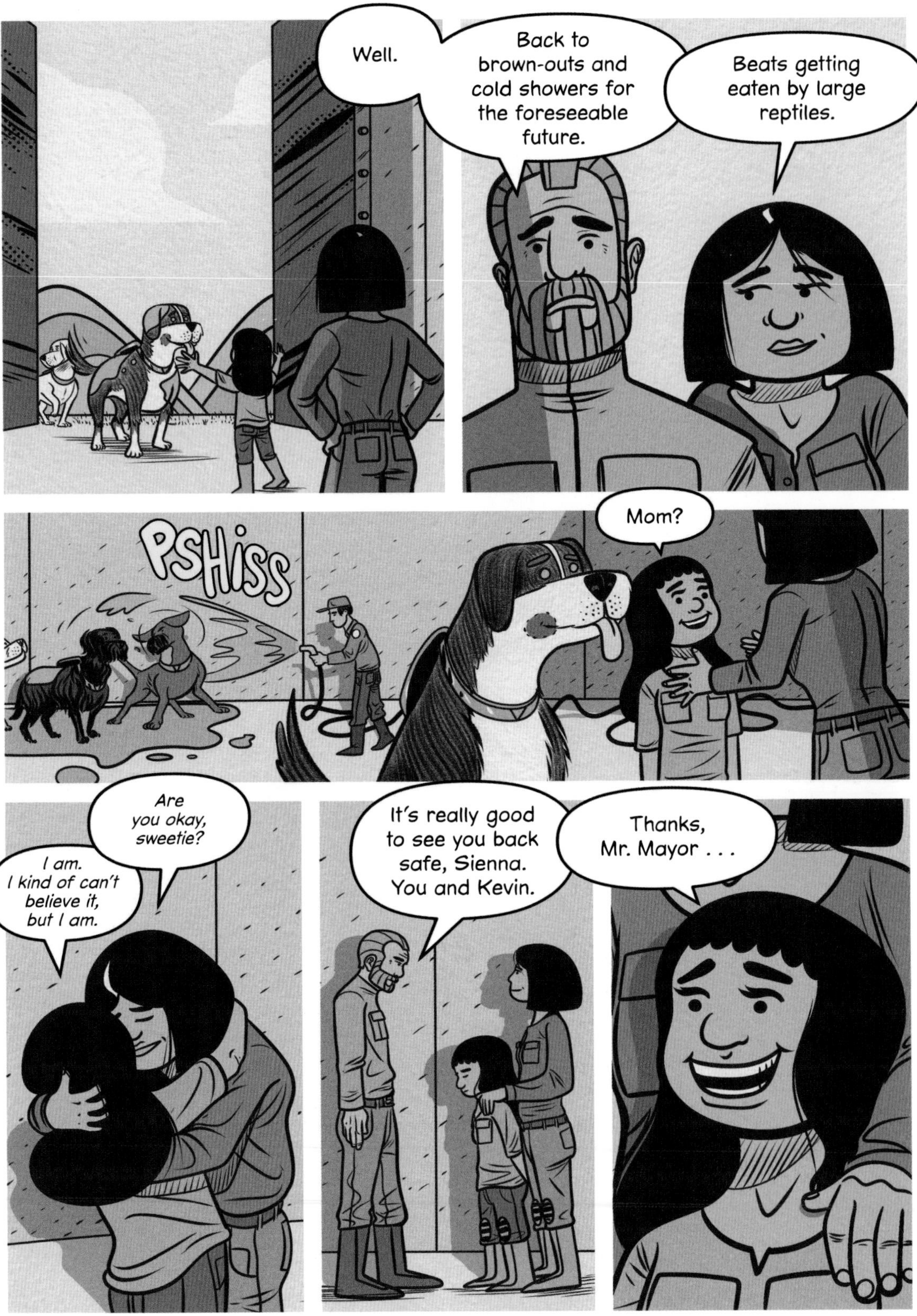
Well.
Back to brown-outs and cold showers for the foreseeable future.
Beats getting eaten by large reptiles.
PSHISS
Mom?
Are you okay, sweetie?
I am. I kind of can't believe it, but I am.
It's really good to see you back safe, Sienna. You and Kevin.
Thanks, Mr. Mayor . . .

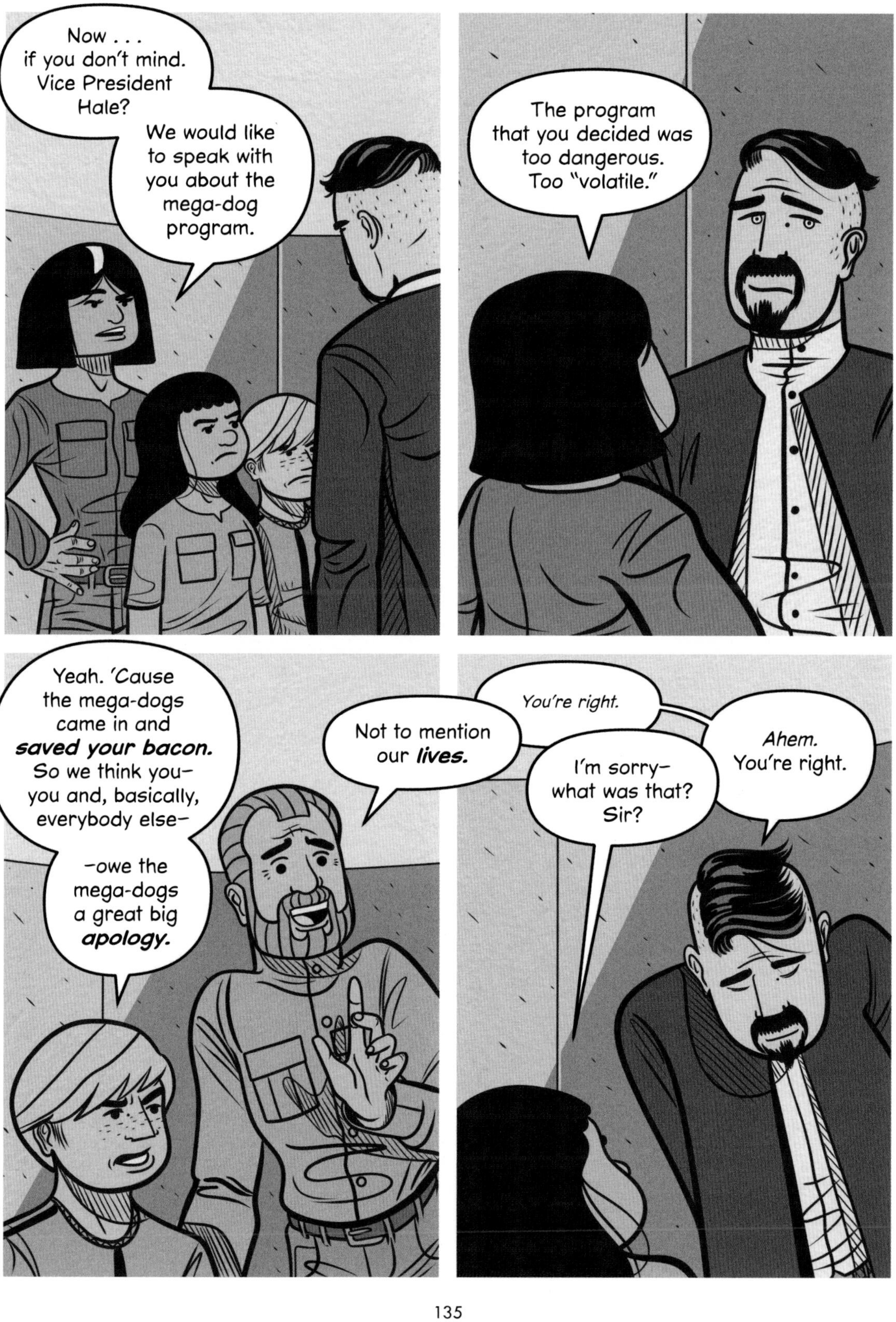
Now . . . if you don't mind. Vice President Hale?
We would like to speak with you about the mega-dog program.
The program that you decided was too dangerous. Too "volatile."
Yeah. 'Cause the mega-dogs came in and **saved your bacon.** So we think you– you and, basically, everybody else–
–owe the mega-dogs a great big ***apology.***
Not to mention our ***lives.***
You're right.
I'm sorry– what was that? Sir?
Ahem. You're right.

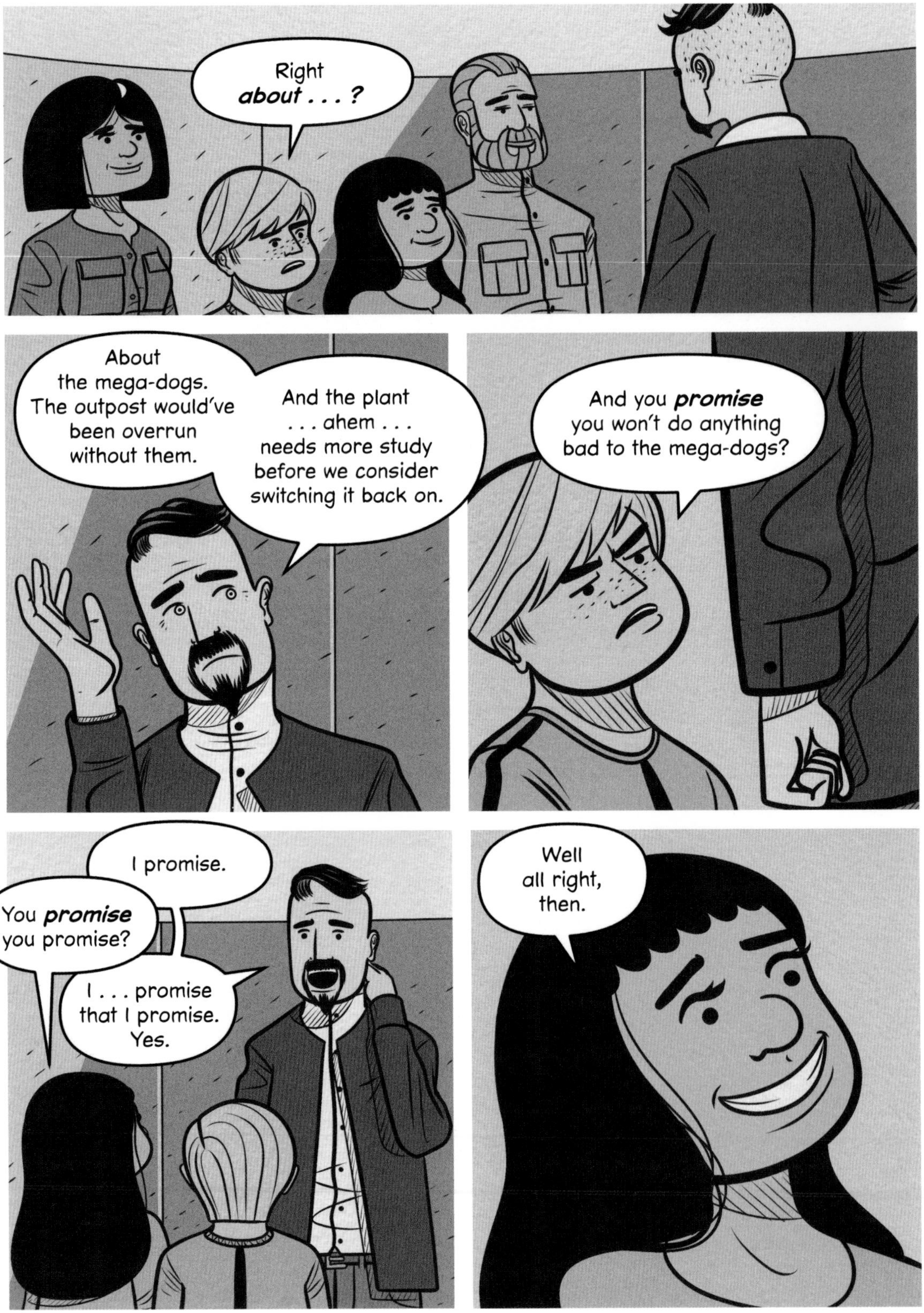
Right *about . . . ?*
About the mega-dogs. The outpost would've been overrun without them.
And the plant . . . ahem . . . needs more study before we consider switching it back on.
And you *promise* you won't do anything bad to the mega-dogs?
I promise.
You *promise* you promise?
I . . . promise that I promise. Yes.
Well all right, then.

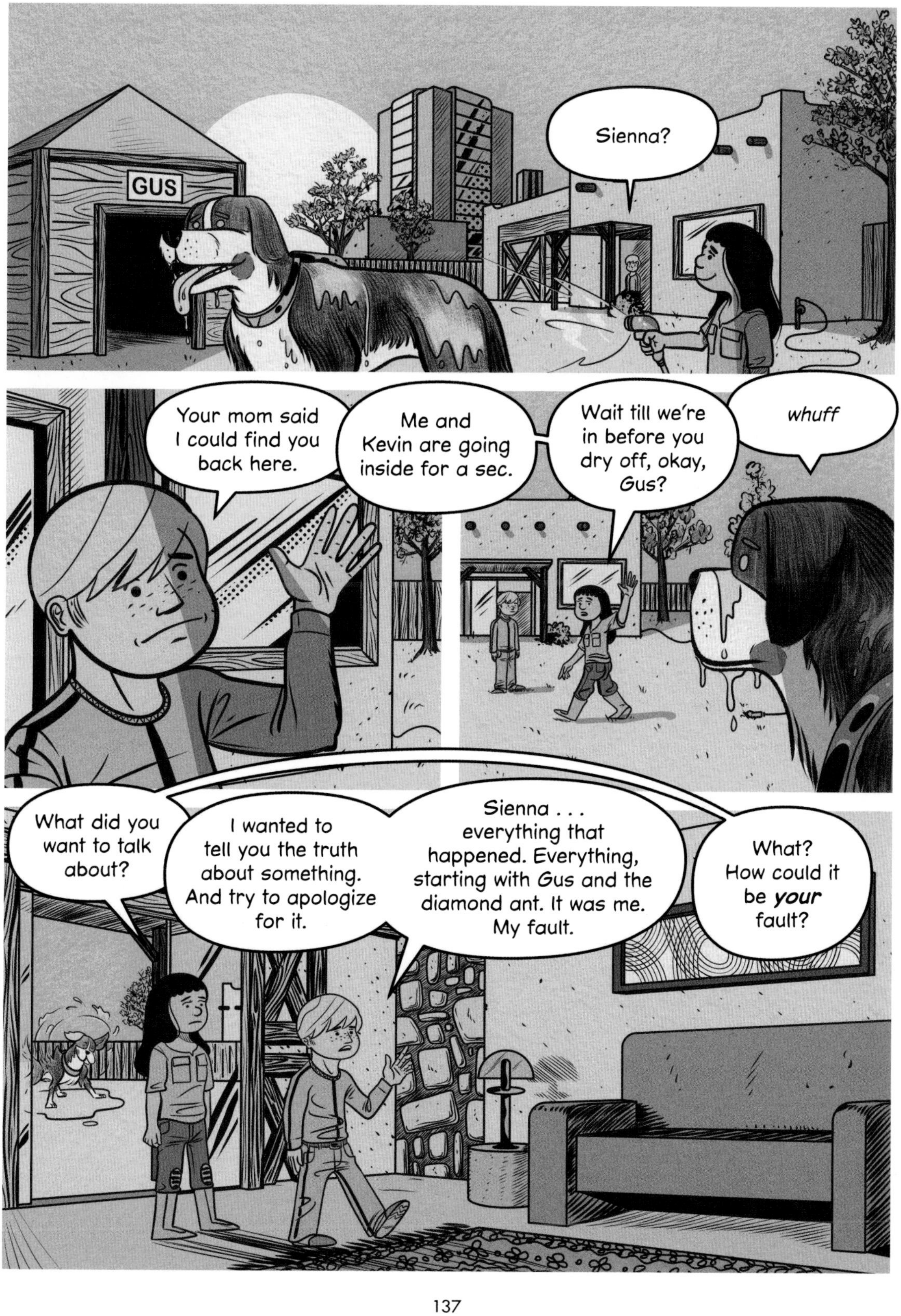
GUS
Sienna?
Your mom said I could find you back here.
Me and Kevin are going inside for a sec.
Wait till we're in before you dry off, okay, Gus?
whuff
What did you want to talk about?
I wanted to tell you the truth about something. And try to apologize for it.
Sienna . . . everything that happened. Everything, starting with Gus and the diamond ant. It was me. My fault.
What? How could it be ***your*** fault?

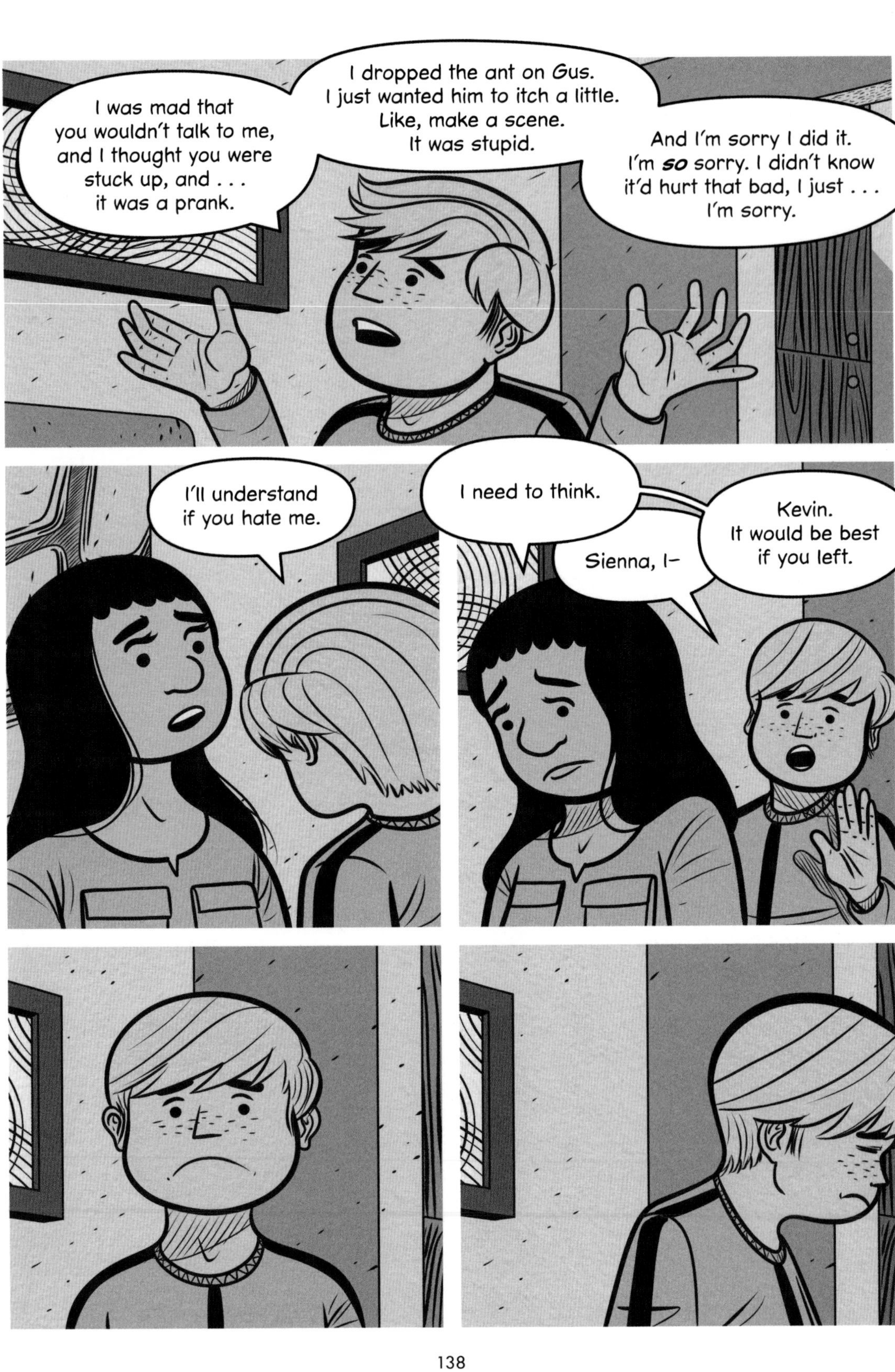
I was mad that you wouldn't talk to me, and I thought you were stuck up, and . . . it was a prank.
I dropped the ant on Gus. I just wanted him to itch a little. Like, make a scene. It was stupid.
And I'm sorry I did it. I'm *so* sorry. I didn't know it'd hurt that bad, I just . . . I'm sorry.
I'll understand if you hate me.
I need to think.
Sienna, I–
Kevin. It would be best if you left.

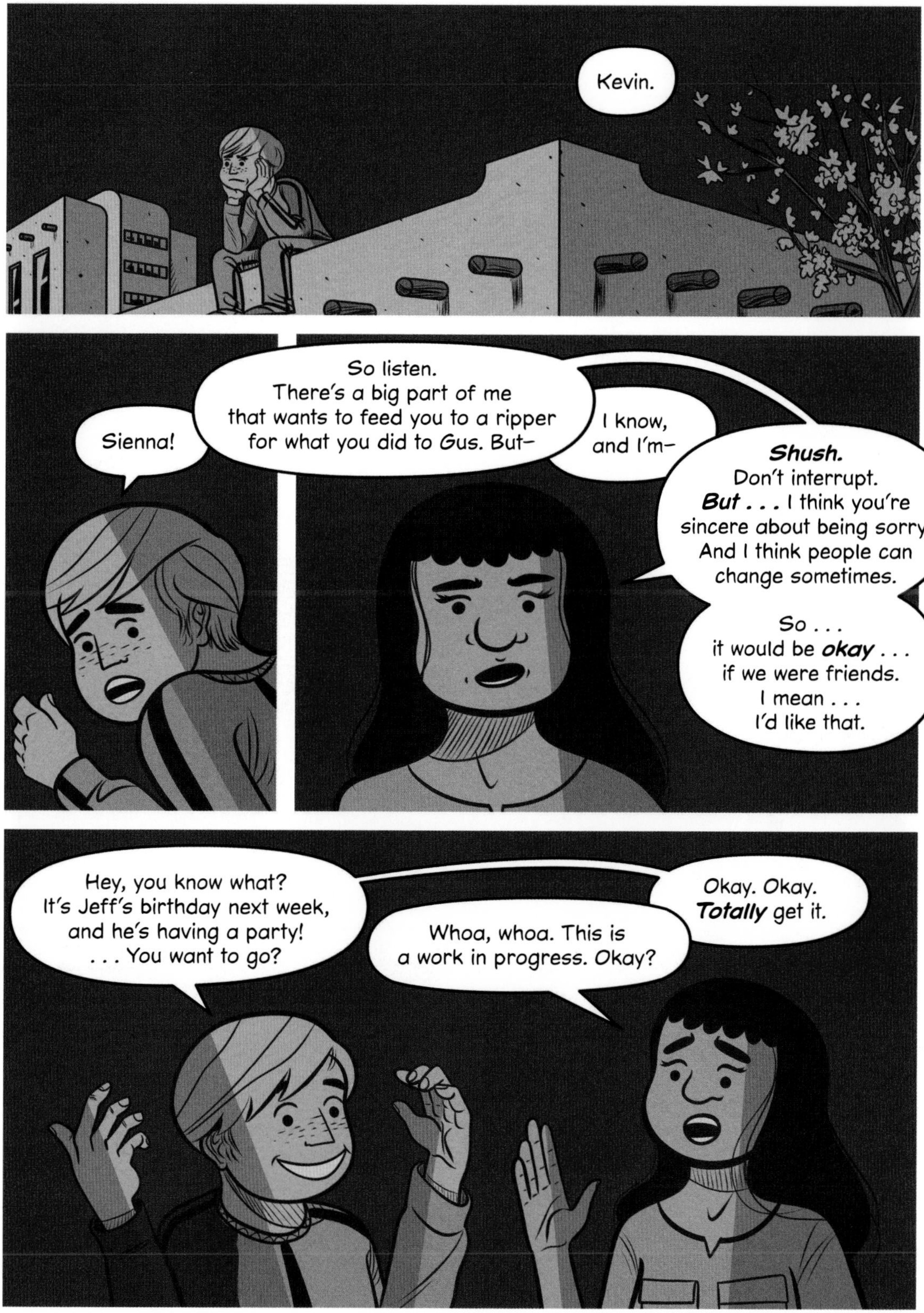
Kevin.
So listen.
There's a big part of me that wants to feed you to a ripper for what you did to Gus. But–
Sienna!
I know, and I'm–
Shush. Don't interrupt. **But . . .** I think you're sincere about being sorry. And I think people can change sometimes.
So . . . it would be ***okay*** . . . if we were friends. I mean . . . I'd like that.
Hey, you know what? It's Jeff's birthday next week, and he's having a party! . . . You want to go?
Whoa, whoa. This is a work in progress. Okay?
Okay. Okay. ***Totally*** get it.

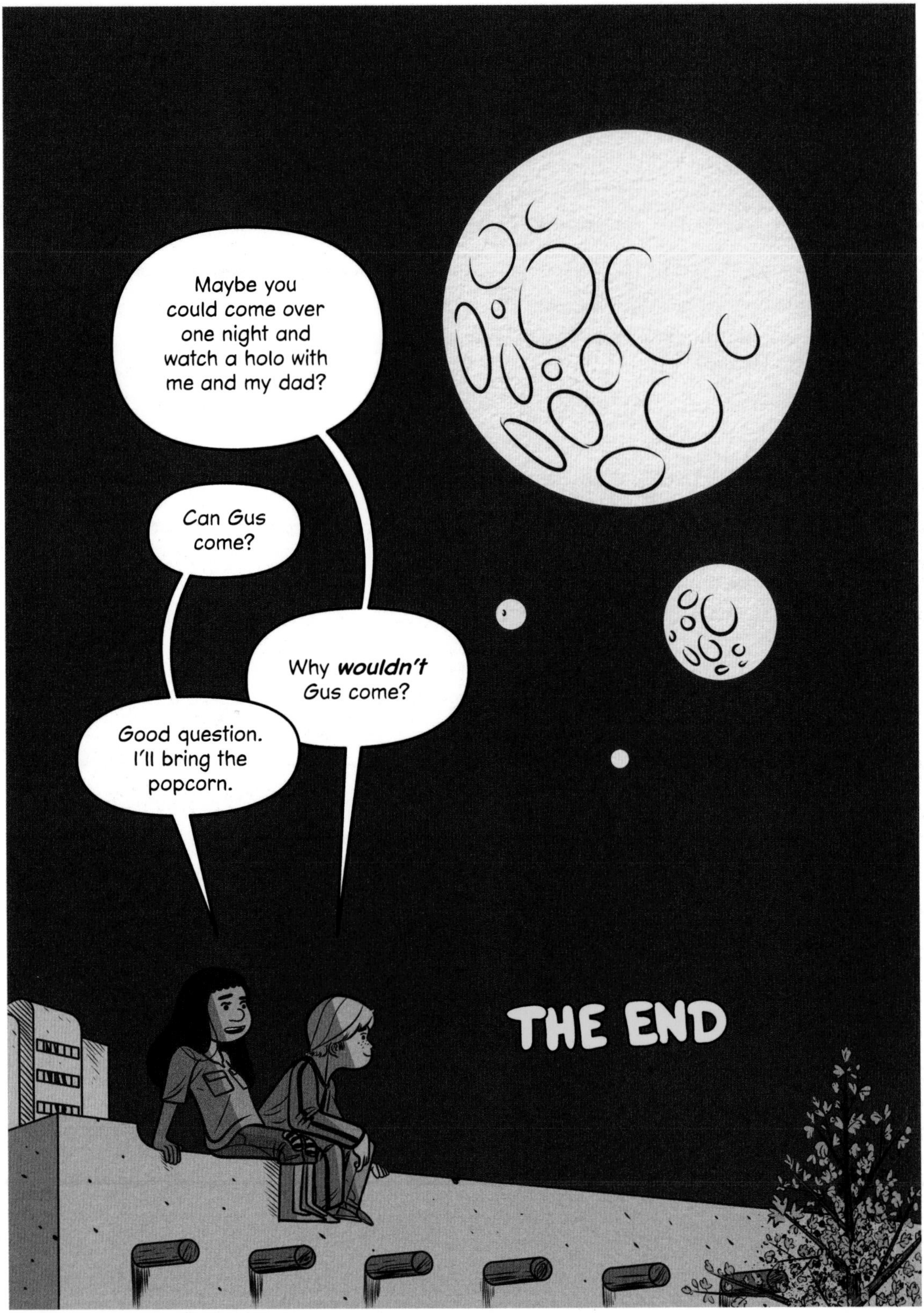
Maybe you could come over one night and watch a holo with me and my dad?
Can Gus come?
Why *wouldn't* Gus come?
Good question. I'll bring the popcorn.
THE END

MAKING MEGA-DOGS

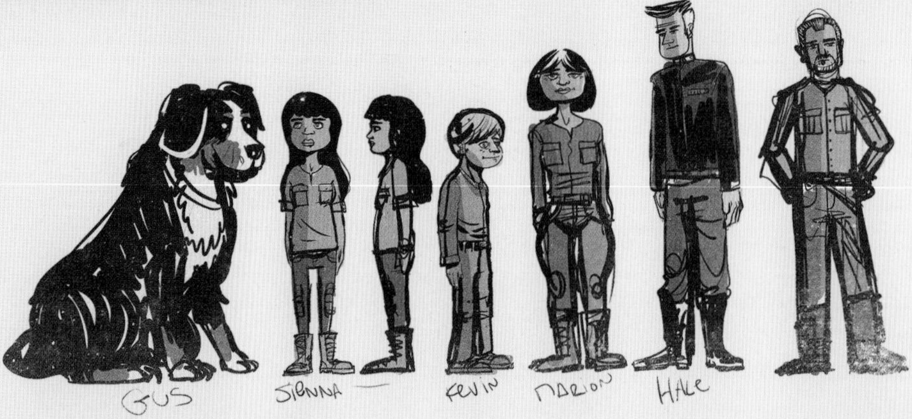
GUS
SIENNA
KEVIN
MARION
HALE

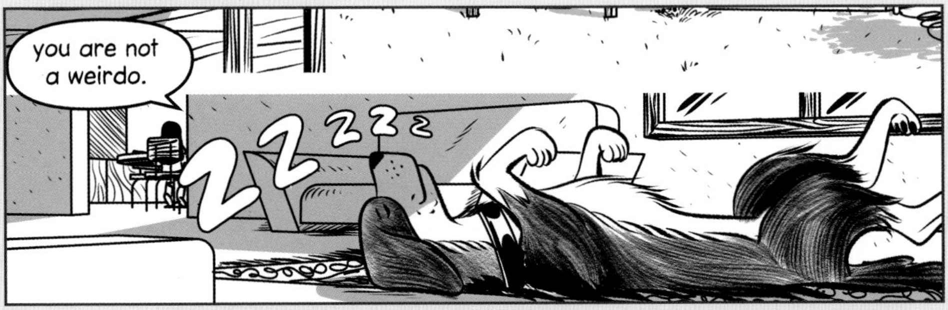
you are not a weirdo.
ZZZZZZ

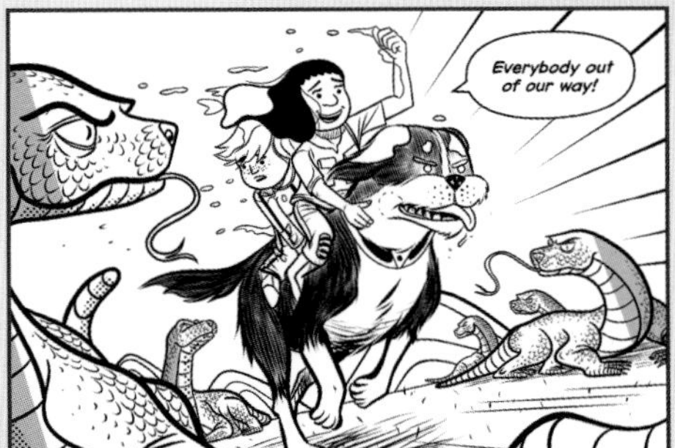
Everybody out of our way!

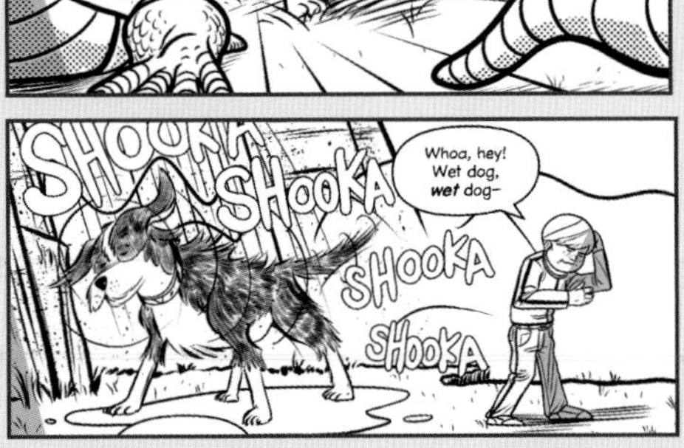
SHOOKA
SHOOKA
Whoa, hey! Wet dog, *wet* dog–
SHOOKA
SHOOKA

Dan Jolley: I'm a pretty huge animal lover, and after working for so long on stories involving the cats of Erin Hunter's *Warriors* universe, I thought it would be nice to write about dogs for a while. A few years ago, I was working on a video game at a development studio north of San Francisco, and one of my co-workers had an enormous Bernese Mountain Dog named Zod who'd come to work with him every day. I loved Zod. He was huge, and very friendly, and he'd go from desk to desk, collecting pets and ear scratches and belly rubs. Zod was my inspiration for Gus, and once I had the idea of this enormous canine, the rest of the story fell into place around him.

For the rippers, I was put in mind of a conversation I once had with a forest ranger. He said he really hated it when colonies of feral cats would show up in the woods, because feral cats are essentially the ultimate killing machines. One cat colony could wipe out an entire species of birds from a forest. I wanted the rippers to have that kind of terrifying, lethal quality, but I didn't want them to be actual cats, because I figured a cat-vs.-dog conflict would be super obvious. Then I remembered reading that some zoologists believe the reason cats hiss is that they're imitating snakes, a known deadly predator. I mixed up cats and snakes in my head, threw in a touch of the crocolisks from *World of Warcraft*, and the rippers were born.

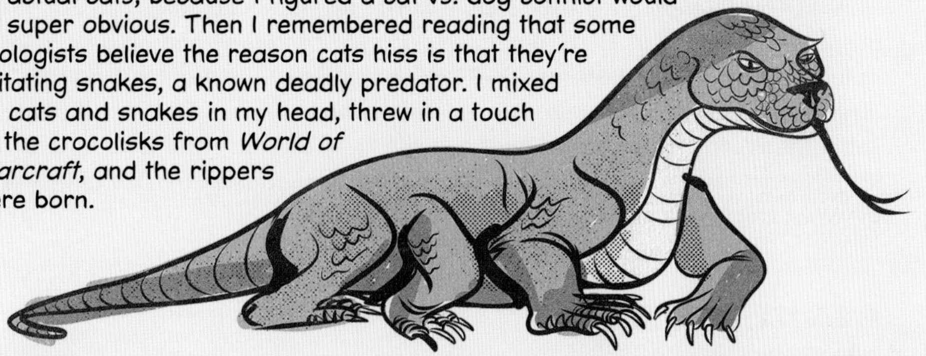

Jacques Khouri: When I was first approached to work on this project, I was enthusiastic and anxious to start on it. I had never illustrated a book starring a dog as big as a pony. The proportions of Gus in relation to the kids were quite demanding, and I had to redraw them a lot of times. It's incredible how our mind wants proportions between familiar elements to look a certain way, like the size of a dog compared to a kid. I had to break away from that.

Another challenge was trying to get clear poses of Gus in action or expressing an emotion. How do you show sadness or curiosity on a dog's face and body? Thanks to the internet, I had the opportunity to learn a lot about canine behaviors and anatomy.

In inking, I find the biggest problem with longer books is keeping a consistent style. For example, if you choose one way to render the trees, then you better be able to do it for the whole book. At the start of the project, I did a lot of inking practice. In fact, one of the biggest challenges was once again Gus. How do you ink a shaggy dog? I tried a crosshatch effect, some patterns, some solid black colors . . . but nothing looked like the fur of a Bernese Mountain Dog. One day I attempted a dry-brush look, and voila! We had a shaggy dog.

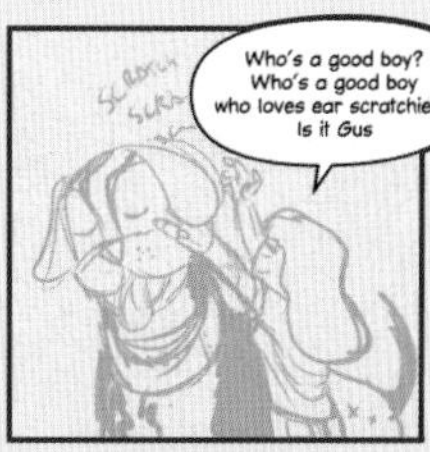
Who's a good boy? Who's a good boy who loves ear scratchies? Is it Gus

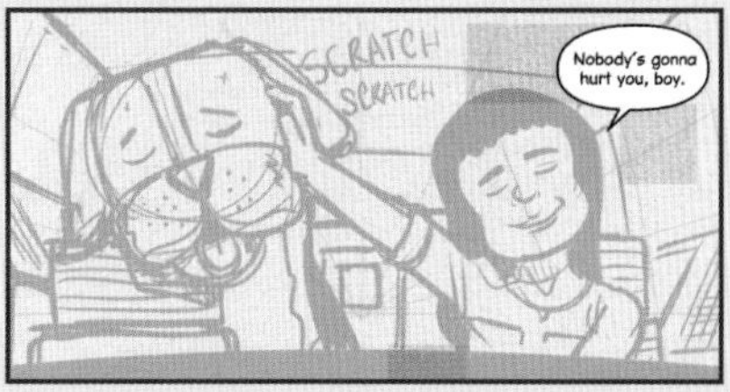
SCRATCH
SCRATCH
Nobody's gonna hurt you, boy.

All in all, I really enjoyed working on *Mega-Dogs*, and have to say I was a little sad when I drew the final panel with Gus in it. Love you, boy . . .

ABOUT THE AUTHOR

Dan Jolley began writing professionally at the age of 19. Since starting out in comic books, he has worked for DC (*Firestorm*), Marvel (*Dr. Strange*), Dark Horse (*Aliens*), and Image (*G.I. Joe*). He later branched out into licensed-property novels (*Star Trek*), film novelizations (*Iron Man*), and original novels, including the urban fantasy series Five Elements and the Audible Original *House of Teeth*. Working with Erin Hunter, he has scripted the manga stories set in the Warriors universe. Dan lives with his wife Tracy and a handful of largely inert felines in northwest Georgia. Readers can learn more about him at www.danjolley.com.

ABOUT THE ARTIST

Jacques Khouri makes animated films, works on commercials, teaches, and draws comics for a living. His influences range from animated cartoons to European and American comics. He currently lives in Montreal. You can find his work at ijotalot.com and jackkhouri.com. Please follow him on Tumblr or Instagram at @ijotalot.